ODD GIRL ROAR

A GOOD LIFE NOVEL

MERREN TAIT

LOLA PUBLICATIONS

Lola Publications. Raglan, New Zealand.

Print ISBN: 978-1-99-118140-4

Large print ISBN: 978-1-99-118142-8

Cover design by Bailey McGinn.

Author photo by Zora Slodicka.

www.merrentait.com

The Good Life series

The Year of the Fox

Bluffing for Beginners

The Misdeeds of Sadie Quinn

The Amateur's Guide to the Art of Running Away: A novella

Britlandia series

Real Life and Other Disasters

Romance is Dead

To all the misfits out there. This one's for you.

CHAPTER ONE

————————

WHEN I CALLED THE MAYOR A "COCKWOMBLE",
it didn't go down well.

In my defence, he deserved it, but a lowly graphic designer for Invercargill City Council was never going to come out of an altercation with the mayor without being forced to eat excessive amounts of humble pie, no matter what shaky ethical ground His Worship stood on.

I know what you're thinking. How could someone drop a verbal bomb that was at once on the limp-wristed side of offensive and able to collect an embarrassing amount of collateral damage in its blast radius?

Here's how.

It was Superhero Day at the library. The library often had theme days aimed at engaging kids. You know, promote literacy and all that good virtuous stuff, and because I designed all the library promotional material, I got an 'invite'. The execs euphemistically called them "team events" because an invitation did not, in fact, offer an attendance choice. All in all, they're pretty generous with throwing out emotive rhetoric, like calling us "the council family", because it made you want to do your job for much less than the private sector would pay.

So here I was. Dancing to the tune of the council panpipes.

I hadn't gone for a full costume because I don't like the pressure of having to act a part. I'm also not partial to embarrassing myself or drawing too much attention or having to, I don't know, actually get involved. So my outfit choice for today was a T-shirt I designed myself from my Empowered Collection.

However, when I saw the average age of the children at this particular event was eight – old enough to read my shirt but not understand it – I realised that maybe it would have been better to have feigned forgetfulness of the *dress to theme* memo and come in a plain T-shirt.

I hid behind a shelf of books and watched the mayor read a superhero themed story to a couple of dozen kids at his feet with all the enthusiasm of a post-Botox-party eyebrow.

Mayor McManus only visited the libraries before an election to help his street cred, which despite being rather obvious, seemed to work. He'd been re-elected three times.

Anyway, at the end of the morning's "super" events, the staff shuffled off to a special morning tea in the library's meeting room. The mayor walked in, gave a short thank you speech, and when he'd finished and the hubbub of cross-coffee talk started up, he homed in on the only other male in the room. Rashid, the newish children's collection manager, who was dressed as Black Panther.

The mayor gave him an *Oh, a male librarian. How novel* look, then slapped him on the back and said, "Good for you," which was reasonably patronising in itself, but the added, "Taking one for the team," really got the emasculation message across.

I caught Rashid's eye and gave him a sympathetic smile.

He widened his eyes as if to say, *Shoot me now*.

Rashid was well over six feet, the mayor well under, but Rashid leant against the back of a chair, so they were pretty much eye-to-eye. The mayor adopted a wide-legged stance and laid a hand on Rashid's shoulder as he talked to him. The body language said, *I am your buddy and the type of man who connects to people in a 'grass roots' kind of way. But you need to know I am still the dominant male.*

Rashid played his part, smiling and nodding and answering questions, and then as the mayor exhausted his male-librarian-inquisitiveness, he looked across the room and spotted me hovering by the Madeira cake.

My T-shirt had a plus-size female superhero on it. Her speech bubble read *Anything you can do, I can do bleeding*. And the mayor didn't even take the trouble to lower his voice because he thought a) the person nearest to him, being male, would agree with him, and b) his brand of witticism wasn't offensive, and he rolled his eyes and said, "Vagina worship. Worst bah-loody thing to come out of the 70s. Apart from The Carpenters."

And I had that thing, where I turned Hulk-like and transformed into an angry, indignant person. Well, okay, *more* of an angry, indignant person than I already was and with much less self-control. And while I was in the green, ripped-clothes stage, I marched over to him, pointed my finger at his chest and said, "We've been subject to the Cult of the Cock for millennia, so deal with it." And the thing was, because his hairline had receded to halfway across his skull, and his very high forehead was shiny and, thanks to my outburst, a little red and veiny, he looked a bit penis-like, so I added, "You cockwomble," and stormed off to immediately regret my actions.

CHAPTER TWO

—————

TWENTY PAIRS of eyes tracked the progress of my death march across the varying grey carpet tiles of the HR open-plan office.

It wasn't my ideal exit scenario, but at least I wasn't facing my professional demise alone. I could cloak myself in the comfort of their, no doubt, well-intentioned voyeurism.

I eyed the crowd and was just about to raise my glower to Incinerate when a woman at a desk to my right raised her hands to her chest, her fingers curled to form a heart.

Behind her, a man smiled and winked.

Huh.

Maybe I wasn't about to go down in a ball of flame. Maybe I was about to get veiled sympathy and an obligatory but metaphorical hand slap.

And yet, judging by the frown Yin-ing the Yang of the HR manager's smile, all possibilities were still on the table.

Summer St. John, dressed in the ubiquitous office fatigues of a grey skirt suit, waited for me at the door to the glass-encased meeting room. Her eyes ran down the front of my shirt and both the frown and the smile deepened. If she intended to be disarming, it worked. I had walked into the office feeling, well, empowered, as promised by the branding of my T-shirt collection and fortified by the finger heart and the wink.

Now I felt too shouty amidst the monochrome.

By the time I reached her, her face had settled into a kind of warm-edged nothing much-ness. If that's a thing. If it is, I had no idea what it meant.

"Have a seat." She indicated the low-backed chair on the far side of the table and closed the door to the fish tank of gawkers behind me.

I sat and swivelled my chair away from our audience so that I could pretend Summer St. John and I were the only parties actively or passively involved in this conversation.

"So, Jules –"

"Jewel."

She peered down at the memo in front of her. "It says Jules here."

"It might do, but that's not my name." I reached forward, turned the paper around, and, grabbing the pen she'd placed beside it, wrote J-E-W-E-L across the top to help her. I mean who was I to question the accuracy of an official document, but I did have pretty good authority on this particular detail.

I returned the paper and pen to their original positions and sat back in my seat.

The frown and the smile returned. "Right. Thank you. Jewel." She sucked in a deep breath, and her nostrils flared slightly. "I would like us to have an open conversation about what happened this morning."

Good.

Summer St. John parted her lips to continue and I said, "Mayor McManus is a sexist Neanderthal who provoked me into saying something a lot of us think but are contractually obligated to bury deep." I sat back in my chair and crossed my arms.

Her brows rose, then knitted together and I understood that she'd thrown out "open" as one of those meaningless corporate *warm fuzzy* type words intended to convey trust and put me at ease.

If there'd been a clue, some kind of face language, I'd missed it. I wasn't awesome on subtlety, but I did excel at the literal.

I uncrossed my arms. This was not a good start.

I tried for a smile. The unused muscles twitched out their progress like an automaton in need of a good oil.

It shouldn't be this hard. I was a business woman after all. Romancing people was part of the job, but I was rusty and, to be honest, not very good at it. It involved words like "effusive" and "charm" and "tact", none of which were in my skill set.

"Look. Sometimes –" By which I meant *often. "*– I have little control over the relationship between my tongue and my brain when I experience emotional spikes. Like anger."

Summer St. John raised her eyebrows. After a pause, she said, "Are you autistic? I can't find your file."

"No. But if putting me in a box helps you to process this situation, then by all means, label me."

I had intended that comment to be helpful, an olive branch to show I supported her in her requirement to carry out this interview. However, the flush that swept up her chest and disappeared into her hairline suggested she did not see it so much as an olive branch but as a switch I'd just slapped her across the face with.

I replayed my comment in my head.

Ah. Yes. I saw it.

It did kind of maybe sound a wee bit like it might belong on the aggressive end of the passive-aggressive continuum.

God I was useless. At this rate I'd be out on my arse with all the other clueless, undeserving people.

Fuck it. Might as well go for broke. I leaned forward in my chair. "I want to lodge a personal grievance against him."

Summer St. John did something I was not expecting. She threw her head back and laughed.

I didn't think I'd said anything funny. What was funny about being so offended by someone that you wanted legal recourse? Or was it bureaucratic recourse?

It was her turn to lean forward. She spoke slowly as if trying to make my inner "autistic" understand the other language behind her words.

My inner whatever understood just fine.

"It's not within your best interest to follow that route," I was fairly certain translated to an approximation of: *The mayor is pretty much untouchable.*

Which was great, because I was not. I was an expendable underling with rapidly narrowing options.

"Regardless of behaviour that could be interpreted as off-colour, you would need a *very* strong case in order for any accountability to be sought."

Translation: *Even if the mayor is an actual dickhead, he's a powerful one. Don't bother with a fight unless you're sure to win. Like making a complaint about him putting his hand up your skirt in the middle of a crowded office with plenty of witnesses. And preferably some CCTV footage.*

Summer St. John splayed her fingers, palms upwards. "But, who knows? There is an election next week." *Cross your fingers and hope the cockwomble gets voted out.*

She leaned back in her chair and waited for my response.

I didn't need to think hard about it. I wasn't actually prepared to go up against a well-oiled council machine, not least because my employment situation meant I probably couldn't even if I wanted to. Which, I supposed, I should come clean about. "You won't be able to find my file because I'm employed as a freelancer."

She twitched her head to one side. "Are you sure? Haven't you been here for a couple of years? I'm certain I've seen you around the building."

"You guys have been giving me contracts for the last eighteen months. I come in every so often for meetings."

"I see." Summer St. John steepled her fingers. "So why are you here and not standing in front of the Communications manager?"

I would have thought that was obvious and told her so. "Because I was told to come here?" Then I clenched my fists until the nails bit into the palms of my hand and waited for the inevitable.

"I'm afraid to say, there's only one course of action, Jules," she said, looking thoroughly relieved she no longer had to initiate any disciplinary procedure or a drawn-out personal grievance process. "I will be *strongly* advising the Communications Manager to terminate your contract and I have little doubt she will put up any objection. You'll have the decision formalised by the end of the day."

I relaxed my hands and peered at the angry half-moons creasing my palms. Then I looked her in the eye and said the only word fitting for such a situation. "Arse."

I DROVE HOME, made a cup of tea, then ignored it while I pressed my forehead to the sticky kitchen table.

In theory, I shouldn't now be melting into a little puddle of panic and self-recrimination, because, as a freelancer, I'd have other contracts. I could 'touch base' with previous clients and see if they had anything in the works. I'd have sensible things that ensured new clients found me. Like a website. And a marketing plan.

The truth was, I hadn't prepared a Plan B: What To Do For Income When I've Squatted Over My Only Source And Shat On It From A Great Height.

Finding a new source was nowhere near as easy as I'd have liked it to be. In the cut-throat, high-octane world of graphic design, designers were two-a-penny. They emerged bawling and hungry from three years in the institutional womb and scrabbled over each other, leveraging themselves off shoulders, hips, heads to get to the top, to prove themselves, to be noticed.

I was not that person. Not least because I hadn't stepped foot inside an educational facility since I left school at sixteen. I just didn't have that fire in my belly that gave me leave to be a shark. My two failings were: I had a love-hate relationship with the capitalist system, and I was not an arsehole. At least, I didn't think I was an arsehole.

Most of the time I was not an arsehole.

The front door banged closed and footsteps approached the kitchen. Two brown legs appeared, the fabric of a denim skirt *fwap*-ing in time with their march.

"Hi, Kaitlyn."

Kaitlyn's acknowledgement was not so much a "Hi" as an expulsion of air that carried the hint of a vowel at its edges.

Her shoes clomped out of view and the jug clicked on.

I sat up.

Kaitlyn leant against the kitchen bench, phone in hand, right thumb swiping up.

I was lucky when I scored the very small third bedroom at 4 Willowbank Way. The house came completely furnished, which meant I got a double bed that left me with just enough space to edge sideways beside it with my back pressed to the wall. And I got Kaitlyn and Brooke.

"I lost my job."

A head nod. Scroll. Pause. Nose-wrinkle smile. Scroll.

"I called the mayor a cockwomble and they fired me."

Kaitlyn continued to furiously text.

I drummed my fingers on the table. "I've got cancer of the eyelash. When all the hair falls out, the follicles will suppurate. I'll look like a crying Madonna. But with pus."

"Uh-huh." With a small smile and a sigh into her phone like she'd just kissed a lover goodbye until the next time, Kaitlyn put her phone down on the bench to grab a mug and spoon vanilla-flavoured hot chocolate into it. "Oh hey, when you clean the bathroom this week, can you pick the hair out of the shower plug hole? It's like having a skin-detritus foot bath in there right now, which is just rank."

I sighed and put my forehead back on the table. "K."

Kaitlyn's spoon *tink tink*ed against her mug, then clattered into the sink. "Thanks," she said as she walked out the door.

I patted the table top until I located my phone and opened my banking app. The situation was just as dire as the last time I checked.

As much as I'd like designing stuff for other people to be the thing that got me out of bed in the morning, it wasn't. Creating my T-shirts was, which meant the graphic design work supported my, as yet, very small business. And as everyone knows, starting a business is akin to taking all your spare money, including the stuff you might otherwise spend on leisure and having a healthy work-life balance, and sometimes your petrol money, putting it in a pile on the front lawn and setting fire to it.

I had just enough in my bank account to see me through one more week of rent and maybe a couple of food. After that, my two choices were: live in my car, or impose myself on the boxes breeding in Dad and Rewa's spare room. I owned a RAV4, which is to an SUV what Danny DeVito is to Arnold Schwarzenegger in the 80s classic, *Twins*. So, either way, a win-win situation.

Forcing myself to stand, I went outside to appraise potential new home number one. Once the ice-cream wrappers and festering damp towel were removed from the back seat, it didn't look too bad. That was assuming after I'd loaded all my crap into it, there would still be enough room for me.

There was another option, a third option, but before I seriously considered it I needed to give notice on my room. Give Kaitlyn and Brooke time to find a replacement flatmate before they were lumped with the extra rent.

I mean, I should do that.

Absolutely.

Even if I didn't technically have the money to cover the obligatory two weeks.

However.

The thing about not being an arsehole *most* of the time meant *some* of the time a bit of arseholery snuck in.

So, I waited until Kaitlyn and Brooke had fallen asleep, then Tetris-ed everything I owned into my car and made a break for option three.

CHAPTER THREE

I WOKE to a muted roar and the orange haze of a candle-wick bedspread, both of which served to remind me of the shameful measure I'd resorted to the previous evening.

Hello new day. Nice to see you too.

I threw the cover off my face, sucked in a lungful of fresh air and contemplated the ceiling tiles.

This person, the one who abused community leaders and ran out on people who almost didn't deserve it, was not the woman I imagined I'd be when I'd entertained my 12-year-old desire for life to hurry the fuck up.

I attempted to make myself feel better by wrapping myself up in that great big, fresh-from-the-heated-rail towel of reason called "You're not as bad a person as them".

It would take approximately the time for my rent to fail to show up in Brooke's bank account before they registered my absence and wondered why they hadn't noticed the smell. At which point I should probably block their numbers.

I mean, it's entirely possible Kaitlyn and Brooke's indifference towards me was down to my inability to "do people", or at least do people in a way that didn't make them think I was both odd *and* lacking basic courtesy.

Or they were just too self-interested.

To be honest, it was fifty-fifty.

Oh, who was I kidding? I was a terrible, terrible person who deserved to be flayed alive and then spat on.

Okay, maybe not spat on.

I gathered my strength to face the day, and possibly my karma-induced reckoning, and tipped my phone towards me.

10:26 am.

A respectful time to ring Dad and confess to having taken refuge in our holiday home. A somewhat shameful time for a twenty-two-year-old trying to pull her life back together to be rising for the day.

Shuffling over to the window, I pulled back the curtains. Framed between the high wooden fences running the length of the back lawn, a gust of wind puckered the mirrored surface of Lake Puhiruru. It pushed the water into a sequence of dimples like something large had moved below.

The lake and the colonial-flavoured town marking its eastern shore, sat deep within the mountainous folds of Fiordland, like the land had gathered it up into a tight embrace.

The mountains rose sharply out of the dark water of the lake and circled towards each other, not quite meeting at the western end. Here, a hanging valley spilled its catchment into the blackness below in a three-hundred metre drop, and the ring of mountains pushed the sound of the waterfall towards Puhiruru township in a steady thrum.

I opened the window to let the roar wrap around me,

and shivered one of those happy shivers dogs, or people in syrupy family movies do.

I loved our crib. I loved the mountains. I loved their cloud hats. I loved the lake. I loved the power behind the waterfall. I loved its ever-present-ness even when you couldn't see it.

I did not love the facilities.

The charm of the crib was that it was a tiny 1960s time capsule. Yellow, orange and green plaid carpet, piped couch edging, a chromed-trimmed Formica kitchen table, candle-wick bedspreads, and dark hardboard walls. All of which was contained within a very cosy forty square metres.

Unfortunately, the charm did not extend to the external bathroom. There was nothing quaint about a long drop you had to make a fifteen metre dash for. Nor a jury-rigged shower that required operating a hand pump to get any water pressure.

My bladder pushed painfully against my lower abdomen and I eyed the wooden shed across the large lawn resentfully.

I pulled on some shorts, pocketed my phone for my Instagram-scroll-whilst-peeing habit that everybody has but admits only to themselves, and headed out to the privy.

It was as I slipped my shorts over my hips and felt the weight of them suddenly lighten, that I considered my folly. The phone took the utterance of every syllable in "Fuckity fuck fuck" for it to reach its soft landing with a shudder-inducing *ploomf.*

Ah, so this was what karma looked like.

I clamped my urethra closed, because the least I could do was not urinate on a phone I could not afford to replace, and pushed my way out the door.

Then I closed it, laid my head against its peeling paint

and watched the veins fattening in my hands. It made a better alternative to, say, having to actually think about what just happened, and even harder, what I was going to do about it.

How on earth did I get here?

It was a question I knew the answer to, and reminded the action-before-thinking Jewel Bauer of, as I squatted in the frigid lake in such a way that almost didn't look like I was relieving myself.

I had neither the genetics, the common sense, nor the luck to invite success.

There was only one of those things I could do anything about and my lack thereof had resulted in me losing a vital piece of moderately expensive tech to a pile of shit not five minutes ago.

I took a moment to enjoy the spreading warmth around my lower half and contemplate the raw beauty of the waterfall.

...

...

...

Then, with an empty bladder making more room for my brain, I snapped a few pieces into logical position to give my middle finger to anyone who'd ever doubted me and set off, dripping, back to the crib.

One sieve duct-taped to a broom handle later, I had my phone back.

Thankfully, because the toilet hadn't been used in nearly a year, most of the liquid had either evaporated or been absorbed in the composting process. My phone was less "stewed" and more "garnished". I shook the earthy-looking clumps off and thanked the Lord of the Telecommunications Universe that I would not be contending with an ongoing leakage problem. But just to be sure, I would wrap it in cling film once I'd sterilised it with toilet cleaner and the best thing for working little bits out of small places.

My tooth brush.

And then I had no excuses not to ring Dad and confess to being both a failure and a bludger. But first I needed coffee. Such a conversation required it.

I opened the blue and white striped coffee jar on the bench top and chiselled a teaspoon-worth off the instant coffee that had been left to solidify sometime around 1992.

The mound rocking on my teaspoon had a bluish tinge to it. I put it back and opted for a greying teabag instead.

It took four rings and twenty-five rapid heartbeats for Dad to answer the phone.

"Hey, Dad."

"Jewelsy!" Dad announced, as if I only rang him at Christmas instead of visiting him every other day. "It's Jewelsy!"

"Jewelsy!" echoed Rewa from somewhere in the background.

"Hang on. Let me put you on speaker."

The line went dead.

I waited, as I always did when Dad attempted to put me on speaker, for the return phone call and the explanation that he forgot to press the speaker button *before* putting the phone in its cradle.

"What am I like, Jewelsy?" he laughed when I answered my phone. "I forgot to press the speaker button before putting the phone in the cradle."

"It's a two-step process, Dad, which means you only have to remember the order of one thing, the first thing, to get the whole thing right."

"Ah well. As long as I remember which order to put my

underwear and trousers on, a little technical ineptitude isn't much to worry about, hey?"

"*Rewa* remembers which order to dress you in."

"Yes, she does. It's like an assisted reverse strip tease. She loves it."

A tongue cluck issued from the background.

"You know what *I* don't love? You telling me that."

"Me either," said Rewa. "Mostly because it's not true. Tell your daughter you've been dressing yourself for several years now."

I said, "I'm calling because I have some news," as Dad told me he'd been dressing himself for several years now.

"Ooh. Is there a boy?" Rewa said before the sibilance of my 's' had subsided.

"Is there a boy?" echoed Dad.

Is there a boy? was default question number one when any kind of space was left for them to guess what was going on in my life. I should have known better and said the whole thing before they had space to push air past their larynx.

"There's no boy." I rushed on before they could ask default question number two: *Have you met the Prime Minister yet?* Because working for local government gives you a direct line to the country's most powerful decision maker. Apparently. "What I have to tell you is..." I rummaged around in my brain for some mildly comprehensive corporate jargon I'd heard in the council offices that might dress the situation up. "I'm pivoting to, ah, nurture my enterprise. Develop things in a more...fruitful direction."

Silence.

"Oh my God, you're pregnant. She's pregnant, Dale."

"I'm *not* pregnant."

"Oh, thank Christ," breathed Rewa. "I can't imagine

where you'd have put a baby in that tiny room of yours. Dangled it from the ceiling in a tiny hammock."

"Or a drawer," said Dad. "Drawers make a good little crib if you've nothing else. You've got a set of drawers don't you, Jewelsy?"

"I don't need drawers for any baby accommodation, Dad. I'm taking time out to concentrate on my business. It's going to be my priority from now on."

"That's what the fruitful talk meant?" said Rewa. "Couldn't you have just said that instead of giving me a near bloody heart attack?"

"Yes," I conceded. "I could have done that."

"*Time out*," said Dad. "Imagine that, Rewa. My daughter. The big-shot business woman. Brains *and* beauty."

I was not a beauty. I had dull hair that at a generous stretch might be called 'golden brown', but which was, in fact, a shade of mouse. My lips were on the thin end and my nose was slightly hooked to one side like it couldn't decide which direction to grow in. At least it managed to get the downwards bit right.

What I did have was large eyes and strong brows. Thick and slightly arched, like Madonna in her plastic-punk years.

"I think this calls for a Green Ginger Wine Moment," said Dad.

"It doesn't call for a Green Ginger Wine Moment," I said.

"It *absolutely* calls for a Green Ginger Wine Moment," said Rewa.

Dad spoke in capitals a lot. Presumably, it was the result of his chronically cheerful disposition, despite a life relegated to a wheelchair courtesy of a small patch of gravel on the shoulder of a sharp bend on State Highway 99. Six years as a paraplegic hadn't dampened his constant jolly-ness.

"It's not even midday."

Dad's chuckle rumbled in my ear. "Worried about the scandal?"

Dad didn't drink as a rule, but when there was something in his daughter's life to celebrate like the loss of a first tooth, the first few spots of menstrual blood, the first sale of a superheroine T-shirt, then the bottle of green ginger wine was brought down from the top of the bookshelf in the lounge, where it sat trophy-like, and dusted off.

"Before you get all celebratory, there's another thing I have to tell you. I'm staying at the crib so I can focus on the business without worrying about finding rent money. I know I should have asked if that's okay before I came, but I didn't." I felt there was something missing. Maybe I should add an apology? "Sorry."

Dad grunted his dismissal. "You're the only one who uses that place any more. I don't mind. I just ask that when you're rolling in the big bucks you move the bathroom inside."

Fortunately for me and my current on-the-precipice-of-destitution situation, I *was* the only one who used the crib any more. It was bought for Bauer family holidays in the early 70s. My grandparents were dead, my two uncles chose to carry out their lives overseas as soon as they were educated enough to ensure a meal ticket, and my father had little interest in travelling to a place where you had to be wheeled across the lawn to relieve yourself.

Glass clinked in the background.

"I bet you sold lots of T-shirts this morning."

"Three yesterday."

"You did?" Dad said like I had won the Nobel Peace

prize. "I knew I'd fathered a genius when you said 'Dad' at two weeks old. Your Nana said it was wind, but I know better."

"Dad," I began, about to unburden myself about the running out on my flatmates situation.

"Hang on, Jewelsy. Rewa's doing finger hieroglyphics in the kitchen. From my extensive knowledge of pigeon sign language, I think she wants to know if you've got any Wi-Fi up and running." He said it like *wee fee.*

"Actually," Rewa shouted, "I was wondering if you've got the *wigh figh* up and running."

"Potayto, Potarto."

"Not the best way to support your argument, my lover. One of those pronunciations is wrong. As is *wee fee.*"

Dad sighed the sigh of the long-suffering, but I knew he was smiling. Being teased by Rewa was one of his top five pleasures.

I, however, was not smiling.

I had two questions for myself: How the fucking hell had I forgotten about a critical online business aid like *an Internet connection?* And: How on earth was I going to pay for it? Out here the only service was rural broadband, which cost double the standard fee for half the gigabyte allowance.

It was official. I was the biggest numpty this side of Planet Spackbrain.

"Um. Not yet. I'm working on it, though."

"Well, that's good," said Dad, "because that would be fairly detrimental to running an online business." He ho ho-ed out a laugh and as much as I would have liked to join him to keep up the appearance that I had my shit together and had this whole *stealing off to the crib to become a badass business woman* thing all worked out, I very much did not have my shit together. So I chose silence. And then panic.

"I should go," I rattled out. "Get some business stuff done."

Dad's lips smacked in my ear as he took a sip of ginger wine. "Okay. Bye bye, Jewelsy. I love you."

"Yep." I hung up.

———

SOME QUICK CALCULATIONS on my phone told me I would be arguably okay for twelve weeks on five dollars a day. As long as I didn't use any water or electricity. Or eat on weekends.

I mean, I made *some* money. I sold a couple of T-shirts a day via a print-on-demand process, so my outlay was minimal, but I had to reinvest that into advertising, so it's not like I could use any of it.

This not having a Plan B thing was really backfiring.

I dictated my new strategy into the note function on my phone:

1. Find a way to access the Internet for free. Illegal options open to consideration.

2. Work out the cheapest way to eat without risking tooth loss or organ failure.

3. Romance some good karma, because the bad kind was kind of shit.

Then I got down with the busy.

I added "toothbrush" and "sieve" to my mental list of shopping items, and placed a jar in the middle of the kitchen table with "For my sins (and Brooke + Kaitlyn)" written in barely legible Biro across a rectangle of duct tape on its front. The $3.70 I had prised from various car crevices made a satisfying series of *clinks* when I emptied them into it. I figured it was approximately six months' worth of coin detritus, which meant at that rate it would take me sixty-seven and a half years to pay my ex-flatmates back.

But, hey. It was a start.

AFTER A...FORTIFYING? but wholly unsatisfactory Marmite sandwich brunch, I set the kilometre counter on my dashboard to zero and drove into town. 3.2 klicks to the Puhiruru Mart and general grocer, or a forty-minute, petrol-saving walk. It would be almost an hour and a half round trip when I needed to make it, but time was the one thing I had.

There were only two parking spaces left in a car park that had clearly been designed to accommodate a fleet of perambulators. I edged the Rav4 into one of them and after briefly accommodating the thought that an exit via the boot might be easiest, managed to extract myself through the narrow door gap without leaving any car-paint imprints on the neighbouring SUV.

The store's automatic door wheezed open and before I could step inside, an elderly man in a mobility scooter rolled up and stopped in front of me, barring my access. The doors shuddered against the scooter's rear end in their attempt to close, then whined a retreat.

He squinted up at me for several seconds before thrusting his head forward and addressing me at the volume of someone who is going deaf and doesn't realise they struggle to hear themselves.

"Loopy."

Tufts of whiskers sprouted in the grooves at the corners of his down-turned mouth from where he'd missed them shaving. As he set his jaw back into place, the slack skin under his chin shook like a chicken wattle.

I could have been mistaken for presuming he was referencing himself, aggressively announcing the unbalanced state of his mind in introduction to a complete stranger. But I knew around here, "loopy" referred to the tourists. Not everyone looked favourably upon the tourist dollar if it meant pressure on infrastructure, walking a block instead of being able to park right outside the store you want to visit.

I couldn't disagree with him. Not really.

I'd only ever interacted with Puhiruru on a temporary basis and could hardly claim residency status after twelve hours of habitation. I certainly felt the actions that had led me here were on the other scale of loopiness.

I did, however, have a driving need to get in the store and buy some coffee that looked and behaved like it was meant to.

A male voice from among the shelves of goods said resignedly, "Mr Hardacre, try not to frighten the customers. They pay my wage."

Without taking his eyes away from mine, Mr Hardacre snarled, "It's *my rates* that pay to flush your turds and take them away to the land of convenience." He held out his hand. "I want a contribution."

"Mr Hardacre," said the disembodied voice. "Leave them alone or you can get your *Hackers' Monthly* elsewhere."

Hackers' Monthly? It seemed unlikely reading for somebody approaching their second century.

Mr Hardacre snarled, reversed two feet, and with a flick of his wrist, accelerated forward, bearing left just enough to make it look like he was making an effort to avoid me, without actually avoiding me.

I had to duck sideways to prevent the basket on the front of his scooter from collecting my right hip.

Luckily for Mr Hardacre, the need to coordinate my body to take urgent action absorbed any energy that might otherwise have been directed to my tongue. By the time my verbal power returned, the window for outrage was lost and I silently watched his scooter speed out the car park entrance.

Then I stepped into the store and wondered if I'd been teleported into another dimension.

The carpark was full, yet the store was devoid of people. The only sound was the quiet hum of the refrigeration units. If it wasn't for the lack of ransacked shelves, I might wonder if I'd missed something big. Like the zombie apocalypse.

I moved through the fruit-laden entry, my Converse high-tops squeaking on the linoleum tiles.

The checkouts were unmanned.

I passed three aisles, looking for one that might house coffee. Not a soul perused the goods, no workers stacked shelves, no undead feasted on cranial matter.

I stopped and listened. The only sign of life was the crunch of gravel as a car pulled into the car park.

A banana skittered across the floor towards me.

I picked it up and approached the aisle it had been jettisoned from. "Hello?"

Silence. Mr Hardacre's rebuker had disappeared into the Twilight Zone with every single one of the car owners.

A car door slammed and an arm shot out from behind a towering display of toilet paper to my right. It grabbed my wrist and pulled me into the gap behind the display.

CHAPTER FOUR

———————

I MANAGED THE "WHAT" of my intended "WHAT THE FUCK?" before a hand slapped over my mouth and a large body pressed against mine.

There wasn't a lot of room between the tower of toilet tissue and the end of the shelving unit. An air bubble at best. I had an eye-full of khaki fabric, a nose-full of lemon fabric softener, and a cheek-full of hard chest. I shifted my jaw, working my tongue up to voice my indignation and a low "Shhhh" issued above my head.

A Vans-clad foot slid one of the tower of toilet rolls across the gap I'd been pulled through.

The entry doors hissed open, and closed again without anybody entering.

The large body tensed.

Now, don't get me wrong, I enjoy a good mystery as much as the next person. I like the mental exercise of working the puzzle out before the answer jumps out at you and shouts, "Boo!" mostly, because surprises were shit. Take my Dad's accident, for example. Or the sudden void where Mum's presence used to be when she decided she wasn't up to potential round-the-clock care for the lifetime of her disabled husband.

So, while part of me was indignant about having been man-handled without being asked first, the far larger part of me was intrigued by what was about to unfold.

I decided to settle in.

From my limited vantage point behind the wall of fatigue-green, I was able to see tiny slices of the outside world. The packets had been stacked to create small windows, like arrowslits in a castle wall.

A hand reached into the crate of bananas at the shop entry, extracting one, before the hand's owner dive-rolled behind the fruit crates further in.

The chest I was pressed against went still and I held my own breath, as if the nervous anticipation was catching.

In the frame of one of the slits, another man commando crawled between the two checkouts, banana cocked in one hand like a gun.

So the bananas were *guns*.

Um.

Had I just unwittingly allowed myself to be a participant in the supermarket arena of The Hunger Games?

A crash from somewhere in the refrigerated goods area sent the commando crawler scrabbling for the cover of the second checkout.

My hair ruffled with a whispered "Diversion".

Diversion? For what? My heartrate shifted into a higher gear even though I was fairly certain no one had ever died from being shot by a banana gun.

But when a middle-aged man with a crew cut and a Clint Eastwood squint crept down the aisle, banana cocked and poised for action, I wondered if I'd underestimated the versatility of the seemingly innocuous fruit.

Two metres out from the tower, he paused, eyes narrowed.

The body edged away from me and a draught of cool air rushed between us. A large fist appeared in front of my face, three of its fingers extended. A countdown. To what?

As the first finger curled into the hand's palm, the stack of beach towels on the shelf behind the crew-cut guy began to quiver.

The fist stilled, the countdown paused.

The towels inched sideways and a hand covered in tā moko appeared, the Māori tattoo unfurling like fern fronds up towards the wrist. As the fist neared the back of the crew cut, the pointer finger extended, its tip glistening, and edged towards a wet docking with the ear nestled beneath the buzz cut.

The banana wielder cocked his head, eyeing the toilet paper out of the side of his eyes, before wheeling around and catching the finger a centimetre from making contact.

"Bumholes," said Mr Hardacre's rebuker. "Nearly got you."

Buzz Cut released the finger, and turned to address the towels. "The point is to get me before I get you, son. 'Nearly' is as useful as using your ballsack as a silencer. On the battlefield, you have to take your opportunity as soon as it waves its red-flagged arse at you, understood?"

"Understood, my captain," the rebuker replied in a sing-song voice.

"Good." The 'captain' raised his head and boomed, "Simulation over, team."

A face appeared between the towels. A man in his late twenties with a wide mouth and deep-set eyes. "Where's everyone else?"

The captain narrowed his eyes. "Still under cover. Not for long though."

I made to edge my way out from behind the tower and a finger appeared in front of my face. Wait.

"Forest?" the captain barked.

A distant "Captain?" sounded from the other side of the store.

"Very impressive, soldier. Full points for stealth."

"Booyah! Did you hear that, Rā? Full points for being a ninja."

Whoever Rā was, they didn't answer.

"No points for initiative, though. You were on the defensive the entire time. You could have ambushed me in aisle one, son. Instead, you scuttled away like a cockroach on a hotplate."

A petulant grunt rolled through the store followed by a "Sir" that sounded like a hasty afterthought.

"Take Liam. He had the perfect set up for an ambush. Liam get out here."

The foot once again slid one of the toilet roll towers aside and large hands steered me sideways through the gap.

I turned to find the face that matched the massive frame.

Dark-lashed eyes flickered to mine before a lock of black, shoulder-length hair slipped forward and curtained them off.

"Perfect set up, son. If it weren't for Joe's attempt to kill me with a wet willie, you would have been upon me. Full points for strategy."

The wall of hair nodded.

"But did your skull jettison its contents when you involved a civilian? Civilians are a liability, trooper. Get them away from the kill site as soon as you can, otherwise they just end up as collateral damage and you might as well use them as meat shields. This one looks like she'd provide good cover for your clackers."

"Thank you?" I said.

"But she's too small for any decent protection."

"I'm actually okay with that," I said, but the captain had already shifted his attention.

"Rānui?"

A "Captain" issued from somewhere above us and a face peered out from between the boxes stacked on top of the shelving units.

"Full points for initiative, but your cover's a liability. You need to be quick and take your target by surprise. How can you do that surrounded by heavy objects you'd have to move out of the way in order to get to me? I'd hear you well before you could do any damage wreaking."

"I could have used my banana grenade."

"Great. Why didn't you?"

A pause. "I only thought of it now."

The captain tapped his temple. "You have to be quick thinking in the field and take the opportunity as soon as it's presented, or they've got you first."

The woman grunted.

"Still, it's a significant improvement on last week, team. Well done." The captain clapped his hands. "Unit dismissed."

"Back on the job, everyone," said the face in the towels as the captain exited the aisle. The face propped a hand under his chin and stared at me in what looked like wonder but could just as easily have been amusement. "*Who* are *you?*"

I would have thought it was obvious, but just in case he was asking because he thought I was a *willing* meat shield for the large guy's genitals, I said, "A customer."

The face laughed. "I understand that, my heart, but you are someone I am going to need to know the name of, because –" he gestured at my torso.

I was wearing one of my designs from my Empowered Collection because going out in public was an opportunity for what should be passive marketing, but actually required me to hand out a business card with my online store's details on it and do some of that "effusive" stuff I was no good at.

It depicted a girl superhero, hands on hips, pigtails blowing in the breeze. Her speech bubble read:

Run like a girl

Throw like a girl

Scream like a girl

Thanks for the compliment!

There was an opportunity here. One that shouldn't be too hard to fuck up. "Jewel Bauer."

"*Jewel Bauer,*" he said, as if rolling it across his tongue and tasting it. "Well, Jewel Bauer, I *love* your T-shirt. Isn't her T-shirt phenom, Liam?"

Liam turned away from me and straightened a shelf of air freshener.

"I design them. My website's shero wear dot com. You should have a look." I pulled a business card out of my pocket and thrust it at the face.

"Shero?"

"Shero. Hero with an S."

"You *design* them? That is a fabulous superpower, Jewel Bauer." The face thrust his hand out towards me. "I'm Joseph Kiriona, but you can call me Joe, and I will definitely have a look."

I took the proffered hand and shook it.

"So, what brings you into the store today, my love?"

"I need coffee and some other food stuffs that meet basic nutritional needs and finite budgetary requirements."

"Oh, goodie. I love a nutrition-slash-budget puzzle. Liam will help you," Joe said in his sing-song voice. "Won't you, Liam?"

"Why?" said the woman as she climbed down using the shelves as ladder rungs. "We don't do personal shopping, Joe."

Joe winked at Liam. "We do today."

Liam swivelled away from the shelves, his black Vans squeaking on the linoleum and disappeared around the end of the aisle.

I presumed he meant me to follow him. So I followed him.

In the next aisle, he stopped in front of a set of shelves, his body half turned away from me. Jesus, he was massive. He had to be six-foot-five with shoulders I could curl up and sleep on.

I thought back to the precarious situation of being abducted behind a pile of toilet paper. Had his intention been less honourable than protecting me from a stray pretend bullet, he could easily have crushed me with those massive hands and no one would have been the wiser.

He raised a finger towards the packets of instant coffee and I selected one based on cheapest-price-to-weight ratio, because extreme budgeting did not allow for qualities like "real" and "decent" to feature.

"What else do you need?" His voice was the low rumble you might expect from someone so very large.

I pictured my mental list. "Sieve, rice, carrots, soy sauce, eggs, bread, and whatever fruit's the cheapest."

Liam backtracked to the store's entrance and slung a basket over one arm. He grabbed five carrots when he asked me how many and I said, "Five," through a mouthful of my banana gun, then he moved on to the apple bin.

He was an odd large. He walked with his shoulders hunched over as if straightening them out caused him pain. And when he squatted down to select a bag of rice from the bottom shelf, his trousers rode up to reveal the tops of frilly socks decorating the high ankles of his shoes.

I mean, who was I to judge how men chose to accessorise, but it did look a little incongruous with the whole *I could snap you in half with my bare hands* thing he had going on.

My list complete, he escorted me to the checkout, placed the basket on the conveyor belt and headed back towards the fresh produce.

The cashier didn't react to my presence. Instead, he blew his long, purple fringe out of his eyes and attempted to peer up at the expanse of his forehead, his eyes crossed. Then he rolled the curtain of hair into a barrel curl, like a rockabilly queen, and took out his phone to peer at himself in it. The combination of purple hair and turquoise fingernails accentuated the dark blue of his eyes.

I cleared my throat.

He jumped as if the sight of two people approaching his checkout and the sound of the basket hitting the rubber belt had occurred one dimension over.

"Sorry." He let go of his hair and it flopped down over his face again. When he made to grab the bottle of soy sauce and missed, as if his fringe-obscured eye had removed his depth perception, I pulled a bobby pin from my hair and offered it to him.

He looked at my palm, then up at me, a smile edging one side of his mouth up. "Can you?" He passed me his phone with the camera app already open.

I held it as he secured his fringe in place and turned his head from side to side. "Do you think I look like Dita von Teese?"

"Who?"

He flicked his eyes towards the aisles. "I'll ask Liam."

A door whined open behind me and I turned.

The captain poked his head out of a door marked "*Staff only*". "Joe, what's the Wi-Fi password again? My computer has the memory of a Day 2 recruit."

"Captainsmart, sir. One word. All lower case. Put it on a sticky note on your computer screen."

The "*Staff only*" door closed, Barrel Curl beeped my first item through, and I once again reflected on the nature of karma.

I FELT GOOD. I had a plan. I was captain of my universe and I could steer my little ship out of its collision course with an iceberg and into less sink-y waters.

After my coffee, I would feel invincible. If for only the amount of time it took for two teaspoons of sub-par caffeine to wear off, but I would take what I could get.

"I got rid of the net curtains," I told Dad. My second call for the day was in case my hurried exit from the previous conversation had raised any paternal concerns. Well, more paternal concerns than normal. "It was like living inside a giant tissue."

Dad's chortle distorted in my phone and I pulled it away from my ear.

"*A giant tissue.* Do what you want, Jewelsy. Any change you make can only improve the place."

It was the first time I'd been able to see out the window, or any of the windows in the living area, since ever.

"Shall I tell you what I can see?"

"I want to know," shouted Rewa in the background.

"There are people beyond the fence. We have *neighbours*. Who'd have thought?"

"No!" said Dad. "*Other people!* What are they doing?"

A digger bucket tore a hole in the roof of a building not too dissimilar from ours. "Demolishing their house. Or someone they've paid to demolish their house is doing it for them."

"There goes another one, Rewa," said Dad.

"Another bloody one," she agreed.

"The gentrification's no longer creeping in, it's at a run," I said. "There's not too many original cribs left now from what I could see on my drive around today. The new builds are all house and no property."

"Holiday cricket on the lawn's a dying art, hey?" said Dad.

Our crib was built on a quarter-acre section. Modest by 1960s standards, palatial by 21st century standards. Due to the small footprint of the building, the section was mostly empty. A large, grassy rectangle.

It used to be that all the sections along the lake front were like that.

On the other side of the house, a double-storeyed, black steel plane hangar stretched the length of the section like a toppled monolith. They'd left just enough room to park a boat out the front, and host a barbecue for six out the back.

"The rising tide of the nouveau riche," said Dad. "Used to be those little houses were castles. *They* were the statement of luxury. The difference is, we knew how lucky we were to have them."

"Well, whoever built the military compound next door is probably appreciating how lucky they *used* to have it. It's up for sale. Can't have been finished more than six months."

"Is that right?

"I don't feel sorry for them. In a few months we'll be completely hemmed in. I have to go all the way down to the lake now to get the view we used to have a year ago." To prove my point to nobody but me, I picked up my coffee and headed out of the crib, across the lawn. "And the town's changing. The craft shop's gone. It's now a café with fake steel ducting and black tiles. A flat white there costs *seven dollars.*"

"Did you hear that, Rewa? Seven dollars."

"Seven dollars," echoed Rewa in her "what's this world coming to?" voice.

"Ah well," sighed Dad. "Tell me how The Old Girl is today." The Old Girl was Dad's name for the lake, as if she was an elderly relative he visited rarely, but had fond childhood memories of.

"She's pensive, but happy."

Today was a typical Murihiku day – steel-grey, calm skies, and low light. The kind of day that might have been depressing in the middle of the Murihiku plains, but was comforting in the close embrace of the mountains, like a thick, woollen rug.

The lack of sun hadn't allowed the dew to lift from the grass and as I sat on the small bank at the end of the lawn, and burrowed my feet into the shore's tiny pebbles, they clung to my skin like raised scales.

I lifted my coffee to my lips, breathed in its bitter steam, and took a sip.

"Give her my regards, won't you, Jewelsy? I bet you've already given yours."

I thought of the only interaction I'd had with her so far. Using her as a toileting alternative was not my first choice in regard-giving possibilities.

"She knows how I feel about her."

A series of splashes broke through the low roar of the waterfall and a woman in a rowing boat emerged from behind a promontory on the shore. Her stroke was strong and smooth and she quickly covered a hundred metres before drawing in her oars and peering over the side.

"Hold your phone out. Let me hear the waterfall."

The boat continued its trajectory for a few metres, and the water dripping from the oars created a series of concentric circles in the still water.

The scene was wholesome. Romantic even.

I raised my arm and turned my phone to face the cascading wall of water.

In the boat, the woman turned towards the bow and knelt. She struggled for a moment with a large object, and then with a grunt, forced it over the side.

The object was wrapped in something pale and had the unmistakable shape of a body.

"Mother of God," I gasped and stood up, my coffee tipping over in the grass.

"What is it, Jewelsy?" Dad's voice sounded tinny from where my hand now dangled next to my thigh. "What's happened?"

My movement caught the woman's eye and she swivelled her head in my direction.

And waved.

"Good afternoon!" Her voice drifted across the still water, the cheer in it clear. "Lovely day for it."

I...slowly raised my hand and waved back.

CHAPTER FIVE

REMEMBER when I said I liked a mystery and that it tended to be on the condition the puzzle didn't scare the crap out of me? I was kinda wobbling on the fence between sphincter malfunction and raising a "Welcome to my brain space" sign. Mainly because this particular mystery involved BODY DUMPING!, which was, somewhat incongruously, being done in broad daylight, in front of a row of houses, and by someone who threw out pleasantries like nothing as untoward as BODY DUMPING! had happened.

I decided to hedge my bets.

"I'm actually...on the phone to the police?"

She flapped a hand. "Oh, I wouldn't bother. I called ahead of time and warned them."

My brain went ??? which caused my mouth to go, "Okay."

The woman reached for one of the oars.

"It's just —"

"If you do get through, tell that delightful Constable Strickland I said 'Hello'." She gripped the other oar and set to rowing back the way she came.

I placed the phone back to my ear. "Dad? What would you do if you thought you saw someone dump a body wrapped in a sheet in the lake and then they waved at you and said 'hello'? And here's the bigger mystery – why on earth would they ring the police and warn them about it?"

"Maybe the eco cemetery's full," offered Rewa.

"I know," said Dad. "She's a mafia boss and has the police in her pay."

"Both of those suggestions are absurd."

"As absurd as dumping a body and warning the police?"

He had a point. "No."

"There you go then. They could be perfectly reasonable scenarios."

While Dad's logic held a small amount of merit, the situation, never-the-less probably called for erring on the side of caution. "Do you think I should phone the police and check?"

"What does your gut tell you?"

"That not is all as it seems."

"I think so too."

"It's also telling me I should find out what's going on."

It wasn't actually. That was one hundred percent my curiosity getting the better of me, but Dad wasn't about to call me out on it. "Imagine that, Rewa. My daughter. A hot shot detective."

Rewa made a noise that could have been mutual appreciation, or the effort required not to roll her eyes.

"Call us when you've got some more clues," said Dad.

"Ae, call us when you've got more clues," confirmed Rewa.

As I hung up and questioned the validity of what I saw, a more pressing thought weighed on my mind.

I'd forgotten to buy a new fucking toothbrush, hadn't I?

————————

THE WALK into town the following morning saved me approximately $1.13 in petrol and took thirty-five minutes. I didn't think the petrol savings was a bad exchange for that amount of productive business time, considering that at my current rate of sales, I was earning forty-three cents gross per thirty-five minutes. I had also single-handedly affected a five second delay in the climate change apocalypse, which made me, for the first time in my life, feel smug for being poor.

When I arrived at the mart at 8:27 am, the car park was once again full. This time, however, the inside of the store hummed. Foot traffic flowed in and out of the door in a steady stream, which was good. My loitering was less likely to be noticed.

The only place to sit was a bench seat on the outside wall between the automatic door and the large windows opposite the checkouts. It was perfect. Unless any of the mart workers came outside, they wouldn't be able to see me from inside.

When I opened my laptop, the Puhiruru Mart network was the first in the list of business Wi-Fis. I typed in the password and watched the spinning dots while my computer attempted to linked to it.

It linked and dropped out. The Wi-Fi icon showed no bands and just the first little dot. I set my computer to connect automatically and watched it link and drop out five more times.

I shuffled along the bench and swung my knees around the end of it so that my computer was positioned in front of the window and more in line with the router.

It made no difference. In fact, it seemed to be worse, as

if the glass was laced with Internet-disrupting titanium particles. Or something.

There was no other option but to risk discovery. I stood up, entered the store amid a scrum of parents and school children and immediately the four bands filled with solid black.

Huh.

Maybe the bench seat was a Wi-Fi black spot.

Exiting, I walked the entire length of the store. The network name flickered and disappeared, flickered and disappeared.

It would seem I was a little hasty in assuming I knew anything about the laws of karma. Whoever stirred that particular cosmic pot was having a right old, thigh-slapping belly laugh.

And yet, there was nothing else for it. I would either have to make myself invisible or make it look perfectly normal to never shop in an environment where the typical behaviour was buying stuff. Perhaps, if I was very lucky, I could get away with it.

It was the never shopping *and* never leaving combination that might be a red flag.

I entered the store on the next wave of harried workers and parents, grabbed a basket to enhance my "shopper" ruse, and set about scouting positions that afforded minimal noticeability.

By my count, and I was pretty good with numbers, I had three possible hiding places. I could squeeze myself into the shelf of chlorophyll powder because while plenty of people had good intentions of adding it to their super food shakes, nobody actually bought it.

The beer chiller was a slightly better option due to not having to contort myself into a small space and nobody buying alcohol before 11 am for fear of looking like a wino. There was, however, a minor drawback in that I wasn't massively keen on hypothermia.

Which left option three. The tower of toilet paper that, blessedly, was still standing despite it having been exclusively designed with the intention of killing someone. Sorry, 'killing' someone.

Due to the narrowness of the display and my ongoing dalliance with Lady Luck, I had just enough room behind the stacks of bleached paper to kneel. I reasoned it would be fine. I only needed blood flowing between my brain and my hands. Legs were frippery to an artist.

I turned around, placed my backpack under my knees, and rested my laptop against the end of the shelving unit so it didn't slide off my thighs. Then I opened up my Instagram advertising account to consider how best to spend the seven dollars I made yesterday in such a way that would make me another seven dollars today.

Somewhere in the back of my mind an image of a hamster whirring out infinity on a wheel attempted to thrust itself forth. I throat punched it like the unhelpful distraction it was and threw my brain power into strategically spending as little as I could to make slightly more than that.

Twenty minutes into my Instagram taking of the world, everything went quiet. The squeak of shoes on the shiny floor ceased, the checkout beeps stopped, the whine of children and the hum of checkout-line conversation died away.

I peered out through the gaps between the rolls and was met with stillness. The store was as devoid of people as when I shopped yesterday, which while slightly disconcerting, one should not, as they cryptically say, look a gift horse in the mouth. Less distraction meant more production, and so, I turned my attention to marketing that had the potential to go viral with the added benefit of not having to spend a thing.

A TikTok video.

My branding across the social media platforms I pushed my T-shirts on was a sort of "geek girl roar" vibe, as in how to be heard without having to do anything nerve wracking like making sounds come out of your mouth.

Part of my look was a pair of black rimmed glasses I only ever wore for marketing purposes and never in my normal everyday life, because the lack of magnified lenses in them would be a dead give away that I was maybe trying a bit too hard.

I recorded a thirty-second TikTok video that featured not only the Empowered Collection T-shirt I wore, but my ability to cast smug, wallflower judgement on the average shopper from the safety of my toilet paper hide. To fortify my social media campaign, I posted a picture of me looking thoughtful against the backdrop of luxury three-ply poo paper on Instagram.

Then, with the marketing tasks out of the way for the day, I started converting last night's sketch into a digital version on my drawing smartpad, whilst intermittently checking my emails for non-existent orders.

At 10:00 am a shadow fell over the tower, blocking the light on one side of the arrowslits. A brown iris framed in impossibly long lashes looked in at me. Then the shadow disappeared and I was bathed once again in the light from dozens of tiny air gaps.

Shit.

If the game was up and I had the time it took for the big guy, Liam, to report me to the captain and for the captain to then march me off the premises, at least I had my social media dignity intact, if...no other type.

In the intervening minutes between discovery and inevitable ejection, I practised my ashamed face. It was sort of a lips turned down look with intermittent big eyes and lowered eyes. It finished with a slow nod of the head/lowered eyes combo.

Nothing happened.

I checked Instagram. A generous fifty-three likes, which I knew from the experience of frustration and disappointment wouldn't convert to a single sale. And a mere fifteen views of my TikTok video, which in the world of viral viewing was akin to a flat lining heart-rate monitor.

A *shuff* to my right made me jump and a cup of caramel-coloured liquid scraped its way across the floor in the narrow gap between the end of the shelving unit and the first tower of paper. A large hand disappeared from around the handle.

Interesting.

Perhaps it was an apology for involving me in yesterday's war game. If it was, it was pretty decent. Protection of my Internet exploitation *and* a cup of...tea?

I picked it up and sniffed its surface. Tea.

There was something written on the side of the mug. It took me a couple of seconds to process the blockish font. *Surely not everyone was kung fu fighting.*

Was it a hidden message? Had Liam recognised me for the lover I was in lieu of the fighter I wasn't? Maybe the war games were not his bag and this was a cry for help.

I had no idea what I could do about it if it was, so decided to just drink the tea.

If it was possible for taste buds to swoon, mine made a pretty good attempt at it. The tea was creamy and full-bodied and unlike any tea I'd ever tasted. Liam may have less social grace than me, but the man knew how to make the fuck out of tea. I stifled an "Ahhh" in case anybody nearby thought groaning toilet paper might be a bit of an anomaly.

Drinking it down, I continued my drawing, and only emerged from the creative vortex when my bladder reminded me I should probably think about emptying it. Crucial bodily functions, like eating and toileting were an inconvenience to the creative flow. If it was acceptable to accessorise with a gastric tube and catheter, I would.

I attempted to stand up, remembering too late that I'd been kneeling for two and a half hours and there was a good chance my legs were not in full working order.

My right foot flapped uselessly as I put my weight on it, the toe of my shoe slipped backwards on the linoleum floor, and I bore down on the top of my foot, the angle of which forced me forward and I fell, face first against the end of the shelving unit, ricochetted off it and took out the stacks of toilet paper on my rebound like a bowling ball scuttling a set of pins to land on my arse.

I slowly turned around. The two staff working the checkouts stared at me, frozen in their between customers tasks.

I got up, scooped my laptop and smartpad into my backpack, and hobbled down the right-hand aisle to the toothbrush section. Plucking a packet off the shelf, I headed towards the checkout staffed by the woman who'd hidden on top of the shelving units.

She had brightly inked tattoos down both arms, a stud in her nose and short, curly silver hair with the tips dyed black. She watched my approach through kohl-rimmed eyes that served to emphasise their narrowing.

So...I bravely adjusted my trajectory to the checkout manned by the guy with the floppy purple fringe and slapped the tooth brush down on the conveyor belt with all the confidence of a decisive, brand-conscious consumer. "I had some trouble finding them. If anyone asks, they're not behind the toilet paper display."

Purple Fringe frowned. "They're in aisle five with all the other sanitary and health care products. Why would I tell them where they're not?"

It was a sensible question and one I didn't have an equally sensible answer for. So, I pulled my card from the Eftpos machine as soon as the word "Accepted" appeared, and made a run for the door.

***

THE FOLLOWING DAY, when I got back to the mart and approached the toilet paper tower from the back of the store, because, you know, stealth, it wasn't there. It must have been packed up after I laid waste to it.

I turned around on the spot, knowing the movement was a waste of energy, because there was nowhere else to make myself inconspicuous as I'd comprehensively established yesterday. The best I could do was ride the swell of 8:30 am customers and settle myself on the bench seat positioned behind the checkouts and up against the windows for people so exhausted by the bagging process they had to sit down afterwards.

I took a deep breath and edged past the two lines of people at the checkout. When I reached the bench seat, I flicked my hair back and sat down. I was simply someone waiting for another someone to do their shopping.

Opening my computer, I crossed my fingers that the

busy period would continue indefinitely, and began my work.

By the time the gentle hum of the refrigerators descended on the customerless store, and Purple Fringe and Tattoo Woman had noticed me and were passing each other various iterations of question-mark expressions between their checkouts, I had spent yesterday's $11 profit on more advertising, improved my toilet-paper hide TikTok views to just over one hundred, and had acquired three more Instagram followers. Considering I'd started my business a year ago, the best that could be said about its growth was "glacial". At this rate, I'd be able to make rent at 63, two years before I retired.

Someone sat beside me.

Knowing the game was over, I chose the mature response of feigning absorption in my work.

The person leant in, peered at my screen, and said in Joe's voice, "Ooh, I very much like that. Come here, Rā, she's drawn a picture of you."

The female cashier scowled. "She better bloody not have or she can reckon with my size 9 boot."

"Come and have a look." Joe held out an arm and beckoned to her.

The design depicted a superheroine with long grey hair and deep happy wrinkles around her eyes and mouth. On her chest it said "Gone to seed", and sprouting from her scalp and flowing over her shoulders were colorful vines and wild flowers.

Rā marched towards us, a frown hovering over her pursed lips.

Joe slid down the bench to give her room and as her narrow bottom hit the wooden planks, she gasped. "Holy shit. That is *so* me. I'm all about ageing gracefully."

"Cigarettes will do that to you," said Purple Fringe. "It's a bugger being thirty-five and looking fifty-five, isn't it, Rā?"

"Easy child," said Rā. "You're not too old to have your hide tanned." Her biceps flexed as she mimed putting him over her knee and spanking him.

Purple Fringe grinned, turned around and waggled his bum at her.

Rā leapt up from the seat.

He shrieked and ducked down behind his checkout, and Rā smirked and sat back down again.

"Chil-dren," said Joe. He lowered his voice. "I love it when they're playful. They're like overeager but *very naughty* puppies."

Purple Fringe popped his head up, his face turned inside out, presumably to show his contempt.

"Don't pretend you don't love being called a naughty puppy, Forest." Joe got up and walked past me to the other end of the bench. "Shove over."

Rā and I slid to our right.

He sat down, leant into me and nudged me with his shoulder. "Are you stealing our Wi-Fi, Jewel Bauer?"

"Yes," I said, because, well, I was. Maybe it was better to lie in these situations. I wasn't always the best judge of when the bald truth would serve better than a lie that was quite obviously a lie.

"Why?"

"Because while I can draw without Wi-Fi, I can't market, update my website, check my orders, or do my accounting without it."

"But why are you *needing* to steal our Wi-Fi?"

I said nothing.

"Honey girl, do you need a job?"

Yes, I probably needed a job. "It would be sensible," I

said before the thought occurred to me that he might be, in a round about way, offering me a job. I wasn't sure that working in a supermarket – *mart* – was a more appealing prospect than eating raw pasta by candle light, given my previous forays into the world of minimum-wage jobs.

I sought clarification so I could have an informed decision-making process. "Are you offering me a job?"

"As it happens, we have an opening at the moment, so yes, it would be mutually beneficial for me to offer you a job. We'd have to go through the pantomime of official recruitment procedure, though, so why don't I knock up a job advert and post it online for too short a time for anyone to take notice, and you go home and pretty up your resumé? Come back at eight tomorrow morning and I'll interview you and pretend to deliberate afterwards."

WHEN I ARRIVED at the mart the following morning, five minutes early and damp under the arms from my walk, the car park was empty except for a lone Mazda Demio.

I waited while the automatic doors met in committee to consider my admittance, and stepped into the quiet of the store when they eventually wheezed their way open.

As I rounded the bin of oranges and stepped towards the checkouts, a tangle of feet came into view, then a tangle of bodies.

Forest, Rā, Liam and Joe lay in a pile as if they'd fainted after a group hug, which was strange enough.

Stranger still was the large pool of blood edging stickily towards the aisles of goods.

Standing over them, carving knife in hand, was a

woman bearing an uncanny resemblance to the cheerful body dumper.

Her free hand covered her eyes and as my insides dissolved and made every effort to make an inconvenient exit, she counted down from three. On "Zero" she removed her hand, jerked her head towards me and jumped.

"Oh, my goodness." She gave a little laugh and placed her palm on her chest. "I didn't see you come in. You gave me quite the fright."

CHAPTER SIX

YOU KNOW when you have that thing when you hear nothing but your blood roaring in your ears, and you get vertigo and you know you're going to fall face first through the floor, and your insides feel pressurised like a house in a tornado the moment before all the windows explode?

I felt that, *all* that, when I got the news about Dad's accident and all Mum could tell me was that he was in the Intensive Care Unit, which I knew from Grey's Anatomy was the fickle intermediary between high dependency and Saint Peter's traffic management of the pearly-gate rush hour.

The current rehashing of that sensation was not something I would wish on anyone. Not even Kaitlyn, or Mayor Dick For Brains. My body felt like it was crumpling in on itself.

Joe cracked an eye.

"Jewel!" he said, beaming at me. "You're early."

The others opened their eyes and peered at me.

It wasn't real. The whole awful thing wasn't real.

I marched over and kicked the bottom of Joe's shoe.

"What the fucking *fuck* is going on you fuckers?" I punctuated my question with another kick.

He sat up and blood dripped from a line across his neck, staining the collar of his T-shirt. "We're staging a scene to help Helena." He waved a hand in the direction of the woman who had slid down the side of the checkout and had her head between her knees. "Evidently it didn't work."

"*Staging a scene,*" I repeated as Liam, Forest and Rā rolled off each other. The pressure under my skin swirled and eddied, gathering strength before reversing in a verbal detonation.

It involved words like "public place" and "traumatised" and "thoughtless asshats" in all caps and with complete disregard to the rules of punctuation. I concluded with "A KID COULD HAVE WALKED THROUGH THAT DOOR" and stopped to pant a bit.

In the ensuing silence came the inevitable question: Did they still like me enough after that to want me to continue working with them? Because in Jewel Bauer world, self-righteousness often came hand-in-hand with crippling self-doubt.

Joe offered me an indulgent smile and walked towards me. "My poor love. Liam'll make you a Rā Special and everything will be alright." He put his arms out as if to embrace me and I stepped back from him.

"Get your realistic fake blood away from me, you faker."

He grabbed my shoulders instead and pushed me towards the bench seat in the window. "It's fine. Nobody in Puhiruru leaves the house before quarter past eight. It's why we have a mad rush at twenty past when everyone panics about how late they are and how they haven't got any lunch for the kids."

I sat down heavily, my anger still pulsing through my

veins, but receding with each slowing heartbeat. "That was really fucking horrible."

Joe made cooing noises and Forest asked, "Did you get a photo?"

"No. Why would I take a photo of a group of people I thought had just been brutally murdered and while the murderer was ten steps away from brutally murdering me? That would be pure twonkery."

Forest grunted and said under his breath, "I bet it looked awesome."

"It did not look *awesome*." What was wrong with these people? I tried to find out by asking them, but they evidently took it as a rhetorical question. Joe patted my hand, Rā helped the woman, Helena, to her feet, and Forest retrieved a waiting mop and bucket, slopping water onto the pool of blood.

Screwing up her eyes as if caught in the beam of a high-powered torch, Helena said, "Can you all unkillify your-selves now? I'll wait with my peepers closed until you're cleaned up."

Rā peered at her from under her brows, rolled her eyes and looked at me. "We're trying to desensitise her."

That made absolutely no sense. "To mass murder? Why? Because of all the instances of mass murder she's likely to stroll across on a daily basis?"

Joe said, "Helena's an author," and nothing else. Brilliant.

"Right. Well, that explains everything. Thank you, Joe."

Patting my hand, he said, "Ooh, you're so acerbic when you're traumatised. I would say I love it, but that would be a lie. Grudging admiration, maybe? I couldn't be acerbic if I tried."

I pulled my hand out from underneath his and shuffled the width of a bum cheek down the bench.

Rā wiped the blood off her face with a towel she'd retrieved from her checkout and threw it to Joe. "You can come out now, Helena. We're back in the realm of the living."

Helena cracked one eye, looked Rā up and down, then turned a suspecting eyeball to Joe. Satisfied, she fixed her gaze on me. "The thing is," she said as if she'd already uttered several sentences. "I'm trying to transition from cosy mysteries to thrillers, you know?"

I didn't know. I'd never read a book in my life.

"It's the fault of this place. The landscape is so moody, so atmospheric." She raised her arms in the direction of the sanitaries aisle, but I presumed she was indicating the lake. "It's the perfect psychological backdrop to books that explore the darker side of human nature. And I really want to give the place the characterisation it deserves." She abruptly lowered her arms onto her hips, making her breasts quiver like a set of jelly desserts. "You know there's a very good reason Ridley Scott chose Fiordland as his location for that last *Aliens* film?"

"Yeah," said Joe. "So we'd have a chance to perve at Michael Fassbender."

Rā emitted a noise like a purr.

"Well, obviously," said Helena a little breathlessly and placed a hand on her bosom. "But it was also because this place has a beauty that is brooding. It can be stunning or it can be sinister. I want to burn the Scandinavian-thriller empire down to the ground. End its domination by making Fiordland the next fictional murder capital of the world."

Joe tutted. "There's just one problem, though, isn't there, my lovely?"

Helena clasped her hands to her cheeks and knitted her brows together. "I can't deal with blood. Never have. Just the thought of it –" she moved a hand to cover her mouth as her cheeks bulged. Swallowing, she flapped her hand in front of her face. "Sorry. I just vomited in my mouth a little bit."

"Hard to write a thriller without blood, I imagine," said Rā.

Helena whipped around to face her and pointed her finger. "Is it though? I challenge that trope. I'm going to prove it's possible to write a fast-paced, murder mystery without ever having to describe a death scene."

Forest wrinkled his nose and "Hmm"ed doubtfully.

"Imagine the byline, Jewel," said Joe. "Nordic Noir. But set in New Zealand. And less stab-y."

"You're mocking me," said Helena, looking thoroughly pleased to be mocked.

"That I am, my cuddlesome." He stood up from the bench, walked over to her and wrapped his arms around her. "Oooh," he said through gritted teeth. "There's just so much of you to love."

Helena tittered. "I hope you're talking about the expansiveness of my mind and not that of my behind."

"The expansiveness of your behind is a beauty to behold, Helena. It's just as exciting as what's under the hood." He placed a palm on her head.

The *Staff only* door opened and Liam ducked under the lintel, cup in hand. He curled himself over it as if protecting it from the glare of the overhead lights, which pushed his hair forward into its customary curtain. It rippled with each step.

God, what I'd give to have hair as effortlessly lustrous.

No doubt he was unaware of any of its qualities bar the face shielding.

My hands shook slightly as I reached for the cup.

"I put extra sugar in it." He said it so softly, I wasn't quite sure he'd said anything at all.

"Good." It took my tongue registering the full-bodied flavour of the sweet tea for me to remember myself. "Thank you," I said, but he'd already stepped away towards the aisle of fresh produce.

I took another sip and eyed Helena over the top of the mug. "I take it you didn't dump an actual body out on the lake yesterday?"

She tipped her head back and offered a tinselly laugh to the ceiling. "Goodness me, no."

"Helena is an artist," said Joe. "Total dedication to her craft. Full immersion."

"Like a method actor," added Rā.

"Except I'd never actually kill anyone. Lord knows my husband tempts me when he goes all Gordon Ramsey, but I wouldn't change him."

I didn't know who Gordon Ramsey was, but Rā said, "Who would have imagined all that bastardry would be the perfect muse?" before I could ask. A bastard presumably.

"You see, Jewel," Helena continued. "I needed to check that a sixty kilogram woman, give or take —" she eyed Forest when he snorted. "— Could lift a hundred kilogram plus man over the side of a boat. I was careful to use a cotton sheet, so it'll eventually rot, but it took over a hundred mother trumpeting swedes to replicate the weight and I had to use nine rolls of painters tape to get it to stay the right shape. I think the tape will be alright." She placed her hands against her chest in a prayer position. "I'd hate to upset The Great Lady, but I think she'd understand. An artist must be true to their art form, right Forest?"

Forest grunted.

"And I can't do that without research."

Joe grabbed my hand and pulled me to my feet. "Come on, let's get the official stuff rolling before Helena's tempted to ask you lots of questions and make you a character in her next novel."

Helena gasped. "I wouldn't do that. Probably."

Joe led me towards the *Staff only* door and through to what he said was his "office".

His "office" was, in fact, a glorified broom cupboard. He had to feed his feet through the space between the seat of his chair and the top of his desk and slide himself in. There wasn't enough room to pull the chair all the way out.

The room also had no windows and was painted a dour muddy grey.

"Welcome to The Hole." Joe widened his arms along the length of the room as if we'd just entered the reception hall of the palace of Versailles. "The captain calls my workspace 'character building'. For two hours a day I endure solitary confinement to strengthen my mind and sharpen my concentration," he said with a bright smile.

"Are you *actually* happy about working in here, or are you doing the facetious thing? Sometimes I find it hard to know."

"Oh, no. I like it. It's amazing how much work you can get done when there's no distractions. You close that door, you can't hear a thing. It's like being in a bunker."

"But...you're not the owner, even though you're hiring me? That captain dude is?"

"Guy Fink. One of the best humans that ever breathed after Nelson Mandela. And Jonathan from Queer Eye."

I was highly doubtful. "Jonathan's a big call."

Joe tipped his head back and laughed. "You are precious.

I'm the floor manager, and yes, I do the hiring." He clicked his mouse and leant over to retrieve a piece of paper from the printer. "Right. Let's have a look at your, no doubt, very impressive resumé."

I hoped he had strategies in place to help him cope with the disappointment.

"I see underneath hobbies, you like 'cooking cats'. I take it that was a punctuation error?"

Ah, yes. The illiteracy gag. I wondered when it was going to rear its ugly head. I didn't want to get indignant about it, because Joe could take his offer of a job away at any time, but indignant was my default position when it came to matters of disability. "Yes. Of course I don't cook cats. That would be a horrible thing to do. I'm dyslexic and make writing errors. Often. So, if you're making fun of me, that would also be a horrible thing to do."

Joe considered me for a beat, gave me a wide smile and screwed the resumé up into a ball. "Never cared much for commas myself. Nasty little things." He threw it over his shoulder where it ricocheted off the wall and bounced to a stop.

I looked at Joe closely for the first time. His *Puhiruru Grocery Mart* emblazoned shirt had been tailored to fit his slight frame. Stretched over the top of them was a set of black braces clipped to a pair of navy pinstripe trousers, which were in turn, rolled up to reveal bright yellow Doc Marten boots.

I think, in the moment he dramatically denounced punctuation, I knew that I liked him. But his style, a blatant disregard for what might be considered standard managerial attire, confirmed it.

Steepling his fingers, he said, "Now. You know this position is twenty hours, four hours a day, five days a week?"

I nodded.

"There may be the odd late shift, depending on illness and annual leave, but most of the evening work and the weekend shift is done by our teen team. High schoolers saving for their escape."

"Escape from what?"

"From the sound of the nowheresville flat-line stifling their celebutante dreams. Selfography has a lot to answer for." He raised one corner of his mouth. "They'll be back."

Then he clapped his hands and I jumped.

"Right! I suppose I'd better make a bit of a pretence at interview formality. So –" he placed a finger on a sheet of paper on his desk. "– Eeny meeny miny mo. Ah!" He tapped the paper with the pointed finger and said, "The 'why' question."

Swivelling to face me, Joe clasped his hands together on his lap and carefully crossed his legs without collecting his shins on any furniture. "Jewel, why do you want to work for Puhiruru Grocery Mart?"

Somebody else might have said they were passionate about customer service and wanted to represent the Mart brand with pride. But I didn't see the point in saying something both of us knew to be a lie.

"I run a yet-to-be-profitable business and I need a support job. Also, I'd really like to eat more than carrot and rice for dinner."

"And *that*," he paused, "is the correct answer." He leaned towards me. "I knew you'd be the perfect fit when I saw your T-shirts. Everyone here has a side hustle. Forest, the rainbow emo at the checkout, makes cosplay outfits. Only way you'd get me into these God-awful shirts is by him sprinkling magic tailoring dust over them."

I wasn't sure if that meant what I thought it might. "Are you saying without actually using any of the words, the job is officially mine?"

Joe offered an indulgent smile. "Of course. There's always room for more colour in our monochromatic world of retail. But, before you say 'yes', I have to warn you I believe in an open and honest culture here. So I'm about to be very blunt. The cons of working at Puhiruru Grocery Mart are as follows" – he counted off on his fingers – "One: you get to wear a sack the delightful colour of cow shit every day. Two: you are paid just enough to meet all your weekly needs but only half a want. Three: the work is repetitive and there are days when you will feel little more than a circuit-board automaton. Here are the pros. One: the team is beautiful." He laid his hands on his lap. "That's all I have."

It wasn't much, but it was leagues above any other option I had on the table.

"I'll take it."

CHAPTER SEVEN

WHEN I ARRIVED for my first day on the job, again five minutes early and just as sweaty, I was, surprisingly, not greeted by a pile of bloodied bodies, or a banana gun showdown.

Liam loaded trays of chicken legs into the meat chiller, and Rā and Forest arranged the packets of confectionery at their counters as if any other workplace possibility was in the realm of the ridiculous.

Before I'd taken a dozen steps into the store, Joe met me with a "My love" and pulled me *by the hand* into the staff room.

I hadn't willingly held hands with anyone outside of my parents since Year 5 folk dancing when I was young enough not to have any notion of personal space, nor that touching other people carried a language all of its own that could be interpreted or misinterpreted in any number of perplexing ways.

When Joe released me, I involuntarily wiped my hand on my trousers because our hands had got a little sweaty. Luckily, his back was to me and he couldn't mistake it for wanting to wipe off the Māori goobies, because I would never think to do that, but, apparently, I could carry guilt for looking like I might think to do that.

The staff room was another windowless box, housing a kitchenette, a small dining table and a set of lockers.

He plonked a cardboard box on the table filled with pre-loved work shirts and explained the "sublime to the cosmically ridiculous" nature of the store's foot traffic.

There was a set of defined rush hours each day: the before work and school; the post-mid-morning-yoga-class/baby-group/book-club/pensioner-zumba; the after school; and the after work. You could set your watch to the consumer patterns of the residents of Puhiruru. Tumbleweed rolled in the minutes and hours in between. "Not that you'd know by the SUV orgy in the car park," Joe said. "People take their two-hour complimentary parking down to the nano-second."

I held the large, shapeless khaki shirt he'd thrust at me against my torso. It had darkened patches under the arms from where a combination of sweat and deodorant stiffened the fabric.

I laid the shirt on the lunch table and unbuttoned it.

"I'll step outside while you get dressed. Holler when you're decent."

He closed the door and I fed my arms through the roomy sleeves. The fabric was soft from wear and smelled of body spray and teen angst.

"Done," I called, securing the last button.

"Excellent." Joe's muted voice carried through the thin wall. "I expect a revelation with a flourish."

"In this?"

"It'll make you feel so much better about wearing such a tragic garment. Like so." He pushed the door wide, one hand on the handle, the other on the door frame, his head thrown backwards and a leg cocked.

"You are *so gay*," I said, and realised that an ordinary person might have thought this and kept it inside their head.

Joe didn't blink. He grabbed me by my hands *again* and pulled me across the room to the door. "Actually, I'm gender blind. Now, your turn. Go on. You'll feel aesthetically invincible afterwards." He closed the door. "On three, two, one."

I pulled the door open and raised my arms in the V of a champagne salute I'd seen on *Next in Fashion*.

Joe applauded. "Beautiful. Don't you feel a million?"

"No. I do feel slightly less repulsed by living in the aromatic fog of romantic aspiration and crippling insecurity, though."

Joe stepped up to me, sniffed and wrinkled his nose. "You'd think they'd have the decency to wash them before they handed them in. Come on, you need to meet Harit."

"Can you really not tell the difference between women and men?" I asked, as he led me to the stock room.

Joe laughed. "Gender blindness means the sex of a person is not a consideration when determining attraction."

"So, you're bi?"

"I'm pan, baby. Man, woman, trans, gender neutral – I love them all." He pointed out the large double bay doors, to where a forklift neatly slid its metre and a half-long forks underneath a pallet and lifted it into the air. It swivelled towards us and approached the inside storage area.

A young man looked over at us, raised his hand and shook it in a shaka gesture. "What's up, Joseph?" he shouted over the beeping of the machine.

"Harit, meet our newest family member, Jewel Bauer. She designs superhero T-shirts and sees bodies being dumped out on the lake."

Harit pursed his bottom lip and nodded as if body dumping was as commonplace as mowing the lawn in Puhiruru. Depositing the pallet next to a set of shelves, he turned the forklift off and stepped down from it. He wore skinny-leg jeans and cheap Converse knock offs. As he approached us, he said, "Ah, this lake. It's the biggest character in this town's story, na?"

Joe clucked his tongue. "You sound like Helena. Jewel, this is Harit, he's from Bangladesh, delivers pizza in the evenings and is the best forklift driver in the southern hemisphere."

Harit put his hands in his pockets and rocked back on his heels. "That's not true. We all know I'm the best forklift driver in the galaxy."

"Now, Harit. That's a pretty big claim." Joe looked at me then. "He probably is. I've seen him load goods balanced on one wheel."

Harit grinned and two dimples appeared high above his cheek rounds. "Next step. No wheels. I'll do it with levitation."

Joe clapped him on the back. "I love your ambition." He turned to me and said, "Ever need a pep up, spend five minutes with this guy. You'll get an energy kick through osmosis," which I knew to be metaphorical, because only plants and paper towels used osmosis as an absorption process.

Joe then led me back up the corridor to a door marked "Command Centre" and raised his hand to knock, before pausing and withdrawing it. He cocked his head to listen, then threw the door open.

Before he had time to fully draw his finger gun and point it into the room, one was placed against his temple.

"Merde," said Joe.

"If you walked more like an SAS commando and less like a tangoing elephant, I wouldn't have been alerted to your presence hovering outside my door." The gun was removed. "Stealth is your best weapon, hmm?"

Joe stepped into the room. "Yes, sir. I'll get you next time."

"Good."

I followed Joe in and chose not to mimic his "at ease" pose in front of the captain's desk. I clasped my hands in front of me and cocked a hip instead. I thought it might signal just enough deference for the boss of a low paying job, while being rebellious enough to preserve my self-respect.

The captain reclined in his leather office chair and dressed his face in a smile that didn't seem to belong to a trained killer. Deep creases fanned out from the edges of his eyes and his cheeks rounded into two plums. He could have been a paediatrician. Or a cat whisperer.

"Captain, this is Jewel Bauer, our newest recruit. She'll be a part-time shelving specialist. Dry goods."

The captain swung his gaze on me, leant forward and offered his hand. "Good to have you on board, Jewel. Guy Fink, veteran, business owner, and reluctant Virgo."

"I'm sorry." I was. Being unhappy with your star sign was like bemoaning a second eyeball.

"Yes, well." He patted his stomach, misinterpreting the object of my sympathy. "Discharged to fatten up in the chair force. It's not all bad. I have Joe here to keep me on my toes." Gesturing to the chairs behind us, he told us to have a seat. "So Jewel, you look fit and healthy. Good, good. We need more capable cadets, pick up the teenage slack." He shook his head. "What is it with the youth these days? Attention span of a blowfly. Couldn't have any of that in the A-stan. It was full battle rattle. Zone out in the conflict zone, you were a bullet catcher. Anyway, where are you from, Jewel?"

"Invercargill."

"Excellent. Good southern stock. We breed 'em to be tough, aye, Joe?"

"No idea, sir. I'm from Wellington."

The captain blinked. "Quite." He turned his attention back to me and blinked again. And once more.

Um.

Was that my cue to say something?

His blinking could have been Morse Code for "The room is bugged" for all my ability to read the situation, or any situation that required interaction with an unfamiliar person.

The captain broke the silence. "In-ver-car-gill," he said as if testing each sound.

"Yes."

Another blink. Perhaps the captain was as bad at small talk as I was.

The way he'd said "In-ver-car-gill" made me think of a funny incident I'd had as a child being billeted to a family in the North Island for a soccer tournament. I thought I could try it out as an offering to the conversation. Or lack thereof.

"When I was eleven, I was staying with a family in Whanganui and I talked about my dog, Gypsy, and the six-year-old boy asked me where Gypsy was now. I said 'Invercargill', and he said 'Where's Vercargill?'"

My anecdote seemed to breathe new life into the verbal desert that had threatened to settle between us. The captain gave an "Oh?" face and pushed out three "Ha"s before leaning forward in his seat. "Little known fact about Invercargill is that it's the German Shepherd breeding capital of the South Pacific. Did you know that?"

"No. That's not trivia that would interest me," I answered while the captain continued.

"Not a very cuddly breed. Our unit had one called Silencer. Very effective at clearing an area. Wouldn't see the squirters for their ghost turds."

I looked at Joe who raised his eyebrows and turned his bottom lip down. I wasn't sure if that meant he didn't understand the captain's lingo, or he did and it wasn't something I wanted to know.

"I...literally have no idea what you're talking about," I said, and added, "sir," as an afterthought. This man would be paying me, after all.

The captain looked unfazed. "Squirters were what we called the insurgents making a hasty retreat."

Joe wrinkled his nose.

"And ghost turds?" the captain continued as if I'd asked the question. "Dust balls, Jewel. You'd be surprised at how careless fighting men can be when struck with a severe case of panic. Made tracking them pretty easy." He waved a hand in the air as if dispelling the kicked-up dirt.

And that, apparently, was that, because he said, "Right, well. Good chat, Jewel."

It wasn't. I'd said a couple of dozen words, pretty much all of which expressed either my lack of comprehension of his conversation or my disdain for it. Five points to Jewel Bauer, queen of the clueless.

With a "Great to have you on the team", Joe and I were dismissed to discuss the art of shelf restocking and after two hours, I was sent to have my morning tea break with Rā, which was, frankly, terrifying. The thought of being enclosed in the windowless break room with a woman who exuded the ferocity that Rā did, *and* having to make small talk with her, made my insides wither a bit.

As demonstrated by my earlier foray into a verbal no-man's-land with the captain, I couldn't make small talk at the best of times. I couldn't be *polite* at the best of times, let alone make polite conversation.

Rā walked into the room, stared at me for three unnerving seconds, then broke the ice by pointing at my white-bread sandwich and saying, "I'll get you a cuppa to wash down your throat glue."

The breeze block-walled room reverberated with the clatter of mugs, and I searched for something to say back.

Surprisingly, it wasn't too hard. There was one thing we all had in common and I genuinely wanted to know what everyone else's looked like. "So what's your side hustle?"

"My what?"

"Joe said everyone has a side hustle here. Forest's is making cosplay outfits, Harit's is delivering pizzas."

Rā grunted. "True. We all moonlight to some extent. The living wage doesn't go very far when you've got a couple of kids or a family to support in another country."

Placing a cup in front of me, she said, "I like that one." She tapped the side of my mug where thick black lettering vibrated against a white background.

I couldn't quite make out all words. "What does it say?"

"It says 'I do not spew profanities. I enunciate them clearly, like a fucking lady'."

I smiled.

"Lord on high, the girl knows how to smile. That's the first upwards-lip motion I've seen you give. You don't find joy very easily, do you?"

"I just –" I stopped, not comfortable explaining my oddities to a woman I didn't know, so I took a sip instead. It was just as good as the last two times I'd drunk a Rā Special. "I find joy in this tea."

"You wanna know the secret?"

I did.

"Lots of milk, but you've got to heat it first so it doesn't make the tea tepid. Just ten or fifteen seconds in the microwave. And here's the pièce de résistance. A quarter of a teaspoon of sugar, not enough to really sweeten it, but enough to bring out the flavour of the tea. Then add a tiny sprinkling of salt. BOOM." She puffed out her cheeks to mime a bomb exploding inside her mouth. "Tea taste sensation."

"It's the best tea *I've* ever had."

"Ruin you for making it any other way."

I swirled my tea, tested its heat, and downed half of it in one hit. Smacking my lips, I said, "You haven't told me your side hustle."

Rā *thunk*ed her mug down on the table and pursed her lips as if sucking on a cigarette. "I organise fringe sports."

"What are they?"

"Stuff that's well outside traditional, institutionalised sport. There's a reasonable demand for them in these parts, especially in the rugby and netball off-season. I think people are hungry for less disciplined disciplines. If you know what I mean."

"Like what?"

"In winter, there's a small lake up the way that we do car curling on."

I wasn't sure I'd heard her right. "Car curling?"

"Yeah, like regular curling. But with cars."

I looked at her for a beat, trying to marry up someone pushing a curling stone across ice with the logistics of doing the same with a car. "How do you curl cars?"

"You have to strip the car of everything non-essential, including the engine, to make it light enough, and then you put one person behind the steering wheel and have nine others pushing the car up to a 'let go' point, and the driver has to try to control the car as it glides across the ice. Generally, it turns into a derby fest, though the speed is too slow to cause much damage." She sipped at her tea in three rapid little *shwurp*s. "I wanted to start an Ultimate Taser Ball league this year, but civilian stun guns are illegal here."

"A *what* league?"

"It's pretty big in Brazil. Your team has to carry a large soccer-like ball to the opponents' goalposts without getting tased." She sighed. "Shame. I would have loved to have seen that in action."

"That's horrendous," I said, despite probably liking to see it in action, too.

"But I bet I'd have had enough sign ups to at least start a social series. Testosterone can make men really stupid. Which means more entertainment for everyone else." She rummaged around in her handbag and brought out a packet of cigarettes and a lighter. Standing up, she said, "Sit with me?"

I followed her through the stock room to the loading bay, where Harit unloaded a pallet of nappies and toilet paper. He straightened up and waved. "Jewel Bauer!" Then his eyes lighted on the cigarette box in Rā's hands and he ran over. "Rānui, let me show you my new trick. I'll light your cigarette for you."

"How long will it take, Harit? My body's starting to suck the nicotine caches in my marrow."

"Two minutes, I promise." He took her lighter and cigarette from the box, grabbed three cartons of cereal from the shelf behind us, and stacked them face down on the ground so that they lay in two adjoining piles – one box against a pile of two, like steps. Then he balanced the cigarette on the higher step so that it jutted out, and placed the lighter on the ground in front of the boxes. "Okay. Wait there."

As he ran in the direction of the forklift, Rā said, "This should be pretty good. He's got a freakish talent for driving that thing. I've tried to get him to design a sport with fork-lifts, but given this is only one of three in town, it wouldn't be much of a game."

Harit swung the machine around to face the boxes and lowered the forks just enough that as he approached the lighter, the right fork rested on top of it. Then with a short reversing maneouvre, he flicked the lighter onto the flat of the steel.

Rā and I clapped and he held up a finger. "Just wait."

With a series of quick ups and downs, he shook the lighter until the butt of it projected over the edge of the fork. Advancing on the boxes, he lined the butt up with the end of the cigarette above it and lowered the steel, laying the bottom of the lighter on the bottom box and raising the fork until he pushed the lighter into a standing position.

I released the breath I've been holding and said, "How does he get so precise with such a clunky piece of machinery?"

Rā shrugged. "It must take hours of practise. But I've never seen him do anything out here other than his job. Kid's a natural."

Harit repositioned the fork so that the edge of it lined up with the ignition switch of the lighter and lowered it. A blue flame flared, the end of the cigarette smoked, and Rā leapt forward to claim it, sucking deeply.

"About fucking time." She enveloped Harit in a hug as he stepped down from the driver's seat. "You are a forklift virtuoso, my lad."

Harit beamed and swaggered over to the cereal boxes, firing a pair of finger guns at them and blowing away the smoke before bending to pick them up.

I couldn't blame him his cockiness. He was masterful. But it was such an extraordinary waste for just a couple of mart staff spectators. At least I could sell my talent to the world and do it over and over again. "You need a videographer."

"My thoughts exactly," Rā said on a smoky exhale.

"In the next life, perhaps." Harit placed the boxes back on the shelf. "God has other plans for me in this one."

Rā looked at me. "We'll keep working on him. "Right." She took a final drag and ground the butt under her heel. "Break over. Back to the meat grinder."

⁂

AT THREE MINUTES to my clocking off time, I removed all the large bags of raisins so I could add the replacement ones at the back.

Between the gaps in the rows of goods in the adjacent shelf, a dark, thickly-lashed eye stared back at me. It blinked once and shifted out of view.

CHAPTER EIGHT

"I GOT A PART-TIME JOB, DAD."

"You did?" Dad said like I'd discovered a cure for cancer. "She got a part-time job," he relayed to a Rewa who'd presumably heard it the first time it was voiced, considering the whole "forgot to press the button before putting the phone in its cradle" routine.

"Yeah you did!" she shouted from somewhere in the shallow bowels of their small house.

"Imagine that. My daughter. An employee." He might have said "NASA engineer" for all the pride he exuded. "Never doubted you could get one if you wanted. Bet you left all the other candidates choking in your dust."

"No one else applied."

"No one else had the required skill set. I expect they couldn't believe their luck when you showed up."

Doubtful. I had a sneaking suspicion my employment was simply Joe's ploy to put me to use if I was going to be hanging around anyway.

"Obviously, the *Dreaded Bauer Curse* didn't rise to haunt you when it mattered." He said "Dreaded Bauer

Curse" in a hammy English accent, like a character from a Hammer horror.

"That I got a job despite it, you mean?" I hated it when he talked about our family's predisposition towards dyslexia like it was some kind of tragic affliction.

"Exactimondo. I'm happy you found a job where it doesn't matter. Hats off to your, no-doubt, very handsome employer. Where are you working?"

"At the Puhiruru Mart. I started a few days ago. My job's to restock the dry goods."

"All of them?"

"A lot of them."

"Sounds varied and interesting."

It was neither varied nor interesting and there wasn't much about the job I could pick out and use as a conversation piece. "The people I work with seem nice. Even Liam, who's only ever showed me one eye at a time."

"Does he wear an eye patch or something?" shouted Rewa.

"No. He hides his face behind his hair, like he's either hideously disfigured or very very shy."

"Poor guy."

"I guess."

Dad said, "It's good you're making friends, Jewelsy."

Is that what was happening? Was I making friends? I couldn't be sure considering my ability to make friends and keep them lasted for as long as it took for my oddities to wear thin.

"I don't know about that, Dad. They're my colleagues. They have to be nice, or their workplace gets polluted with toxic socio-political bullshit or whatever."

Dad rumbled out a laugh. "Work is a great place to make friends. Even special friends. Right, Rewa?"

Rewa had been brought in by the state to care for Dad when Mum left. It had taken them four months to decide they were in love with each other, which, by any standard is rather quick after exiting a marriage, but I didn't care. As long as Dad was happy.

"There won't be any special friend making." And there wouldn't be, even if one of the male members of staff had a brain aneurysm and saw "babe" when they looked at me, it wouldn't take long for my personality, my various idiocies, my difficulty in relating to people, to cool off any initial enthusiasm.

"Never say never," said Dad.

"Never say never," said Rewa.

"Anyway, Jewelsy, how's the crib treating you?"

I peered at the small interior, at the dark walls crowding in on the furniture.

"I was thinking that when I've saved a bit of money, I'll paint the walls cream. Make the rooms lighter."

"Cream? Whoa-ho-ho," Dad chuckled. "Don't go all radical on me, Jewelsy. I'm still processing the lack of window gauze." Which of course, in Dad-speak, meant *Go for your life.*

"It should work in with the carpet and the yellow of the kitchen table."

"Well, you've got the visual intelligence. I'm sure it will look sick or whatever you young folk say."

"Fourteen-year-old skater boys say 'sick', Dad. *I'd* probably say a ubiquitous and misnomic 'Awesome'."

"Listen to that, Rewa. My daughter says words like 'ubiquitous' and 'misnomic'. No dust settling on *her* brain."

"Except I'm not sure 'misnomic' is actually a word," I said.

"Sounds like one. Say it with enough confidence and it's a word."

"As long as it still sounds cool," said Rewa. "I'm not sure 'exactimondo' fits the criteria, my lover."

"What's wrong with exactimondo?" said Dad, as Rewa said, "Oh, hey Jewel, that Brian McManus didn't get in for a fourth term."

My brain revolved with her words and wobbled back into place. The mayor of Invercargill was no longer the mayor of Invercargill?

"Lost to a lesbian from Kai Tahu-Waitaha."

I gasped at the scandal of it. "No. Fucking. Way." A Māori, a gay, and a woman. The custard would be dripping off his face for millennia.

God. If I'd waited a week to call him a cockwomble, I wouldn't have lost my contract.

Still, I supposed in the larger scheme of things, my job loss didn't matter, but his election loss sure did. "Holy shit, you know what this calls for, Dad?"

"Indeed I do – a Green Ginger Wine Moment. We've got two things to celebrate now. You getting your job and a bright, new progressive future for Invers."

I rummaged around in the back of one of the kitchen cupboards looking for the bottle I'd spotted several days ago.

"What do they call politicos like him?" said Rewa from green-ginger-wine retrieving distance. "Male, pale, and stale?"

"I believe neo-liberal, self-interested, power-hungry arsewipe are the words you're looking for," I said. "And let's not forget all the subtle bigotry."

The mayor's vagina worship comment replayed in my head.

And all the unsubtle.

The bottle glugged as I filled a crystal sherry glass. "You want to make the toast, Dad?"

"I do," said Rewa. "To Jewel's new foray into the workforce, and to a new era for our beautiful city filled with hope and rainbow sparkles."

"Mauri ora," said Dad.

"Mauri ora," Rewa and I chorused.

As I slurped back the first sticky mouthful, my phone buzzed. I pulled it away from my ear and looked at the notification.

Brooke: R u dead

My rent was due two days ago. I had to hand it to Brooke, I thought she'd be on my case the moment the amount didn't show up in her account, but perhaps she wasn't as greed-filled money-conscious as I gave her credit for.

I peered at the "For my sins (and Brooke + Kaitlyn)" jar. It didn't have any more money in it than the original $3.70, mostly for two reasons:

1. I hadn't been paid yet.

2. Who pays for anything with cash these days? I'd had no chance to acquire change.

I sighed one of those dramatic sighs where it sounds like your soul is thumbing a lift with your breath. "I better go. I've got something I need to deal with."

"Alright, Jewelsy. Kill it at work tomorrow, won't you?"

Oh, Dad. "Okay. I'll...kill it at work tomorrow. Bye."

I hung up and looked at my banking app. I'd managed to spend a meagre $32.48 since I'd arrived in Puhiruru and had nearly two hundred dollars left in my account. I could *probably* afford to make a down payment on rent owing now that I had money about to come in.

"Soz," I dictated, because apparently we were doing the

"text lingo of the youthful and lazy" thing, and apparently I had appearances to keep up. "Out of town. Not coming back. Will put some money in your account now and cover the rest later." I added another "Soz" to make an apology sandwich.

Brooke: Wot? Neva?

Me: Yes. Never

Three little dots appeared, and disappeared, then appeared again.

Brooke: U have 2 give NOTICE

I was pretty sure the all caps meant Brooke was just a teeny bit mad about me bailing on them in the dead of night nine days ago.

I dictated, "Didn't you get my note: So long, bitches!" and then deleted it. As awful as Brooke and Kaitlyn were, I didn't think sinking to their level would help in the larger scheme of things.

Me: I'll pay for my two week's notice don't worry.

Brooke: But ur only giving notice now!!!!!!

As shitty as the situation was, I didn't think it called for more than one exclamation mark. Also, I knew for a fact my rent was the same as theirs, even though my room was little more than a hall cupboard. As the people who'd signed the lease agreement, they were in complete control of divvying up a fair rent share between tenants. In fact, me giving them a five-day notice period was probably more than reasonable after I'd been subsidising their rent for eighteen months.

Me: Take it or leave it.

Not wanting to put up with more abuse-by-punctuation, I blocked her, which was potentially unfair on my part, but Brooke made it very clear over the year and a half I knew her that she didn't operate by equitable means, so I figured she would understand.

I deposited one hundred dollars in her account and poured myself another green ginger wine.

WHEN I ARRIVED at work the next day, Forest greeted me by placing a work shirt against my torso. He looked me over, nodded, and laying it in my hands said, "You looked like a broom handle in a potato sack in the other one."

I held the shirt up. It had been tailored to have more shape than the original design. How on earth could he work out what adjustments were needed for it to fit me better? "My waist and chest measurements weren't on the employment form."

He raised two fingers and pointed to his eyes. "Don't need 'em." Turning, he walked back to his checkout.

"You have a laser measure embedded in your eyeballs?" I asked.

He flicked his fringe out of his eyes. "As good as."

"It's true," said Rā. "Boy can size anyone up by sight and sew them a form-flattering outfit. See that little swagger he put in his step there? As much as I'd like to tease him about it, he's earned it, so I'll save up my burn for a later opportunity when he hasn't."

From behind his counter, Forest raised his brows. "Was that...a compliment, Rānui Gleeson?"

"If it was, it was the most backhanded one I've ever heard," I said. "Even I could make a compliment less opaque than that, and I'm generally pretty bad at them."

"Yeah, I noticed you haven't mentioned any kind of gratitude yet," said Rā.

I wondered if Forest's apparent act of generosity was for my benefit, or that of everyone else who had to put up with looking at me. Either way, I still got something out of it, I supposed. "Thank you, Forest."

Forest shrugged, which was just as confusing as Rā's 'compliment'. Did he want to be thanked or not?

I changed in the bathroom. While Forest couldn't tailor the unfortunate colour out of it, he had tapered and tucked it in all the right places to compliment my small curves. I almost looked Good.

I emerged on to the shop floor to a series of whistles from Rā, a smile and another fringe flick from Forest, and a dark head disappearing around the corner of the end set of shelves.

IT WAS Joe who joined me on my next morning tea break. He warmed his hands on a takeaway coffee and asked me how everything was going.

"Fine."

"Have you got any questions about anything?"

I assumed the "anything" meant the processes involved in my job. I didn't have any of those types of questions. My job was pretty straight forward. I did, however, have another question that was *kind of* job-related. It was one I'd been thinking about since the day I stepped into the mart and was pulled behind a toilet paper display. "What's with the captain and all his military...stuff?"

"It makes you uncomfortable?"

"I think I *should* be uncomfortable about the military simulation the other day and the fact you all happily participated in play that pretends to hurt people, but I'm not sure how I'm feeling."

Joe poked his bottom lip out and slowly nodded his head. "It's a fair question. The captain's world is coloured by his past. He left the SAS nearly twenty years ago, but *it* certainly didn't leave *him*."

It was half an answer. I sipped my tea and waited for him to redirect his smile energy into padding out the other half.

He sucked down the remainder of his coffee and said, "Did you know the town's food bank is pretty much solely supported by the captain?"

I shook my head.

"You've seen the donations bin by the checkouts?"

"Yes."

"He matches every good donated. Every one." Joe counted off on his fingers. "He also financed the installation of solar panels on the community centre last year, so that the voluntary groups that use it pay little more than a small maintenance fee. Any community groups wanting to fundraise always get whatever they need, the meat pack for the raffle, the sausages for the sausage sizzle, the bottles of wine for the pub quiz prizes, for free. He funds the entertainment at the rest home and hospice. He paid for the new equipment in the Wrights Road playground. He pays us a dollar more an hour than the living wage because he says we should have a quality of life above the subsistence level."

Joe stopped counting off on his fingers and looked at me. "*That's* why we humour him, because he deserves to be humoured." He raised one shoulder. "Also, it's fun and a distraction from the monotony of our jobs."

I did see the truth of that. But I wondered that if I took

part in future simulations, I'd be perpetuating an ideology of violence. Or something.

I wondered it aloud to Joe.

"Look, my love, his games are ultimately harmless. None of us are going to go out into the world and enact for real what we do in here for pretend. If we played paintball for a team bonding session, would you worry about compromising your moral code?"

"Probably not."

He placed his elbows on the table and leant towards me. "Do you know the cost of living in this area has gone up twelve percent in the last year? That's more than four times the rate of inflation. We *need* people like him to help buoy us folk struggling to keep our heads above water."

"Why has the cost of living gone up? Is it all those monied out of towners moving in and tearing down the old cribs to make way for their Mcmansions? Middle class creep or whatever?"

"*Upper class* creep. Once upon a time, and not too long ago, either, it used to be luncheon sausage and fish fingers were our highest sellers. Now its prosciutto and smoked salmon wings. The real estate boom means the town's losing rental houses. Those that are left have increased their rent due to demand and people are pushed into renting places they really can't afford, if they can find somewhere. It used to be a good place to be poor in. Simple living, affordable housing. I'm starting to forget what that place looked like." Joe paused to smile. It was a decent pause, and probably designed to make me pay attention to what he said next. "We need men like Guy Fink. But, unfortunately, I'm not sure many people would understand him. In fact, I'm sure plenty would misunderstand him, so I think he needs us –"

Joe grabbed my hands and gave them a shake. "– this family of misfits, too."

He didn't need to hold my hands to make me have appropriate feelings about the situation or whatever. I got it. The captain was a bit of an eccentric and he was worth making the effort of trying to understand him.

"Okay," I said.

Joe leaned back and pulled his hands back onto his lap. "Have you noticed you've got a food parcel in the fridge?"

"No." I swivelled in my chair and opened the refrigerator door. A plastic, sealed container sat on the top shelf with the word "JEWEL" written on a plaster on the lid.

I pulled it out and opened it. It was filled with deep-red cuts of meat. "Who's this from?"

"Liam. He hunts deer at the weekends. You do eat meat?"

"I'm far too poor to be able to make ethically-based decisions about food." I looked from the container to Joe's face. "Why would he give this to me?"

"A number of reasons. Here's some. One, he hunts more meat than he needs. Two, he's a nice guy. Three, judging by the ratio of instant noodles to food with any actual sustenance in your weekly shopping, you could do with a bit of help." Joe reached over the table and placed a hand on my shoulder. "Why don't you go to the food bank, my love?"

"Because I don't need to."

"You're too proud, you mean?"

"No. I have the money. I'm just trying to make it last as long as I can. I'll buy some proper food on pay day."

"Good." He pushed away from the table and stood up. "That venison will be beautiful. Do it a favour and don't mix it through your instant noodles."

ON MY WAY out of the store, I swung by the fresh foods section to find Liam and ran straight into a wall as I rounded the corner of the first aisle. It "Oomph"ed and large hands grabbed my shoulders to steady me as I staggered back from it.

"I'm sorry," Liam half-said, half-whispered. His Adam's apple bobbed as he swallowed. "Are you okay?"

It was difficult, now that I was standing right in front of him and that his shoulder-clasping meant he was bent into me, for him to do his curtaining-off trick with his hair.

It swung forward from a middle parting, affording me a view of the bits of his face I hadn't yet seen, which was pretty much everything except for his eyes.

He had the high cheek bones, almond eyes and full lips that suggested an Asian ancestor somewhere in his genetic make up. Why on earth anybody who had a face like that spent the energy trying to hide it all the time was beyond me. It was a face that was almost too handsome to be considered seriously. So I decided not to consider it seriously. Ingrate.

"Yes," I said and he dropped his hands, but kept the curl in his spine.

I rubbed the sting from my nose from where it had been flattened against his chest.

"Thanks for the food. It was..." A little weird from someone who spends so much energy hiding from me? "Really nice of you."

He turned and ran his hands over brown onions, squeezing them and removing their loose skins. The curtain fell back between us. "Pan fry it at a high temperature in both butter and oil."

"Okay." I didn't have butter, because it was too expensive, so I wouldn't be doing that.

Pulling over a tall open bin with his foot, he deposited the skins. "Let me know when you've run out and I'll give you more."

I probably wouldn't. It felt too much like taking without giving anything back.

Liam didn't say anything else. His hands worked over the onions in a fast, fluttery motion.

"See you tomorrow, then," I said.

"Yep."

WHEN I GOT HOME at midday, there was a jauntily-angled SOLD sticker covering next door's For Sale sign.

CHAPTER NINE

THE VENISON HISSED as I added it to the margarine
and canola oil soup in the bottom of the pan.

I prodded at the top of the strips, pushing their rounded
middles towards the hot metal underneath. *And* I prodded
at the squishy stuff emerging from my inside places as a
result of Joe grabbing my hands and including me in the
"us" when he said the captain needed the mart family.

I had never belonged to a group. Not a social group, not
an interest group. I hadn't belonged in my last home. Even
my familial group was fractured with Mum in one side of
the Venn diagram and Dad and Rewa in the other.

I kind of gave up trying. It doesn't take too many rejec-
tions before you learn it's better to be lonely than make
yourself vulnerable to disappointment and hurt. And eventually your first true experience of outright ostracism
becomes less important, loses its sharpness in that little
place in your gut where you hold past injustices. Right?

I mean, it's not like I committed it to memory and stuff.

Anyway, it was the 17th of September 2007 and I wore
my green woollen tights that Kimberley Stanton said made

me look like a frog because it was foggy that morning and too cold not to wear tights.

Most of the kids in my class had bought presents for Miss Beecham's birthday because she was young and pretty and nice and we were all a little bit in love with her. You know, things their mums picked out at The Body Shop in the mall. Bath bombs and body butters and shit.

I did not have a mum who bought presents for my teachers from The Body Shop, because my mum was too busy working for minimum wage and saving any spare cash that might otherwise have gone on presents for my teachers from The Body Shop for winter power bills.

So, I *made* Miss Beecham a present. It was a little papier-maché giraffe, because Miss Beecham once said giraffes were her favourite wild animal and I remembered. I had to make all the body parts separately because it was too hard for seven-year-old me to make one cohesive model. The only thing we had in the house that could stick the bits together was Dad's masking tape in the back of his painters and decorators van. The flour and water I'd used to make everything else wasn't strong enough.

Neither, it would seem, was masking tape a day later. I put the giraffe on her desk and the neck, weighted by the bulbous head, promptly swivelled around to rest on the table top. The giraffe looked like it had suffered a brutal vertebrae-severing accident, much to the merriment of the class and my mortification.

But being too poor to afford a real present, or decent glue wasn't the worst of my crimes. Despite Mum writing out the words for me to copy, I had trouble telling the difference between some letters and I wrote "Happy dirthday" in my home-made card, which might have been cute at five, but was unforgiveable at seven.

At morning tea my misspelling was sing-songed back to me, a chorus of "Happy *dirt*hdays" echoing across the playground, which descended to "*Der*" and then "*Der*-brain". It stuck for a little while after. I'd get my new moniker called out to me when there were no teachers to hear it. Eventually, it was forgotten and probably a new one rode in on the back of it. It's hard to recall.

So, yep.

Sometimes I took that little sharp stone out of my gut and turned it over and over in my head until it shone smooth from wear.

And yet, Joe had said in my job interview I was the right shape for the mart's family of misfits.

I turned the meat, the aroma making my empty stomach roll painfully in anticipation. Buttering, or rather margerine-ing a slice of bread, I tipped the venison onto it and blanketed it with another slice. I could have made more effort, but I was too hungry. And who doesn't like a venison butty?

I'd never actually had one before, so it was more of a rhetorical question.

Anyway, I knew what it felt like to be made to feel wanting. That I had parts of me that were wrong.

And yet, nobody at the mart had made me feel I had parts that were misshapen. In fact, they'd all offered something to make me feel welcome. Liam had given me meat, Forest had tailored my work shirt, Rā had shared her tea recipe, Joe had screwed up my error-riddled resumé, Harit had simply been exceptionally nice. I think the gestures were all genuine.

I shoved a corner of the butty in my mouth and bit an entire quarter of it off.

Holy Jesus H. Christ it was good.

Moaning my contentment, I decided if this was the quality of the offerings, it absolutely didn't matter if the gestures were genuine or not.

———

AFTER THE 8:30 am rush, Joe asked me to gather up the trolleys in the car park from where harried parents and workers had panic-dumped their groceries into their cars and fled without carrying out the etiquette of returning the trolley to the trolley docking station.

I stepped outside the automatic doors to find Liam sweeping up the leaves and chocolate bar wrappers gathering in sheltered corners.

His work shirt strained against his large shoulders as he leant forward to pull detritus towards him. The seams looked stressed, like they could split at the pressure of being stretched over such a broad expanse of skin and muscle. They wouldn't. Forest would have reinforced them.

I walked up to him and stood behind him, waiting for him to notice me so I didn't give him a fright by calling out his name.

I gave him a fright anyway.

He did a little jump and I said, "Dinner was really good. Thanks for making it...taste."

He nodded and his hair shivered. I thought I saw a smile behind the curtain, but I couldn't be sure. "Taste is preferable when it comes to food."

"I definitely prefer it."

We fell into silence. Liam ran a hand up the broom handle. And down again.

I thought I should probably say something, but I said the last thing, so it was Liam's turn. Or didn't it really matter about order? I'd never understood the rules of small talk. To be honest, I'd never really understood small talk at all. I knew it was considered polite, but as far as I could tell most people got as much enjoyment out of it as I did and were as bad at it as I was. Why torture yourself for the benefit of absolutely nothing?

Liam placed his other hand on top of the handle and ran his palm over it, fingers splayed. Maybe this was the extent of our chat, which was fine by me.

I turned to start my trolley gathering task.

"Um, what did you cook?"

I swivelled around. "A butty."

"Butties are nice."

"Yep. Bready."

Liam nodded again, setting the ends of his hair wobbling. "I made schnitzel."

I loved schnitzel. "Do you know cornflakes can make the bread crumbs extra crunchy?"

"No, I didn't. I'll try that next time."

It was my turn to say something, but I couldn't think of anything and I also had a job to do. Perhaps I could combine the two. "I have to collect the trolleys."

I turned around and inside the store, Joe, Forest and Helena-the-author whipped their heads around from facing out the window and talked animatedly.

From her checkout, Rā continued to look out at me. She leaned on her elbows, her head resting in her hands. Then she winked.

I had no idea what her wink could mean. She'd caught me chatting and not on task? It wasn't like she never involved herself in off-task behaviour while she was on the clock.

The previous week she'd had an altercation with Forest

and mimed putting a bullet into the nose of her cocked finger gun, because it was "liquidation time".

Forest didn't seem particularly worried about the prospect of being liquidated. "They have magazines these days, Rā," he'd said with a condescending brow wrinkle. "Individual bullet insertion ended with the last ice age."

"I have one word for you, my son. Russian Roulette. Very much still a thing."

"That's two words."

"All right, smart arse. How about we play a game of Russian Roulette with rubber bands? We hold one in one of our hands and take turns to guess which. If you get it right, you get a free shot at the other person's butt cheeks."

I spent the next hour listening to the slap of rubber on arse.

As I stepped down from the curb to retrieve the first wayward trolley, a gleaming black SUV pulled into the car park at high velocity and swung into the space I'd just stepped out on to. It braked an inch from my knees and I staggered backwards, my heart galloping in my chest.

Footsteps pounded towards me on my left, and a pale face stared out at me through the windscreen. The shiny skin and swollen features bore an uncanny resemblance to a figure in my past council life. Mayor McManus's, *ex*-Mayor McManus's wife, Bekka.

I shuddered.

Large hands pulled me back up on the curb. "Are you okay?"

The car was a Lamborghini something, which, quite frankly, looked the same as any mid-range SUV, and bore the number plate BKSLAMBO.

"I'm...fine," I answered slowly as I tried to make sense of the personalised registration number.

"Are you sure?"

I nodded and punctuated the movement with a gasp.

The hands on my shoulders tightened. "What is it?"

It was so awful I couldn't say it out loud. I looked again at the driver who was busy putting things into the handbag slung on the passenger seat. Christ, she must have had a brain aneurysm when deciding to reference the car's black colour in her personalised plate.

She cracked the door, placed a high heel on the bitumen, and turned to us.

"I'm so sorry. It's these new Valentinos. The heels get lodged in the weave of the mat. Are you alright?" Her voice portrayed a concern her features were unable to mirror due to the fact they'd been sealed into the pensive expression of a blow up doll, like she'd been melted down and ironed back into place.

There were few women in Murihiku with the vanity and means to attempt radical age defiance and the arrogance to display her wealth by driving a Lamborghini. It *had* to be Bekka McManus. What on earth was she doing in Puhiruru?

And then I realised I'd swapped letters when reading her BKSLAMBO number plate. "Do you know your car's plate's an anagram of 'black sambo'?"

The back of my hair parted with the force of Liam's snort.

Bekka looked at me for a second, no doubt willing her eyebrows to move in a direction that might convey some degree of mental engagement with what I'd said. Then she pushed the door closed and tottered towards the front bumper.

Liam and I shuffled backwards to give her viewing room.

She stood wide-legged, torso tilted backwards, and scrutinised the plate. "God damn it." She turned to face us and said in a whine, "I'll have to get a new car now."

She'd have to *what?*

As Liam's hands slipped from my shoulders, something stirred and stretched into wakefulness in my belly. "Did I just hear you right?" My voice had a quietness not unlike that period of eerie calm before the tornado rips the roof of your house off.

When it brewed enough that the top of my epiglottis flapped in the rising wind, I unleashed the fury.

"Your crisis de jour is the inconvenience of your car's colour so you're just going to *throw it away?* My crisis de jour is working out how I can cook a decent meal for under three dollars." I stepped towards her as my voice rose in both volume and pitch. "This car that has an aesthetic that no longer *suits* you could pay my wage for a decade. You privileged, undeserving –"

A hand slapped over my mouth and my final words were stoppered, which was probably just as well considering they accused her of being an overstuffed sack of collagen.

"Sorry," Liam all but whispered to the woman and started pulling me backwards. "I'm so sorry."

"No, you're not," I wanted to say to him, but his fingers still hampered my ability to vocalise.

As we edged towards the mart's entrance, Bekka watched us open mouthed, one manicured hand clasping her throat.

Once we were through the doors, she whipped her salon-streaked blonde head around and marched towards the driver's door.

The engine fired as the mart doors sealed closed, and Liam dropped his hand.

I took a deep breath and roared at the closed door, "JUST CHANGE YOUR NUMBER PLATE."

I panted a little in the ensuing silence and turned to Liam, who had forgotten to hide himself behind his hair. His eyes were wide. That I understood. My behaviour could probably have been interpreted as on the alarming side of nuclear.

What I couldn't read was the accompanying curl of the left side of his mouth. It was only *just* there, but it was there.

"Feel better, my pet?"

I looked from Liam to Joe to out the door at the now Lamborghini-less parking space. "No." I'd just shouted at a customer while in a mart-branded shirt and in a public place. There wasn't anything good that could possibly come out of this scenario. Yet again, I had been struck by a case of acute idiotosis.

I sighed and stepped towards the *Staff only* door. "I'll go get my things."

"And why would you be going to get your things?"

I paused and swivelled to face him. "To save you the trouble of firing my sorry arse."

Joe offered me an indulgent smile. "I'm not going to fire your sorry arse without thorough investigation." Then he turned to Liam. "Why did Jewel yell at the plastic lady?"

Liam's eyes flicked from Joe's face to mine, then back again. "Um."

"I'll help you start. Jewel went to collect trolleys and a woman in a very expensive car narrowly missed running her down."

"You saw that?" I asked.

Forest said, "We were still watching you be awkward around each other."

"*Forest,*" Rā hissed.

"Sorry. Liam being awkward around Jewel."

Rā clucked her tongue, Joe shot him a frown and turned back to Liam. "And then?" he prompted.

"And then." Liam pivoted so that only Joe was in his eye line and the rest of us were blinkered from his peripheral vision by his hair. "Jewel said to the woman her number plate was an anagram of black sambo."

A guffaw issued from the checkouts behind me.

Joe's face lit up and his gaze shifted to me. "Did she now?"

"And the woman said she'd have to get a new car. And Jewel..." Liam trailed off.

Joe laid a hand on Liam's shoulder and said gently, "Told her some home truths?"

The black hair shimmered with Liam's nod.

"I see." Joe clapped his hands and said, "Well team, I think there's only one possible *official* explanation. Jewel went into shock after narrowly escaping being hit as the result of reckless driving and got carried away by the emotion of the near death experience. Anybody would have."

"Sounds plausible to me," said Rā.

"And perfectly reasonable," said Helena with a little laugh.

"So," continued Joe. "I see no reason to *fire your sorry arse.*"

I stood absolutely still. As far as I could recall, nobody, outside of parental instinct, had done anything to protect me. "Are you sure?"

"Quite sure. You don't think each of us harbours resentment towards the Have Everythings when we're struggling to meet rent? You've just given us the gift of wish fulfilment by proxy, and quite honestly, I'm looking forward to seeing what else Jewel Bauer is capable of."

"You really don't." I wasn't entirely sure what I was capable of, but whatever it was, it probably wouldn't be good given my propensity for shouting before thinking. Still, if the anticipation of it kept me employed, I'd take it. "If you're not going to fire me, shall I go back out there and collect the trolleys now?"

"That depends. Do you want to hear the local scandal or push around metal cages more?"

"I have no opinion on that." I didn't. Neither sounded particularly appealing.

"*I* want to hear it," said Rā.

"Of course you do, my heart." Joe led me and Liam to the checkouts. "Helena has all the details. Helena?"

Helena placed clasped hands against her bosom and bounced up and down on the balls of her feet. "Would you like to guess first?"

"Hector Norris' Jersey bull jumped the fence and impregnated all Bruce Gainford's wagyu heifers," said Forest.

"Good Lordy, no," Helena said through a laugh. "That was last year's scandal."

"The town hall's being turned into a male knocking shop-cum-champagne bar called 'Gigolos and Piccolos?'," said Rā.

The smile slipped off Helena's face and her eyes darted between Rā and the rest of us. "You know what? I'll just tell you. You know that Trafford what's-his-face who stood unopposed for Fiordland District mayor because the incumbent retired and nobody else was willing to take it on?"

"Yes," said Rā.

"No," said Forest.

"Well, turns out the council didn't do their due diligence and he's only a permanent New Zealand resident." She held her arms wide, palms upwards like she'd done a big reveal we were all meant to have understood.

"And that's a scandal because..." said Rā.

"You have to be a *citizen* to stand for local elections. So we have no mayor."

"Can we have no mayor?" asked Forest.

"I think they'll run a by-election."

Joe folded his arms. "Well, I have to say, my love, that is not a particularly inspiring scandal."

Helena raised her palms. "But we're rudderless. We have no one manning the helm. Who knows what will become of the district in the meantime?"

Rā said, "I bet Forest's laser-measuring eyeballs no one will even notice we don't have a mayor."

Forest whipped his head towards her, his mouth open beneath his frown. Then he closed it, tipped his head to one side and looked up at the ceiling. "No. I have to agree. I don't think I'm in any danger of losing my eyeballs."

I said, "Can I do the pushing-metal-cages-around thing now?" and Helena said, "You guys really can't see the drama in this? The potential for political collapse?"

"No," said Forest.

I turned and followed Liam out the automatic doors.

Joe said, "Please tell me you won't be putting this into a book, my heart. It's hardly *House of Cards*," and the doors closed behind us.

———

THE DAY AFTER THAT, Liam's morning tea break coincided with mine. It'd never coincided with mine before and I couldn't help wonder if it'd been orchestrated in order to help us with our "awkwardness".

I'm not sure what Joe hoped to achieve. If yesterday's attempt at breaking the verbal ice was anything to go by, Liam and I would probably spend fifteen minutes staring at the wall or into our coffee cups feeling inept and wishing it was anybody else but each other we had to share time and space with.

I retrieved my phone from my locker and placed it in front of me so I could use it as a force field. If Liam could retreat behind his hair, I could build an "I'm busy Instagraming" wall.

I guess it shouldn't come as a surprise, however, that I didn't need technology to ruin Joe's intentions. I could efficiently do it by opening my mouth.

As Liam sat down and opened his lunch container, I tried to make sense of the words written in thick white font on his black mug. *I want to ki_ _ you. Options may vary.*

If his choice in mugware was deliberate, I wondered what the options on offer were. I could think of three, but only one of them seemed reasonable, if a little forward after less than two weeks of knowing each other.

When I pointed this out to him, his eyes darted to the writing and he went very still, then very red, then said he had something he needed to tell Harit and left.

He didn't come back.

———

THE FOLLOWING day when we were yet again rostered to share a tea break, Liam chose a mug that didn't have any writing on it.

I understood. Embarrassing people wasn't intentional, but then my social blunders never were. That's the problem with sometimes not being able to read situations and acting anyway. They tended to end up with someone being humiliated, and while that person should, by rights, be me, a lot of the time it wasn't.

I decided I would try my upmost not to make him run from the room again, but there was no guarantees and, to be honest, Liam didn't make it easy. With the combination of sitting opposite me and presumably the desire to not have to strain coffee through strands of hair, the face he put so much energy into hiding was available for scrutiny.

He really did have the kind of features designers would hyperventilate over at the thought of their clothes draped beneath them. He had a light dusting of freckles over his nose and across his high cheekbones. His full mouth was accentuated by a short, wispy beard, and his nose was small and straight.

I'd give a kidney for a nose like that. And yet, he worked so hard to conceal it.

"What's up with your face?"

Liam paused, cup halfway to his mouth, his eyes on me. "What do you mean?" he said quietly.

"Why is it all exotic and perfectly proportioned?"

"Um," he tipped his head forward and the curtain fell again. "Ethnic pedigree. Chinese and Scottish."

"Huh," I said and wondered at the propensity of genes from different races to mix and produce a variance of such beauty. If only my ancestors weren't so ethnically blinkered in their selection of sexual partners, I might be sporting an equally aquiline nose or plump lips.

"It's not..." he fiddled with the mug, turning the cup ninety degrees and back again. "It's not exotic. My Chinese ancestors probably arrived in New Zealand not long after yours."

I thought about this while I chewed on my meat paste sandwich, because it was preferable to wondering exactly what the vague "meat" inferred, and because I felt I probably should think about what he'd said.

I *supposed* he meant Chinese is not exotic because they'd lived here for generations. I was only third generation on my dad's side. He was probably more Kiwi than I was.

"Does that make me a casual racist? Calling you exotic-looking?"

Liam turned the mug in the other direction. "It's probably the 'What's with your face comment' that's more on the offensive end of things."

I sighed. Yes it absolutely was. I wish I had the ability to reflect on my words *before* they entered anybody else's ear canals. I tried, but only sometimes succeeded. "What's in my head and what comes out of my mouth are not always an accurate reflection of each other. Words are hard." People are hard. *Being* is sometimes hard.

"What was in your head?"

I honestly had no idea if the thought behind my words was worse than what came out, but he'd asked the question, so...

I looked him in the eye, which was hard as I had to lean forward and crane my neck to bend my eyesight around his hair. "Why are you so afraid of your beauty?"

Given the amount of eye-widening I'd induced in Liam since we'd known each other, it was understandable that I expected some now. I thought, perhaps, what I'd said might be confronting, because, well, I said confronting shit and often without a lot of forethought.

But Liam didn't flinch. Nor did he look away. It was almost like he anticipated the question.

Eventually he said, "I wish I was more like you," and dropped his eyes to his cup.

I sat upright. "More like me? Why on earth would you like to be more like me?" Plain, friendless, says stuff that makes her even more friendless.

"You're fearless."

"I'm not." I wasn't even remotely fearless.

"You shouted at that woman."

"And regretted it immediately afterwards."

"I could never just...tell people what I really truly thought."

"It's not a good idea. Not if you don't want to die poor and alone because there's nobody left to offend."

Liam raised his eyes to me again. "And your T-shirts."

"Yeah. Aggressive. See the pattern?"

"Unapologetic."

"Shouty and provocative."

"I would love to feel comfortable in my skin and be unapologetic about it."

What was going on? We were exchanging words without having to painfully extract them, just like properly functioning grown ups. "Are we actually having a conversation?"

Liam smiled.

"Look at us," I said. "Words are happening."

"Let's not tell the others. They probably have a bet going about how many words it takes before we implode under the pressure." He tucked his hair behind his left ear and drained the rest of his cup.

Liam had just said two consecutive sentences, which was one sentence more than I'd ever heard him utter. And he'd done something else completely out of character.

He'd forgotten to hide behind his hair.

CHAPTER TEN

THE NEXT TIME Liam and I were forced into close proximity, things were...different.

I made my coffee and sat down with my questionably-filled sandwiches, cut into the triangles you might expect to find in a child's lunchbox.

Liam didn't pass judgement. He nodded at my presentation choice and said, "Geometric shapes make everything taste better."

They absolutely did, but I didn't think anybody else knew that.

"You know the thing I hated eating most as a kid?"

Liam shook his head, because of course he didn't know.

"Swede mash. Tastes like ear wax seasoned with dirt, but if you mould it into a polygon it's like honeyed yams."

Liam rumbled out a quiet, closed-mouth laugh. "I can't imagine anything making swede mash taste nice. I think there's a reason they feed it to cattle. Not fit for human consumption."

Three sentences. This was territory Liam and I had

never travelled before. It felt dangerously like the beginning of something. Collegiality?

I did my best to ruin it anyway, because, apparently, I couldn't help myself. "It is if you're poor enough."

Liam was quiet for a moment. "What does it taste like as a parallelogram?"

"Buttered carrots."

His mouth edged into a smile and he muttered something. It sounded a bit like, "Superpower."

I sought clarification. "Did you say 'superpower' but not want me to hear it? Because if you did, I heard it anyway."

He held his mug in front of his face like a shield. "You have superpowers."

I really didn't. "Having the brain power to make letters dance around in a drunken waltz is less magical than it sounds."

Liam's eyes flickered between mine and his own lunch box like he was too uncertain of himself to let them settle on me, despite the surety of his words. "You can take an unpalatable lump of goop and turn it into a delicacy just by moving it around with your fork."

It was pretty much true. "You make me sound like a food Jedi." I put on my best ghost of Obi-Wan Kenobi voice. "Use the fork, Jewel."

I didn't think what I'd said deserved any better recognition than an obligatory snort, but Liam's laugh actually made it out from between his lips this time. The small collection of "Ha"s rolled and ricochetted around the room like marbles in a jar.

I had to admit, making him laugh felt a bit like a superpower, though I wasn't sure that was something I should share or not.

"What, um," Liam paused as if gathering his words.

"What are you transforming today?" He nodded in the direction of my sandwiches.

"Mayonnaise." It was a new low born of running out of meat paste the previous day and forgetting to buy more.

"Just mayonnaise?"

"Options were limited."

Liam didn't say anything for a beat, no doubt speculating as to why I might have nothing better than a condiment to make a sandwich out of. "And what does it taste like as a triangle?"

"Gruyère."

"Would it...be nice to not have to cast geometry spells on your food and just have it taste good? Of its own accord?"

Yes. "I'm forever hopeful that day will be immediately after my first pay day, but I'm not the best chef, so who knows?"

THE NEXT TEA BREAK, Liam presented me with a container. "It's um...cold venison sandwiches cut into the standard rectangles. Because the taste speaks for itself."

The sandwiches were thick, like they'd been sliced from home-made bread. They looked unbelievably delicious next to my anaemic offerings. My mouth watered and I had my teeth around one before, of course, I'd remembered the courtesy of a thank you.

I took a large bite and had to lean into my swallow to get the mouthful down my oesophagus once I'd chewed it.

"I'll make you a Rā special."

I couldn't wait for a drink before the next mouthful. "I weawy goo'," I said, closing my eyes against the richness of the meat and the tang of the accompanying relish.

"I know," came the quiet reply.

I had upped my game that day by cutting my sandwiches into trapezoids, which is a pretty extreme level of food doctoring for any sandwich whisperer, but I knew without a shadow of a doubt that it still wouldn't have come within light years of Liam's sandwich.

"Would you like to try mine? I entered a whole new degree of geometry today." I slid my lunch box across the table towards his empty chair.

"What's in them?"

"Guess."

Liam turned away from the bench, teaspoon in hand and peered into the container. "I don't even know what that shape's called."

"A trapezoid."

"Right." He turned back to the bench. "I think if a trapezoid is required, I'm going to say 'No, thank you'."

"But you haven't guessed."

The microwave beeped. "Is it...*actual* ear wax seasoned with dirt?"

"No. That would be disgusting. I found some old raisins in the back of a cupboard, so I soaked them in vinegar to make a cheat pickle. There's a layer of mayonnaise, too. I thought it might taste like a ploughman's if I upped the shape stakes."

The little room rang with the *tink tink* of spoon against mug. "Um. I think I'll still say 'No'."

I shrugged. "Suit yourself." And took another bite of the venison sandwich.

Liam placed a steaming cup in front of me and it occurred to me that for a man who was so shy he grew his hair long in order to shut the world out, hunting was the kind of activity you'd expect from someone a little more...testosterone-y?

"Why oo you hun'?" I should probably have waited until I'd finished my mouthful before asking, but I was Jewel Bauer, and when words came, they tended to rush out without consideration for etiquette.

"I've been hunting all my life. My family's always hunted." Liam pulled out his chair, scraping the legs across the floor. "I love being out in the bush," he said quietly. "It's...you know...an aloneness that doesn't feel lonely."

I didn't know. I'd never had that. I'd only ever had the other sort. "It's funny how you can be surrounded by people but still feel lonely, isn't it?" It was the cross to bear of the introverted, or misunderstood. Or utterly clueless.

For the second time ever, Liam held my gaze. "Really lonely."

"But you don't mind taking something's life?"

Liam blinked and reached into the lunch box to take a sandwich half. "I don't mind taking a deer's life."

"Why?"

"They're a real environmental pest here. They eat all the young vegetation and prevent forest regeneration."

"Huh." I peered at the strip of meat between the slices of bread. Any hesitancy I might have harboured about eating a beautiful wild creature, but ignored, vanished. "This next guilt-free bite is going to taste so good."

"It should taste good. She was grazing the tops a couple of weeks ago. She's been fed on tussock and fern."

A couple of weeks ago. "How long do you hang the carcass for?" I asked slowly.

He had to finish his mouthful before answering. "Until it just starts to turn green. That's when it's the perfect degree of tender."

I imagined a skinless, headless deer corpse dangling

from chains, its flesh slick and slimy with the beginnings of putrefaction. "You let it *rot* to perfection?"

"Yeah," he said, taking a sip of his tea.

I eyed the second sandwich in the container and peeled back the top layer of bread. The meat didn't look green or slimy. It was the pale brown of all cold red meat.

I supposed, having already eaten half a sandwich, I had to trust he knew what he was doing if he'd been hunting since he was a kid. I took another rectangle and bit into it with a little more consideration than I had given the first half. It tasted just as good as the first. No fizziness of decay. No taste-bud curling sourness.

Washing it down with a gulp, I noticed Liam had given me a cup that was once again wreathed in writing. "What's with the mugs?"

Liam's gaze shifted to my mug and one side of his mouth tugged up as he read it. "This kitchen is a mug graveyard," he said and took another bite.

"A graveyard?"

He put a hand in front of his mouth so that I didn't have to see his masticated sandwich as he answered me. "All the gift joke mugs you laugh at once and hide in the back of the kitchen cupboard get donated to the staff lunch room."

"The place where cups come to die."

"Or live a fulfilling second life."

Is that what was happening to me? I had been "relegated" to the mart to start again on the path to happiness and contentment? So far the start hadn't been terribly promising. "Well, I'm not going to attempt to decipher this one," I said, thinking of the *I want to ki_ _ you* mug. It might tell me to 'blank blank C-K' something."

Liam picked up his cup and took several gulps before lowering his head so his hair swung forward. He peered out of the narrow window his parting afforded and slid his eyes towards my mug. "It says *And then Satan said: 'Put the alphabet in maths'.*"

I snorted. "It's so true. Geometry is one thing, but calculus is pure evil."

Still hidden behind his hair, Liam twisted his mug in a circle. "You weren't that kid in maths who sat at the front with a hand jerking in the air, begging for the teacher to ask you the answer?"

I was never, ever that kid. "I was too busy drawing the pet sperm whale I'd asked to get for Christmas in the back of my work books. Had to give the other kids a chance."

Liam tucked his hair behind his ear, revealing the cheek closest to me. "Did you get a whale for Christmas?"

"I got a skateboard and a broken arm. Probably just as well. There would have only been enough room in the bath for one of us and I was a pretty grimy kid."

"Dirt behind your knees?"

"Dirt in my eyelid creases." I wondered what a Christmas looked like for a Murihiku kid who never had to worry about eating swedes. "What did you want for Christmas more than anything?"

Liam pushed his lips out while he considered my question, which had the effect of emphasising their plumpness and raising my resentment of such lips on a man. "I can't remember ever desperately wanting something from Santa. I do remember Mum telling me I might, um, confuse him if I put down a Barbie Doll *and* a Transformer on my wish list and I should...probably just go for one."

Interesting. "What did you choose?"

"The Barbie. I got a Transformer."

I clucked my tongue. "We both lucked out. Santa can be a bit of a dick sometimes."

"The Santa of my household certainly was."

I had no idea what a Barbie versus Transformer conundrum meant for a kid, or even if the story was the retelling of an actual event or simply a figurative tale of an unhappy childhood. All it did was emphasise how much I didn't understand him.

"If you find being around people lonely, why did you go into retail where you have to actually be around people and talk to them and stuff?"

"This is just a stepping stone in my career path."

Just like me and my T-shirts. "Where's your path heading?"

He leaned back in his chair with a sharp expulsion of air. "I haven't decided yet."

I did that thing where people don't say anything to force the other person to fill the silence. I didn't expect it to work, but...

"It's one of those Barbie or Transformer moments. Or it could be both."

"Cryptic." It really was. In our tea breaks together I'd learned precisely nothing about him. I already knew he hunted. His loneliness didn't surprise me in the least. All that was left was a childhood preference in toys that might have significance or mean absolutely nothing. To be fair, there was a good chance my lack of knowledge gathering was down to me being pretty shit at the talk thing.

There was one bit of information, however, I didn't know about him and that I was genuinely interested in. "I bet it has to do with your side hustle."

"Maybe." Liam stood up and took his mug to the sink.

Break over. Apparently.

"WHAT DOES it mean if a man had to choose between a Barbie or a Transformer for Christmas?" I took my pasta and sauce off the stove, tipped it into a bowl and walked out the back door so I could eat it looking at the lake.

"Ooh, a riddle," said Dad. "I love riddles. Or is it a joke?"

"Whatever it is," said Rewa, shouting from an adjacent room, "it has the makings of something sexist."

"No. It's metaphorical. At least I think it is." Maybe it wasn't and Liam was just really into dolls as a boy.

I sat down on the bank and dipped my fork in. It was too hot and I opened my mouth, ejecting the contents back into the bowl. "Shit."

"What is it, Jewelsy?"

"Nothing." I flapped my hand in front of my mouth as if the minute amount of air I stirred up could cool my burning tongue. "Too hungry for good judgement."

After a pause, Dad murmured, "Me-ta-pho-ri-cal," like he was chewing it over. "So it *is* a riddle."

"Seems that way right now." I took another forkful and blew on it. "I have no idea how to interpret it." But I was reasonably keen to try. Now I'd been given a glimpse into Liam World, the mystery of it was kind of, a little bit, intriguing?

"Maybe," Dad singsonged the two syllables, "he's torn between two women. One who's really feminine and a bit shallow, but beautiful, and one who doesn't fit the notion of an ideal woman and who is empowered to change and adapt."

I didn't say anything for a beat. "You jumped to that scenario from a toy metaphor?"

"Yes. You haven't explained the context, Jewelsy, so I took the opportunity for some out of the box thinking."

I said, "Okay," because of course he had. Braving

another mouthful, I chewed the soggy pasta and wished I'd had the financial bravery to splash out on parmesan.

The line was quiet as if they waited for me to finish my mouthful.

"What's the bloody context, Jewel?" shouted Rewa. "We're dying from the suspense."

I waited for the time it took to chew a third mouthful and said, "You can't actually die from suspense, but we were discussing Christmas presents we wanted as kids."

"Who's we?"

"Me and Liam. A guy at work."

A series of thuds issued down the line as Rewa made a fifteen-metre dash towards the phone. "Oh my God, there's a boy," she said at the same volume from wherever she was in the house before.

I jerked the phone away from my ear and placed it on my knee with a roll of my eyes.

"That's the second time you've mentioned a Liam. Please tell us there's a boy."

"No, there is *not* a boy. Liam is neither 'a boy' in inverted commas or someone who remotely resembles a boy. He's more a reluctant man-bear if anything."

"A man-bear," Rewa said dreamily. "I had one of those once. Sexy as hell, but you want to be on top. Missionary's like having your beef fillets tenderised from under a slab of concrete."

Dad made a noise like a food waste disposal unit. "Jeepers creepers, love. Do you have to give Jewel sex advice?"

"Well, who's going to do it. You? The man who says 'jeepers creepers' like a Ned Flanders fanboy?"

Oh God, please let this conversation not be happening. "I don't need sex advice! There will not be any sex of any nature with Liam. And if I did need some at an unlikely point in my future, the last two people I'd ask are my dad and step-mum." Gross. "So don't get excited."

"I am most definitely *not* excited," said Dad.

Nobody said anything, hopefully not as a result of the me-having-sex conversation thread still running through their brains.

When I was certain the topic had died its rightful death, I slurped up another mouthful and waited for the next, hopefully benign, one to appear.

"How's The Old Girl?"

The early evening sun glinted across the rippled surface of the lake, the reflected light making her waters seem darker than usual.

"Happy. Sparkly."

It was the hour just before Lake Puhiruru was at her best, when dusk descended and everything, the forest, the water, the sky shifted into varying hues of blue and the air softened, like a light mist had risen from the cool waters.

"Not a bad companion, aye, Jewelsy?"

That's exactly what she was, a companion. I could never be lonely sitting here. "She's my favourite neighbour."

"Speaking of which, you got new ones yet?" asked Dad.

"Ooh, yes," said Rewa. "Any new neighbours?"

"I think so. There's noises next door, but I haven't seen anybody."

"You should go over and introduce yourself," said Dad.

"Why?"

"Because it's considered polite, Jewel," said Rewa.

"You know what will happen. It'll start out okay and then I'll say something impolite without meaning to, or I'll forget to say anything and just stand there staring and the whole thing will be worse than if I'd just ignored them."

"Practise makes perfect," said Dad.

"Practise has never edged me closer to perfection."

A crash followed by the whir of an upside-down plate spinning to a standstill drifted around the end of the new-neighbour shared fence. "Bah-loody hell! Why is there oil on the *outside* of the bottle, darl? It's like trying to grapple a monkey in a condom."

I froze, my fork halfway to my mouth. There was only one person I knew who had a habit of turning a reasonably innocuous swear word into a very annoying, three syllable, verbal tic.

With the kind of realisation that snap freezes your organs, I dropped my fork into the bowl and splattered my singlet top with Cut-Price brand pasta sauce.

Please, no.

It was the singular explanation for the presence of his surgically-enhanced wife in the mart car park.

"Dad," I whispered. "I'll call you back."

CHAPTER ELEVEN

PLACING the bowl on the grass, I tip-toed to the end of the shared fence.

Nothing else was said. Jazz floated softly towards the lake, something clinked, another thing clanged, but no further vocal clue was offered in confirmation.

I would have to look.

Wrapping my fingers around the rough wood, I edged my head sideways until my left eye gained a view of the immaculately landscaped, small back yard.

And there he was.

The cockwomble himself, prodding at a large slab of meat on his, no doubt, twelve-burner, chrome-plated, voice-activated barbecue.

If karma was indeed A Thing, I must have done something truly awful in a past life, like clubbed seal pups, to deserve this amount of shit-filled laughs in the space of a fortnight.

Brian McManus, the man who not only politically represented everything I wasn't, but whose behaviour had been the catalyst for my current dance with destitution, was my new neighbour.

He'd gone and fucking.

Moved.

Next.

Door.

I put my palms together and prayed to whoever wasn't listening up there that it was only a crib – one of perhaps a handful of holiday homes he had scattered around the region and would visit infrequently. Or better yet, he was Airbnb-ing it and they'd be gone by the end of the weekend.

God. *Please* let it be a rental. Having that kind of posturing masculinity in my peripheral vision would sully the beauty of this place. I wouldn't have to see him. Just knowing he was there would be like looking at it through turd-tinted glasses.

I eyed my cooling dinner. It was already fairly unappetising. Now my stomach turned at the thought of forcing it past my tongue.

I tipped it into the lake for the fish and ducks to enjoy and trudged inside to ring Dad and Rewa back.

"You'll never guess who the new fucking neighbour is."

"Brian McManus!" shouted Rewa as Dad asked if I had to express myself with quite so much "swearitude".

I stood corrected. How the fuck did she do that? It could have been anybody I was displeased to have as a neighbour. Mrs Hutchens, my Social Studies teacher, who insisted on doing round robin reading from the class text, despite knowing there was at least one dyslexic in the class. Or Kim Jong-un.

"Yes. Fucking Brian McManus."

Rewa shrieked, "No way!" and whooped. "I am *so* on.

Get a load of this tinny arse, Dale. Feel the awesomeness of its guessing WIZARDRY. Oo yeah, oo yeah."

She was doing that stupid little hoopy-armed dance thing, wasn't she? "Are you finished?"

Rewa let out a final whoop. "Yep."

"Good. I'd quite like to bask in the shittiness of this new reality now."

"Oh now, Jewelsy, you don't have to have anything to do with him," said Dad. "I'm sure it'll be easy to forget he's there."

"It better be. He's not ruining this place for me."

"He's most likely retired from public life. He's probably not even running his businesses anymore. He'll be paying other fools to shoulder the stress for him."

"I'm not sure that's a good scenario, Dad. It means he'll be here all the time." Which would give rise to a rather size-able complication.

How might Brian McManus treat a neighbour who's only past interaction with him had involved abuse? With any luck he wouldn't remember me. Maybe he was abused so often I would blend into the fuzziness of abuse memory.

I also had a fairly nondescript face. There weren't too many times I was grateful for that fact, but I could count this as one of them.

I did not wear nondescript T-shirts, however. My sherowear would be a klaxon-accessorised calling card.

There was only one thing for it. I had my dad handy. I could indulge myself a bit by regressing to a child. Starting ambitiously, I whined out a "Whyyyyyyyyyy?" and followed it up with two more totally useless questions. "Why, Dad? Why does it have to be him?" I even sat down at the table with a "Harrumph" and threw myself across it, because gestures of hopelessness were an important part of the art of the pathetic.

I could almost hear the squeak of Rewa's eyeballs rolling inside her head.

"It's probably a weekend rental, Jewelsy."

"It's Thursday."

"A long weekend rental. He can have them now if he's retired."

"There's a simple way to find out," said Rewa, ever practical.

"I'm not asking him."

"Then you'll have to die in suspense."

I hung up shortly after that, not willing to start another Science of Death debate, and dissatisfied with their level of sympathy.

I consoled myself by sketching a new T-shirt design. It turned into various iterations of superheroines throat punching small, paunchy men with receding hairlines, and I gave up after the fifth paper ball missed the recycling bin.

THE NEXT MORNING, I concentrated on looking on the brighter side of not knowing the McManus living status yet.

I paid attention to the small things I should probably feel gratitude for. Like Liam saying hello to me at a volume I didn't need to strain to hear. And it being pay day, which meant I could splash out on luxuries like proper sandwich fillings. It was also Friday and I had two and a half whole days of not stacking stuff behind other stuff arriving in four hours.

As the first busy period of the morning dwindled to a few remaining shoppers, I emerged from the storage area doors at the back of the store and wheeled the trolley I'd filled with Easter eggs for a display towards the front of the mart.

I rounded the end of the aisle and the entrance doors hissed open. The man I'd spent the last fourteen hours wasting worry energy on stepped through into the age-enhancing fluorescent lights of the store.

My heart drum-rolled and I diverted my trolley into the next aisle, positioning myself to peer around the shelf end.

Brian McManus approached the checkouts and stepped up to Forest's. He paused before making any address, giving Forest enough time to smooth his purple fringe out of his eyes with a hand decorated with gold nail polish. "Help you?"

"Yes, my good man," McManus answered like he fancied himself a peer of the realm. "Is your manager on site? I want to discuss an unfortunate incident that occurred here the other day."

Shit. I hadn't anticipated being forced to reveal my hand with quite so much immediacy. Of course he'd come down to the store and throw his weight around about a peasant who dared to challenge his wife.

The game was already up.

"I'll go get him," said Forest with the air of someone who'd been asked to walk to England.

I spent the time it took for Joe to emerge from The Hole mentally turning around on the spot. McManus was the type to make a fuss. And not just any fuss. He'd swing self-righteous indignation like a spiked club, not caring who he took out or the damage he wrought.

I hoped Joe was up to the parry and deflect needed to avoid being crushed under it. If he wasn't, I'd have to step under the sword.

Joe emerged smiling from the *Staff only* door trailing a Forest who tried to look nonchalant, but the flicking of his eyes between Joe and McManus gave away his enthusiasm for the drama that was about to ensue.

Joe extended his hand. "Joseph Kiriona. How can I help you?"

McManus did the two-handed shake thing, the dominance sandwich, and said, "Brian McManus. My wife and I have recently moved to this delightful town."

Fuckity great. Well, that news was all kittens and moonbeams. Guess I'd be running the discovery gauntlet on a daily basis after all.

"Welcome to the Puhiruru whanau."

Oh, Joe. You have no idea who's just shoe-horned themselves into the fold.

"Thank you, Joseph. I wanted to talk to you about an incident that happened a couple of days ago in the car park –"

Here we go. I gripped the handle of the shopping trolley if just for something to hold on to.

"– which was quite distressing to my wife."

"Oh? I'm sorry to hear that."

I risked another peak around the end of the shelves. Rā's customer had left and the two cashiers watched the exchange. Forest cleaned his touch screen and glanced up every few seconds. Rā didn't bother to hide her interest. She leaned against the rear of her checkout with her arms folded.

"Yes, it seems she might have caused a bit of offence to one of your staff."

Wait. *What* just came out of his mouth?

"I'm sure you're aware of the incident I'm referring to."

Joe nodded.

"I wouldn't want us to get off on the wrong foot when we've only been here a few days. We're very keen to be happy and active members of this community."

My mind felt like it had been catapulted into another dimension. One where Brian McManus was a humble, *reasonable* human being. I clasped my head as if I could hold my brain in place.

"Riiight," said Joe, with a hint of a question mark.

He must see it too. This strange new reality that didn't make any sense. Something was afoot. The power play of a controlling husband, embarrassing his wife and forcing her to be contrite?

"So, I want to offer our sincerest apologies and assure you it won't happen again, if you could pass that on to the staff member in question."

No. Something else. If McManus was truly repentant, he wouldn't be expressing it if he didn't have to, which he didn't. And he wouldn't do it in a public place where he could be overheard. I didn't like it.

"That's very kind of you, Mr McManus."

"Brian, please. Now, if you'll excuse me, I'll pick up a few things before I head out. Bekka and I are big proponents of supporting local."

He grabbed Joe's hand and shook it again with a slap to his tricep. Then he headed towards the first aisle.

Joe's head whipped to me. He eyed me for a beat before walking over. "I take it you heard all that?"

"Yes."

His mouth worked like he chewed something. "You know, that went a lot better than I expected. I mean, I like a good shit fight. Just as long as I'm not involved."

"It makes no sense, Joe."

"No. You did a good yell-job on his wife. I thought

there'd be a bit of a yell-job back." He shrugged. "Maybe there's more to the obscenely wealthy than the vulgar displays of affluence we judge them for."

I watched Joe retreat towards the back offices, trying to marry the evidence with logic. The pieces wouldn't fit into place.

As the *Staff only* door *snipp*ed closed, a voice that sounded like it'd been gargling scoria growled, "Where's my smegging prunes?"

Mr Hardacre, the elderly man who'd demanded a contribution to his rates in exchange for entry to the mart, wheeled himself out of aisle six. He spotted me hovering in indecision about whether to run away and hide until McManus left, and snarled, "Where have you put them now?"

"Perhaps I can be of assistance, good sir?" Brian McManus stood at the end of the aisle with his hands on his hips, like a freshly descended superhero.

Mr Hardacre swivelled his head, making his chicken wattle quiver.

I pulled a Liam and swung my hair over my face.

"I don't work here," McManus continued, "but I'm sure we can work it out together."

Mr Hardacre looked him up and down. "Yeah, alright. I can never find my favourite brand of prunes. I have to soften my stool on account of the haemorrhoids, so I need the kilogram bag. I swear they move it every week just to mess with me."

McManus threw his head back and laughed. "I'm sure they wouldn't do that, my friend." He pointed towards the fresh produce. "Let's head this way and see what we can hunt out."

I looked down at my uniform to check I hadn't accidentally thrown on my Invisibility Cloak when dressing that morning. McManus had wilfully been blind to my presence, presumably so he could stage a "helping the elderly" scene.

At least I now didn't have to run away. The ex-mayor of Invercargill couldn't spot an angry ex-graphic designer in a retail uniform to save himself it would seem. Though, with whatever agenda he had today, it wouldn't have been convenient for him if he could.

I pushed the trolley back towards the end of the aisle, so I could finally construct my display.

An "Aha. Here's the blighter" drifted from aisle three where I knew the prunes were and had always been.

The two emerged out from the shelves and McManus turned and thrust a hand out for Mr Hardacre to shake. "Brian McManus," he said as if it was of great consequence.

"Right." Mr Hardacre allowed his arm to be pumped.

"You're welcome," said McManus, as if gratitude had been offered instead of indifference. He slapped Mr Hardacre on his shoulder. "Always happy to help the handicapped." And with that, he walked back out the entrance without doing any of the local supporting he pledged as a favourite pastime.

Rā turned her back to the store, her shoulders shaking.

"Who's he calling handicapped? I'm old, you cretinous moron," Mr Hardacre shouted at the closed door. "It's only the ravages of time and gravity that have reduced me to a motorised chair."

Rā tutted. "Are the piles weighing you down?"

Mr Hardacre sucked in a rattly breath as Liam stepped up to his mobility scooter.

"The prunes are always in aisle three, Mr Hardacre," he said in a low voice. "We never move them. If you like...I can, um, add the aisle numbers to your usual shopping list, so you always find what you want."

Mr Hardacre grunted. Then he sniffed. "Alright." He handed his list to Liam and followed him down the second aisle.

And in the descending quiet, the thought I had been suppressing after the whole "sincerest apologies" farce, surfed a wave of maniacal, resigned laughter to the front of my consciousness.

Brian McManus, the biggest political douchebag since the Trump presidency, was going to stand in the mayoral by-election, wasn't he?

CHAPTER TWELVE

MY,   "NOOOOOOOOOOOOOOOOOOOOOOO!"
reverberated through the steel beams in the ceiling and set
feet running. Two pairs thudded and squeaked into my aisle
and came to a standstill.

I stood with the heels of my palms pressed to my eyes,
not wanting to emerge into this new Brian McManus-
aroma-ed reality, which smelled of three-hundred dollar
cologne and Satan.

"What? What is it?" Rā asked.

"He's going to run for mayor."

In the pause before her next question, I swore a god-
damn cricket chirped. I kid you not.

"Who is?"

"All his syrupy 'my friend's and 'good sir's. There's no
other explanation."

"Do you know which planet she's hitched a ride in a
UFO from?" Rā asked unseen person number two.

My hands were gently pulled away from my face and
released. "What's going on?" asked Liam, his pupils darting
between mine. I'd never seen his face this close up before.

His bottom lashes were so ridiculously long they brushed the tops of his ridiculously chiselled cheeks. Jesus on high, the man was pretty. It was *almost* enough to derail me from my McManus panic.

"I've just escaped the Brian McManus universe and now he's followed me to taint my new one with his –" I flapped my arms about a bit. "– Dickheadery."

Behind Liam and Rā, Forest emerged from behind his checkout and ambled over, hands in pockets.

"You know that guy that was just in here?" asked Liam.

"He was the mayor of Invercargill until a week ago when he finally got voted out and all the disenchanted people offered salutations to the higher powers. And now he's set his political sights on Fiordland."

"And he's...not someone we want as our mayor?"

Now, I knew Liam was a reasonably smart person, so instead of pointing that the length of my lung-clamping "No" might have been a clue, I chose to interpret his question as a kind of "Are you sure?" type query. "He's not someone *anyone* wants as their mayor."

"He seemed alright," said Forest. "He was polite and helpful and stuff."

"But he's neither. He's doing it to woo people. There's absolutely no doubt that his agenda is the mayoralty."

"What makes him so bad?" asked Rā.

I huffed and peered at the ceiling like it might tell me where I should start. "He's a complete fucking broflake for one."

"A what?"

"A straight white male affronted by any non-straight-white-male activity that isn't aimed at him, because it offends his delicate redneck sensibilities. You know the sort. They say stupid shit like 'if men can be feminists, why don't women volunteer to be masculinists?', or 'when is there going to be a straight pride parade?'."

Liam snorted and Forest said, "Sounds like a douche."

"He's a major douche." I turned to Rā. "You know what he lobbied to get made into a bylaw? He did a needs analysis, which apparently showed a demand for larger parking spaces in the CBD because of the high number of utility vehicles per capita in Invercargill, so he wanted all the disabled parking changed to ute parking because they're bigger and disabled people don't utilise them as frequently as he thought they should. That's the kind of man he is."

A loud *thunk* at the front of the store drew our attention to Forest's checkout.

Mr Hardacre's groceries sat on the conveyor belt and he glowered at us, his eyes obscured by the depth of his frown and the wing tips of his overgrown eyebrows. Then he kicked the side of the counter again, presumably for good measure now that he had our attention. "Can I get some smegging service?"

"Legs not so useless after all," Rā said as she disengaged from our circle and moved towards her checkout.

As Forest ambled back to serve Mr Hardacre, Liam said, "Maybe he turned a new leaf when he moved here?"

It was a generous thought, which while perfectly understandable coming from Liam's brain, required a swift and bloody execution to kill all benefit-of-the-doubt-giving.

"The fuck he has. Nothing that came out of his mouth this morning was genuine."

Liam either chose to take my word for it, or beat a retreat in the face of an angry female, and my day didn't pick up much from there. When I dropped the second five litre can of olive oil on my toe and made a customer yelp with my resulting roar, Joe suggested a pub evening was in order because 1) it was a Friday night, 2) some team bonding was overdue, and 3) I was clearly in need of a liquid sedative.

Harit said he couldn't come due to his pizza delivery commitments, but promised a "drive by", whatever that meant. Rā said she'd come once she'd hidden all the alcohol in the house and made sure her two teenage sons were safely ensconced in the Netflix universe. Forest said he'd come if all his other plans fell through, to which Rā replied that two minutes was more than enough for a wank, and Forest said at least all his working bits were in order. He'd heard smoking caused all small, protruding body parts to go gangrenous and rot off. At which point, Liam asked if he could bring Dana.

It was the first I'd heard of any Dana, which wasn't surprising given the short amount of time I'd known him. Perhaps she was his hunting dog, or the Barbie Doll girl-friend Dad surmised from the toy riddle. Dana had that exotic two-syllable ring to it that a supermodel might have. No last name required. Like Giselle.

I spent the afternoon too distracted to do any creating. I made a strong cup of tea, sat outside on one of the wobbly outdoor chairs and glowered at the dark roofline next door, wishing for the ability to shoot laser beams out my eyeballs.

When it came time to leave for the pub and the ball of angry energy emanating from my core hadn't lessened with my death-ray throwing, I put on skinny jeans, retro yellow and blue Adidas sneakers, and my most provocative Empowered Collection T-shirt. It depicted a female super-hero wearing a bridal veil. Her speech bubble read *Change my name? He didn't buy me.*

It was the kind of T-shirt you might accompany with a swagger and a glare that gleefully invited people to get up in your face. However, once I pushed open the doors to the pub, all my bluster evaporated, because I'm not actually a knobhat.

I took a seat at a table against the wall, where I wouldn't draw attention, and feigned absorption in Instagram until the others arrived. The feed of new posts was punctuated with ads from T-shirt companies thanks to the algorithms, having detected the T-shirt-heavy focus of my posts, deducing I was in the market for buying one. A sensible business person might have actually paid attention because of things like "market research", but as we've established, I'm not a sensible business person, and I was at the end of the fourth worst day of my life. So, I chose to react to their presence like any petulant adult-child might, and offered them a silent "Fuck you" with a swipe of my thumb that sent them to feed history. Or Insta-oblivion as those in the trade called it.

A husky laugh drew me from my Thumb of God-ing.

Rā peered between the frame of my arms at the front of my shirt. "As a divorcee, that is the best titty wisdom I've read in a long time." She laughed again and thumped her chest when it stuttered into a cough. "You are one out of the box, Jewel Bauer."

I tried to keep the resignation out of my voice when I answered, "I know," but it snuck in anyway.

She slid along the booth seat next to me and pushed her packet of cigarettes into my bag. "Now, I'm only allowed one tonight. You need to be master of my rationing and don't give me more no matter how much I beg."

"You're trying to quit?"

"I'm down to three a day. I don't like it. The withdrawal's like undergoing a Brazilian one hair at a time, but they're so expensive now, it's either smoke or feed the bottomless pits that are my teenage children."

"Your blackened lungs will thank you," said a mauve-haired Jodie Whittaker. Forest, resplendent in an outfit he said was an exact replica of the thirteenth Doctor's dress, gave a flourish before doubling over into a bow. "This is what I do."

"Who *are* you?" This confident, theatrical Forest was not the monosyllabic man-boy I'd witnessed in the supermarket.

Rā clucked her tongue as Forest sat in a seat opposite us. "Don't encourage him. He'll start breaking out the 'wibbly wobbly's and the 'timey wimey's and I might have to slap him."

Forest set his face to full wither. "The thirteenth doctor doesn't say that, Rā. That's, like, two doctors back."

I pulled out my phone and asked Siri to "Find me a picture of Jodie Whittaker Doctor Who". I held up the phone for Rā's benefit so we could make a comparison. There was no difference, apart from Forest's lack of boobs. He'd replicated the outfit seam for seam. "It's incredible," I conceded.

Forest beamed. The joy emanating from him rippled outwards and I couldn't help but smile back. I'd never seen him look like that before, so I tried to ruin it by making things awkward.

"You don't care she's a girl?"

The smile shifted, possibly in the direction of amusement. It could equally have been pity at my lack of understanding. "It's the costume I'm interested in, not the gender."

Rā said, "That one's pretty androgynous anyway, but you did go as Gamora from Guardians of the Galaxy to that Armageddon thing a year or so back."

"That is true."

"*She's* quite womanly," I said.

"Yes she is. What's your point?"

"So, you don't mind looking womanly?"

"No. Weren't you listening? I like the outfit, I make it. I like the look, I wear it." Forest flicked his hair back with a jerk of his head, even though it hadn't been anywhere near obscuring his vision. "If I was a woman dressed up as a male character, you wouldn't question her outfit, would you?"

He had a point. I absolutely wouldn't. I tried to make it up to him by asking about his business.

"Don't be coy." Rā reached across the table, grabbed his nose and gave it a gentle tug. "Tell her what you make."

Forest slapped her hand away, but looked pleased she was making a fuss. "I specialise in manga characters."

"Because?" prompted Rā.

"*Because* there's some pretty hardcore fans out there. You can buy ready-made cosplay costumes online, but they're never a perfect fit. The super fans want tailored outfits and there's enough of them that I earn some pretty good pocket money."

If we were having a virtual conversation right now, say on Instagram, I'd write:

LOVE!

My business model might be better in terms of scalability, but his was artistically more rewarding. Full-immersion creativity. "I am in awe and a little jealous."

"The boy's alright, isn't he?" Rā said.

"Yes he is," I said as a movement at the pub's side door caught my eye. It was Liam, clad in a shoulder-accentuating plaid shirt. No Dana. He looked around the room, gave a small wave when he spotted us, and walked over, head bowed.

Forest turned around to see who I was looking at, then he settled back into his seat with a grin in my direction.

I thought I knew what it meant, so I told him, "I was agreeing with Rā about you. I just happened to be looking at Liam when I said it."

His eyes moved from mine to Rā's. "Yep. We believe you."

"Hey," Liam said as he arrived at the table. He slid in next to Forest and fanned his large hands over the empty table top. "You don't have drinks."

"Not yet. We just got here," Rā said.

Liam made to stand. "I'll get the first round then. What do you all want?"

I answered, "I'll get my own," as Forest said, "Beer" and Rā said, "A white." I didn't have a budget that included ten dollar drinks for six people.

"No you won't," said Rā. "This is your first outing with us as a fully-fledged member of the team. We buy the drinks tonight. You can fork out next time."

"Okay." I wasn't going to argue with a free drink or three.

"What would you like?" Liam asked.

"Cider please. A scrumpy. Strong and tart." A joke appeared and I grabbed at it because I wanted to be liked by these people and being funny made you more likeable. "Just like me."

Rā barked a single laugh.

Forest snorted.

And Liam's eyes did that slightly startled thing he tended to do around me and he disappeared towards the bar.

"No, wait," I said to the table. "I didn't think that through properly. I'm not..." I turned and shouted at Liam's disappearing back. "I'm not a tart."

A dozen heads in the busy pub swivelled to look at me and I whipped back around to hunch over the table and shield my face behind my hand.

God I was hopeless. It wasn't enough to be able to unintentionally embarrass other people, like I'd made an art of with Liam, I had to offer some self-inflicted mortification just to balance things out.

"I hear there's a tart at this table." Joe slid in next to Forest with a glass of red wine and winked at me.

"Yep," I said on a sigh.

He patted my hand. "I'm a bit of a tart, too, if it makes you feel any better. In fact, I'm hoping to get my tart on tonight if the opportunity allows." He looked around the room and shrugged. "It's early."

Turning to Forest, he waggled his fingers over him as if miming flames. "Boy, you are sizzling. Is this your latest creation?"

"Kind of. I've been working on bits and pieces of it for the last couple of years. Finished the coat tonight, which was what —" he looked at Rā, his chin jutting out "— my other plans were."

"Mm hm," said Rā. "We all believe you."

"It's kind of my style," said Joe. "If the culottes were stove pipes. Girls'll be falling over you."

"Yep." Rā peered around the room. She poked her bottom lip out and drummed her fingers on the table. "Any moment now."

Forest sniffed and narrowed his eyes at her. "Sorry, how long did you say since your last score?" He counted off on his fingers. "I make it two months for me and five *what* for you, Rā? Days? Weeks? Oh, no that's right." Leaning towards her, he bared his teeth in what might have been a grin. "Years. You even remember how to do it?"

Rā winked at him and Joe said, "What's the tally this week?"

Forest pulled a school-issue red notebook out of his pocket that had BURN TALLY neatly written in the Subject field. He wrote in it, then counted. "Twenty-five to twenty-two. Rā's in the lead."

Joe sucked air between pursed lips. "Close race."

"What is?" I asked.

Forest said, "Whoever scores the least verbal burns at the end of the week has to clean all the finger jam off the checkout computers and the Eftpos machines each day for the following week."

"That doesn't sound so bad."

Rā said, "Imagine a pack-a-day smoker, who's just picked chocolate-laced caramel toffee from his teeth after petting every mangy dog being walked down the main street. Then imagine ten of them. Have you any idea how much gunk builds up on those machines? It's not a quick wipe. That shit builds a crust."

I eyed the Eftpos card tucked into the pocket of my phone case. "I'm getting payWave."

Liam arrived back at the table, balancing four drinks. "I got a couple of plates of wedges, too." He slid my cider towards me and said quietly, "This is what they gave me when I asked for strong and tart."

I couldn't be entirely sure, but was it possible Liam just teased me? The same Liam who could barely string a sentence together and aim it at me a week ago? If indeed he was, then our collegiality had leapt up a whole new level from "How's the missus?" to the one where you laugh and slap each other on the back.

I took a long pull of my drink while watching Liam out of the corner of my eye, but he didn't do or say anything else to confirm or deny the new phase of our relationship, so I asked the table, "Why didn't the captain get invited tonight?"

"He has Rotary on Friday nights," said Joe. "He's the vice-President."

"Oh," I said, like I knew what that meant. Then I thought better of it. "What's Rotary?"

"They raise money for charitable projects, like disaster relief in the Pacific, and giving scholarships for vocational training and stuff."

"That man is a treasure," said Rā. "They should saint him."

"Ah, I don't think saint is a verb, Einstein," said Forest. "But he can be *canonised*."

"Don't you have to be dead for that?" asked Liam.

"That is correct," Forest continued. "Not only do you have to be dead, *Rā*, you're meant to have performed miracles as well, so maybe you should have stopped talking at the treasure bit before all the ignorance fell out."

"Maybe you should have stopped talking before I punched you in the dick."

Forest clamped his hands over his crotch and Rā winked at him while she sipped from her wine glass.

A short, wiry man with an aquiline nose and carefully groomed stubble materialised behind Liam's chair and delivered a kiss to the top of his head. "Sorry I'm late, pumpkin."

"Dana!" the table said as one.

Ah.

I didn't see that coming. Not even with the whole Barbie V Transformer conversation.

So.

Dana wasn't Liam's model girlfriend. Dana was Liam's *boyfriend*.

"We haven't been here long," said Liam. "Get a drink and I'll find you a chair."

As Dana moved off towards the bar, he pointed a finger at Forest. "Doctor Who, right? You totally nailed it. *Nailed* it."

"Dana's so awesome," said Forest, watching his retreating back.

"Yeah," said Joe. "Love that queen. Bless the day you met him, Liam."

But.

I felt like I should get it now. That the toy choice story should fit neatly into this new reality, when, actually, it didn't work particularly well as a metaphor for Liam's sexuality. He wasn't in the least a feminine gay.

When Dana returned to the table and Liam told him I was Jewel, he proffered a hand and eyed my T-shirt. "Yes, you are."

I didn't know what he meant. When I asked, he said, "You're living up to the image of you Liam has inserted in my head, which brings a little thrill to my heart."

Wow.

That was...nice.

I couldn't do any kind of reciprocating, because Liam had done no equivalent image inserting of Dana. I felt it would embarrass Liam if I pointed this out, so I said, "I thought you might be his dog," instead.

Dana threw his head back and laughed.

I glanced at Liam to see if I'd embarrassed him anyway.

His lips were pressed together as if suppressing a smile.

As a waiter slid plates of wedges onto the table, a series of toots out on the street drew our attention out the window.

Someone did a wheelie on a scooter and raised a hand to wave like a cowboy on a rearing horse.

The table waved furiously back.

Right. So that's what Harit meant by "drive by". The image of him peppering us with a spray of bullets had briefly flashed across my mind when he'd said it, but I'd discounted it as a logical possibility pretty quickly. I wasn't going to admit to it, though, even if the saliva gathering in my mouth had allowed me the freedom of speech.

The wedges, in all their bacon-pieced, sweet-chilli-sauced, melted-cheesed and sour-creamed splendour, smelled like a glorious coronary. It was the biggest calorie load I'd had on offer in the last two weeks.

"Dig in," said Liam.

I grabbed a dripping wedge in each hand and shoved one, then the other in my mouth. I raised my eyes when nobody else reached for either plate.

Forest had his brows raised and Rā smiled and winked at me. I wasn't sure I understood what meaning that small gesture conveyed.

I looked at Liam. "Di' you no' mean i'?"

He answered by taking a wedge in each hand and placing them in his mouth.

Dana ruffled his hair, waited for me to stop chewing, and said, "I hear you had a...moment at work today?"

I replayed my shouted denial. I had stretched "No", a pretty short word by single syllable standards, into ten seconds. It was undeniably a moment. "Yes I did." I stuffed another wedge in my mouth.

"So, who's this guy?" asked Dana.

"Brian somebody," said Forest.

I couldn't form the sounds around the cheesy potato glue.

"McMasters," said Joe.

"McManus," said Liam.

"Jewel thinks he's going to run for mayor," said Rā, "but he's not someone we want to run for mayor because he's a broflake."

Dana wrinkled his nose. "I know the sort. Insist some of their closest friends are gay, then tell homophobic jokes around the water cooler."

"Except he's the worse kind of broflake." I said. "One that champions economic growth over community development and thinks "equity" is a dirty word. He's toxic."

Dana spread his palms. "We just have to make sure he's not the only horse to back."

"How do we do that?" I asked.

"Vote for the other woman," said Rā.

"What other woman?" said Forest.

After a pause, Dana said, "Surely someone will stand against him."

"Nobody stood against that other bloke who committed electoral fraud," said Rā.

"He didn't commit electoral fraud," said Joe. "He just wasn't Kiwi enough for the job."

"*I'd* do it if it guaranteed he couldn't get in, but I'm pretty sure I'd be the last horse anyone would want to back," I said. "I wouldn't want to back me."

"I'd vote for you," said Liam.

Joe clapped him on the back. "One pity vote is better than none. You're already ahead, my heart."

"It wouldn't be a pity vote, would it, Liam?" said Dana.

"Yes, it would," I said, as Liam tried to hide his face inside his beer glass. "Anyway, I don't want to devote any more time to Brian Mc-anus. He's not worth ruining our Friday night over."

Joe stood up. "That's my cue for the next round."

TWO HOURS AND THREE, or possibly five rounds later, Dana suggested that as it was a balmy night and we were in the context of celebrating the newest taxi on the rank, which was a metaphor for me, it was only appropriate that we marked the occasion with a skinny dip. "I've never leapt off the pier naked."

"Me either," said Rā a little louder than necessary. "'S on my bucket list."

"Right then." Dana clapped his hands. "What are we waiting for?"

Joe announced he would forego the opportunity for "a rectal lavage" in favour of a decent night's sleep and a clear head. Once he'd escorted us outside, he pointed a finger at each of us. "Drink two litres of water when you get home and take a Berroca prophylactic. You can thank me on Monday."

"Yes, we will. Thank you, Joe," said Dana, before taking off at a run. "Last one in has to marry Vladimir Putin."

The pier, lit with a series of boardwalk-level lamps was a hundred-metre dash down the road. Dana, peeling off his jersey, was already a quarter of the way there before I realised the loftiness of the stakes.

"I'm not marrying that unhinged fucker," I said, taking off at a sprint.

"Wait," shouted Rā. "My blackened lungs!"

By the time I made it to the pier, panting and hopping while I attempted to remove a shoe, Dana and Liam were already in the water and Forest's bottom glowed skinny and pale at the end of the pier from where he bent to take off his culottes.

"Come on, Forest," called Dana from the water below. "No need to iron your clothes before you remove them."

"Two years of work. I'm not wrinkling a thing." He folded his trousers and laid them neatly on the pile of clothes at his feet. Then he leapt into the water, grabbing one knee and arching backwards as he hit the surface so that it exploded in a five metre high splash.

I held my hands out and my face up, and grinned as droplets of lake water hit my skin.

"Here comes Rā, Jewel," said Dana. "Better get your kit off if you don't want to join the Putin harem."

Rā's footsteps clomped on the wooden planks at the base of the jetty and I whipped my T-shirt off before I had time to consider my audience.

The three heads in the water hastily turned away from me, and as I pulled my jeans down and my head dropped to knee level, I realised just how much I had drunk. My head spun and I straightened, trying to pull a foot free of the tight neck of the jean's cuff. It wouldn't budge, and I realised that by pulling my pants down, I'd effectively lassoed my feet, and that by straining against it, particularly when my balancing ability was somewhat compromised, it was inevitable I would topple over.

I managed one hop in the direction of the water before I fell in, bra, underpants, jean ankle cuffs and all.

I almost managed a full rotation. The backs of my thighs slapped the water, and the hurt of it gave me pause to consider the foolishness of a midnight drunken swim in a spot where I couldn't touch the bottom.

Thankfully, the lights from the town gave me a point of orientation in the lake's clear mountain water. I kicked my legs like a mermaid and burst through the surface to a series of hoots from Rā up above.

"I wish I had my camera. That was classic."

I took a deep breath and attempted to wrench my jeans free of my legs, sinking, until I needed air. My jeans wouldn't budge.

When I surfaced again, Rā said, "Help her. She's trussed like a chicken with her jeans around her ankles."

I slapped at the water, trying to push it down and me up and an arm wrapped around my chest and hair tickled my neck and cheek. "I've got you," said Liam.

I brought my legs to the surface and Dana, insisting it was always his pleasure to relieve others of their clothes, wrenched the material from my legs and wrapped the jeans around his neck like a scarf. "I like to keep a trophy of my accomplishments."

Liam let go of me and as my legs sunk to a vertical axis, my thigh brushed against something COLD AND FLACCID.

It shocked us both.

I gasped and Liam jerked away from me.

"What's that look for, lover boy?" said Dana. "Did you do some penis jousting?"

"If I had a penis, the first thing *I'd* do is joust with it," said Rā, who had remained peering down from the pier, fully clothed, and indifferent to the prospect of being Mrs Putin. She bent her knees and wiggled her hips from side to side. "Fwap, fwap, fwap, fwap."

"They should have had penis jousting in Batman's repertoire," said Dana. "Then they could have added FWAP to the onomatopoeic sound effects."

"Bet you can't spell it," said Liam.

"F-W-A-P."

Liam laughed. "Onomatopoeic, smart arse."

"Fuck knows. And I don't feel any less of a man for my ignorance."

"That's seriously the first thing you would do?" asked Forest. "You have your priorities all wrong."

Rā "Hoh"ed and said, "Penis jousting! Next big fringe sport."

I shivered. Mountain water was also synonymous with "frigid" and my skimpy briefs and bra did nothing to shield those small areas of my body from the cold. "Last one to shore has to tell Brian McManus they like what he's done with his wife's face."

"What's he done to her face?" asked Dana.

A flurry of splashes answered him as the water around me erupted.

I wasn't a bad swimmer. I'd had plenty of practise in the lake during our family summer holidays, but I was no match for three stronger men.

I reached wading level as Liam vaulted up the bank at the base of the pier and sprinted awkwardly towards his clothes, his hands clamped to his genitals.

His abs twisted and flexed and his quads rippled with definition with each step. Yes, he was the size of a modest townhouse, but everything was proportioned. *God* it was unfair. How on earth in the vast genetic lottery was it possible for one person to land on the face and body winning combination?

I didn't want to give it any recognition. None at all.

However.

For those of us not blessed with beauty, there is a kind of helpless fascination born of resentment and envy and, okay, admiration. And I couldn't, despite all efforts, take my eyes off him. The muscles bunching in his arse wouldn't let me.

As I stumbled past the water line and Liam reached his clothes, my eyes met Rā's.

This time, I absolutely understood the meaning of her wink.

CHAPTER THIRTEEN

ON MONDAY MORNING when I turned up to work, Liam wasn't there.

It wasn't like him to be late and when I asked Forest and Rā if they knew where he was, I was met with shrugs.

Ordinarily, I wouldn't particularly care if a colleague failed to honour their start time, however uncharacteristic or not, and it did beg a pressing question:

Would I have been this interested in his whereabouts if I hadn't seen him very near to naked three nights ago?

I shouldn't be. The man was gay. I hadn't found him especially interesting before. Well, not in a *your flexing bum cheeks keep popping into my brain* kind of way.

But I did now.

The frequency with which those two rounds of flesh appeared in my mind over the weekend was one thing. The time I devoted to reliving each vision was quite another.

And while I'd pretty much reached a conclusion of, "Great. It's a 'no', isn't it?" on that question, another one rode in on its wake:

Was this something I needed to worry about?

It only took ten minutes for me to find my answer.

When the front doors wheezed open and somebody with Helena's voice – probably Helena – shouted, "I killed Liam," I dropped the bag of flour in my hand.

It exploded at my feet, sending jets of powder out the paper seams and a cloud of bronchial-coating dust into my face.

That. That was the bloody moment right there.

"I gave the full murder scene a dummy run and it went perfectly."

Silence.

"So, is Liam, like, coming in to work this morning?" asked Forest.

"Or have you just done away with our only perishable goods specialist?" added Rā.

A clap and a laugh. "Oh, Lord no. He's not *dead*."

"But you just said you killed him."

I surveyed the damage. The blast radius encapsulated two shelving bays at floor level on either side of the aisle and three rows of goods in each of those shelves. And the entire front of my body.

"Not literally. Though that might be debatable when I come to write the scene." A snort. "Get it?"

"Yes," said an unamused Forest.

I stepped back from the damage. The imprint of a pair of size seven and a half shoes remained, like they'd been cut with a cookie cutter.

"I thought you weren't doing death scenes?"

"I've realised it'll be pretty hard to create a gripping, page-turning read without any of the gruesome stuff. It'd be like a birthday cake with no candles, or George Clooney without teeth. Here's the man himself. See? Not dead."

"Not dead doesn't rule him out from being *un*dead," said Forest.

"True," said Rā. "He does kind of have that head-jutting, hair-swinging thing typical of the zombie gait."

Helena's tinselly laugh sprinkled itself liberally through the empty store. "You guys are such a tease."

The automatic doors opened asthmatically.

"Morning," said Liam and a tiny bird ruffled its stupid, goddamn feathers behind my belly button.

Which was just.

Fucking.

Great.

As if our interaction wasn't awkward enough courtesy of Liam's shy factor one and my tongue before brain policy, it was probably about to reach a whole new level of Let's See How Much I Can Inadvertently Embarrass the Both of Us.

I swivelled from left to right, head and torso locked in the same movement, as if searching for a dimensional portal to scrabble through.

"You look well for having been murdered," said Rā.

"Maybe it's the second coming," said Forest. "He does look a bit Jesus-like."

If I tip-toed to the end of the aisle, I could sidle up the one closest to the *Staff only* door, then turn my back as I stepped free of the aisle for the final two metres of no man's land. The sideways shuffle might look a bit odd, but hopefully they'd be too busy dissecting the death scene and scrutinising the methodology to notice.

Liam said something quietly. It sounded a bit like, "I only perform miracles on Friday nights."

Shoes squeaked across the linoleum floor and I wasn't quick enough.

He glanced down the aisle on his way past and skidded to a stop. "What happened?"

I look down at my powdered front. "Flour bag malfunction."

He eyed me for a beat before bringing a fist to his mouth and chortling into it. As if the weight of the hilarity was too much to bear, he leaned forward and placed a hand on a knee, the chortling deepening.

With a collective scuffing of feet, the faces of the others appeared at the end of the aisle. A chorus of discordant laughter reverberated through the metal beams above us.

I placed my hands on my hips and waited them out.

Rā wiped an eye. "Lucky you don't have allergies."

"It was gluten free," I said, inviting a fresh bout of chortling.

Helena gasped. "That would be a good way to kill someone." She reached into her back pocket.

"Roll them in egg first," says Rā. "Then you could fillet them to death."

"Tastes like chicken," says Forest.

Helena clucked her tongue and lined up her phone for a shot. "How does anyone know that?"

"You finished laughing yet? Or can I go out back and vacuum my lungs?"

Liam held up a finger and twirled it.

"No."

"Oh, go on," said Rā. "We're still recovering from the shock of Liam being killed."

I narrowed my eyes at them, knowing I would acquiesce, but playing my role of resentful victim of unfortunate mishap, anyway. Then I pivoted.

A fresh set of guffaws broke out as I revealed the line of demarcation and a perfect, flour-free back.

"I'll get the bucket and mop," murmured Liam. "You go clean yourself up."

"Thank you, Liam." I strode towards my audience. "Stuff the rest of you."

"Such a good sport," said Rā as I marched past her.

"Don't clean yourself with water," called Helena. "You'll glue the shirt to your body."

More laughter.

"I was being serious. She could pull her skin off."

I closed the *Staff only* door and stalked down the hall towards the delivery bay.

The captain stepped outside his office as I neared it and halted in his tracks. He looked me up and down, then eyed the white walls on either side of me. "I like your initiative of attempting to blend into your environment, soldier, but your timing's all wrong. If I see you move, the illusion fails."

I stopped walking. After a pause, I said, "Yes sir."

He raised a finger and shook it. "You know, it reminds me of summer in the A-stan when the dust would coat all your exposed skin due to the excessive sweat and the seasonal winds. The dirt covered every surface within seconds. We called ourselves 'crumbed drumsticks' because of the gear you had to carry on your back. When you turned sideways you looked like an upright chicken thigh."

I took a step forward in the hope of edging around him, but he continued, "What you didn't want to do was make the mistake of taking a slash into the wind on account of the splash back. Turn your old fella into a crumbed *sausage* before you'd shaken off the last drop. If you tucked that thing back into your pants, the chafing could immobilise you for a week."

I didn't say anything. I wasn't sure I was meant to, and

even if I was, I had no idea what an appropriate response would be.

His eyes lost their glassy, revisiting the past look and refocused on me. "Right. As you were, Jewel." He gestured towards the stock room. "Carry on." He stepped back into his office and closed the door, presumably having forgotten he hadn't actually done whatever it was he left his office for in the first place.

"Jewel Bauer," said Harit in his customary greeting. "You having a good morning, my friend?"

I patted the front of my shirt in answer. Clouds of flour rose from me like dust from a demolished building.

He put the forklift into reverse and said, "You got a little something on your face."

Pulling my hair out of its ponytail, I raked my fingers through it, loosening little white puffs.

I peered down at my front. My black pants were a stubborn grey. There was nothing else for it but to strip them and beat them against something.

"Harit," I called over the noise of the forklift. "I'm just going to take my pants off for a minute. Can you do a job facing the other direction?"

Harit gave me a two-finger salute and swung the machine around towards a pallet of goods in the far corner of the loading area.

I removed my trousers and jumped away from the cloud when I swung them against the side of the building.

Lord help me, how did I get to the point of standing in my knickers beating flour out of my trousers against a wall?

Yet again, the universe was having a laugh at the expense of Jewel Bauer. I mean, how does someone even get attracted to a gay man *after* their gayness has become apparent? Biologically, it made no reproductive sense. There should be a little shutter that slams down over your ovaries when a nice-looking queer guy drifts into range of your baby-making radar. *That one's a lost cause. No zygote creating with him.*

I gave my trousers one last *thwack* and balanced on one leg to redress.

If anything, the whole thing was decidedly inconvenient. I didn't want to waste thought energy on Liam. Mind space was precious. I wanted to waste thoughts on whether electric cars came in teal when my T-shirt business was minting hundred dollar bills. Or whether I should put in massaging shower heads in the new bathroom at the crib.

I unbuttoned my shirt and whipped it against the wall. Half a plastic button clattered onto the concrete.

I'd just have to try and forget about it. Crowbar all naked Liam thoughts out of my conscious brain and hope they didn't settle anywhere else, because I didn't want to waste dream space on him either.

Rebuttoning my defloured shirt, I strode back into the mart and turned into the baking goods aisle.

Liam crouched with a brush and pan in his hand, sweeping up little piles of flour he'd dislodged from the surrounding shelves. His muscles flexed and bunched under his shirt.

An image of those muscles flexing and bunching over me flashed into my mind.

Treacherous, treacherous brain.

Fuck it.

I might as well embrace it. Liam didn't have to know.

Joe stepped into my peripheral vision, but said nothing for several seconds. "You having a good time?" he whispered.

"Yep." I was. Imaginary Liam felt pretty damn nice to the touch.

He waited another beat before grabbing my hand and pulling me back towards the *Staff only* door. "And now it's time to get the mop before it gets creepy. You can pause and look, but being stationary for longer than it takes for a full body assessment is perving."

I'd been there *way* longer than a full body assessment. I should probably feel something more appropriate than turned on. Guilt?

...

Yep. There we have it, folks. One more admirable quality to add to my very impressive resumé:

Jewel Bauer, mayor abuser and unashamed perve.

I DECIDED the best way to start dealing with the new situation was by dashing Dad and Rewa's *Is there a boy?* hopes against pointy, innards-splattering rocks. "Is it wrong to have lusty thoughts about a gay man?"

Dad "Hmm"ed like he gave it serious thought instead of wishing he'd wheeled himself away from the conversation as soon as I mentioned the word "question".

"You asking for yourself or a friend?" said Rewa, knowing very well I asked for myself, not least because it was exactly the kind of question you asked for yourself, but also because I didn't have much in the way of friends. All my school friends stayed to finish their schooling and their lives quickly departed from mine. After that, I had colleagues. They were friendly enough to have a drink with at the end of the restaurant shift, but no one pursued anything closer. I think I was just slightly odd enough for them to not want to make the effort to invest in anything more.

"Myself," I said on a sigh.

"Well, Jewelsy. Sounds like an awful waste of energy to me. Is this the man-bear or a new one?"

"Are you sure he's gay and not bi?" said Dad.

I didn't, but it was moot. "He has a boyfriend."

Dad and Rewa chorused an "Ah" and I tried to see their thoughts. Every possibility concluded in varying degrees of pity. I could almost hear them feeding words through their condescension filter.

"No, there is nothing wrong in having lusty thoughts about a gay man," said Rewa. "You'll forget him soon enough. Attraction can be fickle when there's no substance behind an attachment."

"And I'm sure he'd be flattered to know a beautiful young woman, like you, thinks he's –" Dad said "hot" like trying it out for the first time, prodding the shape of it with his tongue.

"I don't think I'll forget it very easily. I've seen him naked."

Dad gasped like I'd said I let Liam deflower me on the bonnet of his car, which is actually how I lost my virginity. Not that I was ever going to admit that to my father.

I'd also better not tell him I'd touched Liam's penis.

Instead, I said, "That kind of thing burns an imprint on your retinas."

Rewa's voice dropped a key. "How on earth did you get to see him naked?"

"We went skinny dipping."

Her voice dropped another note. "Just...you and him?"

"No. My work team, after a few drinks on Friday."

"Hang on, Jewelsy," said Dad. "Back the truck up a bit. This is the guy who's so shy he wouldn't let you see his face for the first week?"

The very one. "He'd downed a few by then, and he obviously feels confident around his boyfriend, which is natural."

"Still, from hiding behind his hair to showing everything in the space of a couple of weeks."

"What's your point?" Because it wasn't like he'd taken off his clothes for my benefit.

"I don't know. It seems a bit, what's the word?"

"Out of character?" I ventured.

"Disingenuous."

"No, Dale, it's just what young people do when they've been drinking. Alcohol's the great uninhibitor. I remember, or mostly remember, after one particularly sloppy drinking session trying to wear the ring tabs off the beer cans as nipple tassels. Nearly de-gloved my pirate makers."

Dad stuttered a series of "Nguh"s like he'd stuffed his fist in his mouth and accidentally swallowed it.

"Okay. One, de-gloving relates to hands, as indicated by the term 'glove', so you cannot *de-glove a nipple*. Two, your nipples are so large they couldn't fit through a ring pull?" I wasn't sure I wanted to ask about the "pirate makers".

"Yes, I have very large nipples. And I've never had a single complaint, I'll have you know."

Dad managed to pull his hand free. "Jeez, love, do you have to share such intimate details?"

"I'm just making the point that people behave in unlikely ways once the ratio of blood to alcohol in their veins is questionable."

My "Unlikely?" left my mouth with enough dubiousness to pin Rewa to her chair from the G-force. Her ring pull story had enough similarity to other tales of her youth that it couldn't be described as surprising.

"Look, do you want my advice or not? Because I do happen to have some for the case of unrequited desire."

"Yes, I want your advice," I said after a pause and added "Sorry" in case what she had to say was conditional on me being contrite.

"Good. Here's what you do. You find an outlet to redirect your lust energy."

"And this is where I leave to put the jug on," said Dad.

Rewa dropped her voice, despite the clanks in the background suggesting Dad was making every effort to be as loud as possible. "Here are your options. I'll make them diverse so you've got plenty of choice. Yoga, kick boxing, Tinder, base jumping, vibrator, a dog. Any of those sound appealing?"

I thought of Rā's Ultimate Taser Ball league and understood why people might seek the thrill of pain and inflicting it on others if it gave them an outlet for their frustrated, dissatisfying lives.

"Kick boxing?" I ventured and a movement through the open back door caught my eye. A woman, dressed in white, was on the lake shore peering in at the McManus crib. Helena.

"Or a dog sounds nice," I said distractedly as Helena walked on a few paces and stared at our crib. "I better go. Someone's here to see me. I'll think about your advice, though."

"Alright, hon. Holler if you need more ideas."

I hung up and walked down the lawn.

"Jewel!" Helena brought her hands up to her chest, like an excited child. She carried a towel in one hand and something red and white in the other. "Fantastic, I was hoping I'd come across you. I wasn't sure what house you lived in."

"Me? Why?"

"Right-well-so, I need some help with an experiment and my husband has no interest in what I do, so doesn't lift a finger." She turned and pointed a bottle of tomato sauce at the promontory I saw her emerge around the other day in her row boat. "I live just round there, so I thought I'd see what you were up to." She placed a hand on her hip and beamed at me.

"If you need me to help you murder someone, I have a victim suggestion." I tried not to let my eyeballs move to the neighbouring property, but they did so on their own accord anyway.

"No, we're post-murder today, I'm very sorry," she said, as if genuinely remorseful she couldn't offer me an opportunity to do away with someone. "We're going to help the murderer who's just cut the throat of the victim and been sprayed with –" she put her hand over her mouth, swallowed and said thickly, "arterial blood." She turned to face the lake and took a deep breath, before waving her hand in front of her face. "Sorry."

After blowing a breath out through pursed lips, she continued in her sing-song voice, "So as you know, the murderer's then disposed of the body in the lake, but the only problem is, they're covered in –" she waved her hands up and down her body. "And they need to do something about that before heading back to shore in case anybody sees them."

"Right. You're going to use tomato sauce to replicate the –" I paused, not sure if me saying "blood?" would turn her stomach. I settled on "Life juice?" and waited for the expansion of her cheeks.

"Ketchup. Not tomato sauce. I don't know if there's much of a difference, but I read on a science website that ketchup has the same viscoelasticity, whatever that means, as the 'b' word, and I figured at the very least it meant it would be a good substitute – you know how I feel about the stuff – and I thought I'd wear white so I can see if the lake water would do a sufficient enough job of getting the worst of the...stuff off. Of course, I won't have the *killer* wear white. Not a very threatening colour. So anyway –" she sucked in a large breath. "– I need to get my victim murdered and my killer innocent-looking inside forty-five minutes. I've already timed the clothes drying time. I just need you to spray me with ketchup and then I'll take a swim."

As far as experiments went, it wasn't a particularly good one. "There's at least one problem with your plan."

Helena's smile didn't falter. "I knew you'd be the right person to help me. What's that?"

"Has the killer murdered the victim on shore?"

"Yes."

"And then they've wrapped them up and rowed out onto the lake?"

"Uh-huh."

"Well, the b – life juice – would mostly be dry by then. Does this 'visco' thing apply to *dried* stuff?"

Helena stared at me for a beat. Then the smile slipped from her face. "Ahhhh, fudge nuggets." She slapped a hand against her thigh and looked at the water for several seconds. "Let's just do it anyway. I'll wait until the ketchup's mostly dry then take a dunk."

She handed me the bottle. "Shake it at me from up close. The killer's only just –" she ran a finger across her throat. "– So it needs to be close range." Then she closed her eyes and screwed up her face, anticipating the hit of reconstituted tomato.

"Should it be at body temperature?"

Helena cracked an eye. Her features relaxed and she pointed a finger at me. "You're good. You should be my research assistant. You want to be my research assistant? Voluntarily?"

I shrugged. "Maybe." Perhaps researching ways to carry out murder and dispose of bodies would be the distraction I needed.

"Yay," she said, as if I'd given enthusiastic consent instead of apathetic non-committal. "Okay, now hit me." She closed her eyes again. "It's too late for any factual replication like body temperature."

I removed the lid and, holding the bottle by its end, shook out the contents, covering her head and torso in red streaks. It dripped from her hair, her ears, the end of her nose, her chin, and gathered speed as it funnelled into her cleavage.

When I had emptied the bottle, Helena wiped the sauce from her eyes and said, "Now we wait." She eased herself down against the bank and spread her limbs so as much of her clothing was exposed to the late afternoon sun as possible. "I should have brought some wine."

"I'm on the wagon," I said, thinking of Friday night's over-indulgence. After heeding Joe's advice, I had woken with a very full bladder, a mild headache, and the cringe-inducing memory of declaring my lack of sexual prowess to the entire pub.

"Good for you. I wish I had that kind of discipline. I wish *my husband* had that kind of discipline." She whipped her head around to me. "Do you think it would be too obvious if I wrote domestic thrillers?"

"I don't know." It was a reasonable response. I had no idea what a domestic thriller was.

"I could use a pen name, I suppose. Maybe if I'd done

that with my first manuscript, I'd have had the guts to send it to an agent. I've got four more sitting in a draw." She looked away from me and focused on the lake. "I just don't think any publishing house would be interested in me. They want the next Lee Child or Nora Roberts. If it's not set in America or England it's not worth the paper it's printed on. I'd do it myself, but then I'd be responsible for convincing people it was worth buying. I can't even produce something as simple as spaghetti bolognaise with any conviction that it's edible." Her head swivelled towards me again. "Are you much of a reader?"

"No. I'm dyslexic."

"You've never read a novel?"

"I *could* read a novel, but it's a lot of work, so I tend not to."

"You should listen to audio books. They have actors read them and do different accents. I'd have Sam Neil read mine, but he's probably too busy being gorgeous and rich."

"Isn't he, like, in his seventies?"

"Yep." She sighed. "Men are lucky. Their beauty sharpens with age."

I thought of Brian McManus' paunch and rapidly receding hairline. "Not all men."

"Take Guy, for example."

I waited for her to expand on this, frankly preposterous statement, but that, apparently, was it. Guy Fink was an average-looking middle-aged man in good health, sure, but he had no beauty with which to chisel down to perfection as he edged towards old age.

Helena picked at a dried runnel of ketchup on her stomach and it flaked away. "I don't think claret would do that, do you?"

"No."

"I've really fluffed up this whole experiment, haven't I?"

"Yes."

She collapsed back on to the grass and flung an arm across her eyes.

"Just have him wear black. He'd be able to get it all out of his hair and off his face. His clothes won't matter so much."

Helena peeked out at me. "The murderer's a 'she', remember? Number one rule of crime solving. Never assume." She stood up, took off towards the lake at a run and dived in. Surfacing a couple of metres away, she turned towards the shore. "I love her embrace. She's like a rejuvenating balm." She set to work scrubbing her face and tipping her head back, running her fingers through her scalp.

"Aren't you going to turn her into some kind of super villain? Like a dark force?"

"I might make it look that way in the set up, but she'll always be an ally. The Great Lady gives up her secrets in the end. You coming in?"

The weather wasn't quite warm enough to drive the urge for a swim, but it was always hard to deny the incredibly clear water. I stripped down to my bra and underpants and waded in, choosing the path of the masochist and grimacing against the gradual increase of frigid mountain water.

"Do you think there's any truth to what they're saying about the water?" Helena asked once I'd braved belly height.

"I don't know. What are they saying?"

"It's on the Puhiruru bulletin board on Facebook. That the chlorine they add to the drinking water taken from the lake messes with your hormones. It's a...what was the word?" Helena looked to the sky for an answer. "Endocrine! An endocrine disruptor, which means more of the opposite

hormone is produced and why there's a rise in transexu-
alism in teenagers in the last few years."

Right. So that would explain why I'd been replacing
bottled water on the mart shelves with increasing frequency
over the last week. "That sounds one hundred percent
*un*true."

"There's scientific research and everything, apparently."

"Uh-huh." I lowered myself until the water lapped over
my clavicle. "So, you didn't read it?"

"Well, I didn't know if I should pay it any attention or
not."

I breast-stroked past her and turned around to look at
the crib. My favourite view of it was from out on the lake,
even if it wasn't much to look at, with its wide cement
boards and rusting roof. If I raised my hands to either side of
my face, like blinkers, to block out the neighbouring properties, I could pretend it was all there was. The place of happy
childhood summers when the world was simple and all I
had to worry about was making sure I didn't play or swim
out of view of the little crib.

"There's one person feeding all the info. They're getting
a lot of support," Helena continued.

A movement behind an upstairs McManus window
caught my eye.

"They've got some made-up name, like they're doing
everyone a favour by bringing light to the darkness of our
collective ignorance like, Free Your Mind, or The Big
Truth."

The windows were tinted, so that recreationists on the
lake, or people walking along the shore had to battle the
reflection of the sky *and* the darkened glass to be able to see
inside.

"The Unfettered Brain. That's it! It's not very catchy, is

it? I like The Big Truth better. Much more punchy and attention grabbing."

I had to agree with her. If someone wanted to position themselves as the great liberator of the oppressed masses, there were much better options than The Unfettered Brain. Amateur. Even a career muscle like The Rock understood the importance of having a name with impact. But then you would if your birth name was Dwayne.

"You know, Helena, there's one thing I've learned about social media as an observer and as a contributor. Very little of anything posted is one hundred percent true. Photos are filtered and very likely staged. They're simply one extraordinary moment in a very ordinary life curated with just enough regularity to give you the impression that's all their life is. Joy, success, plenty."

Helena tugged on her billowing shirt. "I never thought of it that way. It does sound a bit cynical, though, if you don't mind me saying so."

I didn't mind her saying so. She was right. I, of all people, who didn't fit and only sometimes understood why, was very jaded by seeing the lives I'd never lead of those who did fit. "I do it. I lie all the time about how your world would be better by owning one of my T-shirts." I turned to swim back to shore. "I wouldn't trust anything I saw on social media. Every single one of us is a spin doctor."

AS DINNER NEARED BEING READY, I turned the element to low and approached the back door for my customary, pre-eat bladder evacuation.

I did this to maximise capacity in my abdomen, which

was essential if you tended to eat your head weight at dinner time.

I opened the door to find Brian McManus, hand raised to knock.

My heart galloped with a small kick of adrenaline.

I hoped he wasn't here to do the friendly neighbour-meet-and-greet thing, because I had neither the will nor the bladder space to humour him.

I crossed my arms and arranged myself in the doorway in such a way that it was clear no invitation of any nature was ever going to be issued. Ever.

"Good evening." He stretched his lips around his teeth in a smile a ferret might give to a lost baby rabbit. "My name's Brian McManus and I'm running in the upcoming mayoral bi-election. Is the man of the house about?"

While I might console myself that he wasn't, thank God, doing the neighbourly thing, and that, yes, I had been bang on the money about his political intentions, I didn't, in fact, feel the least bit consoled or smug about the confirmation of either.

As to his question, there was one of two reasons I could think of that would prompt him to ask it. I wasn't going to give him the benefit of the doubt. "Women have been able to vote in New Zealand for well over a century now. We can even make up our own minds about who to vote for without men having to tell us."

His smile hitched, and in that second before he remembered himself, I could see him battling the ferret over the kill switch. "Oh ho ho. I see I've got my work cut out with you. It wasn't a preferential question, my good lady. It saves my time and yours talking to you both at the same time. You are –" his eyes roamed my face "– of voting age? I'm too old to judge young faces these days. Anyone under thirty looks fifteen to me." He issued a string of "Ha"s into the cooling air, which on somebody taller, leaner and hairier might have been charming.

Given he'd so far only hit "mild" on the offensive scale, I had a bit more presence of mind than the last time we exchanged words. Here was my chance to have the kind of interaction I wished I'd engineered the first time around. "If you're wondering whether you should bother wasting your sales pitch on me, the answer is 'no'. I'm old enough to vote, but I won't be voting for you."

He fought to keep the amusement in his expression, which was like watching a colony of worms eating their way out of a potato. "Ah, yes, I imagine someone young, like you, might wonder how a middle-aged man, like me, can possibly represent what's important to them?" He smoothed his features into a mask of earnestness. "How about you tell me. I'm here to listen."

Like fuck he was.

"No, you're not. Your agenda's already set. You'll nod your head, make sympathetic noises, throw some rhetoric my way that makes it sound as if you're listening, but I have it on very good authority that you won't do a thing to represent my concerns." I uncrossed my arms.

Brian McManus' eyes flicked down to my *Anything you can do I can do bleeding* T-shirt and his features slackened in recognition.

"You."

CHAPTER FOURTEEN

"BAH-LOODY HELL. The cockwombler lives next door."
He threw his head back and laughed, bringing his hands
together in a single clap. The solid round of his foie gras-fed
paunch bounced with each expulsion of air, like a twerking
buttock. "What are the chances?"

Unbelievably, ridiculously low. And yet, here we were.

He wiped a finger beneath his eye as if my living-next-
door status held the degree of hilarity that reduced someone
to tears.

I looked on impassively. Impassivity held as much derision
as looking derisive itself did. Or at least when people met my
comments or actions with impassivity it felt that way to me.

Evidently, it didn't have a similar effect on Brian
McManus.

Beneath his grin, he pointed his finger at me and shook
it. "You are bah-loody appalling at expressing censure.
Punctuating your blazing righteousness with a 'cockwomble'. Rather undermines the intended effect."

I recrossed my arms. "And yet, it left you speechless."

McManus' smile didn't falter, but his eyes narrowed. "Not afraid of fanning a flame, are you?"

Ordinarily, I might have said, "It can appear that way, but I have a 'talk first think after' policy that some people might call foolhardy, or idiotic. It's certainly not bravery," but this time I *did* have a presence of mind to maintain a front.

So, I said, "Nope."

He crossed his arms, too. "Good, good." Raising an index finger to pursed lips, he paused before saying, "You know, I really like your pep."

Um...

Had I been sucked through a portal to a parallel universe? Because I could have sworn Brian McManus just told me he liked my pep.

"You're a graphic designer, aren't you?"

Okay. This conversation was not going the way I imagined it would. On the inevitable day Brian McManus recognised me and an opening was given to reminisce on our previous encounter, I would have delivered the lines I'd practised in my head every night in bed for the days following my council exit. I said things like, "Your brand of misogyny lost its used-by date in 1981" and I would have concluded with something dignified, like, "I find your attitudes deeply offensive and I'm ashamed you represent the interests of women in your very privileged position as decision-maker for Invercargill city."

Yes, he would have laughed it off, but I would have made my point without reducing myself to his level of degradation, and had I actually said it when I should have, I wouldn't have lost my job. How on earth was I going to deliver that speech when he'd just delivered a compliment and neatly amplified its disarming nature by asking a question that showed interest in me?

Okay. Well. I might not have been given the opening I hoped for, but I wasn't playing whatever game he was.

"I *was* a graphic designer. A complaint to HR made sure that came to a swift end."

"You lost your job over a 'cockwomble'? Dear me, what is this world coming to if a bit of verbal face slapping can't be indulged when warranted. People are obsessively PC these days. They should call it LI. Linguistic Intolerance."

They should call it AI. *Arsehole* Intolerance.

"Dave accuses Tim of 'having a case of the gaybies' and everyone hides under their desks like a shooter with a semi-automatic's just stormed the building."

I didn't have to be a poo inspector for the needle on my bullshit-o-meter to be swinging to red. *Of course* he made the complaint to HR. And of course, he'd lie through his teeth about it. His prime tactic in connecting to constituents was making them believe he was their mate. The everyman's man.

I narrowed my eyes to convey just how thoroughly I saw through him.

He might have taken notice were it not for his ego eclipsing his view of my face.

"Can we?" He gestured to the two heavy, sun-bleached wooden chairs below the bedroom window.

"No."

Another laugh. "Well, I'd like to. I have a proposition you'll want to hear and when you agree to it, we'll have a few details to work out, which might make standing in a doorway with your hands on your hips tiresome."

I knew he was trying to hook me by dangling some fat and juicy presumption in my face.

Aaaand...he was too well practised for it not to work. I *was* interested, but I wasn't going to let him know that. "There is no conversation I want to have with you that should be held seated."

McManus grinned. "See? There it is. That fire. That fearlessness. That's a rare quality, Jane." My name was a stab in the J-scented dark, but he'd said it with such confidence, it might as well have been my name.

"Jewel."

"Jewel, is it? See? A rare and shining treasure. One I need in my collection."

"Collection of what? I'm not really trophy wife material."

"Fluffers."

His *what?*

"Mirage makers. I want you to join my campaign team."

———

"IT'S JUST SO BIZARRE."

Joe shelved tins of legumes next to me, stacking them on top of each other with a soft *chunk*. "I know. It's outrageous our previous dried goods expert put the chickpeas before the cannellini beans. Who doesn't enjoy a system based on alphabet?"

I glanced at him. His face was set in a frown. "Are you making a joke, or are you genuinely upset over tin placement?"

He sighed. "I wish I could find humour in this situation, Jewel pet, but I believe in order as much as the captain, which is why I am his right-hand man in the trenches."

"Can we focus on my problem, now?" I didn't want to say the word "trivial", but... "Mine's less trivial."

Joe gasped. "Do you know the mart stocks over twenty-five different herbs and spices?"

"Yes. I have to replace them on a regular basis."

"All those tiny packets look the same. Imagine if they weren't arranged in any order. You'd spend half your day trying to find the garam masala amid the tumeric and cumin, when you can easily find it just before the ground cinnamon."

"But here's the thing. If I wanted whole peppercorns, I'd look in the Ps, not the Ws. I don't think the garam masala should be anywhere near the ground cinnamon."

Joe's eyes looked from me and slid sideways in the direction of where the packets of herbs were shelved in the adjacent aisle. Then he clamped his hands to the side of his head. "No! You've just made me doubt the logical nature of my foolproof system."

I let him indulge his crisis for five more seconds, then steered the conversation back on track. "He said I've got an eye for effective messaging, the kind that drills right into the brain and he needs lobotomists on his team to dazzle and stupefy the punters. How could I keep my self-respect if I said 'Yes'?"

Joe shrugged. "Self-respect is easily exchanged for a healthy bank account. Look at Jerry Hall marrying Rupert Murdoch."

It was an excellent point, and one that had bobbed around my consciousness in the hours since my conversation with McManus no matter how many times I tried to hold its head under the surface.

"What did he say he'd pay you?"

"He offered double what I was earning at the council. *Double*, Joe. I mean, that's crazy money. It'd probably only be a couple of hours a day, but I'd earn the same in an hour than what I earn doing my half day here." I placed a tin on the shelf and swivelled it so the label faced outwards. "I don't think he has a concept of money, or what graphic design is. He said double must be a pretty decent rate for a *bit of colouring in.*"

"Then take advantage of his ignorance and accept his offer. It's just a job. Being contracted to do a job doesn't mean you're affiliated to anything. Just because stacking chocolate bars is part of my job doesn't mean I'm pro diabetes."

"Chocolate bars and an aspiring Boris Johnson are not really in the same solar system, Joe."

"I don't know. If anything's going to tempt you to the dark side it's a limited edition Caramel-Pretzel KitKat."

As ludicrous as his assertion was, I had to admit there was some truth to it. Caramel-Pretzel KitKats were pretty phenomenal. "There's nothing Brian McManus could offer to tempt me to the dark side. Apparently, the real estate agent told him the owner of my crib was a paraplegic, which makes me an asset to the mayoral campaign because, and I quote, 'You're a woman with disability in your family. Shame you're not brown, then I'd have the tick box trifecta'."

"He didn't."

"I shit you not. How can I possibly work for someone like that? It's not like I'm mowing his lawns. I'd be dressing up his divisiveness to make it look like it's what everyone wants."

Joe pulled his lips to one side and scrutinised a can of red kidney beans. "Look. surely, he's just another representative of the rich, white boys club. What power to affect real change does he actually have? It's just the council."

Just the council. As someone with brown skin he couldn't POSSIBLY give that little a shit. "That rich white boys club colonised this country, disempowered your people, and a century and a half later still doesn't recognise the damage they've done to an entire race." I *thunked* a can on the shelf. "The ongoing socio-economic problems." *Thunk.* "The cultural displacement that has happened as a direct result of them." *Thunk.* "They're all like, stop whinging about the past and go out and get a job." I turned to face Joe and jabbed a finger into his chest. "You should be making a stand against him on principle. Local council or not."

"Owww." He rubbed his chest and peered up at me from under knitted eyebrows.

"It'd be like handing him a silencer to put on his bigotry gun, so he'd indoctrinate people with his bullshit without them realising they'd been persuaded into dickheadery." I turned back to my task and addressed the shelf of lentils in front of me. "If I did this, and he won the mayoralty, I'd never forgive myself."

"Right. Then why are you verbalising a crisis of conscience?"

"Because you told me I should consider his offer."

Joe wagged a finger at me. "Uh uh. You've framed this whole conversation so I'd have no choice but to play devil's advocate. His financial incentive has tempted you, hasn't it?"

I refused to acknowledge his hitting of the metaphorical nail with a direct answer. "Look, you may think local politicians have little potency in this country, but he got elected three times as Invercargill mayor. That's nine years to slowly bed in, to influence the culture, the mind-set of the council machine. Once he's got his foot in the door, he'll be very hard to shift."

"So, don't work for him."

"I won't."

"Good." Joe twisted a can to align its label with the one underneath. "Helena says the deadlines for nominations is coming up soon and once again we've only got one candidate."

Brilliant. "So he's getting in regardless of me not voting or not working for him."

"Somebody else will step up."

And if they didn't? "Oh, God. I think I'd move back to Invercargill if he got to play at being mayor again."

Joe whipped around and pointed a can at me. "Don't you dare. We've only just welcomed you to our family. Once you're in, it's a lifetime commitment. Like a pre-Gen X marriage."

"I'll be living next door to the smug fucker."

He laid a hand on my shoulder. "Honey girl, I'm not sure why you're making such a fuss. Yes, it would be better if we didn't have a wealthy, old white guy as our mayor, but we've pretty much always had wealthy, old white guys running the show. It's not controversial. At least we know the lie of the land."

"How can you be so apathetic?"

"I'm not at all apathetic. I'm just resigned to the fact that the likelihood of someone like me being chosen by the voting majority is slim at best. If this McManus guy gets in, it's hardly Armageddon. It'll just be the same old shit and we won't even notice the mayor has a new name."

"I want a choice at least. One candidate is not a democracy."

Joe looked at his watch. "Before we're drawn into a debate about what a true democracy is, it's time for your break. But know I'll always have a shoulder for you to cry on when McManus is voted mayor."

I eyed him for three of his lazy blinks. "Your cynicism is disturbing."

"A lifetime of being marginalised tends to amplify the pessimism."

I trudged off to the smoko room, made a Rā special, then ignored it and buried my face in the crook of my arms on the table.

The door creaked open, a shoe squeaked on the polished floor, and Liam said, "Hi, Jewel," in that way of his that is at once deep and soft and rumbly.

I sat straight up like I'd been shocked by a cattle prod.

"You not get enough sleep?"

He walked over to the cupboards and leant over to grab a mug.

I tried to stare at the spot he'd vacated in the doorway, but my treacherous eyes followed his movements anyway. The fabric of his jeans tightened over his buttocks as he bent forward. Buttocks I had seen unclothed and flexing with movement.

An image of them pumping away between a set of legs, possibly mine, wrapped its tentacles over my brain and it took Liam's, "You okay?" for me to shake it off.

I was okay, if a bit hot all of a sudden. "Yep," I said and pulled my tea towards me.

"You're very quiet." The fridge opened behind me.

"I have some stuff going on."

A container slid across the table and came to a halt in front of me. I undid the plastic clasps while Liam made drinking-making noises behind me.

"Would you...like to tell me about it?" He paused, before saying, "It's okay if you don't want to."

I picked up a venison sandwich and sighed. "Basically something's happening that I don't want to happen but I have no control over. Except maybe I do, but it means compromising my integrity." I took a bite.

Liam slid into the chair opposite me. Usually, he sat at the one on a diagonal from where I sat. Today I had an unimpeded view of the ridiculous symmetry of his face.

After a pause, he said quietly, "Don't compromise your integrity. I know you."

Did he? Even I hadn't unlocked that mystery yet.

"You'd be full of resentment."

Yes, I would. I knew that much. "But I can't sit by and watch it happen."

"Then find another way. You have an interesting-shaped brain. You'll be able to do it."

An interesting-shaped brain. What did that mean? A euphemism for 'odd'?

"What shape is it? If I was you, I'd imagine it as an octagon."

"I don't —" Liam peeled back the top of his sandwich, then replaced it. "— need to reshape it to make it more appealing." He put the sandwich down on the upturned container lid and turned his head away from me so his hair walled him off. "I like it in its original form."

Okay. That was...new. Nobody had ever been remotely close to telling me the way my brain worked was appealing, likeable even. I'd only ever been given the impression by anybody who commented on it that it was challenging, required patience.

And yet, Liam had just now said he liked it as it was.

I didn't particularly want Liam to make such declarations. I wasn't sure how it would complicate the whole having lustful thoughts about him thing.

I sought redirection.

"Dana seems nice."

"Dana *is* nice."

I wasn't sure where to go from here. What was the usual line of conversation when talking about someone you maybe didn't want to actually talk about?

"He's a lot shorter than you."

Pause. "Yes." Another pause. "I am quite tall. A lot of people are shorter than me."

"I'm not tall." Jesus wept. What inanity was that? My brain had clearly flat-lined under the pressure of having to make small talk. "I'm about the same height as your nipples." It was true, but only served to make me think of the nipples I'd seen on his perfectly sculptured man chest and Liam to choke on his tea.

"Do you like it? Being tall? You don't look like you like it. You look like you spend a lot of energy trying to make yourself look smaller. Or is that just a confidence thing?"

Liam spluttered out a final cough, his lips twitching towards what looked like a smile. "See? Your mind is like a scalpel."

"Frightening when wielded recklessly?"

He humoured me with a snort. "Slicing to the core of the matter."

That sounded like a bad thing. "Want to take back your liking my brain comment now?"

"No."

"But I've made you uncomfortable."

"I think feeling uncomfortable is good for us."

Before I could ask him to explain the absurdity of such a statement, he took a bite of his sandwich, so I had to wait until he stopped chewing. "It keeps us real. Makes us recognise the stuff in us we weren't aware of and need to be."

That wasn't good. What had I just dredged up from the

id and forced him to confront? "What is it you're recognising now?"

Liam eyed his sandwich and said in a rush, "Um. Actually, I already know that stuff about me. It's more *you* asking me that's got me feeling awkward." Then he shoved the whole thing in his mouth as if it could shield him from whatever was about to ensue off the back of his words.

That I did understand. I'd embarrassed him on enough occasions to keep him perpetually on edge. No point in stopping now. "What stuff do you know?"

Liam swallowed with some effort and downed half his tea. "I feel like I'm in the wrong body." The words slipped out like a sigh.

"Like, you want to be a woman or something?"

Liam's eyes shot to mine. They were wide like he was looking for something in my expression. Whether he found it or not, he looked away again. "Like I'm a small person in an oversized body. So, yes. It's a confidence thing. I'm working at filling the extra space."

I could see it. His personality was very quiet for such a loud body. "You're a raging introvert."

He smiled. "Rā calls it turtling. Hiding in my shell until it's safe enough to come out."

"You turtled with me."

"Yes."

"But not any more."

"No."

I let the significance of that settle, that despite my ability to cause him embarrassment, I was a safe place for Liam to be around. Mostly. He still hid on occasion, but those occasions were becoming less frequent.

Liam reached across to my side of the table and fiddled

with the clasps on the sandwich container. "You don't seem to have any confidence things."

I absolutely did. "I know you think I have, like, anti-vulnerability superpowers. I don't. I just don't make my confidence things obvious, mostly because my indignation gets in the way."

"Indignation about what?"

I pulled the crust off my sandwich and placed it on my tongue. "Being made to feel stupid," I said from behind my hand, my mouth full.

Liam frowned. "But you're not stupid. You're not remotely stupid."

"I know."

"Why is it a sore spot, then?"

"Because I didn't learn at the same pace as the other kids. When most learning is centred around literacy and I had a learning disability that made it very difficult to acquire literacy, it became noticeable pretty quickly that I was progressing at a much slower pace than the other kids."

"They called you dumb." It wasn't a question, because of course they did.

"Being the only kid in the class not able to do what everyone else could? *I* thought I was dumb. Them calling me that just confirmed it. I hated school."

"I didn't like school much either. Kids can be real little dicks."

Of course. There would have been a time when a boy as quiet as Liam was a plum target for bullies. Before he grew bigger than them.

"The school doesn't do anything to stop it."

I shook my head. "Nope. The school I went to didn't have a remedial teacher. We had to pay for tuition ourselves and my parents couldn't afford it."

Liam paused, his cup raised halfway to his mouth. "Your school didn't give you any help?"

"They couldn't. There's very little government funding for kids with learning disabilities. Supposedly, we have one of the best education systems in the world. It probably is good if your brain functions in the way the system's set up for."

Liam's eyes remained focussed on mine, our words spilling into each other's. "I had no idea. It must fail so many kids."

"I think I was only ever going to be an outsider."

"I was *always* an outsider."

"Whenever we had group work at school, nobody wanted to go with me. Who wants to be lumped with the dumb kid?"

"Or the boy who wasn't afraid to cry?"

"What teacher wants to have to devote half their time to one kid out of thirty who also need them?"

"I'm so glad I made it out the other side."

"Me too. Those first few years of school, until my brain finally got its way around deciphering words to some extent, were pretty miserable."

Finally, Liam paused. "And who makes you feel stupid now?"

It was a good question. Since I'd left school and entered the workforce, my disability was less obvious, or if I needed to draw people's attention to it, I did, and it was generally accepted without comment or judgement. And yet, I still regularly felt stupid.

Perhaps it was the result of my own sensitivities, a hangover from that confused, hurt child. It was a reasonable way to react, but the person I aimed my anger at couldn't imply stupidity because of a disability they didn't know existed.

I traced a crack in the table's surface with my finger. "I don't know. Maybe it's something I'll always struggle to shake."

Something flashed across Liam's face. It was too soft, too settled for pity. "You and I are very very alike."

Ah.

Understanding.

Something shifted in me and settled like a Tetrus piece falling into place. It was easy to imagine it shifted between *us*, but it couldn't have, could it?

When Liam started his next sentence with, "You," and his full lips fattened around the shape of the word, I found myself at the mercy of new uninvited imagining. Liam fattening his lips to kiss me.

They were soft and his breath fluttered over my cheek.

It felt far more intimate than the sex tape that had rolled intermittently in my head, and I knew without a doubt that I'd crossed some kind of "got the hots for" threshold that there was no coming back from.

I didn't like it.

I mean, I did like the thought of Liam kissing me. That bit was alright. What I didn't like was the realisation that whatever was happening in the mysterious connection between libido and that murky stuff we call "feelings" – blech – might be just a teeny wee bit out of my control.

CHAPTER FIFTEEN

THE LAST TIME I had an unrequited desire for someone, it was a lot more straight forward. He was the barman at the restaurant I worked at, and he had that 'V' shape of the wide-shoulder, narrow-hipped man, and a very nice nape of his neck. It was smooth and tanned, and his hair licked the top of it with the flick of short hair just beginning to curl.

One night at the end of a shift I told him I would like to have sex with him. He said, perfectly nicely, he didn't want to have sex with me and that was that. Sorted.

Or it would have been if the other barman hadn't laughed, called me a 'tard in the joking way dickheads soften their offence-making, like it's an endearment or something, and said, "Way to get your smooth on."

After I'd finished asserting my right not to be called a retard, which might have involved a bit of shouting, I poured a pint of bitter over his head.

So, with all knob-hattery aside, it was fairly painless. But then, he hadn't complicated things by telling me the shape of my brain was one of my best features.

I didn't mind sexy feelings. It was the other, warmer and

fuzzier, stuff that I didn't know what to do with. Maybe Rewa's suggestion that I needed distraction held merit, even if her list of possibilities offered nothing I wanted to sustain in the long term.

Apart from the vibrator.

"ROLLER DERBY." Rā leant over her cup midway through the following day's smoko. "Violence and theatrics all rolled into one beautiful game. Pun intended."

I sat on the other side of the table in the staff room and stared at her blankly.

"Ever seen that movie *Whip It* with Drew Barrymore and the girl from *Juno*?"

"No."

"Well, can you roller skate?"

"Not since I was twelve." I thought of the Little Mermaid skates I got for my seventh birthday. I skated in them every day after school on our concrete driveway until my feet got too big for them.

Rā sat back. "Riding a bike. You'll love it. As long as you're not scared of a few bruises. There's a league in Invercargill. I'll find the details for you."

I woke my phone and asked Siri to find me images of Roller Derby. "They wear *mouthguards*?"

"Sure. I thought you were after a bit of argy bargy?"

I couldn't recall ever using the words "argy" and "bargy" when relaying my need for a high-focus sport.

"You have a persona, like Hermione Danger or Dora the Destroyer and you spend an awful lot of time trying to psych the other team out. You're a little on the petite side, so you'll have to be quick and look particularly mean. We can get Forest to make one of those Mexican death mask things. Have you look like a skull."

Harit, who'd sat quietly through our exchange, pressed play on a roller derby Youtube video that came up at the top of the search results on my phone. After a minute he said, "Looks kind of like Kabaddi on wheels."

"What's Kabaddi?" Rā and I said in unison.

"Our national sport. It's contact like this one, but not as vicious. You have to tag the opposite team and try not to get tagged or tackled back." He looked at me. "I like this sport." He pointed at the phone. "You should play."

I watched more of the shoving, the falling, the growling. I shook my head. "I'm not aggressive enough. I wouldn't have a shit show."

"Maybe you just have to be fast," said Harit. "Can you be fast?"

"I don't know. I've never speed skated before. Is there something else, where I don't have to be super competitive and drive three hours return to do?"

Rā pursed her lips. "You want adrenaline, right? High risk, high fun?"

"Medium risk. High concentration level."

"There is a sport I've had nothing to do with." She reached for my phone and typed something into the search engine. "But it could meet your needs. Doesn't require much skill, just some imagination and a bit of guts."

She turned the phone around for Harit and me to see and thumbed through a series of images. A woman abseiled down a cliff, an ironing board balanced over her knees. She ironed a shirt and smiled at the camera. In the next picture a scuba diver ironed a garment on an ironing board nestled on the ocean floor. The next one showed a man ironing mid trampoline jump.

"Extreme ironing," Rā thumbed open a picture of a man ironing in the snow wearing nothing except a thong and a scarf.

Harit's laugh blasted in my ear.

It didn't seem *too* dangerous. It just required an element of the ridiculous. Which I was sure I had in me...somewhere. "I think I can do this."

"Yeah, you can," said Rā.

"I'll help you," said Harit. "You can iron on the forklift. I'll raise the forks, so you can do it up high."

Rā leaned over the table again. "Yeeeees. You can put it on TikTok. It'd be an awesome way to give your T-shirts exposure."

It'd have to be better than my Geek Girl Roar approach to selling T-shirts on TikTok. The only way from their stupendous lack of attention-getting was up. "Alright. Let's do it."

"Bring a T-shirt tomorrow and we'll have a go in our tea break."

———

I STRADDLED THE FORKS, an ironing board in front of me, iron in hand, while Rā held her phone out in front of her and counted down from three.

On "one" the forks began to rise. Harit controlled them with such skill that there was no jerk with which to unbalance me or unseat the ironing board.

A metre off the ground, I was reminded to a) iron the God-damn shirt, b) look less like I'd just been cranked open for a cervical smear c) look at the camera, for the love of Christ.

When the forks reach their apex, I waved at Rā and told

myself a three metre fall was perfectly survivable. I could still stack shelves with metal rods in my ankles.

"Bringing you back down now," shouted Harit and the forks smoothly changed direction.

"Keep ironing," shouted Rā. "You're still on camera."

I smiled and ironed and when the forks were half a metre from the ground, I leapt down, the iron in my fist, and threw my hands in the air. "YES! I am an extreme ironing QUEEN." My "queen" reverberated between the metal wall of the mart and the back of the adjacent building.

Rā clamped a hand over my mouth. "You want the captain to hear us and turn this stunt into a daily drill? It'll kill the buzz."

I shook my head and she withdrew her hand.

"Good. Please put the iron down before you brain one of us."

I put the iron down.

"Well?" She handed me my phone. "Did it help?"

It sure as shit did. I hadn't thought of Liam and his lips the entire time. Not even for a split second. Apart from now.

When Harit joined us to watch the footage, he placed a hand on my shoulder. "You, my friend, are going to be a TikTok sensation."

I WASN'T A TIKTOK SENSATION.

In the first twenty-four hours, my video got over 8000 watches, which was more like a TikTok flash in the pan. However, it was light years beyond the number my TikTok videos usually got, so I'd take it.

THE FOLLOWING MORNING, Helena came bouncing into the store in the first tumble weed hour. "Did you hear? There are parents protesting outside the school about the chlorine in the swimming pool."

Rā folded her arms. "Because of that rumour it messes with your hormones or whatever?"

"Yes." Helena clapped her hands and beamed as if she'd just delivered the news that Prince William and Kate Middleton had safely delivered their sixth child.

"What," said Forest, "are you guys on about?"

"Have you been in a 'truth according to social media' vacuum?" asked Rā. "It's all over Facebook."

Forest adopted his customary inside-out disdain face. "Then, yes I have. Nobody under the age of thirty uses Facebook any more."

"It's true," I said. "I had to take Helena's word for it."

Joe pushed open the *Staff only* door and walked towards us, take away coffee in hand.

"Haven't you noticed the sky-rocketing sales of bottled water?" said Rā. "These muppets will happily believe the minute amounts of a sterilising chemical in their drinking water will change their sex, but who gives a shit about the dolphins?"

"Again," said Forest, mid-arm fold, "what are you on about?"

"All the single use plastic they're discarding at record rates to pollute the oceans?"

"What I want to know is," said Helena, "what do they do when they want a shower?"

Rā snorted. "Yeah, I bet the fear of transhood is conveniently forgotten when their pits turn rancid."

Joe leaned against her checkout. "You know, I shouldn't be surprised at the lengths transphobia will cause people to go to, but I always am – this Unfettered Brain person or persons, exploiting it to whip up fear, especially by focusing on children, and how readily people accept lies disguised as fact because it appeals to their prejudices or their wilful ignorance. Transpeople are an easy target. Always have been. It makes me very very angry, which is bad for my soul and my frown lines." He tipped his head back and drained his coffee.

Joe didn't have any frown lines. His face was the kind of smooth Bekka McManus paid thousands of dollars to replicate.

Helena said, "It's two days until the nominations deadline and they've still only got the one candidate apparently."

My groan escaped high in what may, to discerning ears, have sounded like a whimper.

Joe put an arm around my shoulder. "Oh, my sweetness." He kissed the top of my head before I could duck away. "Has McManus approached you again about working for him?"

"No. He won't need a campaign team if no one's standing against him."

Liam poked his head around the end of aisle one. "The guy you can't stand asked you to work for him?"

It sounded as preposterous as it felt. "He said he liked my pep and he needs a graphic designer to make his promotional shit look pretty."

"But you wouldn't, would you?" said Rā. "You wailed like a mother who's just watched their baby's brains dashed against a wall when you heard he was standing for mayor."

"No, I would not. Not that the offer's still on the table.

Looks like he's sitting pretty and I'll, yet again, be governed by a prize dickhead. As we all will."

"Speaking of which, have you seen what else The Unfettered Brain has just 'exposed'?" Rā raised her fingers in the air in quote marks. "There are cameras in all the streetlights watching our every movement."

"Typical," said Forest, though it wasn't clear whether the presence of the cameras was typical behaviour by the higher powers, or the revelation was typical of a conspiracy monger like The Unfettered Brain.

"Apparently, it's a complicated web of conceit designed to bolster bureaucratic oppression. It's no longer about relying on copious amounts of red tape and seemingly arbitrary by-laws to keep us little people too busy to question their agenda. Central government is aiming for total state control and the easiest way to get there is by subduing the regions one by one."

Forest uncrossed his arms and "Ffff"ed his dubiousness. "As if."

"Well, if you think about it," said Helena. "Who puts the chlorine in the drinking water?"

"Um. The local council?"

"That's right. The local council."

"And that proves what?" asked Rā.

"Well, why do they *need* to put chlorine in the drinking water if it comes from one of the most pristine lakes in the country?"

Joe crossed the floor to Helena and took her hands in his. "Because, my pet, they have arses to cover. A whole network of council constructed and maintained pipes to carry that pristine water. Who do you think would get the blame if the water that came out of your tap was contaminated?"

She frowned. "That's a convenient argument if ever I heard one."

"It's a *logical* argument. Only conspiracy theorists argue convenience, mostly because it's very convenient to argue convenience. You don't have to actually prove anything."

"You think anyone will take notice?" I asked. "About the lights?"

"We had a run on baseball caps and sunglasses this morning," said Rā. "And the bottled water's sold out again."

We descended into momentary silence, which was likely a collective rumination on the numbskullery of the masses. At least, that was what *I* was thinking about.

I pushed my trolley of to-be-shelved goods away from me, then back again. "Do you think this Unfettered Brain really believes what he's saying, or do you think he's sitting back enjoying the unrest he's creating?"

"Could be a she," said Helena.

"Could be a whole army of provocateurs for all we know," said Rā. "Whatever's going on, it's good for business."

Helena gasped. "Do you think it's the captain?"

Rā *thunk*ed her bottle of disinfectant spray on her conveyor belt and Forest slapped both hands across his mouth.

Pointing towards the *Staff only* door, Joe said, "Go out the back and wash your filthy mouth out with soap, young lady."

Helena clasped her hands to her bosom. "Well, I know it's unlikely, but I'm just saying...he stands to benefit," she finished weakly.

"Come here, my cuddlesome." Joe wrapped his arms around her. "I know you didn't mean it. Look, at the very least, it's excellent entertainment. Let us sit back and enjoy the effect of the Unfettered Brain's baiting."

Was baiting really what it was? It was just as possible as someone *actually* believing the stuff they posted.

But then.

That begged the question:

For what purpose?

———

WHEN I ARRIVED home from work there was a van wrapped in the turquoise hues of bubbling spa water in front of the McManus house. A young, attractive white couple beamed at each other through the steam, glasses of sparkling wine clutched in their fists. The woman's face traversed the gap between the two rear windows so that her nose had the double-jointed appearance of a boxer's break.

McManus' brief hiatus from local politics was clearly having little impact on his bottom line. I had no doubt his business portfolio was as wide as the fathomless depths of his cash reserves.

Sucks for him.

I'd never been in a hot tub. I didn't know anyone who had one, and I'd never stayed in the kind of accommodation that might offer such luxuries. The closest I'd managed to get was farting in the bath.

I dumped my shopping bag of Cut-price branded white bread, because anything resembling a brown hue was a dollar more, and cage-free eggs, because it soothed my ethical compass when I couldn't afford the free range ones, and trudged across the lawn to relieve myself, because I forgot, once again, there was a flushing toilet at work I could use at the end of my shift.

However, it wasn't without its benefits.

Since the phone dropping incident, and my subsequent

hesitancy to bring said contraption in with me for toileting entertainment, I calculated I'd saved myself approximately twenty-five minutes a day of mindless scrolling, thereby giving me six extra days a year to live life to the fullest, instead of throwing it away in the meaningless social media vortex.

I hoped I would use my six days wisely, but I had a suspicion I'd find something else equally inane to occupy myself with elsewhere.

When I emerged, I was greeted by laughter and the popping of a champagne cork from next door. Mr and Mrs McManus were about to test the trials of spa soaking.

I didn't need to witness their hardship. I crossed the lawn back to the crib to put my groceries away and think about how best to reinvest the record $18.99 – cue the fireworks – I'd made the previous day from T-shirt sales, courtesy of my Extreme Ironing TikTok video.

Half an hour into the mind-numbing process of scheduling ads, my ad copy draft looked like this:

Sherowear. For when "Hey, that's a bit sexist" isn't loud enough.

...

No need for comment.

Tired of giving the one finger salute?

Too aggressive, if entirely accurate.

Sherowear. For the discerning riot grrl

Too sexy.

girl within.

Better. That one I could work with.

All I had to do now was set the ads to run, which required deciphering and deciding on a sequence of actions in the Instagram back end, but my brain was already floppy from all the writing and crossing out.

I took out my sketch pad and drew the bathroom I'd install once I was making $18.99 a minute. It had a one-way floor to ceiling window framing the view of the lake, and a skylight to watch the stars through while reclining in the bath with Liam.

No!

It had a skylight to watch the stars through while reclining in the bath.

With Liam.

Argh.

Get. Out. Of. My. Head.

Soap bubbles slid down Liam's muscular chest, the dip between his pectorals speeding up their descent. He grabbed my hand and traced their path with my fingers towards his belly button and the fine line of hair that disappeared beneath the milky water.

Stop!

"I don't want to stop, Jewel," breathed Liam as our hands sank beneath the surface.

I stood up so quickly my chair fell over.

A walk. I needed a walk to clear my head.

Pushing open the back door, I hurried down the lawn and stopped at the top of the bank. I sat and dangled my legs over it, breathing in the alpine cool as the clouds broiled at the tips of the mountains.

All was quiet next door, except for the hum of jets. Either they'd already departed from the spa, or they'd run out of things to say to each other, which was probably not unusual after a hundred years of marriage.

A fat drop of rain made a cold landing in the part of my hair. I tensed in preparation to push myself up so I could retrieve my raincoat, and the jets turned off. Water swished. And a feminine gasp preceded a masculine growl.

Dear Lord, what hell was this that the McManus', of all people, got to live out the fantasy I'd just attempted to exorcise from my brain?

When Bekka said, "No, just there," and punctuated her instruction with a purred, "Bri," I scrabbled to my feet so I could run to the crib and pour bleach into my ears.

I'd managed two steps, when McManus said, "Talk dirty to me, B. Tell me what you want me to do with my big. Bad. Council. Stick."

I stopped in my tracks. I didn't want to, but my feet were operating independently of my thoughts, which were channelling all energy into an interior monologue of "La-la-la-la-la-la-la-la-la".

"I want you to force the sale of my un-utilised land."

McManus let out a shaky groan and I fought a rising tide of pre-vomit saliva.

And stepped closer to the fence.

"I have a very small allotment. Can you find my very small allotment? Make an assessment with your developer *hard hat?*"

"Yes," McManus said breathily. "God, yes, I can."

Gack.

Was what I thought was going on, actually going on and McManus was getting all pant-y over *council stuff?* Who in their right mind would find council stuff sexy?

Unless.

If the idea of taking control over unused land was so exciting it was a turn on in the McManus bedroom, it had to mean it was part of his mayoral game plan.

So this was what the world had come to. The opportunity the universe gave me to uncover McManus' political intentions was while he had sex with his wife in their new spa pool.

Typical.

"Then you're going to bring in your huge digger and plough my open spaces."

I had plenty of un-utilised land. Well, my family did. The ratio of house to property was at least 1:6. Surely he wouldn't try and make it easier for developers to buy up land, or force the sale of land that wasn't currently being used to its maximum potential? That had to be unconstitutional or inhumane. Or something.

I got very hot. Then very cold. There was less than a day and a half before the mayoral nominations closed, which meant no time to find out what the limitations of local government might actually be.

I threw petrol-consumption caution to the wind, jumped in my car and raced back to the mart.

I had to take three forwards/backwards steps to get the motion sensor above the door to register my presence, and after a shouted, "Come the fuck on!", and some jostling as I attempted to force the doors to open quicker by squeezing my body through, I stood inside and panted.

Liam looked at me wide-eyed, potatoes in hand.

"We have an electoral emergency," I announced to the customerless store and scampered over to the checkouts.

Rā raised her phone to her ear. "Harit? Checkouts. Now."

Once the team had assembled and garnered various expressions of anticipation and alarm, I said, "I have it on good authority that Brian McManus is going to do whatever they do in council to pass by-laws or change policies or whatever to make it easier for developers to develop stuff for rich people." God I wished I was better at words. "I think he wants to force landowners who don't use their properties to sell."

The surrounding faces rearranged themselves into a combination of frowns, pursed lips, and squinted eyes.

"That sounds as ludicrous as the streetlight rumour," said Joe. "I thought you weren't on Facebook?"

"I'm not —"

"On whose 'good authority' did you get this?" asked Rā.

"Mine. I listened in while he was having sex with his wife in their new spa pool."

Liam's head did a little jerky thing.

"Ew," said Forest.

"I know."

"*Jewel Bauer*," said Joe. "I didn't know there was a raging voyeur in you. It's never the shouty ones."

"I didn't know they were having sex until I'd started listening. I'm not a perve! And if I was it wouldn't be Brian McManus I'd want to hear." God. Gag. "They were doing dirty talk. She was commanding him to do stuff to her with his big council stick, like plough her vacant lot, and he was all, like, *yeah* I'm going to plough your vacant lot."

Forest wrinkled his nose.

Rā said, "There's nothing to read into that. It's just weird dirty talk."

"But that's the thing. Sex talk's all about power and submission. Nobody in their right mind would choose council-related stuff as their love language unless they had *actual* ambitions to wield that power in the real world. She asked him to force her to sell her un-utilised land, which got him all groany, even though there's, like, zero innuendo."

"Tenuous," said Joe.

"Actually, she might have a point," said Rā. "All power-hungry people have ambitions that get things boiling in their pants."

"I see Jewel's logic, too," said Harit.

"Yeah," said Liam. "I think it's worth taking seriously."

"You would, my pet," said Joe.

"Think about it," I continued. "There's quite a few unused sections in town, all ripe for development, but for whatever reason the owners have been sitting on them for years. Imagine the kind of money developers could make if all those people were forced to make way for them. People are hungry to live here. Moneyed people. This town would become a high-spec housing utopia for rich, white people."

Joe clucked his tongue. "The twenty-first century version of white imperialism. Forcing land off the natives."

"But they can't do that," said Liam.

"Not under the *current* by-laws, no," I answered.

Nobody said anything.

Rā slumped against the edge of her checkout. "It's already hard to find an affordable rental. It won't be long before people like me are forced out of town."

"So, what do we do?" asked Forest. "Go to the press on the dubious evidence of sexy spa talk?"

With a squeak, Liam rubbed a shoe on the vinyl floor. "We find an opposing candidate."

"With forty-eight hours to spare?" said Rā. "Where are we going to find one and convince them they should stand? There's no way."

"It'd have to be one of us," said Harit.

Rā pointed a finger at Joe. "You're the most confident and can string an intelligent-sounding sentence together. You could do it."

Joe took a step backward. "I *could*. But we should probably choose someone who's already in good standing with the community, has the trust of the people. They don't know me from Brenda and if McManus is going to make it easier for developers, we need to hit the ground running."

"Where are we going to find someone like that at short notice?" asked Forest.

The *Staff only* door swung open.

The captain stood backlit from the bright hall-light behind him. "Joe, there's a large anomaly in the monthly reconciliation for the hardware department. I need to trian-gulate the point – of – origin." He jabbed a finger on the surface of the door in a vague triangle with each word. "Or as we say in the army, 'let's go poo hunting'."

CHAPTER SIXTEEN

"MAYOR?" The captain leant back in his chair, fingers steepled.

"Yes," said Joe. "You'll be amazing at it, sir. You'd be General of the Fiordland District, coordinating manoeuvres that ensured communities in need get the infrastructure, the support they need. While you're at the mart, you can only ever command the territorial army at best. Once you're in office, you'll have a bird's eye view of all the ground troops. You'll be able to change stuff so you can get things like that co-housing project you've talked about happening."

The captain gazed out the window. "I've never been a general before."

"No."

"Not even close. I once led a recon straight into the enemy's fire sack. Got the coordinates wrong. We were out of there faster than galloping dandruff from the chancre mechanic."

"Captain," I said. "When you don't talk English, it's very hard to understand you."

"Mm?" He refocused from reliving the recon to me. "Ah,

yes. Old army saying that one. From one of the world wars, I think. Means crabs running from the VD medic, not that we ever had a VD medic. Or crabs as far as I know." He looked back at Joe. "What do I have to do?"

"Well, think about what your values are, the future you envision for the district, what you'd change if given the chance. Then we'll get Helena to write up the nomination and your blurb about what you're standing for. Jewel can design any promotional material we might need."

I pointed at my chest. "Graphic designer."

"And you?" continued Joe. "Basically, you need to get out there and tell people about your love for this community and how you could make it better if they make you mayor. The whole mart team has your back."

"Will I still get to be captain of the mart team?"

"I believe the civic duties required of you as mayor are not a full working week, so yes, but you'd probably have to reduce your hours here."

The captain smiled at Joe. "About time you stepped up, my lad. You can fill any slack." His eyes fell to me. "Fiordland. It's hardly a political hot zone, but a soldier needs to be prepared for anything. So, who am I tangoing through the mind field with?"

Jesus on a stick. Why could the man not talk in riddles? "Who are you...up against?"

The captain nodded.

"There's only one other candidate. This man." I typed Brian McManus into my phone's Internet browser. No results. "That's odd."

"What is it?" asked Joe.

"It doesn't come up with anything for Brian McManus. How can anybody not exist on the Internet?" I turned my phone around to show Joe.

"Ah. I see the problem. You typed 'brain mcmanus', my love, not 'brian'. Easy mistake to make."

Right. Of course I bloody did.

I withdrew my phone and verbally instructed it to find a picture of Brian McManus. I selected one and turned my phone around. "He's just lost the Invercargill mayoralty. He's a successful businessman with a broad portfolio. He's also a narrow-minded elitist. The only progressive thing he's interested in is increasing his bottom line and those in his rich boys' club."

"He's the last thing this community needs," said Joe. "We have concerns he'll simply quicken the pace of gentrification, dispossess those who have lived here for generations but don't have the good fortune of wealth to protect them."

"A worthy opponent then." The captain looked at Joe. "We've been preparing for this for years. Our drills and simulations have honed our abilities to strategise our play. This is just the next level in the game." He leaned forward in his chair, palms flat on the table. "Where do I sign?"

WHILE JOE GAVE the news to the front of house staff about the captain agreeing to run, I decided to make my exit via the loading bay. I didn't want to get pulled into any debate that might make me doubt my certainty over needing an opposing mayoral candidate, and the captain being the one to fill the brief.

Mostly because I already doubted both those things.

As I stepped into the stock room, I was met with the resonant tones of Amy Winehouse singing 'Rehab'. Three paces towards the loading bay a Liam I could not yet see asked, "I thought about doing this –" pause. "– On 'nothing'. What do you think?"

"Make the duck lower," answered Harit. "You have to widen your legs to get it looking really strong."

I rounded a corner to find Harit sitting on a stack of wooden pallets watching Liam...

Dance?

The song continued to play. And Liam pulled a complex series of moves. His body was fluid, his limbs, his spine, his hips shifting and flexing on the music's cue.

He'd pulled his hair into a bun, the lack of a frame of hair accentuating the angles of a face deep in concentration.

I was shocked into stillness. My left leg refused to lead the right towards the sunshine beyond the stock room.

And I realised two things. **One:** For all Liam's suggestions we shared a burden of being misunderstood, of feeling like social pariahs, that we 'got' where the other came from, I didn't know this man at all. My brain struggled to reconcile the mute, people-shy man I'd met over three weeks ago with *this* being, who moved as if there was no weight on his shoulders, who was so self-possessed that the command he had of his body was mesmerising.

Two: An event of nuclear proportions was taking place in my underpants, which was rapidly diminishing any concern I might have about **Thing One**. Dear Lord of All The Universe's Mysteries, what was it about men who could dance? Biologically, it made little sense. The man who slayed the lion and dragged a wildebeest back to the cave should be far more likely to make women drop their panties on the spot than the court jester. And yet, it was a phenomenon that couldn't be refuted. If a clitoris had an Achilles heel, it was a man with a sense of rhythm.

Liam made two more moves, stopped and shook his head, and shuffled backwards to begin the sequence again.

Then he noticed me.

He went very still and very pale.

I went very hot, despite there being no extraneous blood left in my body to pool in my face. It was too busy keeping my lady parts on the simmering side of boiling over.

Neither of us moved and I realised the only way out of this stand off was to throw dignity to the wind and leg it.

I ran past him towards the car park and out on to the footpath.

It wasn't until I heard the crunch of glass underfoot from a smashed streetlight that I remembered I'd driven down to the mart to deliver the McManus master plan bombshell.

Needless to say, I organised another emergency TikTok shoot.

As soon as the team knocked off for the day, I demanded their assistance in orchestrating a level of Extreme Ironing that raised the danger bar set by the previous one.

Riding pillion backwards on Harit's scooter, I ironed while he weaved between two cars driven by Joe and Forest. Rā brought up the rear, her camera mounted on her dash and I waved and smiled and hoped Harit didn't take it upon himself to show off and pull a wheelie, or attempt his levitation trick.

I got over 3000 views in the first hour. The obsessive watching of that number tick up every minute *almost* provided reprieve from the memory of Liam sashaying around the loading bay forecourt, but when my email inbox pinged with the eleventh notification of a purchase from my sherowear.com website, I forgot about him completely.

I WOKE with a gasp to a room made milky by the waning moon. Taking a large breath to slow the drumming of my pulse, I tried to shake the nightmare from my brain.

I pulled my T-shirt away from my chest, the fabric damp with sweat.

I'd been here before, dreaming I was standing on the stage at school assembly and having to read *Macbeth* aloud. It always seemed to coincide with things in real life that worried me. Like fathers in hospital wards, and running out on your flatmates because you've lost your job and have no money.

It could have been worse. I could have been *naked* and standing on the stage at school assembly and having to read *Macbeth* aloud.

It didn't take too much probing to work out why I'd had an anxiety dream. I was fairly certain my subconscious was doubting my course of action over the mayoral situation because I'd been asking myself the same question ever since the captain agreed to stand:

What have you done, Jewel?

I could, I s'pose, spread the load of responsibility to the wider team, but no. This one was on me. *I* was the one who voiced misgivings about McManus and his political aspirations, his values of profit over people. *I'd* overheard the very private conversation in his back yard and chosen to interpret it as his political strategy.

What was my solution? To throw a generous man with a military obsession people may choose to misunderstand into the lion's den. There was a good chance he'd be eaten alive, despite all his bluster about being battle hard and having a head for strategy.

It wasn't too late to scrap the nomination. The deadline closed in two days. I might be running the risk of unleashing McManus onto the Fiordland populace, but surely that was a better option than bringing about the undeserved humiliation of the captain at the hands of a political veteran like McManus, all for the sake of a suspicion he had nefarious intentions. A suspicion wasn't good enough.

Was it?

...

No.

With a sigh, I rolled over and eyed the moon beating its way onto my face courtesy of the curtains I neglected to close. In the morning, I would call a meeting with Joe and the captain and tell them the right thing to do was not submit the nomination.

There would be objections. The captain appeared buoyed by the thought of being in a position to create greater change than he was currently able to. He was excited by the battle ahead. Joe had the gleam in his eye of someone who might influence change without having to be the public face of it. Or perhaps he was simply roused by the prospect of a promotion while the captain pursued mayoral responsibilities.

And yet, the thought of McManus having an opportunity to shape this community to his political will was disquieting. No. Abhorrent.

I really really didn't want to let it lie. But I think, maybe, I had to.

I turned my mind to the absence of an online presence for McManus my misspelling had wrought. For a split second I had thought the man had created the biggest conspiracy to hit the town yet – a complete Internet vacuum. All for the interchangeability of two letters.

Brian.

Brain.

Brian.

Brain.

Brianbrainbrianbrainbrianbrain.

I sat bolt upright.

I knew exactly who was seeding the paranoia now coursing its way through the town.

The Unfettered *Brian*.

CHAPTER SEVENTEEN

I...DID not call a meeting in the morning.

What I did do was a lot of mind sweating about how I could prove McManus was behind the rumour mongering.

No doubt it was all part of a master plan to create a high level of distrust in the local council, and then he would waltz in, with his decade of knowing how that particular machine worked, and announce himself as saviour.

When Helena stopped by to 'purchase the items she needed for dinner' and spent her entire visit stationed at the checkouts chatting with Rā and Forest, I asked her to show me The Unfettered Brain on her Facebook app. The profile picture showed a brain bursting from a set of chains with a sun rising behind it. Hardly subtle or original.

"What's it say in the About bit?"

"Nothing that would reveal who they are. *The Unfettered Brain seeks to reveal truth and free minds from the tyranny of oppression.* That's all it says."

But it wasn't all that was meant. *The Unfettered Brian seeks to enslave minds to his political will through the tyranny of fear mongering.* Douche.

"Is there any way of knowing who set up this account? Is it linked to other accounts?"

Helena shook her head.

"What about Friends? Who are his Friends?"

She clicked back to the main page of the profile. "He just has followers and good luck finding any info there. There's over two thousand of them." She let out a little laugh like she'd delivered good news.

It wasn't an unreasonable number. I had close to that many followers on Instagram. "Is that a pretty average number?"

"For an area like Fiordland with a small population? I'd guess it'd be well above average."

The number wasn't necessarily the problem. It was the ever-increasing concentric circles rippling out from each of his posts. "How many of those two thousand are then reposting his bullshit?"

"Probably more than you'd want to think. Do you know, I drove down the main street of town last night and every single streetlight has been broken? It was like driving into the bowels of hell. I had to turn my lights to full beam."

I wanted to say it was worse than I thought, but Brian McManus had the ability to engineer the exact degree of disquiet he needed to position himself as the leader the people needed. "How do we find out who he is?"

Helena shrugged. "Probably some kind of computer wizard? Someone who can trace the IP address or something like that?"

I'd heard the term "IP address", but I wasn't entirely sure what it was. When I asked Helena, she said she didn't know, but she'd read it in detective novels, so it was "probably a thing". Nor did she know any computer wizards. "Try a young person. They know all the stuff about technology."

"I'm a young person."

"A boy. Boys have more interest in this stuff than girls."

She was probably right. "Hey Forest, do you know how to trace an IP address?"

"No." He picked at a nail. "Couldn't care less about computer-how."

Liam stepped out from the end of aisle one and Helena shouted, "Liam will know!" as my brain, which was doing so very well up until that point, had a meltdown and produced, "Dance!" at the same time.

Liam, understandably, looked startled and darted his eyes between us.

Helena turned to me. "You want him to dance?"

God yes. "No, I do not. I never want to see him dance ever again."

Two sets of gasps emitted in stereo behind me.

Liam's face took on a ruddy hue. "I didn't think I was that bad." He tried to smile, but it wavered at the edges and he looked past me towards Forest, before flicking back to me again, and then the floor.

"It has nothing to do with your ability. I just found it...unsettling."

His eyes snapped back to mine. An expression shifted across his face. I couldn't be sure what it was. Disappointment? Offence?

It didn't matter. I couldn't do anything about it. I wasn't about to tell him the reason I found it unsettling. *When I saw you dancing I nearly orgasmed on the spot?*

"I thought –" his eyes moved from mine to the three people watching this painful exchange. Then he turned around and began walking back towards the fresh produce aisle. "It doesn't matter what I thought."

"I'll finish that sentence for him," said Rā, crossing her arms. "He thought you were different, Jewel."

"What does that mean?" I *knew* I was different from most women, and I knew he knew that, but there was a subtext here I wasn't privy to. On reflection, I probably shouldn't have said "unsettling". It kind of suggested I was disturbed by it, which I was, but in a sort of good way? But I couldn't let him think there was anything bad about his dancing. That would be arsehole-y and unfair, especially for someone battling confidence issues. "Liam, I thought you were really good. You're a very very very good dancer," I said, like an adverb-depleted simpleton. Walking towards the start of the fresh produce aisle, I paused in front of the bin of kiwifruit.

Liam unloaded pottles of dips into the open-fronted fridge.

"I could never dance like that."

The entrance doors wheezed open behind me.

"I was blessed with a sense of rhythm of a seismograph and five left feet." It wasn't true, but I'd observed lying was a good way of making people feel better. As long as you didn't do it all the time. Or got found out.

"Get out of my way," a voice cracked by age and vice barked.

I turned to find Mr Hardacre glaring up at me from underneath his tangle of eyebrows. He jabbed at a button and a thin electronic note pierced the mart air. "Why are you standing there blocking the entrance like a – skinny – lump – of – uselessness?" He accentuated the last four words with jabs to the mobility chair's horn.

I stepped aside and looked to where Liam had been by the refrigerator units, but he was gone.

Mr Hardacre rolled towards Forest's checkout. "You. I

want my computer magazine. It should have come in yesterday."

As Rā located the magazine underneath *her* checkout, walked over to Forest's and slapped it on the conveyor belt in front of Mr Hardacre, my first encounter with the miserable antiquarian smacked me in the think box, as the captain would say. Joe had threatened to stop sourcing *Hackers' Monthly* for him if he wasn't more polite to the customers.

Once the mobility scooter rolled out the automatic doors, I sprinted over to Forest's checkout. "Give me your doobie."

"My what?"

I whipped around. "Rā, write on a piece of paper, *The Unfettered Brain, Facebook. Who is he?*"

I turned back and leant over the conveyor belt towards Forest. "I know you smoke it. I smelled it on you at the pub. Can I have a spliff now and pay you back later? Please?"

Forest's face crumpled in on itself. "*Spliff?* Wait there while I reset the DeLorean from 1952." Despite the sneer, he pulled a tin out of his back pocket and opened it. Raising an eyebrow, he said, "You *sure* you want a piece of this?"

"Yes," I hissed and glanced out the large shop front windows. "Quick!"

He slapped a long, skinny joint in my palm. "Race horse. It'll burn fast, but the hit is quick."

"Excellent." I snatched the piece of receipt roll Rā held out for me and ran for the automatic doors, sliding through sideways as they edged their way open at my approach, and pounded up the pavement towards Mr Hardacre's receding back.

"Mr Hardacre. Mr Hardacre!"

He halted and did an about turn.

When I reached him, I placed my hand on my knees and gulped at the air.

"What do you want? Did I forget something?"

I put my hand up to signal him to wait, sucked in a breath and righted myself. "My dad's in a wheelchair too. He's a paraplegic. He gets a lot of phantom pain in his legs, but he finds a bit of this helps." I held out my hand and opened my fingers. "It's a...medicinal cigarette."

Mr Hardacre eyed the joint in my hand. "It's a reefer."

I shrugged. "Same thing. It'll go nicely with that bottle of red you bought the other day."

He glared up at me, his eyes narrowed. Then he "Hmph"ed and reached out to slide the joint from my hand. His papery skin was cool against my palm.

"You know computers?"

Mr Hardacre's head jerked back up towards my face, setting his chicken wattle quivering. "I was one of the first computer engineers in the country. I helped install the IBM 650 in Treasury in 1961."

"Treasury? As in the government?"

"Yes, *Treasury as in the government*." He sniffed. "Kept my hand in ever since."

"So you know coding and stuff?"

"I know all the stuff, girl. Why are you asking?"

I handed him the note and pointed at the joint. "Let me know how you get on with that. You know where to find me."

Mr Hardacre opened the piece of paper and read it. Then he scowled at me before turning his scooter around and speeding off up the street.

DURING MY BREAK, I hit Harit up about doing another Extreme Ironing stunt.

I told him it was to continue the sales momentum the videos had given my T-shirts, which was true, but also a big fat lie by omission because it made me feel better about having upset Liam.

Well, maybe not *better*. But it meant if I didn't acknowledge it, it didn't exist.

Right?

I told him it needed to be bigger than the last. More entertaining, more dangerous.

Harit nodded and said he had something he'd been working on. How did I feel about transitioning towards comedy *and* dare-devilry?

"I'll take anything as long as it's soon. Like in the next few hours."

Harit gave me two thumbs up. "Bring a change of clothes."

AFTER WORK, I met him and Rā down at the pier in my bridal Empowered Collection T-shirt. There were a few tourists scattered along its edge eating fish and chips and watching the water shift beneath their dangling feet.

Harit stood, dripping wet, in front of what looked like a surfboard mobile.

"What's this?"

"It's a go-kart, stripped down to the frame and engine, with two surfboards balanced on top."

It gleamed wetly. "I'm going to ride that thing into the water, aren't I?"

"Just the surfboards." He bent down and picked up a long towing cable. "This will stop the go-kart at the end of the pier, and your momentum will carry you and the surf-boards off the end and into the water, God willing."

"*God willing?*"

Harit walked around the contraption pointing out features that proved he hadn't, in fact, left my fate to a thing as fickle as God's will. "I've joined the surfboards together to provide a bit of stability for you and I've put polystyrene on the underside of the ironing board, and attached the electrical cord of the iron to the surf boards so we don't lose it. Everything should float."

"Will it drive straight?"

"Yes. I locked the steering and did a dummy run." He grinned. "It was fun."

OH GOD. I WAS GOING TO DIE, WASN'T I?

He laid a hand on my shoulder. "Really important thing. Jump clear when you're airborne. It's a bit of a drop down to the water and if you land on the surfboards, you're more likely to break than they are. And duck deep. In case they skim across the surface."

Yep. I hoped it would be painless. Quick was prefer-able, but I didn't think that was how drowning worked. "How fast does it go?"

"How fast do you want it to go?"

I considered the degree of madness in his smile. "Slow enough to be safe, fast enough to impress."

"Got it." Harit picked up what looked like a skate-boarding helmet and fastened it under my chin. "Once you start, I can't stop it, but if you need to abort, jump, crouch and roll."

I stared at him and he repeated "Jump, crouch and roll" as if I was deaf instead of frozen in alarmed incredulity. I shook it off and pulled up my big girl pants. "I won't need to abort. I'm going to execute the best fifteen seconds of extreme ironing Puhiruru has ever seen."

He slapped me on the upper arm. "Jewel Bauer. Totally fearless." Then he turned and shouted at Rā who was rummaging in the boot of her car. "Rānui. Time to mount her up."

THE SURFBOARDS SHUDDERED as the cart rumbled over the wooden boards of the pier.

I crouched in a 1960s surfer stance, one arm ironing, the other straightened in front of me, adrenaline pumping through me like an electric pulse. I hoped the smile I'd adhered to my face was less rictus grin and more self-assured excitement, but I couldn't be sure due to the concentration required to multi-task with maintaining the seal on my sphincter.

I turned to salute the video streamers and then I was airborne, pushing away from the surfboard underneath my feet, windmilling my arms and kicking my legs for dramatic effect.

I hit the water and sank, watching the surfboard raft above me skate across the water and the ironing board flip over from the load of its iron anchor. The iron hung suspended in the lake's blue as if weightless.

When I surfaced and cheers and whoops met me from the few onlookers, I knew I had a video that would leave the last record of 12,000 views in twenty-four hours in its lung-clogging dust.

Plus, for the three minutes of pre-ride anticipation, the twenty seconds of ride terror, and the five-minute post-ride come down, I'd forgotten how much I cared that I'd upset Liam. It was a decent reprieve if it also meant I got to bask in TikTok viral video glory and enjoy the ping of new mail notifications when the T-shirt orders started rolling in.

There was only one way to express how GOOD I felt:

Squeeeeeeeeeeeeeeeeeeee.

If only I could make it last indefinitely.

CHAPTER EIGHTEEN

THE FINAL DAY for mayoral nominations dawned crisp and clear, which in no way suited how I felt about having to make a decision to intervene before Helena submitted the forms that afternoon. I still had nothing truly tangible about McManus' political agenda, except for his track record as Mayor of Invercargill, which while highly objectionable, indicated a wholly predictable ambition to protect and project the interests of the money makers in town.

Why, why, why did I not explain the urgency of the situation to Mr Hardacre?

Without that evidence, there was no point in offering the captain up to McManus' wolf. I indulged in some teeth-gnashing and forehead smacking, and then, five minutes before my shift was due to end, a phlegmy throat cleared behind me as I stacked chicken-flavoured – *kack* – potato chips.

"Your man lives in the proximity of Lake Parade between Kea and Kākāpō Streets."

Brian McManus lived on Lake Parade between Kea and Kākāpō Streets.

"Man?"

Mr Hardacre grunted. "I say man because he is one. Thanks to his use of Google Internet searches, and Google helpfully scraping a whole lot of data about his search habits for the benefit of advertisers, I can tell you his approximate age, his probable ethnicity, his penchant for Hawke's Bay riesling, and that he prefers *Friends* highlights over funny cat videos on YouTube."

Nobody preferred *Friends* highlights over funny cat videos. Further proof Brian McManus was a sociopath.

"You hacked Google? That's like hacking Nasa, or the Kremlin, or something."

"Yep."

I let the awesomeness of his computing dare-devilry sink in for another second, before allowing disappointment to wash over it. "It's not enough, though. I need a name. Or something that's specific to him."

"I take it you have someone in mind already?"

"Yeah, Brian McManus. The guy running for mayor who called you 'handicapped' a couple of weeks back."

Mr Hardacre's veranda of eyebrows lifted a centimetre. "*That* cretin." Rasping a liver-spotted hand down his stubbly cheeks, he gazed over my right shoulder for the length of two blinks before refocusing on me. "How much do you know about him?"

"He's my next door neighbour."

The wing tips flew up again.

"And I worked under him for —"

"Did he recently get a spa?"

"Yes."

"It has to be him, then. He's been looking at luxury hot tub sites for the last couple of weeks."

I punched the air. "Yes! I bloody well knew it was him.

Only Brian McManus could have an agenda of making people want his leadership without realising it." I grabbed Mr Hardacre's hand, raised it into the air and slapped it in a high-five.

Mr Hardacre managed a look of outrage and a "Get off" before I continued my victory burble. "The Unfettered Brain unmasked. Not that we can publicly unmask him without risking exposing you."

"No one will be able to prove I've done anything."

Now we had a chance at preventing McManus from winning the mayoralty, which meant I didn't need to intercept the application. The captain would run and we'd just have to make sure he had all the support he needed so he could play the game. Whether that meant playing by the rules.

Or not.

"Mr Hardacre," I said, my voice low. "How would you like to take it to the man?"

He frowned up at me. "Take what to who?"

"Help in getting rid of the cretin for good?"

The frown deepened before lifting. "I've never snuffed anyone, but I'm only eighty-six. There's always time."

"No! I'm not asking you to *kill anyone*." I whispered the last two words as a man in gumboots *fallump*ed past. "Let's meet at the prunes and I'll tell you more."

I headed up aisle two and came to the prune section in aisle three from the back of the store, while Mr Hardacre wheeled his way slowly from the front, looking at the products on either side of him as if considering their shopping-list worth.

He squeaked to a stop beside me. "Ahhh, there they are. Miss, could you pass me a kilogram pack of the Sunbaked prunes?"

I hesitated, shocked to hear him behave so politely, when I remembered he was playing a role. "Certainly, sir." I took a bag off the shelf and placed it in the basket mounted at the front of his scooter. Then I leant towards him. "How do you feel about seeing if there's anything untoward the general public should know about a mayoral candidate, like tax fraud, or insider trading?"

"And why would I give you my help? I haven't given anything freely, except abuse, since 1984."

"Because he offends you, because you get to flex your IT muscles in a covert operation, and because we can keep you in a steady supply of medicinal cigarettes."

Mr Hardacre pointed his finger at me and opened his mouth.

The finger quivered.

Then he retracted it. "How many medicinal cigarettes?"

"Two a day."

"Three."

"Done."

"I might need to get direct access to his devices. His laptop, his phone."

"You can get what you need off a phone?"

"I could make his phone put on arseless chaps and line dance, lass. Just get it for me. Hone up your cat burgling skills." He reversed backwards a foot and did a three-point turn.

Cat burgling? I didn't particularly want to hone any skills that had the word "burgle" in it and therefore "arrest" and "prison".

There had to be another way.

IT TURNED out there was another way.

If I recalled correctly, McManus himself had given me a direct route to access his stuff. All I had to do was wait two days until news of a new mayoral nomination reached the McManus stronghold, then I walked to its front door and knocked.

He opened the door, a wide smile already stretched across his round face in case the caller was someone with district voting rights. It slipped ever so slightly when he saw it was me. "Jewel from the little house next door. What can I do for you?"

I decided to dispense with pleasantries, mostly because he didn't deserve any, and get straight to the point. "You can add me to your collection of fluffers."

McManus raised an eyebrow.

"I'll join your campaign team."

CHAPTER NINETEEN

I SPENT my Saturday night trying not to undress Liam with my eyes whilst rallying the troops in the field HQ.

Which was the pub, because Puhiruru wasn't a literal war zone and I didn't have a tent.

Everyone sat around a table in the corner, sipping their drinks while I doled out our roles in the captain's campaign team.

I meant "everyone" without any kind of descriptive accuracy. Harit had pizza-delivering commitments, and the captain was visiting his mother for the weekend and had a role anyway.

"Joe. Campaign manager."

Joe beamed. "I have no idea what one of those does, but I'm happy to make it up as I go along."

"Rā. Strategist. You're the game maker."

She fist pumped. "Hell yes, I'm the game maker."

I placed a hand on my chest. "I'll design anything promotional." Then nodded at Forest. "Stylist."

"Oh my God, yes. I've been dying to see the captain in a tailored suit."

"Harit will be the captain's driver."

Everyone nodded.

"Helena?"

She sat up straight, smile wide, brows raised.

"Speech writer."

She hugged herself. "Oooh, yes. Speech writer."

"Liam." I had nothing for Liam. Flash mob choreographer? Catering?

"Security," I said with all the conviction I didn't feel.

Forest laughed, Joe said, "Why would we need security?" and Liam looked at me like I'd betrayed him in some unforgivable way.

"You don't have to do any...securing stuff. You just have to look like you could."

"Because," he said, drawing out the word, "I have the body for it?"

"Well, yeah."

He shook his head and his hair danced and shimmied.

God, it was beautiful, beautiful hair.

"No."

"You can do it, Liam," said Rā. "Put on a suit and stand around not smiling at anyone. Easy."

"I'm not doing it, and I thought," he dropped his voice, his confident indignation receding, "Jewel understood me enough not to even entertain the idea."

The workings of my insides ground to a halt with a sound that was kind of, *a;kdlsjgi;oanv;lkadg;harghx!*

He was so right. I was a blundering, thoughtless idiot.

"It fell out of my brain in a panic, because I don't have a role for you."

Liam blinked. "There's no place for me on the campaign team?"

"No. That's not what I meant. I don't know your

strengths apart from hunting and dancing, and neither of those lend themselves well to a political campaign." Wow, I was awful at apologising. I felt sorry. I just had to string the words together. "I'm sorry for being a dick." It was a start, but I could do better. "What would you like to do?"

"I could...help you with the PR stuff? Write the copy?"

"Okay." I knew what gave him such glorious hair. It was all that virtue radiating out of him. No wonder mine had the colour and shine of the mummified rodent found during stove removal. What did I do? Suggest an entirely inappropriate role for him by being insensitive to his insecurities, and what does he do for me? Offer to help in the one area where he knows I'll struggle. He was a way better person than I was. "Thanks."

"Wouldn't it have been best to discuss this with the captain?" asked Helena. "He's the most important part of this operation. Shouldn't he have a say?"

"I deliberately held this meeting without him, because I have a couple of developments that are controversial, and I'm not sure the captain would be okay with," I dropped my voice, "playing dirty."

"Playing dirty?" Rā smiled and narrowed her eyes. "What have you done?"

I made a beckoning gesture and everyone leaned in.

"I've recruited Mr Hardacre as a clandestine computing professional."

Joe sat back. "You've got him to hack something, you bad girl."

"Shhhh." I looked around us, but everybody at the pub was too busy with their own conversation or sinking their beer to pay us any attention.

"Oh my goodness," Helena said, fanning her face with her hands. "The intrigue."

"What did you get him to hack?" asked Rā.

"Google."

"No!" Forest flung himself back on his chair and Helena gasped.

"Mr Hardacre, who's only five-star rating is on the quality of his abuse, hacked Google?" said Rā.

"I needed to confirm my suspicion that Brian McManus is behind The Unfettered Brain, so Mr Hardacre traced the IP address and looked for clues in his browsing history."

"I told you the IP address was a thing," said Helena.

"I can confirm it is Brian McManus."

"But...why?" asked Liam.

"Clever man," said Joe. "The best way to get people to vote in a particular direction is to seed doubt. Do it strategically and they'll be hungry for stability and security. Then the candidate swoops in and vows to provide it."

"The sly asshole," said Forest with something that might have been wonder or admiration.

"Surely, that's unlawful, or something," said Helena.

Joe raised his palms. "Politics can be a very dirty game."

She gripped his hand. "So, what are we going to do? The captain would never agree to sink to those kind of measures."

"No," said Liam. "It's hardly an even playing field."

I took a sip of my cider before answering. It was something I'd seen actors do in movies to raise tension. A dramatic pause.

And a fairly dickish move, now that I'd done it. "The captain doesn't need to know. Let him think he's up against a regular opponent and he'll handle this with the confidence he has to have to win the election, because his lack of experience is a big disadvantage. In the meantime, I gather intel."

"How are you going to gather intel?" asked Helena. "Mr Hardacre?"

"No," Liam said. I couldn't really tell what his face was doing as a whole, but his eyes looked all shiny. "She's joined the McManus campaign team."

Helena slapped a hand across her mouth and Rā raised her hand for me to high-five.

"Jewel Bauer," said Joe. "I knew you had it in you."

"You," said Forest, holding out a fist for me to bump, "are a total double agent. Respect."

"So, we'll get to know exactly what he's doing before he even does it?" asked Rā.

"I have to be careful. He's going to get me to sign a non-disclosure agreement, so I can't just take stuff and publish it to out him. Or at least, if I do, I have to be very careful it can't be traced back to me. If he discovers I work at the mart, it'll be obvious." I gasped and slapped my hands to my cheeks.

"What is it?" asked Liam.

"She's met me at the mart."

"Who has?"

"Bekka. His wife. Fuuuuuuuck." I placed my thumbs against my eyelids. "I won't be able to do it. She'll spot me in a hot second."

"It was only for like, a few seconds," said Forest. "She's not going to remember you."

"I shouted at her and kind of called her a selfish, vacuous rich bitch. She's going to remember."

"Could you wear a disguise? Your face isn't *that* memorable," said Rā.

No, it wasn't. And yes, I could.

I thought of my Geek Girl Roar persona. "I've got some fake reading glasses I could wear, but it won't be enough."

"Hide your hair," said Liam. "People look very different when you can't see their hair."

I took a moment to think it through, which was a very short one because what choice did I have. I had a fashionable loose beanie I could tuck all my hair into. "Okay. Do you guys think that will be enough?"

Joe shrugged his shoulders. "If she recognises you, we think of some other way."

"I'll have to remember to wear the beanie and glasses whenever I'm at home in case they look over the fence or he comes round."

"It's only until voting closes. Not long," said Liam.

Thank goodness she wasn't home last night. It would have been over before it began.

"What's this McManus guy got you doing?" asked Helena.

"All we've discussed are the terms of the contract and that I'm to join his 'Think Tank' on Monday to start building a cohesive campaign strategy. So, I have nothing yet." Though it might provide an opportunity to grab the phone Mr Hardacre wanted.

Rā downed the rest of her wine and placed the glass on the table with a *thunk*. "I have a pressing question. How on earth did you get old haemorrhoid face to do your hacking for you?"

I shrugged. "I asked and it appealed to his tech ego. It's been a long time since he's had an opportunity to do anything like this."

Rā snorted. "He probably leapt so fast at the chance, his chin reabsorbed his chicken wattle with the G-force."

"Also, I bribed him with medicinal cigarettes."

"Where'd you get those from?" asked Liam, who'd sat up a bit straighter.

Rā and Joe looked at Forest.

"What?" Forest's eyes flickered between them. "They're medicinal cigarettes. I use them...for medicinal purposes."

"Well, whatever," said Joe. "If it means we've got him on our side, we have a valuable weapon. As long as we aim it properly."

"I just," Helena started. "I mean, I'm really into the intrigue of all this and I get that this McManus bloke might not be the nicest person, but most politicians aren't. Sure, we'll get a few more expensive houses whacked up, but change isn't all bad. Why are we having to do this? Bribe hackers with cannabis and risk Jewel being sued for breach of contract?"

"Because, my heart, this little scene right here," Joe gestured to the table, "or the one at the checkouts where you pretend to be a customer, but are just having a good old chin wag, might not be possible in the future McManus envisions for this place. You think someone like Harit, who works two jobs so he can send money home will be able to stay? Lord knows how McManus thinks he's going to get his trim latte, or his house cleaned if the lowly paid can't afford to live here."

"But." Helena glanced around the table. "You guys are my family. I'd go mad if I had to rely on my husband for company."

My insides did a little buzz thing as if Helena's words had reached behind my ribcage and jostled my organs like Joe ruffling Liam's hair.

Because.

When she said "family", she meant everyone at the table. Including me.

!

"Then you understand why we have to do this," said Joe.

Helena blinked rapidly at him. "Okay. Yes." She gave a series of little nods. "I'm one hundred percent in."

Rā stood up. "Right, if that's the main business done, I'm off. I'm not risking a repeat of our last night at the pub. I had bags under my eyes for a week afterwards. That shit tends to hit you in the vanity."

"Before you go, strategist," said Joe, "what's our game plan over the next few days?"

"Wait to hear what went down in the McManus think tank, so we know the lie of the land? Then form our own game plan and somehow make it look like the captain's driving this thing, because we all know he'll want to."

"The poor captain," said Helena. "Keeping him in the dark."

Joe patted her hand. "It's better this way, my lovely."

It had better be. He didn't deserve to be used as a political pawn, and I wasn't entirely convinced that's not exactly what we were positioning him as.

BRIAN MCMANUS' "Think Tank" was three people around his massive dining room table, and Bekka, who fussed about in the open-plan kitchen making coffee in their gold-plated espresso maker.

Okay, it was black and chrome. But I bet if they could get a gold-plated one, they would.

McManus didn't seem to notice I looked any different to when we last met, and Bekka behaved exactly how a person meeting someone for the first time would, so for the five minutes I had been there, I had got away with it.

I was introduced to Jess, his campaign assistant. McManus didn't have a need for a campaign manager or any other political specialist because, he said, he already knew it all. A dog's body with a bit of nous was all that was required, and Bekka could plug any other gaps. Despite appearances, Bekka did not exist for the sole dedication of keeping Queenstown's boutique stores in business. There was a fully-formed brain behind the excessive collagen.

I'm paraphrasing, but that's pretty much what he said. He punctuated it with a kiss to her artificially-plumped lips and a slap to the arse.

Bekka didn't bat an eye. Presumably that was because her husband was master of the credit card, and not because she'd had her lids surgically sealed in an expression of the perpetually surprised. Or maybe she did actually love him.

Jess's great-great-grandfather, according to McManus, was "a Māori" of no specified tribal affiliation, but that, apparently, got her the job over her less tick box-y competitors.

She had dark brown hair scraped back into the kind of ponytail that made your eyes water and wore a pants suit and heels like she assisted a Prime Ministerial candidate instead of a mayoral nominee in New Zealand's sparsely-populated mountainous back blocks.

She brought her hands to her chest and offered rapid applause when McManus announced, mid-pace, "My campaign slogan will be 'Protecting and preserving the integrity of this community'."

I had two issues with his slogan. Firstly, it wasn't remotely true. Secondly, it had an unnecessary use of two similar words. I chose to only voice concern number two. "You don't need the word 'protecting' *and* the word 'preserving'. Choose one and keep it snappy."

McManus paused in his pacing and placed a finger to

his lips. "You're absolutely right. One of them is completely superfluous. Which one?"

"'Preserving' is less aggressive," suggested Bekka. "You're the nice guy that people want to invite into their houses for a cup of tea, remember? Relatable."

"But 'Protecting' suggests you'd fight to keep what's important to this community," said Jess.

"In the art of persuasion, you go for emotive every time. Which one has the greatest impact?"

"Protecting," I said in a monotone, knowing McManus already had his answer, but wanted to enjoy some kind of wisdom-imparting of the master.

"Exactly. So, our slogan is 'Protecting the integrity of this community'. Even though the campaign is district-wide, it makes the residents think I'm dedicated to their specific interests."

"Are you not?" I asked.

"You're dedicated to *your* interests, aren't you, darling?" Bekka said over the top of her enormous latte mug.

"I wouldn't put it quite like that. I'm happy to represent the interests of the community. As long as they align with mine." He placed a hand on the shelf of his belly and tipped his head back in laughter. It might have seemed villainous had it come from someone who looked less like a gnome.

Jess laughed, presumably because she was paid to.

I did not.

"It's nothing so shocking, Jewel. All politicians are the same."

He was probably right, though I didn't know enough about the political arena to cross-reference his statement.

"Right." McManus clapped his hands, which seemed unnecessary since he already had all our attention. "What are the core interests I'll be representing? They'll drive our campaign policies."

"Rates," said Bekka.

McManus pointed a finger at her. "That's right, my love, there's no better way to gain votes than to reward voters' wallets. Now, every other political aspirant touts the idea of rates cuts. It's nothing new and there's the potential all voters hear is white noise when the words 'rates cuts' are uttered. So, we need to do something that'll hit them between the eyes. Who are our rates payers in this district, by and large?"

"Um," said Jess, eyes raised to the ceiling.

"Are they residents?" prompted McManus.

"No?" said Jess at the same as I said, "Some are."

He paused in his pacing and gripped the back of a dining chair. "You're both right. Only thirty-five percent of rate payers are permanent residents. The rest of the houses in the district are rentals or holiday homes. That's a majority of house owners who pay full rates for benefits largely enjoyed by the permanent residents. Are you with me?"

Jess nodded while I chose to channel my energy into working out where he was going with this and what personal benefit it would be to him. "Are *you* a permanent resident?"

McManus' eyes flicked to Bekka. He answered, "For all intents and purposes, yes," which I knew from experience of taking people at their word and then discovering they'd lied through their teeth, actually meant, "No, not really."

So, McManus intended to be an absentee mayor. It didn't surprise me, given the little interest he had in representing anybody's concerns but his own. The mayoral crown was a prize he could casually drop into conversation at the golf club.

I steadied myself for his rates cut bombshell.

"I'll campaign for making rates proportionate to occupancy."

"So, the less time you spend in your house, the less rates you pay?" asked Jess.

"Exactly. Genius, no?"

I admit, it was genius, if he could make it work without hamstringing council services in the process by stripping away too much revenue. It was sure to attract voters. And it financially rewarded people who absolutely didn't need it. An effective rates rebate for people who were so wealthy, they could afford a second property, while punishing those who absolutely did need the support council gave, because if rates were cut, something had to give. Community group funding, safer roads, free programmes at libraries.

And then, the full impact of proportionate rates hit me. If people were incentivised to minimise occupancy of their houses, long-term rentals would disappear in favour of short-term. Every landlord in the district would turn their rentals into AirBnBs.

Almost everyone I knew and...cared about? would be homeless. They'd be forced out of the district.

All of the fears the mart family had expressed based on reasonably tenuous spa sex talk, were now firmly realised. It would be the end of the mart, the end of everything, everybody I had gained since moving to Puhiruru. The end of acceptance, of...feeling like I might actually belong somewhere.

I couldn't let it happen. McManus must not be allowed to win the election.

As the roaring in my ears died away, McManus' voice pierced the static.

"...interesting things happening on social media, which are ripe for us to leverage off. You two on Facebook?"

"Yes," said Jess.

"No," I said.

"For Jewel's sake. There's someone stirring up discontent. Calling themselves The Unfettered Brain."

"I've heard about it," I said. I'd be in a hearsay vacuum if I hadn't.

"They're pushing a few conspiracy theories about central and local government. You know the kind of thing. 'Your local council is the front guard for a state-wide agenda of totalitarianism'. Absolute rubbish, but political gold if it creates enough fear and you can use it to your advantage.

"Now, I like conspiracy theories because they're easily exploited. They appeal to two types of people – those who already distrust the government, so the hippies, the anarchists, the colonised. And the spoilt middle and upper classes who haven't had anything real to worry about in their lives since the cold war. Biologically we're hard-wired to expect to have to fight for survival. At the end of the day, we're just another animal running from the lions. Except there are no lions any more, and what happens when that daily fear of being eaten is removed? Our brains look for something to fear. If we can't invent it ourselves, we're perfectly happy for someone to do it for us."

"It's true," said Bekka, as if she sympathised. I imagined the chosen fear of someone with such a taut face would be their skin bursting under the pressure of all the tension, like a sausage cooked too fast on high heat.

"And here's why The Unfettered Brain's stirring works so well for our campaign," continued McManus. "Statistically it's the educated and financially privileged who tend to vote in local elections, a mere thirty-seven percent of those eligible. And it's the educated and financially privileged who gravitate towards conspiracy theories, so all those people out there currently feeling angry and anxious are our voters, ladies. And how do we secure their vote?"

"Lower their rates?" said Jess.

"Well, yes, we've already established that, but there's something else. Which of the two mayoral candidates knows local council like the back of their hand and can position themselves as the man to free the rate payers from supposed bureaucratic oppression by creating effective change from the inside?"

I didn't bother answering. Surely it was a rhetorical question.

"You, darling."

I stood corrected.

"That's right. Me. So, we'll use social media to indirectly allay any fears the guy's followers have. I couldn't campaign outright on them, but I can use the power of suggestion. Are you with me?"

Bekka nodded. "A two-pronged approach."

"That's right, my love. Get their attention with the campaign policies, push them towards the voting booth with some subliminal messaging."

And there was the opening to get McManus' phone. "Speaking of messaging. TikTok would be a good way to expand your reach. It's popularity as a platform is growing exponentially. You should post daily videos to get exposure. I could set it all up on your phone after the meeting if you like. I'll do it from home and bring it back in a couple of hours." It was a long shot, but I needed a reason for him to hand his phone to me and it was all I could think of.

McManus flapped a hand. "No. Bekka does all the

social media stuff. She can sort it if we decide to go down the TikTok route."

Great. That was that idea nuked on the spot.

"Now." He clicked his fingers at Jess. "What do we know about this Fink fellow?"

She tapped the screen of her tablet. "He's fifty-four. A widower. Two adult children. Owns Puhiruru Mart and a couple of rental properties in the town. Vice-President of Rotary. Does quite a bit of charitable work, donating food to the Puhiruru Food Bank, funding various community projects, supporting the Puhiruru hospice etcetera."

"Right. So he gets to play the good Samaritan card, which is a pretty decent one. It's an advantage we don't have, but it doesn't make up for his lack of experience. We can out-manoeuvre him in a heartbeat as long as we get the coverage. Nobody outside Puhiruru knows this guy from bah-loody Tom, Dick or Harry, so his advantage is only local. I'm not particularly concerned, but just in case – Jess? See if you can rake up any skeletons in the guy's closet. Nobody's squeaky clean."

"That's right," I said, looking at McManus, then flicking my eyes to Jess in case anyone heard the added "Nobody is, Brian, *nobody*" I thought but didn't say.

Jess ran a finger over the tablet screen. "I believe he's ex-military, Mr McManus. Served for fifteen years. Rose to the rank of captain in the SAS."

"Did he now?" McManus stroked his chin. "That could be useful. Well done, Jess. Proved your worth already."

Jess' lips twitched in her effort not to beam.

"Let's see what Jewel's made of."

Metal, wankstick. Titanium-plated, rich-boy-arse-kicking, fucking ninja-ry. Just try me.

"We need to get our campaign posters ready to go asap,

so they can be mounted around the district. I've already had my publicity shots taken, so I'll get Bekka to send them to you for you to start on them."

Bekka gave a series of small nods and offered a smile that pushed her taut skin to the squeaky limits of its stretch-ability.

"Now, this is important. I want to look as everyman as possible. There needs to be something in the image that appeals to most voters, yes?"

God I hated when people did that. Anybody who ended statements by unnecessarily turning them into a question should be taken out back and put out of everyone's misery. It might *look* like they were seeking affirmation for something they had doubts about, but were in fact patronising you into complicity without giving you the time to think about what was being asked of you.

"But mostly the white middle-class ones, because they're the ones that'll actually vote. Make sure I'm smiling, and use one where I've got my hands on my hips. I need to look as open as possible. Kind of grass roots –" he wrinkled his nose like he could actually smell the crap he believed the concept of "grass roots" to be "– but professional, yes? And powerful. I need to look like I can actually do what I say I will. Widen my shoulders if you need to and get rid of the tum." He slapped his stomach. "Nothing says 'can do' less than an overstuffed one-pack."

AS THE MEETING drew to a close, Bekka having long since saved her ears from bleeding from the campaign minu-tiae and departed, McManus ushered me and Jess towards the front door. Amongst the campaign notes and empty coffee cups on the table lay his phone.

THANK YOU, HIGHER POWER.

At the door, I clucked my tongue, said I'd forgotten something, and retraced my steps.

The living area remained mercifully empty.

It was too easy.

I grabbed the phone and as I dropped it into my tote bag, Bekka emerged through a side door.

Our eyes met.

CHAPTER TWENTY

MY STOMACH DISSOLVED into my bowels. Through the wave of heat threatening to broil my organs, I said, "Forgot my phone. What am I like?" like a teenager in the early stages of brain development. I even threw in a giggle for good measure.

Bekka looked at me for a second before saying, "I'm always doing that. Brian says I might as well have my phone surgically grafted to my hand, the amount of time I'm on it. Then I'd never lose it." She gave a little laugh and I took that as my cue to leave.

I had to move fast. It wouldn't be long before McManus couldn't find his phone. Or Bekka put two and five together. Hopefully she thought it was a case of mistaken identity rather than theft.

Once I was out of the McManus eye line, I ran for my car and turned both phones off. They'd both be ringing before long and it would be hard to lie about why I hadn't heard anything.

I drove to the Mart and ran inside to Rā's checkout. "I need Mr Hardacre's address. We've had a development."

Rā looked at me blankly. "Why on earth do you think I might know where he lives?"

A disparaging grunt issued behind me. "You don't have to know, Rā, you just have to be resourceful, like all ninjas. Behold". Forest tapped on his phone. "8 Brancose Crescent."

As Rā argued that using the White Pages was in no way akin to ninjary, I ran for my car, then drove the short distance to 8 Brancose Crescent in a way that might have been described as "somewhat reckless".

A Zimmer frame-assisted Mr Hardacre opened the door and I slapped the phone into his hand. "You've got about five hours. I'm pretending I'm driving to Invercargill and I always turn my phone off to avoid distraction. Apparently."

"It's no use to me if the phone's off."

"Well, think of a way. You said you could make it put on arseless chaps and line dance. I'm sure you can work around a phone behaving like it's turned off."

Mr Hardacre narrowed his eyes at me. Then he grunted and did an about turn.

I took that as confirmation he could.

He disappeared through a doorway off the hall without closing the front door, which presumably, in Hardacre land, was an invitation to come in.

I followed him into a small, very tidy, open-plan living area. When I shared my surprise at its neatness, he said, "Home help's just been."

I would have thought Mr Hardacre too proud and stubborn to accept charitable assistance, but then I wouldn't have picked him as a computing virtuoso, either.

"Tea making stuff's in there." He nodded in the direction of the kitchen and sat down at the dining table.

Admiring his presumption, I set about making tea. It was a small thing to do for someone who was doing a big thing that might otherwise cost several hundred dollars an hour. Admittedly, it could have been more than that, but I hadn't trawled the dark web lately looking for the going rate on hackers.

"Make sure you turn off Find My Phone."

"You teaching me how to suck eggs, girl?" Mr Hardacre said, thumbs swiping the small screen.

"I'm just aware that once you've done all your wizardry, I'll have several hours to kill while I supposedly do whatever I need to do in Invercargill and then drive back again. I can't run the risk of being discovered I've just been hanging about town."

"You're not hanging here for five hours. Have your cuppa then bugger off for two. I'll have what I need by then."

"You can look through all his stuff by then?"

"No. I'll have access to all his stuff by then as long as he's not using a password manager. Most people are lazy with security, so I have high hopes your man is a typical techno monkey."

I didn't think he'd be disappointed. Given the lofty heights of McManus' arrogance, he probably thought himself impervious to cyber-espionage.

I drank my tea, bid goodbye to an unresponsive Mr Hardacre, and went outside to lie on the back seat of my car for two hours. With any luck I'd fall asleep and my waiting time before I could go home would be halved. Or two-fifthed if we're aiming for accuracy.

Of course, I didn't sleep. I stared at the sagging underside of the Rav4's roof and invented sixteen different ways of how I might be discovered for what I'd done and whether my fair skin would look washed out in an orange jump suit.

An hour and a half after leaving the McManus house, I

turned on my phone. Six missed phone calls and one message: Hi Jewel Bekka here I think you have Brian's phone

I waited the time it would take to rummage in my bag before replying.

Me: Oh yes! Sorry!!!! Our phones are the same model lol

They weren't. His was a nondescript black and the latest iPhone. Mine was a cheap Chinese make in a turquoise case.

I'd have to remember to never use my phone in their presence.

0271991354: I rang it several times but it was turned off?

Me: I turned it off because I was driving

Me: I don't like to get distracted

Me: I'm in Invercargill

Me: Back tonight

Me: So sorry

0271991354: No worries see you later

Well. So far so good.

I knocked on Mr Hardacre's door again. He handed the phone over without a word and closed the door before I had the chance to do something courteous, like thank him.

Turning around, I peered at my car. I still had two or three hours to kill and I didn't want to do it imagining my downfall in an ill-conceived shoot out with the Armed Offenders Squad.

I drove back to the mart and entered the post-after-school-rush lull. Helena stood opposite Rā at her checkout, reading from her phone, while Forest listened, elbows propped on his conveyor belt, head in hands.

I couldn't see Liam.

"Oh, Jewel. I'll read it again. You'll want to know this."

"Know what?"

"The Unfettered Brain is really ramping things up. He's gone on a bit of a rant today. He says, 'The people of Fiordland must fight for justice, fight the rising tide of authoritarian aspiration. Fiordland will be a pocket of freedom amid national tyranny'."

"What tyranny?"

"Apparently, the government wants to strip everyone of their assets. The only ownership will be state ownership."

"What, like communism?" said Forest.

"Won't be much different for the poor people, then," said Rā. "My heart will bleed for the middle and upper classes."

"*I'm* middle class. I don't want to lose my house," said Helena.

"You won't," I said, "because it's not true, remember? The Unfettered Brain is McManus' insurance policy. Get the financially comfortable and the rich to come scuttling to him in the face of dispossession. I went to my first meeting with him today. He said, get this –" I beckoned them to gather round and lowered my voice. "– It's the privileged who vote in local elections, and the privileged who believe in conspiracy theories because humans are hard-wired to have to fight for survival, right? And those people who have everything don't have to worry about survival any more so look for something to worry about. So, the conspiracy theories will push the voters towards voting for him, and all he has to do is look like the guy who will save them."

"So, he's totally open about it?" said Rā.

"Kind of. Though he's pretending The Unfettered Brain is some other guy. But listen to this. His main campaign policy is making rates proportionate to occupancy, so if you own a crib, you only pay rates for the days of the year you use it."

"How will they police that?" asked Forest.

I turned down my bottom lip and gave a little shake of my head. "That's the least thing to worry about. It means property owners will be encouraged to lower occupancy."

"No way. The long-term rental market will disappear."

"The worst thing," I said, "is that he's only doing it to save himself rates money. The house he's bought is a holiday home for him. And renters are once again powerless to do anything about it."

Rā crossed her arms. "We didn't have a homeless problem here until rents went up with property values. Now it'll be rife, or people will just have to leave. People who have lived here their whole lives."

"Like me," said Forest.

"And me," said Rā. "And everyone else who's made this place home, like Harit and Liam."

"And Joe," added Helena.

Rā slapped her counter top. "We have to get the son of a bitch if it's the last thing we do."

"Speak of the devil," said Forest.

A gleaming Ford ute pulled into a parking space outside the window, McManus at the wheel.

"Fuck." I ducked down and squat-walked to the entrance of Rā's cubicle-shaped checkout and nestled myself at her feet.

Thankfully I'd had the forethought to park my Rav4 round the back in the loading bay. All I needed to worry about was whether he'd seen me.

"Act natural," I hissed at the group. "Start chatting, or look like you're actually doing your job or something."

The doors wheezed open. "Good afternoon, ladies."

Helena answered, "Afternoon."

Rā said under her breath, "I'm not a bloody lady."

And Forest said, "Really?" as McManus said, "Can you

tell me where the bay leaves are? The wife needs them urgently for the poached trout she's making for dinner."

Nobody said anything.

"I'm not showing him," said Forest without bothering to lower his voice.

"I'll show you," said Helena in a girlish pitch. A series of small scuffs *shished* their way over the vinyl floor as she, what, *shuffled* over to him? "They're in aisle four."

McManus's Italian loafers clomped after her. I couldn't actually see if they were Italian loafers, but like everything about him, even the noise they made as they contacted the floor sounded expensive.

After several seconds, Forest hissed, "He called me a lady and didn't correct himself even after I spoke. Even if the visuals were in doubt, and they are not, I have a man's voice. Right?"

"Yes, you have a man's voice," said Rā.

"Do you think it was deliberate?"

"Probably," I whispered. "As a checkout guy, he'll have discounted you as a voter, so what does it matter if he looks like he intended to cause offence, or not?"

"Oh, *here* they are." Helena's giggle fluttered among the rafters. "I couldn't find my nose if it wasn't attached to my face."

"Thank you, young lady. The missus would have been very unhappy if I returned home empty handed."

Helena tittered this time. "You're welcome, young man."

They were coming back. My pulse threatened to hammer its way through my skin.

"Rā," I hissed. "Bugger off and look like you're straightening a display or something. He can't come to you. He'll see me."

Rā clucked her tongue, but did as I asked.

The foot steps – McManus' six-hundred-dollar-cushioned stride and Helena's little shuffle – neared the checkouts.

"Just that please, sir," McManus said. "I hope I didn't cause any offence earlier. I saw the long, purple hair over your face and thought you must be a girl." He bellowed out a laugh.

Forest waited the length of a hard stare before saying, "That'll be three dollars, nineteen."

"Thank you, my man. You have a good evening." The loafers *clumped* away.

Once the doors closed, I poked my head over the top of the checkout to find Helena breathing hard, hands clamped to her cheeks. "Oh my God, swoon."

"Oh my God, gross," said Forest.

"I swear you have the most appalling taste in men," said Rā, who'd returned to her checkout.

Helena pivoted from watching McManus' receding back. "Spritz my face, spritz my face."

Rā picked up her spray bottle and said, "You know this is several parts disinfectant?" before squeezing the trigger.

Helena flapped her hands in the direction of her head. "More. I'm burning up."

"No. I'm not sure how I feel about being responsible for melting your face off. Best to err on the side of caution." Rā didn't elaborate what, exactly, she was favouring caution over – disfiguring Helena's face, or entertaining her own morbid fascination with the outcome.

"I mean, he's a bit of a D-I-L-F," Helena continued, spelling out the word.

"He's a bit of a D-I-C-K," Forest corrected.

"Am I safe to come out now?" I asked.

"Yep. His unnecessarily large and planet destroying car

has left the car park," said Rā. "What does an aspiring mayor need with a ute?"

"Farmers are voters. It's probably his way of connecting to them," I said. "If he looks like them, he must understand them."

Rā grunted, Helena sighed, and Forest waggled a pointer finger. "You know what I should have said when he did the whole 'no offence' bullshit? I should have said, 'I don't mind being mistaken for a girl. Girls are cool. I mind if the mistake is weaponised, as if being compared to a woman somehow makes me lesser. When, in fact, being compared to a woman makes me *more*'. Why is it you only think up awesome come backs after you need them?"

"I don't know," said Helena, gazing at the parking spot vacated by McManus' ute, before wandering towards the automatic door.

"A good come back needs crafting," said Rā. "You need that T-shirt of Jewel's. The 'Thanks for the compliment' one." She raised a hand to wave at Helena's back. "Bye, then."

"Where's Liam?" I asked.

"Where's Liam?" parroted Rā and nudged me with her elbow.

"He's out the back helping Harit," said Forest. "You should go find him."

I thought back to the last time Liam was out the back helping Harit, and how well that went. "Why would I do that?"

"Because you want to."

I did.

And I didn't.

The Liam Thing was like scratching a mosquito bite. You know you shouldn't because it makes the itch worse, but the temporary relief is too much of a temptation. I needed to put a slab of ice on it and calm the whole thing the fuck down.

"I'm not going to."

As it turned out, I didn't need to. Liam emerged from the back of the store before Rā and Forest could say more coercion-y stuff and my blood fizzed. His step faltered when he saw me. "Hey Jewel, what are you doing here?"

"Hiding out."

"From what?"

"Brian McManus. I stole his phone so Mr Hardacre could do covert techy things with it."

"Isn't that illegal?"

"Yep."

Liam stared at me for a beat. "Your lack of fear is admirable and kind of...scary."

"Oh no. I'm bricking it. You don't have to lack fear to be courageous."

"You do have to be stupid to lack fear," said Rā.

"Exactly," I said.

"And Jewel is anything but stupid," said Liam.

"Okay." Rā clapped her hands. "As much as I love the J and L show, it's ten minutes to finishing time, which means Forest gets to clean the finger cheese off the Eftpos machines because he came second in last week's burn-off."

Forest threw his head back and groaned at the ceiling before snatching his spray bottle and narrowing his eyes at Rā.

"What are you all doing after work?" I asked. "I have about three hours to kill before I can go home and hand McManus his accidentally taken phone."

"I'm going on a date," said Forest. "I'm not inviting you to that."

"I wouldn't get in the way. I'd just sit there and pretend not to listen."

"Still not inviting you."

I turned to Rā. "Rā?"

"I'm coaching the over 60s cheerleading team with hot Philipe."

"Can I come?"

"No."

"What if I say 'please'?"

She turned her back to me and moved things around under the baggage packing area in a way that looked deliberately unnecessary.

"Um," said Liam. "It's picnic dinner night...if you want to come. It'll just be me and Dana."

Great. Date night. That won't be like taking a hunting knife to my heart or anything.

"I don't want to be the third wheel in your quality time together."

"We do it every week. You won't be a third wheel." His eyes flicked to Forest and I could see the little glint of hurt in them. I practically begged to be the third wheel on Forest's date.

I couldn't do it to him.

"Okay, I'll come." It might be good to bear witness to Liam's gayness. They might hold hands. Maybe they'd kiss. It would be like a bucket of iced water over whatever this squishy thing was metastacising in my insides.

WE AGREED it was safer to leave my car at work and when we arrived at his house, Liam told me to wait in the ute. He wouldn't be long.

Two minutes later, Dana exited the front door and I got out to sit in the back seat.

"Hello gorgeous, kick-arse Jewel." He grabbed me for a hug and I let him because I thought I should, even though hugging anybody but my mum and my dad seemed a little unnecessary.

"Hi, Dana."

"Don't bother changing seats. I'm not coming."

I didn't know how to take this news. It wasn't what I wanted to happen at all, so I was mostly "Ngar!". But I was also a little bit "Yay".

"I'm up to my Him-scented pits in work and have to catch up tonight. You know how it is."

I didn't. I'd always been very effective at meeting deadlines. I had to because pulling extra hours on contract work meant unpaid hours, so I said, "No," then wondered if I should have lied to make him feel better about not being efficient.

Dana didn't seem upset by my honesty. "I'm sorry we don't get to hang. Liam's prepared a delish spread, so you're in for a real treat tonight."

"Sweet," I said, as Liam appeared at the front door dressed in jeans and another form-fitting plaid shirt and my ovaries orgasmed.

I didn't understand it. It was just an ordinary wardrobe choice. Why did my body have to react like he was bare chested and greased up for a Fireman's calendar?

Except.

I did understand it. I knew what the flesh pressing against the denim and cotton looked like and it was pre-tty phenomenal.

I turned away from him and climbed in the car.

Liam loaded the picnic gear onto the back seat and Dana called, "Have fun, kids," when Liam fired the engine.

I waved to him as we drove off, then turned to Liam. "I'm sorry you don't get to spend time with Dana tonight."

"Yeah," said Liam with a smile that suggested he wasn't terribly unhappy about missing out on a romantic evening with his boyfriend.

Weird. Maybe things weren't all well and good in Dana-Liam loveland.

A small glow ebbed in my chest.

I gnashed my teeth. Mostly metaphorically. It wasn't useful for me to be entertaining such thoughts, especially as I actually had no idea what the reality of their relationship was. Maybe Liam was just happy he was spending time with me, which was a little more likely than it would have been a few weeks ago.

"So," I said by way of something to say that might keep my thoughts trained on the Dana/Liam as one picture. "Picnic night."

"Yeah." Liam smiled and raised a shoulder. "You know."

"No."

"We try to make the most of the warmer weather before winter sets in. It's a couple of hours for us to hang out, listen to the evening chorus and remind ourselves we live in this awesome place."

"Where do you go?"

"A spot most people don't know about."

Where you can make out and say sexy stuff to each other while stags roar in the background.

The little smile didn't disappear from Liam's face and I knew it to be true.

He turned off down an unmarked gravel road cut

through dense, fern-studded bush. It ended at a little, secluded beach behind a small arm that hid the town.

It was early enough that the sun hadn't dipped behind the mountains and the air was golden in the soft evening sun, and the only sounds were the birdsong and the steady thrum of the waterfall. I'd choose this spot for romantic dinners with my boyfriend, too.

Liam handed me the carton of food and followed me down to the beach with a rubber-backed picnic blanket and a couple of camping chairs.

The chairs were slung so low, my arse was suspended just above ground level, which didn't make getting into them with any kind of elegance easy. Liam had to catch the chair leg to stop me tipping over after I threw myself into it, bum first.

Our laughter frightened a couple of ducks, who flapped off in a frenzy of outraged quacks.

"You'll be wanting this before you settle in." Liam handed me a bottle of insect repellent from the carton.

"Yes," I said, slapping at a sandfly on my ankle. "Not good for hand taint on a picnic, though."

"We'll be eating with all four cutlery sets of fine dining. I'm not a savage."

Four cutlery sets? I hoped he didn't expect me to know which went with what course. Then I understood. I smiled at him. "Did you just crack a joke?"

Liam turned from me to riffle in the box. "I do have joke-making abilities buried deep in my skill set. I bring them out from time to time."

"What else are you going to surprise me with?"

Liam looked across at me sharply, which was a little odd.

"You can probably juggle flaming knives or something."

He did that rumbly laugh thing that sends shivers up my spine and I wished he brayed like a donkey when he laughed, even though I liked the fact he didn't.

"I can't juggle flaming knives. And even if I could, how do you set fire to a knife?"

True. That was a stupid thing to say. "If you *could* set fire to a knife, Rā would start a flaming knife juggling league. Though Puhiruru's probably safe given she never got anywhere with the penis jousting tournament."

The smile slipped from Liam's face and he busied himself pulling items from the box.

"What are those?" I asked, pointing to a jar of what looked like pickled chilli peppers.

"Stuffed jalapeños."

"Will I like them?" Good one, Jewel. Of course he couldn't know that.

"I want to say 'yes' with confidence, but the best I can do is 'I hope so', because they're really good, especially with a thin slice of venison wrapped around them." He opened a container, made a blanketed jalapeño and handed it to me.

I eyed it, then I eyed him in an attempt to convey suspicion, but he chose that moment to flick his hair out of his face and my pelvic floor tightened while my brain went ------ ------ and I shoved the whole thing in my mouth, which meant there was no room for any air with which to cool THE FUCKING INFERNO INCINERATING MY TONGUE.

Liam beamed and said, "Isn't it amazing?" and I answered by wiping my knuckles across the tears making a desperate bid to parley with the fluid leaking from my nose.

I stood up and flapped my hands a bit.

"It's not that bad," said Liam, laughing at my pain like a...ridiculously beautiful sadist.

I swallowed, wheezed out, "You've probably killed all your pain receptors off," and made a little tunnel with my mouth to suck cool air over my tongue.

"Here." He pulled a bottle out of the box. It hissed when he opened it and he poured some into an enamel mug.

"Wha' ith i'?"

"Fizzy water."

Swallowing the saliva that had gathered, I said, "No way. That'd be like trying to calm a homicidal maniac by making him sit through a tap dancing recital."

Liam grinned and popped a jalapeño in his mouth.

When he had finished showing me even his tongue was manly, he passed me a sliver of cheese on a cracker, then looked at me with a raised brow as I chewed the final bit of crunch out of it.

"What?"

"You were humming."

Oh God. "Was I?"

"I haven't heard anybody out of childhood hum while they chewed." He raised a palm. "It's not a judgement. I think it's...cute."

I didn't. "I don't want to be cute. I want to be all Sasha Fierce and shit."

He rumbled out another pelvic-tightening laugh. "You are Sasha Fierce and shit. But that's not all you are. You have a, kind of, naive side too. The humming-while-chewing Jewel."

I wrinkled my nose.

"It's nice. You know...endearing." He tailed off at the end as if unsure of his words.

Endearing? Was he patronising me? I checked by asking him.

"No! I don't mean to. I really like your naive side. A lot."

He looked away when he said the last two words, letting their sounds bend and amplify in the mug he took a sip from.

I didn't like naive. Naive was often mistaken for stupid. "I think I'd rather be world wise and jaded."

"No you don't. Everything would lose its colour. And then you'd lose yours. Keep your colour, Jewel."

In the short few weeks since I'd got him to talk to me from out behind the wall of his hair, Liam had been reasonably complimentary. Take right now for instance. He'd thrown two at me in the space of a minute, which I shouldn't be surprised at. Not because I unquestionably deserved them, but because gay men were probably thoughtful like that.

I supposed I should have a go at returning one, so this wasn't a one-sided relationship.

The problem was, there were just so many to choose from, though admittedly, I'd have to cross most off the list for fear of revealing my wanton thoughts.

I found myself focused on the frilly socks poking over the top of his Converse boots. He often wore them and I failed to notice them most days. I mean, I *saw* them. It was impossible not to when you were watching someone bend over or squat down and their trousers rode up. But I didn't *notice* them anymore.

"I really like your socks. They look cool with your bad boy shoes. Kind of like a 'Fuck you' in a 'That's right, I'm totally rocking a contradiction' kind of way."

Liam beamed at me for the second time that evening. He didn't do it often, as clearly I didn't please him to the extent of extreme happiness that much.

"How do you find ones that fit you?"

"I don't. Forest sews the frills on to the top of normal

socks for me."

Huh. "You must really love them."

"I really love them."

"See? You talk about me being bold. That right there is some bold as shit. You need to give yourself more credit."

Liam gazed out over the darkening water. Then he gave a single nod. "Okay, thank you. I should."

I reached for another cracker and filled the silence with the crunch of vigorous masticating.

A bellbird chimed its evening salutations above our heads and Liam said, "How's the T-shirt business going?"

"Good. Really good, actually."

"I'm not surprised. It was a really smart move to take advantage of a trending platform *and* a trending gimmick to grow sales."

Oh. "You know about that?"

"Yeah, I know about that," he said with a small smile. "I might hide behind my hair, but it doesn't mean I'm not watching or noticing stuff. I feel a bit left out, actually."

My stomach listed and my organs felt too big for my ribcage, which seemed one sensation too many for the situation. "Yeah, you are left out." I couldn't tell him why. *I do the TikTok videos to distract myself from wanting to run my tongue over your perfectly-proportioned buttocks?* He'd probably say something nice back, because he was Liam and exceptionally nice, but it would be the kind of humiliation neither of us would recover from. "Sorry."

Liam's smile tipped to one side. "It's alright. I figure there's a good reason for not including me."

From anyone else that would have sounded passive-aggressive, a manipulative statement to force an answer.

"There is. I just can't tell you."

"Okay. I respect that."

I wouldn't. I would be all pissy and "Why don't you like me?" and stuff, which Liam might be feeling on the inside right now but would never ever show on the outside. I owed him more than an "I can't tell you".

"I will when I'm ready." On the day in the, hopefully, near future that I no longer look at you and think *Please take me now*, and we both roll around laughing about it.

"See that ridge over there?" Liam pointed to a knobbly arm of land, like a spine curved towards the water. "Really good hunting."

I held up the piece of meat I'd just plucked from the container. "Is this where this tasty fellow came from?"

"This tasty felless came from several valleys that way." He pointed over his right shoulder.

"How do you know where to go? The wilderness is so large out here."

"Deer leave pretty distinctive signs, but I use hunting cameras too. They record when they detect movement and I can see if a particular spot has a lot of deer activity, if there's a stag in the area. Males are the ideal target. A female can have only one baby a season, but a male can father several fawns."

"What's it like taking a life?" I realised after I said it that I didn't actually want to know. "Don't answer that." I searched for a diversion to the conversation. I landed on, "I think it's really sweet you and Dana have a weekly date night."

Liam's face did something in between what might have been amused and confused. "Yeah, I guess it is sweet. But, um, can I answer your question, because I don't think it's as messy as you think it's going to be?"

"Okay."

He gazed out over the water. "It's...a complicated set of

emotions. There's power in having the ability to kill something and...I can't deny there's a bit of joy in having that power." He whipped his head around to face me. "But I never ever take ending an animal's life for granted. It's a massive thing to be able to end something's existence so easily."

"I don't think I could do it."

"No. They're beautiful creatures. It's not like killing a rat or a fish. They're a bit, I don't know, emotive." He let out a sigh and gripped his knees. "But, you know, my meat is ethical. The deer have no idea they're about to die and I'm conserving the environment by helping to reduce their population."

"I never think about taking a life, like a cockroach or a spider. Maybe I should be more mindful. I mean, I'm still going to kill a cockroach, but I could at least appreciate that my action is creating an end for a creature who's just doing their thing for survival or whatever."

"Humans aren't always very mindful. We can get pretty wrapped up in our own existence, which is kind of biological, I guess, but we have so much power, so much privilege. We have a responsibility to be more than self-interested."

"Look at us getting all philosophical. The Liam and Jewel of a few weeks ago couldn't have blundered into this conversation if they'd tried. I'd have been all like 'What's your deal with the killing?' and you'd have been all like mumbly and stuttery and it would have been over in ten seconds before we got to the philosophising because you'd have probably run away."

Liam snorted. "It's true. It's like we're proper adults now. We've graduated from our awkward teens."

I grabbed the mug I'd refused during the jalapeño incident and raised it. "To our maturing relationship."

Liam raised his mug and *clunk*ed it against mine. "To our maturing relationship."

WHEN THE SUN dipped down behind the mountains and the light grew thin and the cold thickened and the bird-song blazed, Liam handed me a hunting fleece he had in the car.

It was big enough to fit two of me inside it and I pulled it over my knees and breathed in the Essence of Liam suffused through its weave.

It smelt of smoke, like he'd been sitting by a fire, and the saltiness of being worn against skin.

Sweet mother of God, it was heady.

I conveniently forgot to take it off and hand it back to him when he dropped me off at my car.

I hugged its roominess to me like protective armour when I returned McManus' phone with profuse apologies, which were met with far more good grace than I deserved.

I then *conveniently* forgot to hand the fleece back to Liam for two days.

It was a drug.

I kept it on the back of a dining chair so I could bury my nose into it whenever I walked past.

And then I conceded defeat.

I was officially Jewel Bauer, slave to The Liam Effect.

CHAPTER TWENTY-ONE

MCMANUS DIDN'T WASTE TIME. No sooner had I created the campaign posters according to his stipulations and added a couple of touches of my own, he had them printed and ready to be staple-gunned to people's fences.

I took a corflute poster to work with me so I could 'Show and tell', just like I never did at school.

"I like what you've done with the colour saturation levels," said Joe.

"Thank you." I'd given McManus the complexion of someone who slept in a sun bed, and whitened his teeth to the point where if you turned off the light, they glowed in the dark. I'm not joking. I tested it out. I even threw in a sparkle over his right incisor for good measure.

"He looks like a chat show host," said Forest. "Or a motivational speaker."

"He looks like he's been rolled in powdered turd," said Rā.

"I know. I couldn't have made him more of a parody. He absolutely loved it. He used the words 'excelled yourself'. I s'pose that's a good thing. He could have thrown it back at me and asked for something less show-business-y."

"At the end of the day, it doesn't matter what *he* thinks," said Liam.

"No," agreed Rā. "It's the people out there who are going to be the judge of this."

"You did good, my heart. It's going to alienate all the people he's not interested in trying to get to vote for him. It might just push them to vote."

Something large *thunk*ed against the window behind us.

Helena was pressed to the glass, her eyes on the poster. With a squeak, she dragged her face a foot to the left to get a clearer view, leaving a greasy nose-streak on the pane. Her lips, pale from the pressure of being jammed up against the glass, pursed slightly before she pushed herself off the window and scuttled in the direction of the automatic doors.

Once through, she ran towards us and squeaked to a halt with a series of pants. "Can I have this?"

"Sure." I had no need for the poster.

"Thank you." She ripped it from my hands and ran out of the door again.

"Hi, Helena," called Joe after her.

"I worry about her," said Rā. "That is one love starved woman."

Joe put his arm around her. "Aren't we all a little love starved? It's harmless."

"Not if she ends up voting for him," I said.

"She won't," said Forest. "She's on our team. That would be, like, sedition, or treason, or something."

"What? Just like Jewel's doing?" said Joe with a smile.

"That's different. She's a double agent."

"Jewel's head is clear. Helena's is not. She's our weak point," said Rā.

"Apart from the captain having no experience in politics," I said. "And using inappropriate military anecdotes."

"Okay, so there are several weak points. Helena's is the most volatile at present."

"She'll be fine," said Liam. "She's just wobbling slightly off course."

God he was sexy when he was all generous of spirit.

"While we're on the topic," said Joe. "The captain's asked that we all come in an hour earlier tomorrow to have a strategy meeting in his office, which he's renamed The War Room. Can you all make it?"

We all could, but not without a bit of groaning about the early hour.

I ARRIVED the next morning with the suggestion we should change The War Room to Fink Tank. I thought it was almost Green Ginger Wine Moment-worthy, but was met by a chorus of groans, which I hoped had more to do with coffee depletion than an inability to recognise genius when they heard it.

Forest looked like he'd showered, dressed and breakfasted the night before to save time in the morning, and Helena arrived at the shop floor with a dreamy smile on her face and a glaze across her eyes.

"You been handing out more of the electric puha?" Joe asked me.

I shook my head. "I only give Forest's race horses to Mr Hardacre."

"What's wrong with her?" asked Forest.

"Nothing," said Helena. "I am very right in every way."

Rā narrowed her eyes at her. "What did you do with that sign?"

"Gun stapled it to the ceiling above my bed. Husband didn't even notice, as I knew he wouldn't. Normally, I lie back and think of The Great Lady." She clucked her tongue and put a hand on her hip. "You know those romance books that end with the love-making scene and it says something like 'All the colours of the rainbow exploded behind her eyes?'" Extending a pointer finger, she gave it a shake. "Those writers knew what they were talking about."

One of the fridges rattled and gasped before joining the collective silence.

"Everything about that is so ew," said Forest.

Rā's mouth turned down in distaste. "I sincerely hope you're talking about a migraine, Helena."

Helena's eyes settled into the hardware-aisle middle distance. "Nope. Not a migraine."

Joe wrapped an arm around her and walked her towards the *Staff only* door. "My love, you are wondrous."

Liam shuffled sideways through the automatic doors. "Morning, Jewel," he rumbled and my stomach did a little fluttery thing.

I didn't want to make a big deal of an innocuous greeting, so I said, "Hi, Liam," in a squeaky, sort of breathy voice and attempted to nonchalantly walk towards the *Staff only* door. Except knowing he could see me doing this and was possibly watching me, my limbs felt like they were stuck together at the joints with drawing pins, like a paper puppet or something. I had to concentrate very hard to get them to coordinate while wondering what the fuck was happening to me.

I managed to make it to the captain's office without

stumbling or collapsing under the weight of Liam's non-existent gaze.

The captain greeted us with a "Righto, troops" and a "Settle yourselves in" and I made sure I was neither next to Liam, in his eyeline, or he in mine by hiding behind Joe and Helena. Thankfully Liam found a chair, which meant I didn't have to crouch to compensate for his height and, therefore,   being-able-to-see-over-the-top-of-people's-heads factor.

An engine whined past the window and a moment later, Harit rounded the doorway at a run. "Sorry I'm late. Had to stop for petrol."

"Nonsense, lad," said the captain. "You're just in time for the best bit. Which is all of it." He turned to the room. "Now, I've never been much of a PowerPoint Ranger myself, so I haven't organised a five-point presentation of our attack strategy, or most efficient deployment of personnel. To be honest, I wouldn't know where to start with the campaign Flail Ex."

"The what?" asked Helena.

"I think," said Joe. "We need to have a clear view of the political landscape, so we can tailor our campaign accordingly."

"Good idea. What intel have you got?"

Joe glanced at me before answering, "We have a fairly good idea of McManus' agenda, turning Puhiruru and perhaps other places in Fiordland into a playground for the wealthy through changing by-laws around development and lowering rates for holiday homes. The potential issue for us is that this Unfettered Brain is continuing to gain popularity, and he's beginning to explicitly push McManus as the candidate to vote for – the person with the political experience to withstand pressure from central government and to overhaul local government from the inside. McManus himself has visited the page and promised an investigation into both the treating of drinking water with chlorine and the street lights, so he's playing along, because why not? He can only gain from doing so."

"Urh," Forest grunted. "We're screwed."

"No, we're starting at a disadvantage, my boy," said the captain. "Nothing like having a muzzle resting against your clackers to put a fire in your belly. Tactical retrograde are not words in our vocabulary."

"Ah. They're not in our vocabulary anyway?" I said.

"Beat a retreat, Jewel. No defeatist lingo of any sort shall pass your lips. Got it, everyone?"

Everyone did get it, especially Helena, who answered, "Affirmative, sir."

"Excellent. We must keep our values in mind at all times, who we stand for. We can't let the little guys down, team. We're playing for the underdog, which means this other guy will underestimate us, and if there's one mistake you never make on the battle or playing field, is to underestimate your opponent, right Rānui?"

"Absofuckinglutely."

"So, considering our values and who we represent, what are the policies I want to be pushing?"

"Affordable housing," said Rā.

"Taxes on holiday rentals," said Joe, "so there's actually somewhere for renters to rent."

Liam said, "Co-housing development. Houses on shared spaces with shared amenities."

"Like a commune?" asked Forest.

"Kind of. Get rid of elitist covenants, so the houses can be small and built of recycled material."

I said, "Community consultation on any large-scale

development," and Rā said, "Maximum housing footprints. Nobody needs a four-hundred square metre house. It's greedy and wasteful."

"Rent caps," said Harit.

Joe put a hand on his shoulder. "I'm not sure local government can control that one, my love."

"Rates means testing," said Helena. "Rates are proportionate to income."

The captain clapped his hands. "I love it. I asked for ideas and you strafed me with your thought guns. What I'm hearing is housing concerns. Is that what most people are worried about?"

"Everyone except those who don't have to," said Forest.

"Housing is the biggest change McManus wants to implement," said Joe. "He's going to disempower more people, not just the renters."

Leaning back in his chair, the captain said, "Okay, so we've got a lot of responsibility on our shoulders. There's a huge amount at stake if we're talking disenfranchisement. We need to be clear about our objective, what we represent, so we need a campaign slogan that reflects it. What's McManus' slogan?"

"Protecting the integrity of this community," I said.

"He missed a trick there," said Helena. "If he'd used 'our' instead of 'this', he'd have connected himself to his voters, implied he and they belonged to the same place."

The captain placed a finger to his lips and tapped them. "I thought 'Gunning for you'. It says I'm fighting for you and supporting you and championing you and all that good stuff."

"It also kind of has connotations of taking out a large crowd with an AK-47?" said Forest.

"Except I'd use an M2 Browning if I was going to fire on a crowd, not that I ever would. Much more effective."

"Okay. I still really really don't think we should use that slogan."

"Ooh, I know," said Helena. "What about 'Ground Zero hero'?"

"No!" I said a little too loudly. "No military allusions."

"But it's catchy." She folded her arms and added quietly, "Because it rhymes."

"It's very catchy, my lovely," said Joe. "But we don't want to push the military thing. This isn't an American political race. New Zealanders have much more mixed feelings about things military, and promoting the fact the captain's a veteran may not work in our favour."

"I don't think we should hide it," said Harit.

"We won't hide it, we just won't use it to try and attract voters."

"There's not a lot of time," said Rā. "Council want a mayor pronto, so we've only got a couple of weeks until voting closes and only a week and a half until the Meet the Candidates event. Ballot papers go out in the next few days, so we need our signs up yesterday."

"We could do one like that mug in the staff room," I said. "'F_ _k for mayor = F_ _k you white elite'."

The captain steepled his fingers and nodded. "I like it. Could be a bit base and aggressive for the average voter."

"Could we do a 'rising tide lifts all boats' type of thing?" said Helena. "'Empowering the under represented' or something?"

"You could have a clenched-fist salute in your photo," said Forest.

"We're not fighting segregation," said Joe.

"Not yet, we're not."

"What about 'For a Fiordland we can all call home'," said Liam. "It's simple, but it makes a direct stand against what McManus is campaigning for."

A silence descended on the room. It might have been awe.

"Yes!" said Helena.

The captain pointed his finger guns at Liam. "That's the one."

"And have a Māori translation," said Harit.

"Yeah," agreed Rā. "Next to the English. Not underneath it like it's secondary or an afterthought. It's so culturally patronising when they do that."

"A slogan isn't going to be enough, though," said the captain. "Not with McManus being endorsed by this Facebook guy, so what can we do to make Fink a household name?"

The room paused. Helena tapped her pen against her pad and pursed her lips. Forest pulled at a wayward thread on his work shirt. "I've got it!" he said. "A Guy Fink blimp floating above the main street. You'd be hard to ignore when you're blocking the sun."

The captain nodded. "I like it. Could be fairly expensive and take some time to make. How large are we talking?"

"You could have a Fink air dancer," said Helena. "You know, those tall wavy guys outside used car sales yards. The turn around on that would be quicker."

"It's good," said Rā. "Except for the fact they look really fucking stupid and they'll make a mockery of the captain."

"*I* like them," said Helena. "They're funny."

"Exactly."

"An ice cream truck," said Harit. "You could hand out free ice creams and tell everyone your campaign policies over the speaker."

"It would save all the door knocking," I said. "Just drive up every street."

"Who doesn't like ice cream?" said Forest.

"You guys are forgetting we're not just persuading Puhiruru voters," said Rā. "This initiative has to be district wide. You're going to do that all over Fiordland?"

"Also," said Joe, "it's a little 'bribery and propaganda rolled into one family-friendly package'. I'm not sure it's completely ethical."

"Especially for the vegans," said Helena.

Rā clapped her hands together. "Naked Liam and Jewel wearing 'Vote Fink' sandwich boards. Sex sells."

I had no idea what Liam was doing. Probably finding a dark, quiet corner of his mind palace to curl up and die in, but I was busy imagining what that might look like.

Liam was large. Sandwich boards were small. There would be a lot of exposed skin, and muscle. Muscle that flexed when moving. Muscle with defined lines and curves and planes.

"Jewel likes the idea," said Rā. She clasped my shoulder and gave it a squeeze. "Don't you, Jewel?"

"I could make it work," I said.

"McManus might spot you," said Harit. "It would compromise your mission."

The captain said, "What mission?" as Joe said, "It would compromise your *values*. We're not going to objectify people to get votes."

"McManus is doing it," said Helena.

Forest pulled his chin into his neck and frowned. "Who's he objectifying?"

"Himself."

"Gag, Helena," said Rā. "The man is not objectifying

himself because there is nothing remotely attractive about him to objectify. You need to get your eyes checked."

The captain looked at his watch. "Right. We've got five minutes 'til operation time." He looked up at us. "I appreciate all the idea throwing. I'm not sure which has stuck to the wall, but time is of the essence and I need to choose one." He tapped a finger against his lips and Joe huffed. "I do like a well-turned out sandwich board myself..."

"Right." Joe clapped his hands and stood up. "As campaign manager, I'll be taking over from here. Jewel, you'll take photos of the captain this afternoon when you finish work and have the poster finalised and off to the printer by the end of business hours. Can you do that?"

"I can do that."

"Helena, you need to write copy for a flyer drop and get it to Jewel tonight, so she can work on making it pretty. I'll be assigning streets to you all for delivery. You'll have two evenings to get your quota done."

"Two evenings?" said Forest.

"Two. Captain, can you get your Rotary colleagues to help deliver around the district?"

"I could, but Rotary's a-political. The chaps might refuse."

"You think McManus is playing by the book, essentially supporting the fear-mongering of The Unfettered Brain just to win votes? They might help when they understand what he's doing. In the meantime, you need to go door knocking. We need to convince the politically apathetic that it's within their interests to get interested. I can come with you. We need to make it clear that you are not another typical white politico. A brown face will help you get a foot in the door. We won't get around the whole district in three weeks, but if we do it every night, we can cover as much ground as we can. We'll have to rely on the pamphlets for the rest. Sound good everyone?"

Of course it sounded good. It wasn't ground-breaking or out-of-the-box thinking, but it was tried and true and sensible and the rest of us were muppets.

As everyone filed out of the room to begin the working day, Joe placed an arm across my shoulders. "Sorry about ruining your sandwich board dreams, honey girl. Want me to make it up to you by taking you out on Friday? Well, me and Forest and a couple of others, like Liam and Dana?"

It would be a Friday and I was still in my twenties, which meant it was a life requirement to go out. "Yes."

"Excellent. We're going to Invers. To Tokyo Steamroom."

Tokyo Steamroom was Invercargill's premiere gay bar and cabaret club. A night out there presumably meant a night watching Liam and Dana be a couple. Liam and Dana tripping the light fantastic in that small, closed-off world all loved-up couples seemed to have when dancing together. Liam and Dana sharing cocktails and whispering in each other's ear.

It was exactly the shot of medicine I needed and I was Ready For It.

Bring that bad boy on.

TOKYO STEAMROOM HAD both the chicness of a modern bar and the cosiness of a Victorian boudoir. Large candelabra dangled from a high ceiling supported by metal beams, and the industrial-cum-parlour look continued with brickwork walls and velvet curtains draped between booths.

When Joe, Forest and I arrived, unfashionably early at

10:00 pm and shaking rain from our hair, the place was only half full and devoid of either Liam or Dana. But with a cabaret performance scheduled in half an hour, patrons trickled in through the door in a steady stream.

I hadn't worn one of my T-shirts that evening, wanting to prove to everyone that I had more in my repertoire. I chose an off-one-shoulder, bat-wing, elbow-length top, black skinny jeans and beaded ballet flats because I didn't do heels. I wasn't a great dancer at the best of times, and giving myself the added disadvantage of raising my heels and throwing my weight forward tended to make me perform my limited dance repertoire with all the grace of a giraffe on ice, which ironically, was a cocktail Tokyo Steamroom served.

Despite my wardrobe endeavours, I was completely outshone by Joe and Forest. Joe wore a slim-fitting, cream, double-breasted three-piece suit with a dark blue shirt. And over the top of a black shirt and trousers, Forest wore an elaborate silver-ribbon-edged black jacket and skirt that belted at the waist with an open panel at the front, so that it looked like the beginnings of a train. It was, he said, an outfit that belonged to an anime character called Kirito.

They both looked incredible. I looked like I'd made eight seconds of effort.

Ten minutes before the cabaret was due to start, a Liam-less Dana edged his way into our booth, an electric blue cocktail in hand. As Dana talked through who he thought might be performing tonight, the purple layer at the bottom of the glass gradually encroached on the blue.

"What are you drinking?" asked Forest.

"A Galaxy Magic Vodka Moscow Mule. The colour changes as the ice melts."

Forest slapped his hands on the table and pushed himself up. "I'm getting one. You guys want one?"

"Yes," I said.

"Not if you want a sober driver," said Joe.

"Why didn't Liam come with you?" I asked Dana as Forest disappeared to the bar.

He laid a hand across mine, which wasn't really necessary given the total lack of gravity of the conversation. "He's here. You'll see him soon."

I peered around the room. No Liam. Perhaps he had a bathroom emergency? I swivelled my head back to face him. "You guys come here often?"

"I don't. Liam does."

"You're okay with that?"

"Sure." Dana offered both a smile and a frown, which meant something beyond my capacity for interpreting face speak. "I support him all the way."

As I wondered if open relationships were so normalised in the gay community that it would be unusual of me to question them, the music stopped, the house lights went down, and a spot light hit the centre of the stage.

The hubbub of the audience ceased, and my next question for Dana died on my lips as a leg appeared between the curtains. It was trousered, the material striped length-ways in red and orange and yellow. At the end of the leg was a red, stilettoed boot.

One finger at a time, a hand curled around the edge of the curtain. Then a top-hat of the same material as the trousers appeared, as if floating, before a face revealed itself. One of its eyes was monocled, and its lipsticked mouth formed a scarlet "O" beneath a long, waxed moustache.

The face pantomimed a resigned expression before

stepping out from the curtain and revealing the rest of the body attached to it.

Beneath the top hat was short hair, Brylcreem-ed to a wet shine. One hand rested on the top of a cane. A set of tails completed the bright suit, a suit tailored to fit the curves of the body wearing it.

A drag king.

"Ah, the colonial rabble riseth again," he drawled in an upper class English accent. "I hoped you'd all gone home, taking the bitter stench of blue collar desperation and Kardashian pipe dreams with you."

"Never, Sir Dapper," called a man in the audience, and the initiated part of the crowd, knowing their silence was part of the act, erupted into cheers and whistles.

"That's the MC," Dana said in my ear. "Frank Dapper. It's him as much as the performers that draw the punters."

"Fuuuuuck," Frank Dapper said, head sunk to chest. Then he raised his face to the ceiling. "Mother, do I have to?" He listened, then clucked his tongue and rolled his eyes. "Mother says I've been a naughty boy and I have to see out eternity in the wastes of the antipodes. Be a good little remittance man or she'll cut orf my allowance." He turned, bracing himself on his cane and waggling his bottom. "Do I look like a naughty boy to you?"

"Yes," the crowd called back.

He pivoted back around and spread his arms. "You know what I look like? The love child of an enthusiastic coupling between a dandy and a ring master."

Someone near the front shouted something.

"What's that you say, my little keening plebeian? You want me to master *your* ring?" The MC pulled a polka dotted hanky out of his breast pocket and mopped at his brow. "Oh, you colonials. You're so coarse. So –" he fanned his face with the other hand "– rough around the edges." He looked at the same man in the audience. "I suppose you're going to offer to rough up my edges in exchange for a bit of ring mastering?"

Hoots rang out around the bar.

"I must remember to write to mother and tell her I'm having thee – most – awwwful time."

Forest slid my blue cocktail towards me and I took a sip. It was at once sweet and tart, the zing of the ginger beer hitting the tip of my tongue as the sugars exploded at the back of my mouth. It was de-fucking-licious.

I told Dana, except I removed the "fucking" because I wasn't seventeen or drunk enough yet to be using expletives as extra syllables.

"I'm glad you're enjoying yourself already, gorgeous girl," he said, patting my knee, which seemed kind of...paternal? and a bit unnecessary.

Onstage, Frank Dapper had shifted gears and now smiled broadly at the audience. "Our first queen of the night needs little introduction because her reputation is so stratospheric, her name is bandied about across the galaxy. Please welcome our very own skag hag, Stellar."

The spotlight cut to bright stage lights and the curtains cinched open to expose the back of a tall male figure dressed in a business suit and Converse high-tops.

"Stella's not a very good name for a king," I whispered to Joe amid the applause.

"Stell*ar*. And just wait," he whispered back. "Prepare for your mind to be broadened."

When Amy Winehouse broke into the first refrain of 'Rehab' and the king turned around, my mind wasn't so much as broadened as split wide open as if cleaved with an axe.

I realised what I'd been witnessing the other day.

Liam was practising for his cabaret performance.

"Mein Gott," I said, standing upright and sending the icy contents of my Galaxy Magic Vodka Moscow Mule across the table.

CHAPTER TWENTY-TWO

A PAIR of hands on either side of me pulled me back into my seat and as the purple slurry of vodka and ice inched its sticky way to the edge of the table, the man on stage lip-synced a series of "No"s through a rosebud mouth. *Doll lips* beneath a mask.

I sucked in a lungful of air, but before I could do anything with it, a finger sealed my lips.

"Just watch," said Joe. "Put your fist in your mouth or something."

"But..." My brain didn't know what to do with the visual information it was receiving. The masked man in front of us was dressed as an ordinary working man might. If it wasn't for the mask. And the lips.

This was no drag king or queen as I knew it.

When a man and a woman, made up to look middle aged, appeared on stage imploring the business man, I understood what was being referenced in the song.

And I understood what was coming.

Striding to the beat of the music, the pair advanced on the business man, forcing him to the end of the runway.

He made a show of nearly teetering off, wind milling his arms. But with the next set of "No"s, he regained control. He shook his finger at the pair, taking a step towards them and loosening his tie.

When it hit the ground, the parents flinched, shielding their faces with their hands. The suit jacket was shrugged off, then the domes unpopped on the shirt in time to the beat of the song and with each act of undressing, the parents retreated to the main stage, their faces contorted in fright.

On the next "No", the business man tugged the shirt off and the mother's hands moved to cover her mouth, the father's, his eyes.

Beneath the shirt was another one. Peach-coloured with branching leaves and blue fuschia-like flowers.

The trousers were ripped off in a single flourish, like a male stripper might, and the parents turned away.

And...

The shirt...was in fact...a dress. Mid-thigh and loose, collared with cuffed sleeves. Frilled socks appeared above the top of the Converse boots.

A. Dress.

Then, as the parents cowered in front of him, the ex-business man turned to face the audience and removed his mask, and the couple fell back through the curtain, and Liam remained, illuminated in the bright eye of the spot, and the entire table gasped.

His face was exquisite.

He'd been made up to look like a doll. The skin underneath his lower lids was painted to look like his eyes were twice the size of normal ones. Lines down the sides of his nose gave the illusion of a slim, petite one, his lips were rounded and the sides of them narrowed to appear cherubic. To allow room for a dark outline to his cherry-red lips, his moustache had been trimmed, and the skin above his beard was paled to make it look as if the hair was a prosthetic. A beard wig.

And then he changed gears, moving to the music with loosened limbs, as if released. His movements were feminised, his hips swinging as a model might on the catwalk in choreography that was sure and full of attitude.

And I stop breathing.

Liam was a face-hiding, shoulder-curving introvert. The sassy doll lip-syncing about refusing to exorcise his female persona and gyrating in front of me was so far removed from the image of Liam I had in my head that my brain seethed and hummed.

I held my hands to my skull as if to keep it from peeling open and purging the pulsating cerebral mass onto the table in another sticky mess.

Dana's shouted, "Doesn't she look incredible?" did nothing but raise the humming to a high-pitched buzz.

She?

My thoughts swirled like a flock of starlings at dusk.

Liam a queen.

Stellar the woman.

Liam a she.

Liam is a woman.

But the bear.

He's a bear.

He's gay.

Oh.

My brain shuddered back into stillness.

Gay men did drag. Not all gay men, but drag was a gay expression.

I sat up in my seat. I needed to pay attention. Absorb the performance, soak my brain with the fact Liam was a homosexual man with such strong feminine tendencies he had a female persona. He was SO far off the unobtainable scale I might as well fancy him from the confines of another universe.

This. This story on stage was exactly what I needed. It was as if Liam performed it just for me.

And yet, Stellar was unlike any queen I'd ever seen before. She had no breasts and the loose dress did nothing to create an illusion of hips.

"I thought drag queens were all sequined and wigged," I whispered to Joe. My eyes dropped to the dark fuzz on Liam's legs. "And waxed."

"Cross dressing comes in all shapes and colours, my green friend. You heard Frank Dapper call her a skag hag?"

I nodded.

"Skag is a type of drag where the queen does nothing to feminise her body. No hair removal, no shape padding. Many skag queens have facial hair, like Stellar."

My mouth made an "O", but I wasn't sure any sound made it past my lips. It wasn't so much what Joe said, as the performance on stage.

Liam was mesmerising. He made full use of the stage and the short runway at its centre, appealing to the crowd to applaud his gender-crossing empowerment. Liam's body was capable of performing both the technically challenging maneouvres that required several moving parts in one beat and the subtlety of moves that isolated individual body parts.

I was dazzled.

When the final chord played out and the lights cut to black, the house erupted into cheers and whistles.

The spotlight came on and Frank Dapper stood where Liam had been. He urged the crowd to give Stellar another round of applause for her "astronomical performance" and when the clapping died down and the MC began to harry a woman in the crowd who'd dared to stand up to head to the bar just as he came back on stage, three heads leaned over the table and swivelled in my direction.

I continued to stare at the stage, at the spot Liam had thrown his final pose in.

Joe gave me a nudge.

"I just..." I said, unable to begin to articulate...well, anything.

"Bit different from everyday Liam?" Joe prompted me.

"Yeah."

"Here." Forest passed me the remains of his Galaxy Magic Vodka Moscow Mule. "Finish this."

I slugged it back and hoped the alcohol fumes burned their way through the cloudy mess in my head, so I could start to make sense of what I used to know about Liam and what I knew now.

"Think of it objectively," said Dana. "It's a performance, right? He's playing a role, a character."

I let his words seep through my brain fog. "He was amazing," I said slowly.

"Yeah, he was."

A thought wormed its way out of the fug. "Was it ironic? Is he taking the piss?"

Joe laughed. "That wouldn't be very Liam like. Can you imagine him taking the piss out of women, or men who dress as women?"

"No, not from what I know of him. Which is actually very little, apparently."

Joe leaned over and kissed me on the side of the head. "Oh, my innocent cherub. You seem so scandalised. So betrayed."

Dana said, "Liam is very serious about his performances. He might be playing a role, but it's part of who he is. Liam is a cross-dresser. He likes to dress up in women's clothes and perform as them. You'd be surprised at how many men do."

"I have," said Forest. "I already told you I went as Gamora from Guardians of the Galaxy to Armageddon last year."

"And that female Doctor Who," added Joe.

"Yeah, and Jodie Whittaker."

I turned to Dana. "You must be very proud of him."

"Sure. It's taken him a long time to get the courage to do this."

I sunk lower into my seat. "You're a good boyfriend. A better boyfriend than I would be."

Dana gave me an odd smile. "Liam's not my boyfriend, Jewel. He's my flatmate."

I frowned back at him.

"He's as straight as...a very straight thing."

"A ruler?" said Forest.

"I didn't want to be clichéd."

"But..." I looked between Dana and where Liam had been onstage.

"You think because he likes to dress and perform as a woman he has to be gay?"

"No. I mean...Wait." I put my hands to my cheeks. "I'm really confused right now. Let me just shuffle my brain around a bit." I closed my eyes, running through the bits and pieces of information I'd gleaned from comments and behaviour. I opened them again. "OK. So, you kissing him and calling him names like 'pumpkin' and 'lover' is because you're his flatmate?"

Dana shrugged. "I'm a demonstrative guy. And Liam's a close friend. It's never been an issue for him."

I slurped the last of Forest's Galaxy Magic Vodka Moscow Mule as the two halves of my brain *fallumped* open again.

"I can see how that might have been confusing for you. Believe me, Liam's only ever brought," he raised his eyes as if counting. "– A woman home. He's never once looked twice in the direction of a man and believe me –" Dana cast his eyes around the club. "– He's had plenty of opportunity here." Then he swivelled his head back to me. "Jewel."

"Yes."

"Listen very carefully. He's never allowed a girl he likes to watch him before."

If my head had been thrown into a spin already from the steady stream of revelations that evening, Dana just reached in through my ear and whirled my brain like a roulette wheel.

I felt motion drunk, like a sailor who still rolled with an imaginary ocean once on land. "He likes me?"

"It's the best performance I've ever seen him give. It's not a coincidence, Jewel. Tonight was for you."

I gripped the side of the table to steady myself. Tonight I'd been privy to the revelation Liam was a drag queen. And not only that, my belief he was gay and Dana's boyfriend had been atomised with a new truth that Liam was not only heterosexual, he wanted *me*.

On the face of it, I should be ecstatic.

I stood up. "I need to get some air."

Dana shuffled off the bench seat to let me out, but before I could walk away he grabbed my hand. "He'll come looking for you. Think through your reaction very carefully. He's made himself very vulnerable tonight."

I nodded and navigated between the tables as the next act started.

Outside, the sky had cleared to reveal a smattering of stars twinkling determinedly through the competition of street lights and illuminated windows. The wet skin of the road gleamed with the wink of neon signs and the glare of passing cars.

Placing a hand against the bar's wall to steady myself, I dragged it across the rough surface until I reached a power supply box several metres from the entrance. I hoisted myself on top of it, and as the cold soaked through my jeans, I drew my knees up to my chest and peered up at the sky as if it could somehow ground me, stop the earth beneath my curled-up form from ducking and diving.

Tonight was...a lot.

I needed to recalibrate, I don't know, everything? And come out the other side being one hundred percent cool with this new picture, because what choice did I have if I didn't want to be an arsehole?

Someone exited the club and walked up the street towards me, their shoes splashing in the small puddles in the pavement. A tall figure with a pale and billowing, short dress.

"Liam!" My heart lurched and I sat upright. The smooth soles of my ballet flats slipped off the edge of the power supply box and I nearly toppled forward. Or...should I have said..."Sorry, Stellar."

He smiled. "I'm only Stellar when I'm on stage. Off stage, I'm Liam in a dress. There room on there for me?"

"Um." My brain struggled to catch up with real time events and I shook my head as if to clear it. "Yes. You can have this bit." I shuffled sideways. "I've already dried it with my bum."

Liam squeezed on next to me, our shoulders and thighs

pressed together. Locking his elbows, he placed a palm on each knee.

He looked out over the road, waiting or thinking or both, and I studied the side of his face, ran my eyes over the intricate paint work, the expert mix of bold lines and softened contours.

"You do your own make up?"

The corner of Liam's mouth curled and he turned towards me. "I know the basics, but one of the other queens does the really difficult stuff. I'm just learning."

"You look amazing," I whispered.

Liam shifted his eyes to his hands. "Thanks," he whispered back. He took a breath, exhaled, and took another one. "I *think* I know why you're out here. There's a lot to process, and I'm guessing you have some questions for me. Beginning with a 'why' one."

"Yes."

He nodded. "Well, I've, ah, always been drawn to women's clothes and make up. Ever since I was a little boy. My older sister would dress me up to be her doll or her fellow princess or whatever and we'd play for hours. I loved it and that desire to continue playing dress ups never left me." He smoothed out the bottom of his dress. "I don't want to be a woman or anything. I just...like to wear their clothes from time to time."

It sounded too simple. I opened my mouth to speak, but before I could, Liam said, "But Stellar isn't just about dress ups. Stellar exists for a number of reasons."

I could guess one. I'd branded my entire business with it. "She's empowering."

"Yeah, she is. When I get on that stage, I feel invincible. Stellar's...Stellar's like a layer of impermeable skin, the bold, I-don't-give-a-fuck person I'm not. And since she's come into my life, I'm more confident. But –" Liam rocked from one buttock to the other as if finding a more comfortable spot. "– It's also partly sexual. Not like a kink thing, more that...I feel sexy wearing feminine clothes."

"You don't feel sexy in masculine clothes?"

"I don't think many heterosexual men do, unless they're the medallion, open shirt-front types. Women can, like, bare some skin and wear figure-revealing clothes and feel sexy. Most straight guys don't even *think* about looking sexy. It's not in our mindset. We think about looking *good*. And...I want more than that."

"And...do women find you sexy?"

"One or two who are, I don't know, bi-sexual? Have sexual fluidity? But it's not so much about other people finding me sexy, it's about how *I* feel."

I ran the bottom of his dress between my thumb and forefinger. "I like your style."

"Thanks."

"It's cute and feminine. But not what a lot of women would choose to look sexy."

"Not figure hugging and skin revealing?"

"Yeah."

Liam bumped his shoulder against mine. "You're not wearing a tight dress tonight and I think you look..." He waved his hand up and down my body as the conclusion to his sentence.

I thought I knew what he meant, but I wanted to check anyway. "What?"

"You know. Sexiness can be subtle. Your jeans hug your curves, your top reveals the skin of one shoulder. It's alluring. And," he dropped his voice. "Sort of very sexy."

A ball of light unfurled behind my belly button and seeped under my ribcage.

"I know I'm a bit unusual. A lot of drag queens make their performances quite sexualised. They present a particular gender stereotype for comic effect. That's not my bag." He nudged my thigh with his leg. "If I was a woman, I would want to be...more like you."

I did a little internal "Squeeee" and nudged him back.

A car passed with a *shhh* of displaced water.

"Do you cross dress at home?"

"Sometimes."

I waited for him to say more and when he didn't, I said, "Dana says I'm the first woman you're interested in that you've allowed to see Stellar perform."

Liam swivelled his head to watch a passing car before answering. "It's just..." He exhaled heavily. "I have to be careful. Not all women understand the desire to cross dress, because I don't fit in with what their idea of being a man is."

I understood that. I wasn't about to say it though, because if I did it might be an expression of how I felt and I didn't want to feel that.

"I think some women find it threatening. Like they're not enough or perhaps their man isn't happy with his gender. But you –" He turned his head to look at me. "You are so fierce in your gender identity and so unapologetic about who you are. I knew, I mean, I hoped you'd be open to accepting this part of me."

Right. So that was what shame felt like. A curling up of your insides, a backwards scrabble from the Jewel who made that decision in that moment.

Liam had so much faith in me that he opened up the most vulnerable part of himself to my scrutiny and what did I do? I excused myself and walked out the door before he had a chance to gauge my reaction.

It must have felt awful to have given his best performance, for me, and then find that I'd left immediately afterwards.

"I'm sorry I wasn't in there for you when you came from back stage."

Liam mirrored my pose, pulling his knees towards his chest. "You know one of the reasons I do this is for validation? That finally, after twenty years desiring something heteronormative society tells me is wrong, I have absolutely nothing to be ashamed of?" He smiled and his eyes flicked to mine before refocusing on the shop over the road. "I stopped playing dress ups with girls' clothes when I was teased by my friends. I never talked about it with *anyone* since for fear of judgement and rejection. Now...I'm making up for lost time. Stellar is an expression of that hurt and confused little boy. But none of that's on you, Jewel. I'm not going to snap my fingers and expect you to accept all this –" he gestured to his clothes "– in an instant. I know you'll understand in your own time."

I thought I probably could, but, quite honestly, I didn't have the same level of confidence. When Liam looked at me he saw something different to the sometimes disappointing person I saw when I looked in the mirror.

The best I could do was, maybe, try to live up to it?

As we sat down next to Forest and Joe and Dana to watch the rest of the cabaret, I reached across in the dark space between our thighs and sheathed my hand inside Stellar's, lacing my fingers through hers.

CHAPTER TWENTY-THREE

"I'M MAKING a few hundred dollars a week on T-shirts." I sat in an outdoor chair wedged into the pebbles of the lake's shallows. A mist rolled down the valleys to the north-east and spilled onto the lake, its ragged edges like fingers feeling their way over the surface.

"Whoa. Hold the phone," Dad said. "Did you hear that Rewa? My daughter. The multi-hundred-making business woman."

It sounded better when I said it, but I was. It wasn't enough to give up my job at the mart, but I was on the cusp of bringing in more money than I was earning there, and it meant I could finally afford to pay Brooke and Kaitlyn out.

"I heard it, my lover." She said, "I'll get the glasses," as Dad said, "I think this calls for a Green Ginger Wine Moment."

I already had the crib's bottle to hand and tipped out two shots' worth into the glass nestled between my thighs.

"How have you managed it, Jewelsy? I mean, I'm not surprised you're – what do you kids say – *killing it*, you being a genius and all, but have you done something different to crack the market?"

"TikTok."

Silence.

Rewa said, "Why are you impersonating a clock? Or are you just being a smart arse?"

"TikTok's a social media platform. Like Instagram, but for video."

"Insta-what?"

"You know Youtube?"

"Of course," said Dad, like I'd asked him if he knew water quenches thirst. "It's how I watch pirated copies of my favourite BBC shows. You have to be quick though, before they take them down."

"TikTok is a video platform, too, but for fifteen second videos. I've been posting some of me wearing my T-shirts and doing crazy stuff and it's been driving traffic to my Instagram page, which has been driving traffic to my online shop. T-shirt sales have gone through the roof. Admittedly a pretty low one, but I'm selling at least twenty a day."

"Did you hear that, Rewa? Twenty a day."

"No, I'm trying to download the TikTok app on my phone. I can't listen and type at the same time."

Nobody said anything to allow her to concentrate.

Dad took a sip of his wine. His slurp was loud and wet in my ear.

"How do I find your videos?"

"Search for Extreme Shero."

"Ex-treeme She-ro," said Rewa, sounding each syllable out as she typed. "Huh. You've done quite a few. 104,000 followers!"

"That sounds like a lot, Jewelsy. Let me see."

A death metal riff distorted in my phone's speakers.

"Are you ironing while balanced on a motorised scooter?" asked Rewa.

"Who's that man you're straddling?" asked Dad.

"Mr Hardacre. And I'm not straddling him, I'm standing on the back of his chair."

"Looks like a straddle to me," said Rewa. "If he looked up, he'd see what you had for breakfast."

"I don't eat with my vagina, Rewa."

"Ladies!" said Dad. Then, "Are you *head banging?*"

"Is that...?" Faltered Rewa. "He's giving a devil horn salute, isn't he?"

"Ah." I screwed my face up and wondered why she couldn't have chosen a safer one. Like the burnout video. "Yes he is."

"That poor man," said Rewa.

"It was his idea."

"He looks too old to have ideas like that," said Dad.

"He installed the first computer in New Zealand in 1961."

"Ahhh," they chorused, as if that explained everything.

The music ended and a silence descended.

"Well," said Dad after five long seconds.

"Indeed," said Rewa.

"It's fun," I said.

"If it's selling your T-shirts..." said Dad.

"But why *ironing?*" said Rewa.

I took a sip of the sticky syrup and smacked my lips. "Not just any ironing. *Extreme* ironing. It's a worldwide phenomenon. Groups of people jump out of planes and iron in formation."

"You're kidding."

"No. I'm not kidding."

"Please don't jump out of a plane," said Dad.

"Okay." I scratched my nose. "You might not want to watch any of my other videos."

Another silence descended.

Somebody slurped at their wine.

"So," said Rewa.

"Yep," I said, though I had no idea what I had just agreed to or confirmed, as it was simply a word to help fill the verbal emptiness.

"What else has been happening, Jewelsy? Anything interesting going on in the hood?" Dad said, like the Puhiruru lake front was some sort of middle class ghetto.

"Yes." I wasn't about to play the "Guess what Brian McManus is up to now?" game, given Rewa's history for wildly stabbing in the dark and getting it right first time. So, I gave it to them straight. "Brian McManus is running in the local by-election for mayor."

"You're joking," said Rewa.

"Nope. He's not in yet, but he's trying very hard to manipulate the voting populace into thinking they need him."

Rewa sighed. "I really thought he'd run off with his political tail between his legs after his humiliating defeat here. Obviously not."

"He's had a taste of power," said Dad. "I bet it's highly addictive."

I didn't actually want to talk about it with them, but it was a handy stalling tactic for discussing the thing I'd *really* rung them about. "I have some other news."

"*More* news?" said Dad, like I'd brought out the bottle of dessert wine after a five-course meal.

"It's not the Transformer *or* the Barbie Doll, it's the Transformer *and* the Barbie Doll."

"Is that the riddle you couldn't solve, Jewelsy?" said Dad.

"Yeah."

"The 'and' doesn't make it any clearer," said Rewa.

I attempted to clarify. "Do you think guys get a bum deal with the types of clothes they're allowed to wear?"

And evidently failed.

"You've lost me," said Dad.

"Women can wear skirts and dresses as well as shorts and trousers. Men don't have the same freedom of expression. Unless you're Scottish or a Pacific Islander."

"I'm not sure. I don't feel like I'm missing out, but I've never had the chance to feel the wind up my skirt, feathering my whatsit. And I buggered up any chance of that six years ago."

"But would you, if you *did* have the chance?"

"I don't know. I guess so, if it was normal."

"See, there's the thing. Men don't feel they can wear dresses because it's 'not normal'. Women don't have the same dilemma. At least, not any more."

"But they can get criticised for looking *too* masculine. For being 'butch'," said Rewa.

"What's this all about, Jewelsy?"

I took a deep breath. "How would you feel if I brought home a man in a dress?"

"The gay one?" asked Dad.

"He isn't gay. I got that wrong. He likes me, and he also likes to wear dresses."

"And have you definitely got that part right?" asked Dad.

"Oh yes. I'm one hundred percent sure about that."

I shivered at the cold air the mist pushed before it.

"And how do *you* feel about him wearing dresses?" asked Rewa.

"I don't know. I want to be okay with it. It's just so far out of my experience. I can't look at him and be dress blind."

"Not yet, you can't," said Rewa. "It's just different. Do you look at me and see brown?"

"No. Maybe when I first met you. I can't remember thinking 'she's Māori', but I probably did."

"Wait," said Dad. "You're Māori? All this time and I thought you were just from solid Sardinian fishing stock."

"You're an idiot," said Rewa, a smile in her voice. "The same thing'll happen with your man and dresses, Jewel. Just be patient."

"I'm assuming you like him back, Jewelsy?"

"I like him back."

A *pop*, like someone had clapped, issued from the speaker and I jumped.

"You know what this calls for, Rewa?"

"Indeed I do. I'll do the honours for the second glass."

A series of glugs issued down the phone.

"Okay," said Rewa, "I can't contain it any longer."

Here it came. I braced myself for the blast.

"THERE'S A BOY. DALE, THERE'S A BOY."

"There is," agreed Dad, "at long last, a boy."

"When do we get to meet him?"

"Oh my God. I haven't even kissed him yet. At least wait until I've done that."

"Well, hurry up. How come you haven't kissed if you both like each other and you both know you like each other?"

"All in good time, aye, Jewelsy?"

"Yes. He's not the type to be rushed into things. It took him three weeks to look me in the eye."

"Does he...wear dresses all the time?" asked Dad.

"No. I've only ever seen him in one when he was kind of playing a role, but I think he'd like to wear them more."

"Is he, what do they call them?" said Rewa.

The line went very quiet.

"Gender fluid!"

"I don't think so. I think he firmly identifies as male. It's his dress style that's gender fluid."

"Huh," said Rewa.

"Interesting," said Dad.

"I know," I said.

"Well, if it's taken you this long to ring home about a boy, he must be worth wrapping your brain around the cross-dressing thing for."

I thought so too. How someone so beautiful could look at me and see the same beauty, I had no idea, but he did. Which meant that every time a text had come in from Liam over the weekend, my organs flopped around under my skin like a fish that had been pulled from its underwater world.

I'd never reacted in any kind of excited way to words before and I wasn't sure if I was completely Team Romantic Feels. I liked the rush. I didn't like the feeling of not having control over it.

There wasn't anything I could do about exploring this uncharted territory. Liam had family commitments the whole weekend and we'd have to wait until Monday to see each other again to find out if it had all been a terrible mistake.

IT TURNED out it hadn't all been a terrible mistake.

At least, I'm pretty sure having your brain turn to a soupy mess and your tongue forgetting how to turn sound into decipherable syllables whenever the guy who held hands with you two days previously came near meant it hadn't all been a terrible mistake.

Liam's tongue wasn't working either. Instead, his chosen expression of communication was a poke in the ribs whenever his route to the stock room required him to walk down the aisle I worked in, which was pretty much every time he needed to restock. His route had never been via my aisle before.

It was very childish.

And kind of wonderful?

Horrifyingly, I chose to express this by alternating between shrieking and giggling.

However, the mid-morning arrival of Mr Hardacre threw a cold bucket of "snap to your senses" over all the gooeyness.

He rolled up to me at a speed entirely inappropriate for a narrow supermarket aisle and braked with a violence that set his chin skin wobbling. "He's clean."

It took me five long seconds to calibrate to this new non-Liam context.

Mr Hardacre narrowed his eyes at me like I was some kind of imbecile, which, given the morning's carry on, was only fair.

"You've got nothing on McManus?"

"No Ponzi schemes, no business fronts for laundering money, not even a sext from a mistress. On paper he's an upstanding citizen. His tax is all in order. His businesses are legit."

"Shit." This wasn't what I expected. I thought Mr Hardacre would be our magic bullet, to find the vulnerability in the McManus armour.

"No business deals with developers that would mean a monstrous conflict of interest?"

"If there are, he's not holding any records of them."

"Bugger. So we've got nothing."

Mr Hardacre shrugged. "Doesn't mean the game's over. Just means you have to play harder, especially with what's been going on on Facebook in the last half hour."

"What's been going on?"

"The Unfettered Brain's gunning directly for your boss. Saying he's ex-military and the state are supporting his candidacy because they want to militarise Fiordland."

"You have to be joking. No one in their right mind would fall for that."

AS IT HAPPENED, plenty of people in Puhiruru functioned on a completely different level than their right mind. The post-mid-morning-yoga-class/baby-group/book-club/pensioner-zumba rush was half its usual strength, which raised the concern that half of Puhiruru was under the spell of The Unfettered Brain. If so, how long would their boycott last? Because losing half our customers would severely affect the business. It might mean that not only was our ability to call Puhiruru "home" at stake, but our jobs might be, too.

We'd have to wait and see.

As the last Zumba-loving pensioner exited the shop, a flushed and ecstatic Helena spread-eagled herself against the glass of the automatic doors. She forced herself through before they'd barely opened enough to let her do so and stood panting, hands on hips. "Is it still adultery if your husband's only purpose in life is to be a sack of meat?" A large, brown and still-wet stain covered the front of her white shirt. The material clung to the heaving rounds of her breasts.

Joe walked up to her and placed an arm over her shoulders. "Firstly, my heart, having your husband as your authorial muse is probably not reason enough to put up with him. And secondly, who are you adulterating with?"

Her hands slipped from her hips. "Oh no. I'm not adulterating with anyone yet. I'm just putting it out to the universe for consideration."

"Right. Yes, it would be adultery."

"And thirdly," said Rā. "Why do you look like you've been in a cross between a mud wrestling match and a wet T-shirt competition?"

Helena looked down at her front and pulled her shirt away from her breasts with a *shluck*. "Oh this! I bumped into Brian McManus. Literally. Tipped his entire take away trim latte down my cleavage. I'd like to think it was an accident, but I can't be sure on either of our parts. Took him twelve serviettes to staunch the worst of it." She laid a hand against her forehead. "I've been in a bit of a swoon ever since."

"I hope you took the opportunity to place incriminating evidence in his pockets or something," I said from where I stacked herbal teas on a display at the end of aisle four. I didn't want to have to resort to dirty tactics. Okay, dirtier tactics than we were already using, but at this point, all options were on the table.

"Why would I do that?"

"Because he's the opposing candidate?" said Rā. "We don't want him to win, remember? Or have your misguided lady parts swallowed your brain?"

"Not that we would resort to planting evidence," said Joe. "Right, Jewel?"

"Right," I muttered. By now, the team knew about Mr Hardacre's failure to secure anything that would hamstring the McManus campaign and that the entire success of the captain now rested on us. Typical.

"My lady parts are in my pants where I left them, thank you very much."

"Look hon." Joe took a step backwards, holding her hands and pulling them out from her sides as you would someone in a beautiful dress. "You've at least proved that you are spectacular in translucent clothes, no matter what the liquid."

Helena beamed. "Do you think Brian thought *spectacular* when he tried to sponge me down?"

Joe dropped her hands. "I wouldn't pin my hopes on it, my love. Judging from his marital standards, he prefers women who bear an uncanny resemblance to a blow up doll."

"Oh," Helena said, her mouth an unconscious mimicry of said doll. "Do they make plus size sex dolls?"

"Helena!" growled Rā. "The man is a power-hungry arse. If he didn't shower in Hugo Boss he'd probably smell like arse, too."

Helena's eyes widened. "But he's so magnetic. And he fondled my breasts."

"He dabbed at spilt coffee with napkins. Your breasts just happened to be in the way."

Fortuitously, or arguably fortuitously, Liam put an end to the conversation by sneaking up behind me and tickling my ribs. The screech I emitted made everyone jump and plug their ears, which meant that half an hour before I knocked off for the day, the team petitioned Liam and me to do something about the incessant squawking and giggling.

The options presented to us were: go on a date, release our tension on the 20 kg bags of rice out the back, get married already.

So, I made an attempt to put everyone out of their misery. It went something like this:

"Hi."

"Hey."

"Um. Do you wanna, like..."

"Do I wanna, like, what?" Rib poke.

Shriek-giggle. "I don't know, like...hang out?"

"Yeah."

"At, like, mine, or something?"

"Okay."

"Like, tonight?"

"Yeah."

"Like, eight? Or something?"

"Okay."

"I'll get some wine. Or, you know, like, whatever you want to drink."

"I like wine."

"Me too."

"Cool."

...

"OK. Well, see you then."

"Yeah. See you then."

So. Yeah.

Clumsy, but effective?

Thankfully I didn't have too much time to torment myself about how many "like"s I could fit into a single conversation, as McManus called a meeting for that afternoon.

WITH EIGHT DAYS until the close of the election, Jess and I were once again required to fight motion sickness by watching McManus pace backwards and forwards while he "thought big".

Bekka leaned over the kitchen island that was almost as big as my entire kitchen and watched with an expression of ....

Let me start that sentence again.

Bekka leaned over the kitchen island that was almost as big as my entire kitchen and watched.

"I want to keep the momentum of the popularity this Unfettered Brain is creating for me. Jewel, let's get some sappy emotive publicity images I can use on my own social media, which is getting more and more attention every day. I don't have time for the inconvenience of a photo shoot, so I want you to find pictures of a white guy holding babies and shaking hands with brown people and just Photoshop me in. Give me an ethnic buffet to choose from and make sure there's some Chinks in there too. They're business people. They'll tick the McManus box if we can sucker them in with some good old fashioned image manipulation."

"It won't work," I said.

"Why won't it work? I've seen what you're capable of. Bah-loody make it work."

"I'd need photos of your face at the right angle, and in the same light as the other people in the photo. It would be easier if you hired some babies and did an actual photo shoot."

McManus stopped pacing and sighed. He looked at me for a few seconds. "Do you know any brown people?"

Yes. But I wasn't going to coerce them to help promote him. "No."

"See? That's the thing, isn't it? White liberals can bleat on all they like about equity, but at the end of the day they don't actually have anything to do with brown people because in reality they move in entirely different circles, which they're secretly happy about. It's all just tokenism."

"My cousin's got a three-month old baby," Jess said brightly.

"Is it brown or yellow?"

"Ah. It's kind of pink."

"Organise a meeting anyway. Now, I've read Fink's candidate statement. He's pushing community and family values, and some socialist clap trap like affordable housing. It might persuade some of our more left-leaning Unfettered Brainers. Have you dug anything else up on him, Jess? Anything that we could use against him."

I didn't even bother narrowing my eyes at her. There wouldn't be anything.

"There is a report of him double parking outside the bakery two weeks ago to purchase –" she looked at her notes. "– A mince and cheese pie."

"Inconsequential. Give me something good."

"Oh, um." Jess scrolled through her tablet. "Well, one of his neighbours told me he had his sprinkler going on his garden for ten minutes after the stipulated 8 pm shut off time during last summer's water restrictions?"

"No, no, no. We're not looking for minor by-law infractions. We want something juicy. Like he has a criminal record for embezzlement or he has a wife on every continent."

"Okay." Jess carefully placed her tablet on the table and said with decreasing volume. "I think he might actually just be an average guy with no...juicy...ness."

"Well, no matter. We've got him where we want him, which is lagging behind in popularity so much he'd need binoculars to see how far ahead I am."

How could he know that? "Have they done preliminary polls?"

McManus snorted. "There's no budget, or frankly,

interest for that. We don't need them. I have the perfect tool to test the temperature of the general populace. Social media. And my popularity is soaring. I don't even have to try. Thanks to the Unfettered Brain, my posts are getting so many impressions and likes and comments that the Facebook algorithms are doing the work for me in getting them in front of people. Facebook's like the Nor'east-er to my wild fire. Right, Bekka?"

"Exponential organic growth, darling."

"What are you doing about the younger demographic?" I asked. "The twenty-somethings who aren't on Facebook?"

McManus flapped a hand. "Not concerned. They're the group with the largest apathy towards local elections. Not worth wasting time on. Has Fink got a Facebook page?"

"Facebook, Instagram, and Twitter," said Jess.

"Spreading himself a bit thin. What's his follower numbers?"

Jess tapped on her screen. "One hundred and fourteen on Facebook, fifty-six on Instagram, and nine on Twitter."

"*Nine*. See? This is why you concentrate on one platform and do it well. What are my followers at now, my love?"

Bekka pulled her phone along the marble bench top towards her. "One thousand, five hundred and forty one."

I crumbled a little inside.

"Not quite at the levels of this brain chap, but I think we can confidently say we've got this election in the bag."

CHAPTER TWENTY-FOUR

I IMMEDIATELY GOT HOME from the meeting and started wearing my own hole in the carpet. I had two things pressing on my mind and I couldn't decide which required more brain space. One was slightly less self-interested than the other: How were we going to play catch up to McManus's popularity? The problem was the more I tried to tackle that issue, the more the other shouted its way over the top, which meant my thoughts were a little fractured and therefore solutions were hard to find:

How on earth are we going to get Fink to be a household name?

LIAM'S COMING OVER.

We've got less than two weeks before the election closes. It's a postal ballot. People can already vote.

EEEEEEEEEEEEEEK.

There's no time. We have to do something momentous that outshines McManus, or we need to take him down.

I AM VERY VERY VERY VERY VERY NERVOUS. And just a tiny bit EXCITED.

How is the objectionable, megalomaniac fucker not take-

downable? He's an awful person. He cannot be squeaky clean.

HE MIGHT WEAR A DRESS.

We'll have to play him at his own social media game. Get Mr H back on board.

AM I GOING TO BE COOL WITH IT?

Get into the Unfettered Brain account and control the content. Yes. We have to do that.

I'M NOT. HE'S GOING TO FEEL JUDGED AND LEAVE AND NEVER WANT TO SEE ME AGAIN AND I'LL FEEL LIKE A MASSIVE ARSEHOLE AND I'LL NEVER KNOW WHAT IT FEELS LIKE TO HAVE MY BEEF FLAPS TENDERISED BY A SLAB OF CONCRETE. BUT MOSTLY I'LL FEEL LIKE AN ARSEHOLE.

I decided to go for a calming walk around the lake edge, only remembering to put my beanie and glasses back on as I pulled on the back door.

I got home around dinner time and cracked the fridge to begin the mental challenge of what to cook for dinner. Its yawning emptiness met me.

Fuck.

Despite working in the perfect environment for memory jogging about purchasing groceries, I had neglected to do so for several days, because I suffered from moronitis.

I took stock. Half an anaemic-looking broccoli head, four slices of bread including both crusts, some sun-dried tomatoes, five lonely-looking capers floating in the bottom of a jar and a heel of mouldy cheese. A palatable dinner would require pulling a culinary miracle.

I set to work surgically removing the green fuzz on the cheese.

I'd just put my creation into the oven, when someone knocked on the door.

Scrambling to put the beanie and glasses on in case it was McManus, I put my hand on the snib to unlock the door.

The shape through the textured glass was far too tall for McManus. My heart imploded and then tried to hammer the pieces back into place.

"Liam?"

"Yeah. I'm, um, very early."

Sweet Mary's tears he was. It was only just gone six. I wasn't ready. I wasn't anywhere near ready.

"Just...give me a minute." I scampered off to the bedroom to turn around in circles.

Then I thought better of it and pulled the curtains closed so Liam couldn't watch me freaking out or see me strip down to my underwear once I'd thought my way through a casual but subtly suggestive outfit. I couldn't even go to the bathroom to brush my teeth and put make up on. Why would he turn up so early and not warn me?

I peered down at myself. I wore high-waisted jeans, a black long-sleeved shirt and bare feet. I pulled off the beanie and glasses, swapped out the shirt for a striped one, put in a pair of hooped earrings, and slapped my cheeks for colour. It was the best I could do with a limited time frame and resources.

Then I ran back to the door, sucked in two lungfuls of air, and opened it.

Liam was not wearing a dress. He had on a raglan sleeve T-shirt and black jeans. His hair was tied up so that his face was free from its usual shadows.

He was crushingly beautiful. I felt a little breathless under the weight of it.

"I'm really sorry. Eight o'clock was too long to wait." He thrust a container in my hands. "In case you haven't eaten."

Shit. I whipped around, made a dash for the oven, and peered inside to make sure my dinner hadn't caught fire. It hadn't. I turned the oven off.

"Smells good."

I unclipped the lid of the container. Schnitzel. "Oh, thank fuck. I only have fridge dregs."

"Can I, ah, come in?"

I turned around. Liam stood just outside the door, his hands in his pockets.

God, I was useless. "Yes, sorry. Come in." I waved an arm in invitation.

He took a step inside and peered around the door, his hands still in his pockets. "Whoa. This place is an epic nod to the sixties. It's like a time capsule."

"It's not by design or anything. Mostly neglect and lack of money."

"It's really cool."

"Yeah, I like it. Which is just as well, because I can't do anything about it at the moment."

Liam nodded.

And stared at me.

"Do you want to close the door?"

"Oh, yeah." He turned and snibbed it very carefully and softly, and then we were in a world all of our own. It was much more terrifying than being in the enclosed space of his car with him. Now that our feelings were out in the open, there seemed to be more at stake.

He stared at me again.

I didn't mind that much, but I wasn't entirely sure why. His view wasn't anywhere near as appealing as mine of him.

He grinned. "Sorry. I'm really nervous." Then the grin was gone and he looked at the floor.

"I think we need some help." I squatted to retrieve the bottle of green ginger wine from the cupboard and poured an inch into two sherry glasses. Handing him a glass, I downed mine and watched his very lickable Adam's apple bob as he swallowed. "Better?"

"Can I have another one?"

I thoughtfully waited until he was in the middle of tipping his second glass back to say, "I thought you might be wearing a dress."

Liam swallowed and coughed. Moisture gathered in his eyes and he thumped a hand to his chest. "I, um —" he put a fist to his mouth and swallowed again. "I tend to only wear dresses in places they're normalised. I mean, where a man wearing a dress is normalised. At the moment. I'm not ready for anywhere else."

"Like Tokyo Steamroom?"

"And madi gras, festivals, not that those opportunities come up that often. How would you have felt if I *was* wearing a dress?"

"I don't know. Hopefully cool about it. I want to be cool about it, but it's very different. There'd be a bit of recalibrating."

"Yes."

"There shouldn't have to be."

"No. But we've had a lifetime of being conditioned that men wear pants."

I knew what that was called, so I said, "Gender normative discourse," in the hope of impressing him.

He smiled and said, "Exactly," which probably meant he was?

"Do you wanna...sit down or something?" I gestured towards the kitchen table.

"Actually, can I...?" He pointed through the bedroom doorway.

"Sure. Don't get lost. Take your phone with you just in case."

Hovering in the door frame, he asked, "Do you sleep in the bunks or the double bed?"

"Guess."

"If I was you, I'd sleep in the top bunk. But that's just because I haven't been able to fit in a bunk bed without a shoe horn since I was sixteen."

"I don't think you'd fit very easily in the double bed either."

He disappeared and mattress springs squeaked.

"You're right."

I followed to find him lying on the bed, his feet dangling off the end. "People were shorter in the sixties."

My feet were nowhere near the edge when I lay down on it. "How do you get women's clothes to fit?"

"Plus size. Forest takes them in for me. Sometimes he has to lengthen them too." He sat up. "Where's the bathroom?"

I walked over to the window, pulled open the curtains and beckoned him with my finger. "Behold."

Liam didn't say anything for a moment. "That must be character building."

"The novelty wears a bit thin when you have to beat your way through the grass you neglected to mow to get to the toilet. And by dubious lamp light because you forgot to replace the batteries."

"Come on. You wee on the lawn in the middle of the night. I saw the bald patches."

There were no bald patches, but I did wee on the lawn to save braving the long drop in the black of night. "The en-suite's going to have a bath you can roll outside and soak in by star light."

"Minimum requirement."

"I should probably prioritise a flushing toilet."

"But a bath by starlight..."

Liam was so close, if I leant a centimetre to the left, our arms would touch. The air crackled in the small gap. Not literally. But whatever was happening in the tiny space between us, was distracting and I momentarily forgot how to add words to his.

Liam did not have the same problem. "So. What did you cook?"

"I'm going to ambitiously call it 'gourmet cheese on toast'." I pushed away from the window and edged past him towards the door. "I would like to say, 'a sixties' classic', but I have no idea if it was or not."

Liam magnanimously did not question the extent of my culinary abilities. Instead, he said, "I love doctoring cheese on toast. It's like cheat pizza." Admittedly, it was after a short pause in which he was, no doubt, gathering his generosity.

I reached for the container on the kitchen bench. "Do you have a particular way of cooking these?"

"I can do it. I'm well practised." He stood very very close to me and my thoughts stuttered to a stop while my pulse roared from first to second gear. He smelled of lemons and temptation.

"What?" I said when my olfactory system calmed down enough for my hearing to return.

"Where's your oil? And a pan."

Pulling them out of various cupboards, I busied myself pouring the wine I *had* remembered to buy earlier that day.

"I, ah, added cornflakes to the crumb mix like you said."

"Yum," I said, because that was all my brain was capable of producing while watching a man capably handle food at my stove. A man cooking shouldn't be sexy. We lived in liberated, gender equality-ed times and a man doing a domestic chore should be normalised and incapable of rousing anything other than hunger pains.

And yet, my temperature rose several degrees and I had to turn around and place the cold wine bottle against my cheeks and hope he didn't notice I was melting into a little pile of pathetic.

The pan sizzled. "It shouldn't take long to cook."

I turned back around and handed him his wine glass.

"We should eat your cheat pizza as an entrée before it gets cold."

We probably shouldn't. "I can't guarantee it's quality."

Liam pulled the tray out of the oven and sniffed deeply. "Smells good. Looks questionable."

"I've run out of food. This is improvised."

He nodded. "Fridge dregs. Good game that. Calls on your powers of invention. And desperation." He smiled at me. "I'm...game if you are."

I decided not to tell him about the cheese and retrieved two plates.

Once seated at the table, I watched with something akin to morbid fascination as Liam took a bite.

He crunched through a piece of warmed but entirely uncooked broccoli. "It's an interesting flavour combination with the sun-dried tomatoes and the capers, but I like it. Tangy and salty."

I didn't quite manage to bite down on my tongue before "Just like me" popped out.

Liam eyed me for a second, flushed an alarming shade of crimson, and choked on a broccoli floret. His cough sent it skittering across the top of the table where it hit the edge of the chrome and spun itself out.

We stared at it for a bit.

Eventually, Liam kind of giggled? which may have been nerves and was somewhat charming coming from such a large man. He said, "Can't waste it," and popped the piece of broccoli into his mouth.

"No," I agreed, the giggle catching. "That's an eighth of a fridge dreg. Worth its weight in gold in a food-starved house."

"Best thing worth two hundred dollars I've ever had on my tongue."

"You've had others?"

His smile froze, his cheeks coloured again and he got up to turn the schnitzel.

So, I attempted to dispel his embarrassment by saying something comforting and, "I thought you were gay," popped out.

Liam prodded at the meat with a spatula. "Dana told me."

"He kissed you and called you 'pumpkin'. What else was I going to think?"

There wasn't really anything for him to do at the stove except watch the meat cook, but he didn't turn around. "I...thought my interest in you was pretty obvious." Meat prod. "I felt like a bumbling idiot every time I went near you." He risked a quick glance at me. "How could you not have noticed?"

"I thought that was you being normal."

Liam's shoulders gave a little shake like he was crying, but I thought it more likely to be a silent laugh. "Yeah," he said on a sigh. "I can see how you thought that."

I took a bite of my cheese on toast. It wasn't actually that bad once you got over the shock of the crunchy broccoli. "Did you think I might like you?" I said through a mouthful.

"I saw you staring a couple of times. I guess I hoped rather than thought." He brought the pan to the table and tipped the schnitzel onto our plates.

I wasn't surprised. "I have done a lot of staring at you."

Locating cutlery in a drawer, Liam sat back down at the table. "I wasn't sure after you said you never ever wanted to see me dancing again ever, though."

Sawing at the schnitzel, I said, "Do you know what you look like when you're dancing?"

"No."

"If I hadn't run away, I would have thrown myself at your feet and offered to birth your children."

He raised his brows. "Oh."

"And because I thought you were gay, I had to run away. Escape my body's reaction to your body."

After a beat, Liam said, "Right."

My teeth *clink*ed against the tines of my fork as I pulled the piece of schnitzel off. It was good. Liam had cooked it for just the right amount of time before it got chewy. The hum emerged involuntarily like a cat purring beneath stroking fingers and Liam smiled at me.

I washed the mouthful down with a sip of wine. "I didn't ask you to help with the TikTok videos because they weren't just about T-shirt sales. They were about distracting myself from you."

Liam's head jerked up, fork in his mouth. He chewed hurriedly and swallowed. "Really?"

"Yes."

His lips tugged upwards. "Cool."

AFTER LIAM HAD INSISTED on doing the washing up and I watched him from behind my wine glass, I said, "Wanna see my tricks?" and walked into the bedroom without waiting for an answer.

The bunk beds were metal with a rounded rail on the top one designed to prevent sleepers from rolling into the void. I grabbed it, put my feet on the top bed's frame, and hooked my legs over the rail to dangle, hands trailing on the carpet. "I used to be small enough that I could get a bit of a swing going." I locked my arms and pushed away from the bunks with my legs so that I dismounted like a gymnast. When I straightened, I threw my hands into the air and bowed to the imaginary crowds to my left and right.

Liam clapped from his seat on the double bed. "What else can you do?"

"I'm so glad you asked," I said, already climbing onto the top bunk. "Be prepared to be amazed." I held on to the bar, pushed my torso out and over it and flipped to the floor.

He held up nine fingers. "That's for technique. You get eight of ten for difficulty."

"Eight?" I said, climbing back up on to the top bunk. "Robbed. You might want to get out of the way."

Liam narrowed his eyes. "Why?"

"Do you want to see my corkscrew flip or my triple back?"

"How old is this bed?"

"1600s. Made when beds were the singular heirloom. Designed to last a millennium."

Liam leaned back and surveyed it with a finger to his

lips. "I'm not convinced. You could be impaled by a wayward spring."

"Only one way to find out." I launched myself into the space between the two beds as Liam scrabbled to his feet, and landed a starfish with a *whoomf*.

"Holy shit, my stomach just dropped through my feet. That was the most terrifying thing I've seen since you nearly drowned yourself with your jeans ankle cuff."

I rolled over and looked up at him. "That terrified you?"

"You were down for a while." He sank back down on the bed.

"What have *you* got?"

"I think I'd break the bunk if I dusted off my tricks. But –" he held up a finger. "– I know how to make an excellent bunk hut."

He grabbed my hands and pulled me off the bed, gathering in the corners of the bed spread. "You take that end." He handed me a hunk of material.

The candle-wick was heavy, but Liam easily threw his end over the top bunk. I had to grunt to pull mine over.

Once the bedspread was taut, Liam asked, "Pirates or astronauts?"

"Both. I get to be Han Solo."

"Ah." Liam lifted the edge of the bedspread. "I see what you did there. Best pirate astronaut in the galaxy. Does that make me Chewbacca?"

"You do bear a bit of a resemblance."

He climbed in and sat hunched at one end of the bunk. His neck was forced into a curve by the bed above, his knees up around his ears.

I clambered in after him and sat cross-legged at the opposite end.

We were thrown into an orange half-light from the

bedroom light pushing its way through the little squares in the candlewick pattern.

"You don't look very comfortable," I said.

"I'm not really. I don't remember the Millennium Falcon being this small."

I slid forward, stretched myself the length of the bunk and patted the bedding in invitation for Liam to do the same. "We're in an escape pod. Ship got hit by Star Destroyer fire."

"Bummer." He unfolded his legs and shuffled down the bed, before lying down next to me. His feet dangled off the end, pushing the bedspread out and creating a column of light and fresh air.

The bed wasn't very wide and our bodies pressed pretty much the entirety of their lengths.

Liam's breath shook a bit on his exhale.

Little fires flared beneath all the skin that was pressed to Liam.

The whole thing was INTENSE, and I wanted to move away from him and press more of myself against him all at the same time.

I turned my head towards him. If he did the same, our mouths would come within millimetres of touching, but he stared at the rusty springs of the bunk above, not blinking.

When I was sure his eyeballs must have dried out from all the staring, he finally blinked and asked. "Do your parents come here very much?"

I shifted my head to gaze at the springs too. "No. My dad's in a wheelchair and the facilities aren't fit for purpose."

Liam rolled his head toward me "Your dad's in a wheelchair?"

"Yeah. Car accident six years ago."

"Whoa. I'm sorry. That's tough."

"It got tougher. Mum decided she didn't want to live the rest of her life looking after a cripple and left, which, you know, is fair enough. I guess. But still a pretty shitty situation. Dad didn't hold it against her. Imagine leading a life lived for someone else and resenting it the whole time."

Liam didn't say anything for several seconds. "That must have been really difficult for *you*, though."

"Yeah," I said on a sigh. "I was pretty angry at her. It was about the time I decided to drop out of school." I turned my head towards the bedroom and ran a finger over the knobbles in the orange bedspread. "I was already having a hard time, and then having the shock of the crash and Dad's terrible injury."

"You stayed with your dad?"

"She didn't go straight away. She made sure I was on my feet. You know, had work, and that Dad had support, and then she went to live with her sister in Christchurch."

"So, you didn't look after your dad?"

I shook my head. "We got Rewa and everything changed."

"Who's Rewa?"

"The woman who was employed to care for him. She took the tragedy out of the situation. Normalised it, because she'd spent a lifetime working with people with disabilities, so it was normal for her."

"God," he said. Then, "I can't imagine it. It must be awful to see someone you love reduced like that. Dependent on others and not being able to do the things they used to love."

"It was. Dad had to get over his sense of indignity at having somebody doing stuff for him that he used to be able to do on his own. But you know, he never ever saw it as a tragedy. It's not in his make up to be any kind of a victim.

And he's got a lot of his independence back now, like working and stuff."

I rolled my head towards Liam and he turned his away to look at the springs again. "They're together now. Dad and Rewa."

Liam's head swivelled towards mine. "Really?"

He was very close. I could smell the wine on his breath, the heat of it across my cheeks.

He shuffled sideways and put his back against the wall and we were still close, but no longer in danger of accidentally kissing, or purposely kissing without having to make much effort.

"Yeah. They're really happy."

"What about your mum?"

I offered a one shouldered shrug. "She's good. I see her from time to time. Rewa helped me forgive her."

Liam watched me, biting his cheek. "You're a lot like your dad, aren't you?"

"What do you mean?"

"Proud. Not afraid of a fight."

The thought was warming. There were so many things about my dad I'd have been happy to inherit. Knowing I had two of them...

Well.

I was pleased.

I rolled over and snuggled my back into Liam's front and he inhaled sharply and I pulled his arm over me and weaved my fingers through his. Then I listened to him tell me about his family and his childhood, and I told him more about mine. It felt right and good and ...

I woke up to find us in the inverse position. I was curled around Liam's broad back, my hand over his shoulder and resting in his hair.

Raising myself on one elbow, I peered into the orange gloom to check the time on his watch. 6:30 am. Given we'd forgotten to fill the oxygen tanks before launch, it was a wonder we made it through the night without asphyxiating in our own carbon dioxide fug.

I wanted to stay longer. Have him roll over so I could nestle into his shoulder, or into the crook of his neck, but I needed to pee, so I peeled back the spaceship hull and startled at the crispness of the air.

Hooking a corner over the top bunk to let the fresh air in, I headed towards the back door.

When I re-entered the house, Liam stood with the fridge door open, peering inside.

"Morning," he said without looking at me. "You really weren't joking about having no food in the house."

"No."

He closed the door. "Come on. You can have a decent shower at mine and I'll make you a breakfast fit for superheroes."

WHEN WE GOT TO WORK, the team were huddled around Helena, peering at her phone.

Joe lifted his head at the sound of our footsteps. "Come and look at this, lovelies. Mr Hardacre's having some fun with The Unfettered Brain."

"What do you mean?" I asked.

"He's hacked the Facebook account. See?" Helena spun her phone around. On the screen was a picture of one of McManus' campaign posters with the words "Who are you really voting for?" written across it. Helena beamed. "It's a post on The Unfettered Brain page."

Excellent. It seemed Mr Hardacre had read my mind. The next step to regaining some control over the electoral race had to be infiltrating McManus' social media content and I hadn't even needed to ask.

"In terms of gauntlet throwing, it's not much of one," said Rā.

"He's warming up," said Forest. "That won't be it."

Helena turned her phone around. "He's posted something else." She peered at her screen for several moments.

Rā clucked her tongue. "What? What did he post?"

"Oh. Shall I read it out aloud?"

"*Yes.* Everyone here wants to know."

"'As mayor of Invercargill, Brian McManus' total sum of "win"s for the people included successfully lobbying against the creation of a Māori ward, meaning no guaranteed indigenous representation on council. A continuation of post-colonial disenfranchisement? Modern imperialism? Racism? Heck yes'."

"Wow," I said, because that definitively upped the ante.

"There's more. 'He lowered rates on commercial properties to stimulate the local economy, despite no evidence it was failing. Who benefited? Rents rose 3% and the five wealthiest commercial property owners collectively pocketed an extra \$4 mil per annum. Meanwhile, council funding to community groups was halved'."

"What a total douche," said Forest, and Helena said, "Ooh good. He put the last one in."

I opened my mouth to ask for clarification on her statement and she said, "Listen. 'He also committed two million dollars of rate payers' money to a failed bid for Invercargill to host a tournament in the PGA Tour'." She looked up. "There's a few exclamation marks after that sentence." Then dipped her head to read again. "'Meanwhile, twenty-five council-owned houses sat empty due to being classed unhealthy, despite a housing shortage in the city'."

"He didn't really, did he?" asked Rā. "The PGA Tour in *Invercargill*? What a muppet."

Liam said, "What do you mean 'He put in the last one'? Did you give him this info, Helena?"

"I put together a dossier, yes."

Joe wrapped an arm around her. "Helena, you dark horse."

"Well, research is in my skill set and I wanted to do my bit. Brian might be a beautiful face, but I try not to suffer fools."

"No. You only marry them," said Rā.

"There's a few comments popping up." Helena's eyes darted backwards and forwards as she scanned them. "A bit of confusion about the mixed messaging, because The Unfettered Brain had been saying to vote for Brian, and a few coming in saying it's all bogus even though Mr Hardacre's provided links to council documentation that proves it."

Rā pulled out her phone and thumbed it into wakefulness. "All The Unfettered Brain's proved is that people will believe anything, even if the truth's staring them in the face."

Helena gasped. "Mr Hardacre's posts have been deleted." She looked up, her eyes wide. "It's working."

It most certainly was. Brian McManus was finally, *finally* on the back foot.

"The Unfettered Brain's made an announcement," said Rā. "He says 'My people - my account's been hacked. The state are frightened of the truth and they don't want you to know it. They will never allow freedom of speech.'"

Helena squeaked. "Hardacre's deleted it. Just like that."

"McManus won't like that," said Joe. "He's losing control."

"No," said Rā. "Though he's trying to use it to his advantage. He says 'Proof they are running scared. They want to silence me because I am the voice of light in a world of darkness. They don't want you to have hope'." After a couple of moments, she continued, "Aaaand post deleted. Mr Hardacre's having fun."

Helena jiggled excitedly. "It's going to be a war about who gets in first."

"It's going to tie McManus up," said Rā. "He won't be able to run his campaign *and* do damage control. Hopefully he'll give up and shut the account down altogether."

I said, "He can't be surprised someone would want to do this. His claims are so inflammatory. I'm amazed more of a fuss hasn't been made earlier."

"Well," said Joe. "People are sheep. Which is, ironically, an argument *they* have. Those of us who believe in the democratic process and dare to read the newspaper are, apparently, brain dead fools."

And yet.

Now that it was unfolding, I wasn't so sure about its efficacy. "But, it might just fan the flames. People are watching as the posts are deleted. What else are they going to think is happening if it's not government intervention?"

Rā shrugged. "We have to let it play out. See where it gets us."

As it turned out, not very far.

I had only been home for one minute after I'd finished my shift before someone knocked on the door.

I pulled on my beanie and glasses and opened the door to a smiling Bekka McManus, which I shouldn't have been surprised at. She was my neighbour after all, and neighbours sometimes called on each other. Except I wasn't the kind of neighbour she might need anything from.

Before I could open my mouth to ask her what she was doing here, she said, "We need to talk."

She walked past me and sat down at the kitchen table. "This place is cute."

Ordinarily I might have responded, or found the coordination to close the door and sit down at the table with her, but my brain was too busy imploding from the panic setting in.

She knew, didn't she? She knew I was a spy for the Fink camp and bad stuff was about to happen.

"Why don't you close the door and take a seat?"

I...closed the door and took a seat.

Her smile didn't shift as she said, "I need you to stop hacking The Unfettered Brain Facebook account."

Okay. That wasn't quite what I was expecting.

"Um..." Did I deny, or ask how she knew?

Wait a minute. Bekka McManus operated The Unfettered Brain Facebook account?

Of course she did. She was in charge of social media for her husband.

"So, you're actually admitting Brian is The Unfettered Brain?" Why would she do that?

Her cheeks bunched into tight, painful-looking rounds as she laughed and reached across the table to clasp my hand. "No, darling. I'm admitting *I'm* The Unfettered Brain."

Well shit.

CHAPTER TWENTY-FIVE

"BRIAN HAS NO IDEA. OBVIOUSLY."

It wasn't obvious. Was it? Had I missed something big? Like the possibility of Bekka McManus BEING THE FUCKING UNFETTERED BRAIN?

Yes. Because I was a moron. "How...is that obvious?"

"He'd never think to do something like that. He might push the rules, test their malleability, but he plays the game by the book. An open book. His brand of manipulation is always available for scrutiny by those who can recognise it."

My thoughts were still too scattered to comprehend exactly what was going on and how deep into the shit I currently stood. I pushed up from the table. "I need a drink."

Digging the bottle of Green Ginger Wine out of the cupboard, I poured myself a generous glass. "Want one?"

"No, thank you."

I downed half of it and eyed her.

If it was possible for a face whose muscles had been poisoned into immobility to look smug, hers was it.

I didn't know what was coming next. So I continued to lean against the bench. And wait.

It didn't take long.

"It took me a little while to place you," she began. "The beanie does an excellent job of concealing your hair, but the glasses don't hide your extraordinary eyes. The frames are too big. Fashion can be a bugger like that, and I wasn't going to forget your face easily after the shouty thing in the car park. So."

So indeed. I did think the minimal disguise was a long shot. I just thought that if it was going to fall down, it would have done so as soon as she laid eyes on me at the first meeting.

"It's a logical leap to put you behind the hacking. I have to say well played. Hacking! Extraordinary."

I downed the rest of the wine and realised what it was she was saying. She'd come over to ask me to stop said hacking. That was it. No "I will expose you as a spy and send you to prison" or whatever she was capable of doing with that information.

I sat back down at the table. "You're going to let me continue...working for both camps?"

She waved a French-manicured hand in the air. "There's no hope of Fink winning now, Jewel. Why take away the fun? I had thought creating The Unfettered Brain would be entertainment enough, but you –" she pointed a finger at me. "– have made this election wondrous, which I am very grateful for." She dropped her finger and sighed. "I had thought politicking was behind us, but no, Brian *had* to drop his hat into yet another mayoralty bucket."

Ah.

She wasn't evil. Okay, she wasn't *only* evil.

She was bored.

Did that make it worse?

"So...you want me to keep pretending I'm on your team, but you don't want me to actually do the stuff you've found...entertaining?"

"Oh no. By all means, do your stuff. Just not the Facebook hacking. It's not a good look for The Unfettered Brain. It's undermining, and I don't want the hold I have over those people to lose its potency. It's good for Brian, and it's good for my ego. I've never had that kind of power before, Jewel, and for the few remaining days of The Unfettered Brain's existence, I'd quite like to keep it."

I think I understood. Her feelings weren't necessarily born of megalomania, but a lifetime of being just an attractive face in the background. Or maybe it was megalomania and she didn't deserve my understanding.

"And if I don't?"

"I doubt there's any way to prove I'm the Unfettered Brain, but it won't be very difficult for me to prove you've been working for both camps, which would probably disqualify Fink from the election. Don't you think?"

THE MORNING of the Meet the Candidate event, four days out from the close of the election, dawned dark and wet.

I chose not to interpret it as an ominous sign, but the fact was Brian McManus was a political veteran with at least a decade of experience in talking the sweet voter-enticing talk and being able to answer curly questions without actually answering them.

The captain had half an hour of going over the critical "touch points" with a bunch of supermarket employees, and an opening address in his pocket written by an aspiring thriller writer.

The odds were not in our favour.

The event was, apparently, always held late in the run to the close of voting, because most people didn't bother to tick a box until the deadline. It was a ploy used as a 'final push' to remind people there was an election, and it had, in fact, attracted a fair amount of attention. Every chair was occupied in the town hall and people lined the back wall.

I donned my beanie and glasses and sat hiding behind the McManuses so the captain wouldn't see me, while trying not to make eye contact with anybody from the Fink camp. Liam was dressed in a suit and looking every gorgeous bit the security personnel he didn't want to play, which meant my eyes involuntarily gravitated to him every few seconds despite my best intentions.

I had told the team about Bekka's threat, but what could they do except try to whither her to death with narrow-eyed antipathy.

What we did have going for us was a relatively short event agenda. The captain and McManus were to deliver a prepared speech, no longer than five minutes, then take turns answering questions from the floor.

The first part was easy enough. The thinking had already been done. All the captain had to do was look confident and project his voice, and he had little time to dwell on it because he was first to speak.

I crossed my fingers and hoped he didn't fuck it up. Then I thought better of it, because I sat next to Jess, who might have little eyes, but they were still capable of spotting a treacherous finger cross. I used the tops of my knees to wipe the stickiness off my palms instead.

The adjudicator introduced the captain, who stood, straightened his tie, and made his way to the podium at the front of the stage. He took a moment to arrange his papers and do officious-seeming things like clearing his throat and, thank fuck, he remembered to smile when he raised his eyes to the crowd.

The sides of my lungs clamped together.

"Tēnā tātou katoa," he said with the ease of the well-practised and I remembered how to breathe again. Joe's schooling on Māori pronunciation had paid off. So far so good.

"Hello people of Puhiruru and the Fiordland District. Who am I? I am Guy Fink, mart owner, vice-President of Puhiruru Rotary, veteran, and your –" He peered closer at the paper, then raised a finger and jabbed it at the audience. "– biggest fan."

Dear God, why hadn't anyone checked the speech for Helena-flavoured cheese? And, more importantly, why did the captain look like he hadn't practised it? If there was one way to romance disaster it was blind-reading something prepared by someone else.

My scalp prickled with sweat under the beanie.

"It is a privilege to be nominated to represent you." He glanced twice at his notes and jerkily raised his lips into what could, unfortunately, be best described as a smirk. "Now, Brian McManus might have a gorgeous smile and expensive lapels you want to curl your fingers around to pull him closer." The captain cleared his throat and flicked his eyes towards Helena who nodded her encouragement. "But beauty is only skin deep. What do we really know about this man? He's been a member of our community for all of ten minutes. What actions have proven himself to be someone who loves this district, who is invested in who we are and what we want this place to be, who is one of us and will do the best by us? There are none." The captain drew in a deep breath and scanned the crowd before continuing. "Yes, he might have a proven political track record, he might have first-hand, intimate knowledge of the way council works and know the best ways to bring change at the policy level. Yes, he's been a mayor before."

I had to close my eyes against the urge to slap my forehead, or better yet, Helena's.

"But he is not us. I was born here and I know what the heartbeat of this community sounds like. I know the names of your children, I remember your grandparents, and I put everything I have back into making my community the best, the strongest it can be. And I've been doing that for a lot longer than I've had a political agenda, which is twenty years more than the fellow standing, er." The captain's eyes flicked down to McManus, seated below him. "Next to me. I've watched our district change faster than most of us would like. I know first hand how higher house prices have driven up rents, how many of you are struggling to afford to feed your children."

He flipped the page, flipped it back again, then placed it under the one beneath. "Why would we want to benefit the people responsible for that by dramatically lowering their rates? Only two things can come of that. Compromised services and severely reduced social initiatives from council because the income stream will be strangled, *and* there will be fewer places to live. Every owner of a rental property in Fiordland District will terminate lease agreements and turn their houses into short-term accommodation. Why? Because the council will reward them for it and because they can charge premium price for a night's stay. The tourism in this district is growing, and that promise of extra dollars will be very enticing."

Reading silently for a moment, he placed a hand on his chest and continued, "How do I know first hand that people are already struggling? Because the food bank is asking for more donations, because more community groups are asking me for support, because Rotary has more applications for funding in the last two years than it's had in the last ten.

"Yes, I own my home. Yes, I won't be adversely affected by McManus' main campaign should it succeed, but I am a family man. And you, you all, are my family. You all make my home what it is. I don't want to watch the soul of this place being sucked dry to line the pockets of the privileged. I don't want to..." The captain broke off and peered at his speech. When he spoke again, it was with a quiet, cracked voice. "I don't want to lose my family."

Well.

Who knew Helena had *that* in her?

It was rousing. I was roused. I blinked rapidly and forced myself to clap limply as a member of the opposing campaign might.

The Fink camp stood and applauded. Several hoots sounded from the back of the hall amid the clapping. Feet stomped.

It was going to be a hard act to follow.

But the captain had the disadvantage of going first and therefore the effect of his words being forgotten first.

For the first time, I studied the audience. They were mostly white. They were mostly turned out in smart-casual attire, collars over cashmere jerseys. They looked like the kind of people who would vote for McManus, but it was impossible to know for sure. The test would be in the reaction to his speech.

McManus had chosen his "Just an average guy" look for the event – rolled up shirt sleeves, no tie, top button undone – and walked to the podium smiling at the crowd as if he knew each and every one personally.

A round of applause met him, applause that did not greet the captain when he stepped up on to the stage, and McManus waved it down with a smile on his face that said "Come on, guys. It's just me".

He reached the podium and clasped it with both hands, leaning over it, leaning into the audience. "Thanks everyone for taking time out of your busy lives to come and hear a couple of old white dudes drone on about themselves." He rolled his eyes and a smattering of laughs met him.

It was his old game of "I'm simply someone you'd have a drink with at the pub, talk over the fence with" that he'd employed with great effect in Invercargill. The unprofessionalism of it *might just* work against him here, but I had nothing to base that on apart from my own desperate hope.

"I know, I know. You've heard it all before – the promises for better roads, more car parking, public toilet upgrades. It's all wah, wah, right?" He made a duck beak with a hand, opening and closing it. "Truly uninspiring stuff. But you aren't here because the waste water system needs upgrading. There are bigger things at play, yes?"

A murmur rippled through the audience. An affirming one. And I knew McManus wasn't going to address the proposed rates policy. The captain had already done the advertising for him.

He was going to use all the leverage The Unfettered Brain had given him.

"You're here because this little piece of paradise, this

small corner of the world most people would give their first born to live in, is no longer the place you thought it was. Something rotten has crept in, sullied the water. You're here because your trust of the administration meant to protect your interests, your well-being as a citizen, has been eroded. Am I right?"

This time the agreement was clear. The sibilance of a hundred "Yes"s rolled around the room like cicadas waking for the day.

"You feel powerless. What can one person do in the face of a large-scale agenda? I know what's being said. I know how far reaching the political will potentially goes, how small Fiordland feels in the face of it. But you, my friends, have all the power. The power of a tick box. And it's a mighty one."

McManus pushed away from the podium and dropped down from the stage onto the hall floor. Walking towards the first row of seated people, he gestured towards the captain. "Guy Fink might be a military veteran. Make of that what you will, but I am a *political* veteran. Fifteen years in local politics – six as a councillor, nine as a mayor. I know how the machine works. I know how to staunch the rot before it creeps in under the door, how to sweep out the decay that's already snuck in."

He walked down the aisle dividing the audience into two. "You, sir. What's your biggest concern right now?"

The man said something inaudible.

"The council losing its autonomy?" McManus repeated. "As long as I'm standing, your local council will never be a pawn of central government. It will always represent the interest of its rates payers and residents. No. One. Else." He punctuated each word with a slap of his fist into his palm, then he moved down the aisle.

"You madam, what's your biggest concern?" He nodded as he listened, one arm across his belly propping the elbow of the other, a finger placed against his lips. "A safe water supply." He turned in a circle, addressing everyone. "That is a fundamental right. Not a privilege. A *right*. We all deserve a water supply we don't have to fear and I will make sure it happens. There will be total transparency. You will all bear witness to *every, single, step* of the process."

He was a motivational speaker working the crowd, an evangelical church leader stirring the congregation. They craned their necks towards him, eyes following, mouths slightly ajar in anticipation, excitement.

He made his choices carefully, only giving voice to the people who looked like they were already won over by him.

The sweat that had gathered at the nape of my neck turned cold.

"My good man, what worries you?" He cocked his head as he listened. "Big brother, aye? I can tell you, sir, Under the Local Government Act 2002, the council has a statutory responsibility to, and I quote, 'sustain the well-being of the district'. Anything that compromises the well-being of the Fiordland district is therefore unlawful. I will ensure the territorial authority we pay our rates to will *only ever* act within the confines of that piece of legislation."

My insides listed like a sinking ship.

The game was up.

McManus was just too practised at it. For all the emotion the captain had managed to stir, McManus was better.

Even during question time afterwards, he effortlessly deflected the angry questions about his rates policy. He never once mentioned a conspiracy or made any direct promises to address any of them, but the promises were made never-the-less through suggestion, through indirection, through all the tricks of rhetoric in his political veteran book.

It was like watching a goddam conductor command an orchestra.

CHAPTER TWENTY-SIX

ON MONDAY MORNING, two days to the close of the election, nobody said much to anyone except to wish a good morning no one felt.

Votes were already being cast and we hadn't done anything definitive, except rely on the captain's reputation and hope people didn't use his flyers as fire starters, to shift public opinion on McManus.

I shuffled off to my locker with a cursory hello to Forest and Rā and stared into its depths. I wouldn't have minded if the metal maw swallowed me whole. I could curl up and ignore the world, and let it spit me out when all this was over.

I threw my bag in and scuffed my way to the shop floor. As I opened the *Staff only* door, Liam bounded through the automatic one. He held something up between his thumb and pointer finger. A memory card.

"I have it. This is how we take him down."

"What is it?" I asked.

"Footage of Brian McManus putting chlorine in his spa pool."

I gasped.

It was utterly, as in, *utterly* brilliant.

"How'd you get that?" asked Rā.

"I set up a hunting camera on the fence between his house and Jewel's. It records when it detects motion."

Rā walked up to him and clasped his head between her palms. "You clever, clever man."

"What do we do with it?" said Forest.

"Get Hardacre to put it up on McManus' Facebook feed," answered Rā. "Bekka only made The Unfettered Brain an exclusion zone."

Forest glanced at me. "Won't it compromise Jewel anyway, seeing as it's from the top of her fence?"

"Does Jewel care?"

"I don't care." I couldn't care. We now had absolutely nothing left to lose.

Rā gave a single nod. "Ring Mr Hardacre now. Let's take this fucker down."

MR HARDACRE HAD the video uploaded within twenty minutes of him peeling into the store to retrieve the memory card.

The video showed Brian McManus pulling back the cover on the spa pool, placing a white bucket on its edge with the label *Spa Mate Chlorine* helpfully facing the camera, opening the lid and sprinkling two scoops into the water.

Hardacre had edited the video so that it played on a continuing loop. McManus pulled back his spa lid and tipped chlorine into his hot tub over and over and over again.

The response was slower than it was on The Unfettered

Brain's page, presumably because of the fewer followers, but the first response from a Damon 4 Realz received a flurry of likes and angry faces and a healthy amount of assenting and outraged comments.

Deep fake. The label on the bucket's probably photo-shopped on. Also the head isn't right. It's too large for the body. Amateurs

"Well," said Joe. "I didn't see *that* coming."

"We're fucked if we do, fucked if we don't," said Rā.

I chose to deal with this further failure by lying on the floor. It wasn't particularly helpful for the store's spotless health and safety rating. Customers who wanted pickled onions had to straddle me to reach the shelf.

I finally chose to move when a child pushing a trolley decided nudging the lady on the floor with the front wheels was a fun game of "See What Happens When...".

I bought a bottle of wine, went home at midday and despite the chill of the day, proceeded to do my best to empty it while watching the brooding sky float on the surface of the lake from the end of the lawn.

I WOKE to something crawling across my face.

I brushed it away with a groan.

Opening my eyes, I then wished I hadn't as daylight pick-axed my frontal lobe.

I snapped my eyes closed against the image of Liam gazing down at me.

"You need to be careful. Your hair's sticking out from under your hat." He placed a finger on my forehead and poked the offending hair under the edge of my beanie. "McManus could see you."

I didn't particularly care. "Why are you here?"

"I saw you buy the wine. I came to check up on you."

It was a nice thing to do. It showed he cared more about me than I did right now.

"I don't want to talk about it."

"Okay. Do you want to continue to feel awful, though? Or would you like to drink this water?" Something round and cold was placed in my hand.

"I don't want to think anything. I want to go back to sleep for as long as it takes for all this to go away."

"But it's not, is it? So, help yourself by drinking this." He lowered his voice to an almost whisper. "One step at a time."

"No."

"Yes. Feeling shit isn't going to help the situation."

"Will you go away if I do?"

Liam was magnanimous enough to laugh. "I'll think about it."

I cracked my lids and pushed myself up to sitting. My head throbbed with my heartbeat. "I need to lie down again."

"Not until you've drunk all of this." Liam closed his hand around mine and lifted the glass towards my lips. The warmth and strength of his grip was, admittedly, reassuring.

I downed it and wiped my mouth on my sleeve. "We're not going to win, Liam," I whispered.

"You don't know that."

"I do know that. We haven't done enough to convince the non-voting majority they need to vote. We're too inexperienced to know how to make them care enough, or to get them to believe they have some power in this process. We're going to have to watch that smug fucker make his acceptance speech at the election day rally, and I'm going to have to listen and not punch him in the face."

"You could be underestimating all we've done, all the captain's *already* done to create a name for himself in this community."

"I don't think so." I pushed myself to my feet. "I need more water."

My head weighed heavily on my shoulders as I stumbled across the lawn and into the house. I filled my glass from the tap, downed it and refilled it again.

Liam hovered in the doorway, his head bent to avoid the lintel. "When did you last eat?"

I smacked my lips, placed the glass on the bench and walked to the couch. "I had an apple for breakfast." Collapsing onto it, I closed my eyes against the light. I had no idea what the time was now, but it had to be close to 5 pm if Liam had come around straight after work. It was a wonder my insides hadn't been turned inside out with that much nothingness in my stomach to meet the best part of a bottle of wine.

The door snibbed shut and the fridge whined open.

"What are you doing?" I asked uselessly, knowing very well what he was doing.

"Making you a meal. You'll feel better."

"I won't. I will never feel better. We have no time left to change the voting tide. That smarmy arsehole is going to systematically ruin this place. He won't even see it happen. He'll be too busy polluting the neighbourhoods of his other holiday homes."

Pots clinked. "I don't think it will come to that *if* he gets in. The mayor of any place can't just click their fingers and get what they want. Won't the councillors have to agree, too?"

He might be right. I hoped he was right. All that time working for council and I hadn't bothered to learn how the place worked. "Just wait. He'll bed in, get re-elected, turn them all one by one."

"I don't believe that will happen. I can't." Something hissed on the stove.

"He managed to get lots of self-benefiting by-laws and policies passed in Invercargill."

"But nothing of truly significant consequence. Nothing like what he's trying to do here."

I turned my head to watch him and my brain rolled sideways, thudding against my skull. I closed my eyes and groaned against the pain. "I need drugs."

"Okay. Where are they?"

In my toiletry bag, next to my contraceptive pills. I wasn't going to do that to either of us. Rummaging around in someone else's toilet bag seemed like a violation of something very intimate. "I'll get them," I said as I rolled off the couch.

Liam reached me in four strides. "Don't be silly. Tell me where they are."

"No."

He stood very still and didn't say anything as I crawled towards the bedroom door.

I'd done it again. I needed to give more than I had. "I don't want you to see where they are."

With a quiet "Okay", Liam's footsteps *shuffed* back to the kitchen.

By the time I'd swallowed two paracetamol and crawled back to the couch, the aroma of buttery eggs filled the small living space and my stomach growled in appreciation. It was as empty as everything else inside me. I felt hollowed out, a void growing within me. The certainty that the captain could never out-best McManus pulled me towards it and I teetered at the edge, fighting the vertigo.

A knife scraped across toast, the jug bubbled to boiling.

We'd done everything we could and it wouldn't be enough. If McManus' policies went through, there was *so much* to lose.

I cracked an eye and watched Liam scrape a wooden spoon across the frying pan. Despite my objections to him being here, I was really glad he was. His presence and his fussing stopped me from that long fall into the pit.

"Dinner's ready," Liam said softly. "You need help crawling to the table?"

I didn't. The desire to fill my empty stomach was strong enough to have me sitting upright and pushing myself up into a walk.

Dinner was scrambled eggs and a Rā Special. Saliva gathered under my tongue and I had the first forkful in my mouth before I'd thought to use it to express gratitude. I chewed and swallowed. "Thanks, Liam. It's really good."

He gave me a little smile. "I know."

We ate in silence and when one piece of egg-covered toast was down, a wave of exhaustion hit me, despite my alcohol-induced afternoon nap.

I pushed my plate away, the food only half finished.

Liam looked up from his eggs. "You don't want any more? You haven't eaten much."

I shook my head. It was him. I needed him. His warmth, his solidity. I needed to feel him wrapped around me. "Can you make the escape pod?"

He stopped chewing and blinked at me. "Sure." Shovelling the last of his eggs into his mouth, he pushed up from the table and headed to the bedroom.

I grabbed his half-drunk tea and followed him, handing it to him when he'd finished pulling the edges of the bedspread into place over the bunks. Then I picked up a corner and crawled inside. "Join me?"

The springs protested against our combined weight as Liam climbed in after me. He sat cross-legged next to the pillow and looked at me, waiting.

I lay down and curled my knees towards my chest, and Liam followed.

His knees brushed the back of mine and his arm rested on my rib cage.

Interlacing our fingers, I shuffled back against him so my back rested against the solid plane of his torso.

Liam's breath warmed the back of my head and I closed my eyes against our small orange world, feeling the edges of sleep pulling me down.

"Jewel?"

"Hmm?"

"Are you okay?"

It took me a moment to swim back up through the fuzziness of half-sleep. "No."

He tapped my chest. "What's going on inside here?"

"A pit of despair."

"Why? Why are you feeling it that badly? I know you think we've lost, but it's not the end of the line. Any changes he wants to make, we can protest, lobby the councillors."

It was out of me before the thought had fully formed. "It's all my fault."

"What's all your fault?"

"This whole thing. It's all on me. I'm so stupid. So fucking stupid to think we could take him on."

Liam didn't say anything for a couple of breaths. There wasn't anything he could say. It was true.

"Do you remember when we talked in the staff room

and you said you didn't know who made you feel stupid now? Now that you're an adult and school's in the past?"

I remembered.

"Maybe." Liam swallowed, the noise loud in the small space. "Maybe it's you."

My eyes flew open.

But. I didn't think I was stupid. I made a point of making that clear if it was ever called into doubt.

My "No" came out as if it had a question mark at the end of it.

"You just called yourself stupid. Right now when you said it was your fault."

The world came to a standstill with a little shudder and my only thought was *Oh*.

I didn't even have a "But" to start my next sentence with.

"I..." I didn't want it to be me. I had enough battles without having to go up against myself.

"What went on in your head after you yelled at Bekka and assumed you'd be fired?"

I opened my mouth and closed it again. I had *absolutely* berated myself for being an idiot.

"People aren't stupid for making a stand, Jewel. In fact, they make a stand because they *aren't* stupid." Liam sucked in a breath and my scalp turned cold against the pull of air. "When else? When else do you tell yourself you're dumb?"

Closing my eyes, I searched for the moments I *felt* dumb.

Every time I made a social faux pas, every time I misunderstood someone's meaning, every time I got something wrong.

And I knew. I knew in those moments I told myself I was stupid.

"God. I am an awful, awful person."

Liam's arm tightened around me. "No, Jewel. You've just never learnt how to change the narrative."

And it was all too much. The revelation I was my own worst enemy, the abject disappointment of knowing we were going to lose the election, the possibility of eventually losing all the people that mattered to me, the exhaustion of it. I started to cry. I sniffed wetly and Liam said, "Hey. It's okay," in that redundant way people do when it never ever actually is okay.

He snaked his other arm under me and pulled me tightly to him. "I'm here." His breath was hot across the top of my head. "Let it all out if that's what you need."

It probably was what I needed, to give release to everything swirling around inside me, but his gentleness, his care, his ability to see parts of myself I didn't even know, drove me to do something else.

I twisted myself around and pressed my mouth to his.

Liam sucked in a breath as my lips sunk into the cushion of his. He smelt of tea, and flushed skin, and everything that was right and good and wholesome.

"Jewel," he whispered.

I didn't answer. I pressed myself closer and kissed him again.

Liam didn't say anything this time. He placed a warm palm on my spine and kissed me back.

It was a gentle kiss. Just lips and shared air. But it was if all the energy we'd spent in the last few weeks, circling around each other, of waiting, of building anticipation, was distilled down to this single point of contact.

I'd never experienced a rush like it. How something as simple as the press of mouths could at once strip everything else away until it existed in its own orbit, and light the streets of cities. We could destroy worlds with this kiss.

Um.

...

It's possible I got carried away with my metaphors, but it was a

Really.

Fucking.

Amazing.

Kiss. Okay?

Liam drew in a shaky breath and asked, "Are you sure you want to be doing this?"

I answered by running a finger across the soft pad of his bottom lip.

"I mean." He swallowed. "You're upset and—"

I pulled his hand from where it rested against my back and placed it on my breast.

The rest of Liam's words appeared to fall out of his brain. His tongue worked behind the gap his teeth left when he failed to close his mouth, but didn't shape any sounds.

My nipple tingled under the heat of his large palm and I pressed my fingers into the back of his, encouraging him to squeeze.

And then his mouth was on mine again, open, warm, the press of lips harder, the first tentative touch of his tongue.

Heat gathered in my belly, swirling and eddying downwards until it settled between my thighs. I raised a leg to rest across Liam's hip and the touch of tongues became a press of tongues, an urgent need to taste, to feel as much as possible.

Liam ran a hand up my thigh and tightened it around my buttock before pulling me into him. As our hips met, my gasp sucked Liam's groan into my mouth.

I needed to touch his skin. I slid my hand beneath his

work shirt and ran my palm over the knobbles of his spine. It wasn't enough. My other hand was trapped between us, useless to help me feel him, to explore the skin, the muscle, the contours I'd seen all of before and desired for so long to touch. I needed him closer.

I pulled him over, on top of me, and felt the heavy, delicious weight of him.

His hips flexed and his eyes widened, as if the movement had been involuntary and taken him by surprise. It pressed his swollen bits into my swollen bits and...wow. I think my eyes rolled back in my head a little bit.

Liam didn't move. He gazed down at me, his eyes still large, his breath coming in ragged little gasps.

I knew what he meant.

It was a little overwhelming. Exciting, and scary, and self-conscious, and not wanting to lose control and wanting to lose control all at the same time. But mostly self-conscious.

I didn't want to fuck this up as much as he didn't want to, but given my limited experience and my general ability to excel in the human-interaction-fuckupability stakes, there was every chance I might.

My lizard brain took over. You know, the one that says, "Fuck it," to thought and chases base need. It ran my hands up the sides of his ribs and over his chest, because, apparently, it needed to, and Liam stuttered out an exhalation.

That right there. That moment where Liam struggled to make his lungs work properly settled the ball of freak out pinballing off the walls of my chest. If I could do that by running my fingertips over the least erogenous parts of his body, what could I draw out of him when I touched the most secret parts of him?

Freeing my hands from his shirt, I placed them against

his jaw, my fingers in his hair, thumbs framing his ears, and pulled him down to me.

Sweet Jesus, the man could kiss. It might have taken a couple of months for him to work up the courage – or me to work up the courage for him – but the wait was worth it. He was all tender and firm and gentle and a bit bitey. It might have been the result of indecision about what he thought I wanted, but, holy shit, it dinged the dial on the Drive Jewel Insane-o-meter.

He drew away slightly, his lips red and glistening, and I chased after him, nipping at his bottom lip to pull him back to the pillow with me.

He "Mff"ed and thrust again and my focus shifted to an entirely different part of where our bodies met.

It was very very warm down there, the heat inching towards boiling point.

I wanted more friction, to chase the pleasure that came from that friction. I planted my feet on the mattress and pushed up against him and a sound came out of my mouth that could best be described as mewling.

Awesome. I made sexy sexy cat noises when I made out.

Liam didn't seem to mind. His hips pressed down to meet mine and he made a little "Uh" noise that disturbed a shoal of minnows in my stomach.

And all I could think about was how I could get all of his fingers all over all of me.

I grabbed his hand from where it was bunched in the blanket we lay on and moved it to the bottom of my shirt. Pincering the fabric between my thumb and forefinger, I guided his hand up my belly, the fabric gathering in front of our fingers.

Liam looked down, watching our progress, and looked up at me once my bra was exposed. "Jewel," he said as if he'd run a hundred-metre sprint. "Are you sure you...want to?"

"I'm sure I want to have sex with you, yes." My voice sounded all breathy like I'd just run a hundred-metre sprint, too.

"Okay." Liam's eyes slipped to my lips before meeting mine again. "It's just, um, I'm not, you know."

"I'm not massively experienced either."

Liam's face relaxed a little, before tightening up again. "I don't wanna." He closed his eyes momentarily. "I'm scared I'm gonna..."

"I don't care, Liam. Whatever happens I'll enjoy." I mostly meant it. We were both probably beyond the clumsy fumbling of teenagers, but neither of us had the confidence in ourselves to set expectations beyond that.

My bra had a front clasp. So I unclasped it to take his mind off how he thought he could fail me.

His head jerked down, then he looked at me, his mouth slack, eyes wide.

It was too much looking and not enough touching. So I arched my back and pulled on the back of his head.

His hand enclosed one breast, his mouth the other.

He whimpered, or I did, or both of us did.

My nipple ached under the pull of his lips – that exquisitely sweet ache of wanting more, that the slide of his tongue would never ever be enough.

I said something like, "F-fuck," and he hummed out a growl, which was so un-Liam-like and so SEXY that my toes curled. The vibration that travelled from his throat to his mouth to my skin sent an electric charge to my groin. I jolted at the shock of it.

Liam pulled his mouth away with a little pop. "You okay?"

I answered by wrenching open his top button. "Take your shirt off."

He pushed himself up and fumbled at his buttons with shaky fingers and I helped him by working my way up from the bottom one.

When our fingers met and there was nothing left for him to do but remove his shirt, I held my breath.

His stomach muscles flexed as he shrugged it off and it was total *ohmyGod*. It had been weeks since I'd viewed them in the near dark, at a distance, and under the blur of motion. They were pre-tty fucking fabulous up close.

My fingers sought them out before I realised my brain had issued instructions to them and I traced their lines and firm little curves.

His skin goose-bumped and he sucked in a series of tiny gasps and I needed to have him on me, to feel the press and rub of our exposed skin.

I shucked my shirt and bra and hooked my fingers around his waist band, pulling him towards me. Meeting him halfway, I arched my back so that my breasts were flush with his chest and with a tugging of my arms and a wrapping of my legs, I was pinned into the bedding by the glorious weight of him.

I had to breathe in shallow sips. It was wondrous.

He placed his elbows on either side of my head and removed some of his weight before he crushed my ribcage. And then my hands were in his hair and his mouth was hot and his tongue slid against mine and our teeth clashed a bit, but it was okay, because things were needy and urgent and teeth-clashy, and my fingers were on the domes of his jeans, and his lips were on my neck and I had him gripped in my palm and everything stopped.

Liam's muscles bunched against me and his breath stuttered near my ear. With a slowness that was almost measured, he drew back his head and looked down at me. His eyes were large. It could have been anticipation, or fear, or both.

I hoped it wasn't pain. I relaxed my fingers in case it was and his eyelids fluttered closed. With another small stomach-fluttering "Uh", he ground against my hand, flicking his hips in quick, shallow thrusts. Six, seven, eight.

Then, with a groan that sounded like deep regret, he shifted out of my reach and rolled on to the mattress, his hands at the waistband of my trousers.

I kissed the little frown of concentration creasing his brow and tried not to melt into a little pile of *holyfuckingshit!* at the proximity of his fingers to my vagina.

When he had freed all the domes, I wriggled out of my pants and waited to see what he would do about my very near nakedness.

Liam's eyes were very dark. His lips were very red from all the desperate, bitey kissing. He looked down my body and up at my face again.

He needed help.

I gave it to him by removing my knickers.

Liam said, "J–" which could have been "Jewel" or "Jesus" or "Jiminy crickets", but I swallowed the rest of the sounds with a kiss and placed his fingers to my opening, letting him feel how ready I was.

I inhaled a chain of tiny tiny breaths, a sort of hitchy, hiccupy thing, and Liam's mouth made a little "O". He can't have been surprised. I'd been grinding and mewling and generally making a desperate mess of myself for the last ten minutes. Maybe it was wonder. Maybe he struggled to believe he had the ability to do that to me.

He was going to be *very* surprised, then, at all the other

things he could make me do. Seeing he was already in the vicinity, there was no time like the present. I trailed his fingertips up to my clit.

"Like tha-hat," I whispered, moving his fingers in slow, gentle, ever-decreasing circles and suddenly the escape pod was a ridiculously tiny, blanket-covered, child's bunk.

We needed the big bed.

With immediate effect.

With a "Come on", I pushed through the candle-wick wall and pulled back the bedding on the double.

The escape pod hull shivered into stillness.

I arranged myself into a sexy, leg-cocked pose, then pulled the blankets up under my armpits when Liam still hadn't emerged. "You okay?"

Liam's voice sounded strangled. "Yep."

"Is there anything I can help you with?"

He waited the length of a calming count to three and lifted the bedspread. "I'm really really nervous."

"I am too, but the ache between my legs is bigger." I stood, walked over to the bunks and reached my hands out to help pull him up.

"God, you're perfect, Jewel," Liam whispered.

I wasn't, but it was very nice, particularly in this moment, that he thought so.

He stood without needing me to lever him up, and I led him to the bed, fingers curled around his.

I didn't get back on the bed. Not yet. I turned and pulled his head towards mine, lips and tongue seeking, while I slid his jeans and his trunks over his hips and ran my hands over the swell of his buttocks.

"I want you inside me, Liam," I said as he stepped out of his clothes.

I gathered his "O-ho-kay" between my lips and reached

behind me for the bedside drawer and the packet of condoms I'd placed within, with wishful thinking, on my arrival to the crib.

It wasn't the sleekest of moves in the world of seduction techniques. I had to duck down and sort of turn my head sideways to see what I was doing, which meant Liam had to bend over and try to keep contact with my mouth with pursed lips.

But honestly, in the long list of the afternoon's awkward moments and potentially awkward moments, it wasn't much of a scale-tipper. I tried to regroup some of the sexy by tearing the condom wrapper open with my teeth in a, well, sexy way, but it didn't really matter. We were already at the point of no return.

Liam rolled it on without breaking eye contact with me, which *definitely* regrouped the sexy and I pulled us onto the bed and kissed him until we were gasping for air and my hand found his hardness again.

"J-Jewel."

"Yes?" My voice was little more than a whisper.

"Are you...are you sure?"

I was so desperately sure that I guided him towards my entrance and raised my hips so that his tip rested just inside.

This was it. This was the moment I would discover what it was like to have him. I attempted to gain control of the shivery things my body was doing in response to the feel of him, but my "Now," came out plead-y and question-y.

Panting into each other's mouths, Liam slowly pushed against me, stretching me. He paused, lids heavy, to check if I was okay, and when I hissed out a "Yes", he shifted his hips forward until he filled me. He lay very still on top of me, eyes closed, breaths shallow.

"Okay?" he asked again, his voice husky.

Before I could answer he rolled his hips forward and grunted.

I gasped. A good gasp, not a "what have I got myself into?" gasp, because it felt pretty fucking amazing.

"Sorry," he whispered.

"Do it again," I said, and he did it again.

On the fourth one, I raised my hips to meet his, and then we were both doing the thrusting, and our bodies slid and dragged against each other and Holy shit...

"Jewel," Liam panted, his rhythm increasing. "I can't..." He swallowed and chased a breath. "I can't..."

He did his little "Uh" as the conclusion to his sentence and I clamped him to me. I wrapped my arms and legs around him and pulled down on him with all my strength. "Stop. Just...stop."

Liam lay still and his bottom gave a last, rebellious half roll.

I didn't mind if Liam lost control. There would, I hoped, be other opportunities for him to take his time. But it mattered to him. So I had to help.

He panted against the side of my head, his heart drumming a beat on my clavicle.

When his breathing was measured, I pushed his chest until he knelt, my thighs over his knees. "Give me your thumb."

He reached forward.

I grabbed his wrist and took his thumb into my mouth, working it with my tongue. Then I pulled it from my mouth and placed it on my clit. "Do you remember how I showed you before?"

Liam moved his thumb in a circular motion.

I gripped his thigh. "Lighter."

He eased off, the pad of his thumb brushing, teasing my sensitivity.

"Good," I breathed and mewled out a string of "Just...yes...oh"s and some other things that were more noise than words.

A storm brewed under his thumb and I wriggled, impatient for its unleashing. I arched my back.

"Jesus." Liam's thrust took me by surprise. His thumb paused.

"Don't stop."

His thumb swept another circle and he thrust again. "I have to."

"Faster. Do it faster," I urged, concentrating on corralling the storm clouds, of gathering the building energy.

Liam's thrusts quickened. "Jewel."

I couldn't...whatever he needed of me right now...I couldn't.

"Jewel!"

Liam began to thrust wildly, his thumb barely able to maintain contact with my sensitive flesh. It didn't matter, I was so close, he could have breathed on me to make me come.

I twisted the sheet in my fist and convulsed as the first wave hit me.

Liam let out a string of "OhGod"s and gripped my thighs to pull me in harder to his thrusts. I reached down and stroked myself through the final combustion and, with a sigh, melted into dissolution as Liam sucked in a sharp breath and shook with his own orgasm.

His eyes remained closed for a few seconds, his chest heaving. When he opened them, he smiled down at me and collapsed onto the bed, our faces a stolen breath away. "Alright?"

"Yes. I had an orgasm."

He grinned. "Me too."

We lay in silence with our hands clasped, allowing our heartbeats to slow, the sweat to cool.

"How's your headache?"

"Good. You sexed it out of me."

His grin returned. "I didn't know my penis had that kind of power."

"I like your penis. It can come back for a return visit." I yawned. I had no idea what the time was, but the daylight outside the window was bright enough that it had to be early still. And yet, I felt the drag of sleep again. I pulled the blankets up to cover us and Liam nestled me into his shoulder. His heartbeat was a metronome, sinking me further.

Liam's "Jewel?" jolted me into wakefulness. "I feel like we were only halfway through a conversation before you leapt on me."

Oh yeah. That.

It was absolutely a conversation I needed to have with myself, but I was warm, and after-glow-y, and I was pressed against a naked Liam. I didn't really want to have it *now*. "I didn't leap on you."

"You would have if the escape pod wasn't designed for Ewoks."

"Be thankful we landed on Planet Bedroom, then."

"I don't know. The local lifeforms are pretty short." Liam waggled his feet from where they jutted out off the end of the bed.

"Perfectly proportioned."

I could feel Liam smile against my forehead. "Yes, perfectly proportioned." He laid a hand on top of my head.

"Including your brain, which is so ridiculously far from stupid it's laughable."

In principle I knew it. I did. But I still did stupid things on an alarmingly regular basis.

When I told him, he gave me a little squeeze. "Everyone makes mistakes, everyone does little things they regret. I do plenty of them." He placed his lips against my hair so that his next words were muffled. "It doesn't make them stupid, it makes them *human*. Nobody gets it right all the time."

"No, but some of us struggle a little harder to get it right more of the time."

Liam let this sit for a second or two, then raised a fist in front of my face like he intended to beat the sense into me. "Let me tell you how intelligent you are." He raised a finger. "You anticipated Brian McManus' intentions to run for mayor and were right." He raised another. "You knew that whatever he campaigned for, or whatever he wants to do once in council would be to the detriment of this community." A third finger extended. "You organised us to run a campaign against him." He shook me. "Run a campaign, Jewel!" With finger number four, he said, "You got the most miserable, self-interested man in town to do stuff that benefits everyone but him. Mr Hardacre, an *actual* hacker. Who would have guessed?"

I couldn't deny it. I one hundred percent did do all that.

"You are one of the most intelligent people I know."

"And yet, I can get it wrong with people. Often."

He pulled away from me and met my eyes. "Yes, maybe you lack some social intelligence at times, but nobody is master of all the intelligences. We have strengths in certain areas. That's all. I can dance really well, but I couldn't be a double agent in a mayoralty race. So..." Liam's eyes flickered backwards and forwards between mine, "I don't know, give yourself a break." He placed a finger on my temple. "Turn that little voice off."

"I'm not going to be able to turn it off just like that."

"I know. But if you're aware of it, you can start telling it what you actually are, which is a mistake-making, intelligent human. It'll learn to shut up."

I hoped he was right. I mean, I thought he probably was. I just wasn't sure I could pull it off after a lifetime of self-talk.

As if Liam read my mind, he said, "It'll take practise, but you can do it, Jewel."

I snuggled back into him and asked, "Is there such a thing as empathetic intelligence?"

"I don't know. Probably."

"If there is, you've got it. And you've got social intelligence."

He didn't say anything for a beat. "I'd love the confidence to go with it."

"You will. With more Stellar in your life."

Liam said, "I think so, too," and I wanted to be more for him, just as he'd been so...everything for me. "I think you should wear more dresses. Like, you could wear one when you come over. If you wanted."

I waited for two of his slow breaths.

Then he gave me a squeeze. "Thanks, Jewel."

I turned my head up to his and kissed him.

We kissed for a long time, trailing our fingers over each other's bodies, stroking, cupping, until Liam turned hard again and we played another game of goosebump-inducing Can Jewel Come Before Liam Does?

As our sweat cooled, Liam nestled against my breasts and I stroked his hair. His slowing breath skittered across my chest. On his fourth exhale, an idea took hold and refused to shift from my thoughts. "He really loves her, doesn't he?"

"Who?"

"Brian McManus really loves Bekka."

Liam was quiet for a moment. "That's...really what you're thinking about?"

It was a fair question. I should have been basking in a hazy afterglow, being present in our moment, not somebody else's. If I was Liam, I'd be very offended.

And yet...

I scraped my fingers lightly across his scalp. "Liam?"

"Yeah?"

"I know what we have to do."

CHAPTER TWENTY-SEVEN

OUR WINDOW WAS VERY VERY VERY small.

Like election-day-rally small.

The election day rally kicked off half an hour before voting closed. So yeah. If we were going to change the course of Fiordland history, there wasn't a lot of time to execute something definitive that would make up for the fact the captain, according to the tally on the council website, still only had half the votes McManus had.

But we had to give it a shot, because the Trying to Get More Votes Than the Other Guy thing hadn't worked.

When I arrived at the town hall with the McManus entourage, it was mostly full. Supporters milled about, nibbling on the finger food they'd brought courtesy of an unsaid "Bring a plate" etiquette. The captain chatted with the chief electoral officer, Mr Simms, a very pale man in a well-worn grey suit that only served to make him look paler. And the real-time vote count, broadcast on a large screen on the stage, confirmed McManus' lead was still, damningly, a couple of thousand votes ahead. It would take a miracle to swing things the other way. Like several thousand Fink supporters mailing their votes in on the final day of voting, and having them counted the following week thanks to the postal system shutting down over the weekend. Which was not a miracle I could rely on.

In another reality, where the votes were closer, people would stay into the night, drinking from the hip flasks they'd smuggled in pockets and handbags until a winner was declared.

Tonight was not that night.

At 5:00 pm, the captain would be forced to concede and McManus would deliver his victory speech and all the Fink supporters would go home to leave everyone else drinking from the hip flasks they'd smuggled in pockets and handbags.

Unless...

What I had planned somehow worked.

I chose to spend twenty minutes of the final half hour of the election eating my way through eleven asparagus rolls and avoiding eye contact with Bekka, because it seemed a good use of time when potentially waiting for the world to end.

Also, *if* my move to stop McManus from winning succeeded, waiting until the last possible second, when expectations about the election outcome were firmly concreted in, kind of made it more awesome. Like raising your hand to high-five someone and pulling it away at the last second so they only slapped air.

Alternatively, if it failed, we only had to wait a couple of minutes before McManus crowed his triumph and we could escape to cry in the car park.

At six minutes until the captain's concession speech, I climbed the stage and switched on the waiting microphone.

I gave it a couple of taps, and when two *doofs* sounded

through the amplifiers, I cleared my throat and said, "Kia ora, Puhiruru."

The hubbub of chatter died and a couple of hundred pairs of eyes turned on me.

A wave of heat rolled up my body and eleven asparagus rolls pushed against the top of my stomach like they were thinking about making a quick exit.

Dropping my chin, I closed my eyes and sucked in a shaky breath.

"Jewel?" said McManus a moment after the captain did. "What are you doing up there?"

I opened my eyes and peered down at my front. I was wearing an Empowered Collection T-shirt featuring female reproductive organs in the shape of the Superman logo and the words *Grow a pair* underneath it.

Time to be a Shero.

Raising my head, I said, "It's been quite an election, hasn't it?" I attempted a smile as if I'd said something amusing, or was actually enjoying myself, and not crapping my pants.

The crowd murmured half-hearted responses, which was understandable. They had no idea who I was and I didn't really look like I knew what I was doing.

"Most of that's been down to one person." I peered down at McManus, who puffed his chest out in arrogant assumption.

I waited a beat.

"The Unfettered Brain!"

The murmuring rose.

McManus' smile slipped, but only fractionally, because he was a semi-decent politician.

Bekka hissed out a "Jewel" that had a large "What the fuck are you doing?" hidden within it.

I ignored her and said to the crowd, "Whoever they are, they've provoked thought and debate and won your trust, haven't they?"

The crowd mostly agreed.

"They've been a complete enigma. It's been the most exciting mystery this community has seen. *Who is the Unfettered Brain?*"

A plate crashed to the floor.

Shards of porcelain lay at Bekka's feet and she looked up at me without any pretence it had been an accident. She narrowed her eyes and cocked her head ever so slightly before bending to pick them up.

I considered what I imagined to be the message she'd been attempting to communicate. And disregarded it.

I took a step towards the crowd. "I have exciting news for you, Puhiruru." I paused again, pulling their curiosity to loftier heights. Or so I hoped. "The Unfettered Brain has decided to be an enigma no longer. Would you like to finally meet them?"

"I would," said McManus as the sibilance of a hundred "Yes"s gathered strength. "Bring him out."

"Jewel!" hissed Bekka again as I gestured off stage.

"I give to you The Unfettered Brain."

Mr Hardacre rolled out from the wing.

The excited murmuring died.

"Him?" said McManus and answered himself with a disappointed grunt.

"Yes," said Mr Hardacre in the monotone of a rehearsed line. "I'm The Unfettered Brain, because most people are so stupid they need someone to do their thinking for them."

Several people gasped.

I didn't bother to see how Bekka was reacting, considering her confused face was most likely identical to her understanding face.

Then Helena pushed away from the cluster of the Fink camp and turned towards the crowd. "No. *I'm* The Unfettered Brain. I did it for research for my next novel. It's about a politician who manipulates the public into voting for him through espousing conspiracy theories."

"Actually," shouted Rā over the gathering drone of confusion, "*I'm* The Unfettered Brain. It's a new fringe sport. See how many followers you can get on Facebook through spreading disinformation. I won, by the way. You lot are total suckers."

A motor whirred at the rear of the hall and people scattered as a scooter mounted the steps and drove through the open double doors. It wove between startled onlookers and came to a skidding halt beneath the stage.

Forest unclasped his arms from around Harit's waist and climbed off the back. He was dressed in a masked superhero costume with a large "UB" stitched onto the chest. Placing his hands on his hips, he announced in the deep voice befitting a superhero, "*I* am The Unfettered Brain. The people's champion. Your saviour from the tyranny of bureaucratic opp–"

"What the bah-loody hell is going on?" McManus roared, swinging his head from Forest to glare at me.

Excellent.

I'd needed a bit of chaos, and I'd got it.

I looked at Mr Simms, the chief electoral officer, whose open-mouthed perplexity showed me he was paying the attention I needed him to. It wasn't *his* confusion I needed, but I hoped it helped to amplify the bewilderment in the person that had to feel it the most. It was the only way I could think to get a very necessary reaction to what I was about to throw out into the world.

"Jewel?" The captain's voice was a fraction of the volume of McManus', as if he anticipated the inevitability of betrayal. "What the foxtrot is happening, trooper?"

"I'm sorry," I whispered to him and looked back at the crowd. "The Unfettered Brain could be several people –" I waved an arm at Forest, and Helena, and Rā, and Mr Hardacre. "– all these people, but I know the big truth, Puhiruru." I scanned the room, drawing out my dramatic pause. "Your future mayor, Brian McManus...is The Unfettered Brain."

The murmuring died before swelling again.

McManus frowned. "I'm *not*."

"But you have to be." I looked from his bemused features to the people in the hall. "He has to be, Puhiruru. According to a local...data analyst, the Internet habits of people are like a finger print. The person who operates The Unfettered Brain account lives somewhere between Kea and Kakapō Streets, has recently bought a spa, loves Hawkes Bay riesling and watches Friends highlights on YouTube." I turned back to him. "Is that not you?"

McManus puffed out a single "But" before comprehension rolled across his features.

He turned to his wife who attempted to shake her head at him in a way that wasn't obvious to everyone else, but considering we were all looking at her because he was, it was pretty obvious.

He placed his hands on her shoulders, his eyes wide. "*You're* The Unfettered Brain?"

Bekka's head shake lost all its pretence at subtlety. "No...I..."

"Bah-loody hell, darl." He pulled her into his arms. "I had no idea you had that in you."

"*Shut up*," she hissed as McManus drew his smiling head back and shook it in wonder.

She attempted to wriggle free and her eyes darted from her husband, to me, and then Mr Simms. "Jewel's a spy for Fink!" she shouted, her words high and hurried. "She works at his store." She wrenched herself out of McManus' grasp and pointed at me. "She's been pretending to be our Creative Director, or whatever, but she's been working for the Fink campaign the whole time. Jewel Bauer –" she stabbed the air with her finger "– is an employee at his supermarket."

I had no intention of denying it. "It's true," I said into the microphone.

The captain, watching the exchange with his hands on his hips, gasped.

"Surely that's gross misconduct," Bekka continued, "or electoral fraud, or something. It's *way* beyond a conflict of interest."

It sure was.

However.

I had a big "But" in my arsenal. "Is it as bad as posing as a supposed truth sayer and spreading conspiracy theories to get votes? You weren't even subtle. You specifically pushed McManus as the candidate to vote for." I turned to Mr Simms, my voice amplified through the speakers. "The council must have been aware of what was going on with The Unfettered Brain. Bekka was saying the council was doing a whole lot of evil stuff."

Bekka stepped towards the stage. "You *hacked* stuff. That's illegal." She jabbed the finger that had been pointed at me towards the electoral officer. "She's broken the law."

I held a hand up. "Nope, not me. I haven't done any hacking. Wouldn't know where to start."

Before Mr Simms had a chance to pass comment, the captain said, "Why would Jewel need to conduct espionage?" at the same time as McManus looked up at me and said, "You were *spying on me?*"

And all hell broke loose.

The crowd shifted forward with people pushing to the front to fling their indignation at Bekka. *She'd made fools of them. Their trust had been betrayed.*

She tried to make herself invisible by hiding behind her husband, and as the wall of people advanced, made a dash for the stairs to the stage.

As she disappeared, their fury increased.

And the pandemonium swelled.

McManus shouted at Mr Simms. Rā and Forest shouted at McManus. Bekka shouted at me from her hiding place behind the gathered stage curtain.

The noise was glorious.

There was only one more person to play their part.

I jumped down from the stage and handed the microphone to Mr Simms.

He looked from it to me to out at the frothing tide of angry voters and back to me, his eyes wide. Then he cleared his throat and leaned into the microphone, as if moving his hand towards his mouth was counter-intuitive. "Ah. Can everyone please calm down?"

Not a single person had the presence of mind to do as asked.

He tried again.

The fracas continued to rage.

Taking the microphone from his hand, I shouted "Hey!" into it. Then "Everyone SHUT UP for a second."

The sudden boom over the speakers shocked people into a hasty silence.

"Thank you. The chief electoral officer has something to say." I handed the microphone back.

And waited.

Mr Simms cast his eyes around the hall. He ran a hand through his hair. He opened his mouth to speak and had to unglue his tongue from the roof of his top palate.

I willed him to pull through. He had to pull through, for the sake of everyone here, even if they didn't know it yet.

"I just..." he began quietly, then shook his head as if trying to shake the vision before him from his mind. "In the whole of my eighteen years of overseeing elections I've *never* seen anything like this." He gave a little laugh, then cut himself short and frowned. Waving a hand over the heavily breathing people before him, he continued, "I'm not just talking about this...this circus." He turned to look at Bekka, his voice a rasp, barely more than a whisper. "I have *never* encountered such a shocking abuse of local democracy." Then he looked at me. "It's so utterly disrespectful of the process and the voters, I'm...appalled."

"No argument here," I said.

Somebody offered a "Too bloody right" and Mr Simms' eyes shifted to McManus, then the captain. "I'm sorry, gentlemen." He raised his chin and said with more force behind his words, "I have no choice but to disqualify you both."

CHAPTER TWENTY-EIGHT

"YES!" I squealed over the top of McManus', "No!"

He stepped towards Mr Simms, his finger pointed up at Bekka. "I had nothing to do with it. I didn't know she was doing it."

I *kind of* hoped Mr Simms didn't dignify that with a response, but, to be honest, I didn't really care. I was too busy being overwhelmed by the reality of

WHAT. THIS. MEANT.

We had won. We'd lost the battle, but we had comprehensively won the motherfunking war.

With a whoop, I punched my fists into the air and turned to look for Liam.

He stepped away from Joe, who had his head bent in solemn conversation with the captain, and swept me up in a hug. "I knew you could do it," Liam said. "Smartest person I know."

And then Forest and Helena and Rā and Harit were there, joining the huddle.

"Holy shit, guys," I said. "We won!"

"*Yeah* we did," said Rā. "Wiped the smile right off that smug fucker's face."

"You, Jewel Bauer," said Forest, "are a total election-wrecking ninja. Big ups, girlf–"

"What *on earth* are you all on about?" Bekka's voice cut through the renewed din of the voters. "You haven't *won*, Jewel." She stood on the edge of the stage, her tone putting the frown in her words that her eyebrows couldn't. "Didn't you hear him? You got Fink disqualified."

"Yep," I said, still enfolded by the arms of the group. "But more importantly, *you* got *your husband* disqualified. I'd say a McManus-free Fiordland is a pretty fucking epic triumph."

Note from the author: If you liked this book, may I ask three things? **First,** *please rate this book. I appreciate your opinion and what I focus on next depends on you, the reader.* **Second,** *please consider joining my reader group at LeeGabel.com/join. Once a month I share little details of my life (the fun stuff, that is) and keep you informed of future books. Plus, I'll give you a* **25% discount** *on all my ebooks.* **And third,** *if you liked this book, please recommend it to your friends. You can also ask your local library to order it for you if they don't have it yet. My sincere thanks.*

One more thing: *This book features music from the 1980s and earlier. For a playlist of all music referenced, please go to: LeeGabel.com/music*

Titles by Lee Gabel

Dreamwaker Saga
Lucid Bodies
Lucid Revenge
Lucid Fate

Detest-A-Pest Series
Vermin 2.0
Arachnid 2.0
Molerat 2.0

Standalone
David's Summer
Snipped
Tied

Afterward

Like it? Rate it. Share it.

If you enjoyed *Lucid Fate*, please rate it and spread the word. With your rating, you take part in this book's success. If you're interested in joining my Reader Group for fun chit-chat and advance notice of upcoming releases, please sign up by going to LeeGabel.com/signup.

Note from the author

Whew. What a journey 2021 (and part of 2022) was. I began this three-book saga in January 2021, smack in the middle of the COVID pandemic. The idea of lucid dreaming had remained in the back of my head for a number of years. I've tried to direct my dreams before and have never been able to. But the few dreams I remember are usually quite vivid and I thought, "What would it be like if I could make a dream real?" I refined the idea further by focusing on making a single person from a dream real. It seemed like a cool idea and, if really possible, probably one that would get me into a heap of trouble. Perfect story material. The Dreamwaker saga was born and it represents my seventh, eighth, and ninth novel.

I decided to write all three Dreamwaker books back-to-back, unlike writing and publishing stories one at a time, like my earlier books. Stories change as they're written, although the Dreamwaker saga did stick largely to my outline. Writing the books back-to-back allowed me to refine details in earlier books to reflect the minor changes that had worked their way into the story later on.

The Dreamwaker saga takes place over the summer of 1986 and contains many pop culture references. I give sincere thanks to the many creators of the film, television, music, and magazines of the era that helped enhance the fictional world I constructed for this story. I hope you enjoyed the indirect ride down memory lane. I certainly did.

I am eternally grateful for my wife and editor Sheila. I couldn't do this without her, nor would I want to. MJ Mumford, while spinning your own time travel suspense novels, your eagle eyes and honest feedback elevated this book to a higher level. And I owe a debt of gratitude to David Hoselton for his feedback on my earlier work as a screenwriter. He helped me gather the courage to take on this novel writing journey on my own. Watch David's work on *The Good Doctor,* which airs on ABC. And to my family and friends who supported my decision to quit my job to write full-time, you were right. I am your number one fan now.

About the author

Lee reads practically any genre. Plus, he's a movie junkie. That's a dangerous combination. Traditionally trained as a screenwriter, Lee moved to writing multi-genre books in 2016 and is the author of nine novels.

Lee once walked 63.5 kilometers in thirteen hours. Why? Ask him. He loves to hear from readers. Past lives include working within the visual and dramatic arts landscape as a graphic designer, illustrator, visual effects artist, animator, and screenwriter. In 2005, he contributed to an Emmy award (LOST; "Pilot; Part 1 and Part 2") for Outstanding Special Visual Effects for a Series.

In reality, Lee lives on an island in the Pacific Northwest with his wife and son. In his head, he lives wherever his characters are.

CHAPTER TWENTY-NINE

SIX WEEKS LATER

WITH A CLICK, Dana ignited the barbecue and scraped a wire brush over the grill. "Your delightful neighbour gone yet?"

"Sold sticker went on this morning, so it won't be long, thank fuck." I took a sip of my beer. "Hopefully they're retiring to the glitz of Queenstown and won't ever think of this place again."

"Not after the humiliation you handed them. I bet they're desperate to make their escape." Dana raised his head and peered over his shoulder at the cars parked in the small beachside parking bay. "Where's our man of the moment?"

It wasn't like Joe to be late. Everyone else was here. The captain stood in ankle-deep water, cuffs rolled to his knees, beer bottle in hand. He chatted to Forest and Helena and their laughter rolled out over the still water.

It was good to see him relaxing with the team, being

part of the "us" he had created, after, no doubt, feeling rejected by it.

I had expected to be fired on the spot after the election day rally. I'd made a fool out of him. All of us had. We'd used him to meet an, admittedly well-intended, end with little regard to his feelings or any respect for who he was to us.

Which made us all, for that moment, terrible terrible people, even if we'd never set out for it to end the way it had. I had thought we could make him mayor.

But he hadn't fired me. Or any of us. He'd been angry, yes, and hurt, but ultimately, his understanding that we'd done the right thing for our community, and his admission that he was actually relieved he didn't have to be mayor, won out.

And we all loved him a little bit more for it.

A vehicle pulled into the car park with a bit more speed than was necessary for a sleepy Sunday.

The three at the water's edge turned at the crunch of gravel, and as Joe cracked his door, Helena said, "Good afternoon, Your Worship. Nice of you to join us."

Joe stepped out of the car and placed his hands over his heart. "Hello my lovelies, sorry for being tardy. My excuse is I'm a very busy man now, because I'm very important."

It hadn't taken much persuasion for Joe to throw his hat in the ring of the second by-election for Fiordland District Mayor. He had the ability and the passion, and it ended up being an uncontested election, which meant no campaign pain for the rest of us.

"I hope you're prepared for competition, Captain Ego," said Forest. "Now that Helena's going to be, like, a famous writer and everything." He nudged her with his elbow.

Find Lee on the Internet:

Want to join Lee's Reader Group or find out more about Lee and the books he writes? Please go to:

LeeGabel.com/links

An infestation of supersized vermin with a hunger for raw meat? CHECK.

An estranged son staying for the summer? CHECK.
An intense fear of rats? DOUBLE-CHECK.

Sam Shaw's life has flipped upside down. Pets and tenants in his Bronx brownstone begin to disappear. Left behind is a wake of carnage.

All evidence points to a hybrid colony of vicious white-tailed rats that has moved into the basement – genetically superior with intelligence to match.

When his ex-wife dumps his son Bradley on his doorstep, Sam must switch into protection mode, if his son will let him.

Faced with impossible odds, Sam hires Bertha O'Connor from Detest-A-Pest Exterminators Inc. She runs the only outfit brave enough – or crazy enough – to take the job.

With help from the Detest-A-Pest crew, Sam must face his fears or the white-tailed mutants will eat him alive. Because this horde of super-rats are smarter than anyone had bargained for...

Detest-A-Pest #1 (304 pages)

Spiders. Over 35,000 species. Every person on Earth eaten in one year. Now there's one more... a ravenous eight-legged hybrid thousands of years in the making and bigger than a dozen burritos.

After a summer of exterminator training in New York, Bradley returns home ready to face his senior year with renewed confidence. But fate gets in the way of his grand teenage plans – especially when eight legs attack instead of four.

And these aren't your typical, everyday spiders. Their newly acquired taste for raw meat has them casting a wide net over Bradley's sleepy San Fernando suburb. It doesn't take them long to scramble up the food chain.

Add a vengeful ex-girlfriend casting a web of lies into the mix, and things get downright sticky.

But Detest-A-Pest can't resist a challenge. Sam and O'Connor rejoin Bradley and his inventive friends as they wage war on an infestation of spiders poised to swallow not only the high school, but the neighborhood and everyone within...

Detest-A-Pest #2 (504 pages)

A playground for the rich. A genetic mutation a thousand years old. A relentless hunger for human flesh. What could go wrong?

Harry Harcourt has a problem. People are dying at exclusive golf resort Mar-A-Verde. As head greenskeeper, it's up to him to "fix" the problem and keep the course open... or face termination. But it's not one problem, it's a vast network of vicious problems, all under the turf.

As bodies pile up, resident doctor Daniela Trejo joins Harry in the fight. Together, they capture a creature unlike anything on Earth – acid skin and razor-sharp fangs with agility that matches its appetite. But the creature escapes.

Outmatched and outnumbered, Harry seeks outside help. No one wants to touch the job – no one except Detest-A-Pest. O'Connor, Sam, and Hope hit the road for what looks like an easy payday in a tropical paradise. What awaits them is a journey through hell that has gruesome death hiding in every shadow...

Detest-A-Pest #3 (340 pages)

A family in crisis. An impossible choice. A race against time.

An unplanned pregnancy turns the lives of Deanna, her husband Max, and her teenage son upside down. But there's something else wrong...

After baby David receives a cancer diagnosis, Deanna drops everything to focus on finding a cure. Max has other ideas.

Based on his own troubled past, Max challenges Deanna to consider quality of life versus quantity. Their opposing opinions throw their marriage into chaos and Deanna seeks treatment options alone.

Caught in the middle, Alex must navigate this family crisis on his own. An unexpected friendship with a cancer survivor may offer the perspective he needs.

With the clock ticking, Deanna stops at nothing to save baby David's life... but her relationship with her family may not survive the process.

David's Summer (310 pages)

Two sisters. One wants in. One has a plan. But gang loyalty cuts family ties...

Jess works, spends time with friends, and earns good grades in school. But she's also sole provider for her drug-addicted mother... And she hates it.

Her sister Nova holds a high-profile position in the Dynamite Queens. Within her turf Nova enjoys fame, fortune, freedom, and respect – at a cost of family life.

But Jess wants what Nova has and is willing to do anything to get it. After one explosive argument, Jess joins a rival gang, a decision that leads her down a path of brutal consequences.

South Central L. A. erupts with violence as two gangs – two sisters – wage war on each other. For the winner, victory could be unforgiving...

Tied is a fast-paced look at family, friendship, betrayal, and revenge through the lens of tough Los Angeles girl gangs.

Note: This novel contains strong language and gang violence.

Tied: A Street Gang Novel (316 pages)

"Get snipped," they said. "It will solve all your problems," they said. Unfortunately, Ted listened...

Five years ago, it was love at first sight. Now, it's life on autopilot as tumbleweeds roll through Ted and Iris's bedroom. Their lackluster love life is driving Ted nuts. Iris's solution to their bedroom blues: get snipped.

Kunal and Ray, Ted's best friends and sworn enemies of Iris, agree with her for once. All roads seem to lead to a surgical solution, but Ted's not going there... until an explosive argument changes everything. A vasectomy seems like Ted's only play to win Iris back.

The antics of his precocious next-door neighbor complicates matters. Ted's ill-conceived decisions jeopardize everything important in his life, including his nuts.

But life was about to throw Ted a romantic curve-ball aimed straight at his heart...

Snipped: A Cutting Comedy (300 pages)

Helena placed a hand on Forest's shoulder and threw her head back, offering her tinselly laugh to the heavens. "You are precious. I've submitted a manuscript to some agencies, guys. It doesn't guarantee a thing."

Joe wrapped an arm around her. "But it was a very brave step, my heart. I'm proud of you."

It was incredibly brave of her. But it wasn't why we were here. Nor were we here because I'd just had a record sales week with nearly three hundred T-shirts sold, which was rather a momentous Green Ginger Wine moment. Liam and I had almost finished the bottle.

Okay. It *mostly* wasn't about that. We were officially here because Joe had just finished his first week balancing his mayoral and mart-floor-manager duties, but it also provided an opportunity for the Liam/Jewel social media partnership to keep building momentum.

Helena raised a pair of binoculars she had slung over a shoulder like a handbag and looked out over the lake. "Ooh, they've started. Have a look, Jewel."

Taking the binoculars from her, I peered at the magnified short causeway on the southern side of the lake and the car, driven by Harit, roaring across it. Rā hung out the back window, her phone raised.

From the car's tow bar, a cable ran out on to the water to where a figure wake boarded, one hand on the rope's handle, the other ironing a deep red garment.

She was rather striking.

She had the face of a doll above a neatly trimmed beard and the power to pull a TikTok audience of nearly 350,000 people courtesy of her ability to dance like she owned the world.

Above a vintage swing skirt, she wore a new T-shirt

from the Empowered Collection. It had a glasses-wearing superheroine on it, face screwed up, mouth wide open.

Her speech bubble read *Odd Girl Roar*.